AN ORNAMENTAL WIFE, A MARRIAGE UNCOMPLICATED BY LOVE.

That was Ben Franklin's advice and Lion Hampshire took it when he engaged himself to socialite Priscilla Wade in hope of securing his reputation and winning a seat in Congress.

But with Priscilla came a raven-haired minx of a lady's maid who tumbled all Lion's calculations with her outspoken manner and daring ways.

Threatened by scandal, hounded by his bitter rival Marcus Reems, pursued by voluptuous Clarissa who laid prior claim to his bed, Lion tried to hide his love. But as a new nation prepared to celebrate its hard-won independence, love, too, struggled to break the chains that bound it, to dispel the dark secrets and vaunting ambition that clouded its glory, to stand free and . . .

TOUCH THE SUN

Also by Cynthia Wright
Published by Ballantine Books:

CAROLINE

TOUCH
THE
SUN

Cynthia Challed Wright

BALLANTINE BOOKS • NEW YORK

Library of Congress Catalog Card Number: 78-60700

ISBN 0-345-27512-8

Manufactured in the United States of America

First Edition: December 1978

For Thomas R and Margo-Starr,
who made it from cherry pie to
wedding cake in only eight years.

PART I

COME muster, my lads, your mechanical
   tools,
Your saws and your axes, your hammers
   and rules;
Bring your mallets and planes, your level
   and line,
And plenty of pins of American pine:
For our roof we will raise, and our song
   still shall be,
Our government firm, and our citizens
   free!

> —FRANCES HOPKINSON
> "The Raising: A New Song
> for Federal Mechanics"
> (March 1788)

Chapter One

WINTER SUNLIGHT GLANCED off the last bits of melting ice that hung on the pecan trees like diamonds. Meagan Sayers, astride her gray gelding Laughter, rode under the dripping branches and on into the open fields beyond.

The muddy ground made riding conditions less than ideal, but in comparison with the rest of this miserable winter of 1789, this early January day seemed like paradise. At least the sun was out, and it was warm enough to go without a heavy coat. Meagan rode every day unless the weather threatened the footing of her horse. She insisted that it was for Laughter's sake, but in truth, she grew more restless than the dappled gray gelding when forced to stay indoors, and these past weeks had yielded an unbroken procession of rain and snowstorms.

Pecan Grove was one of the largest Tidewater plantations in Virginia and boasted the area's finest mansion, next to Mount Vernon. However, by no stretch of imagination could Meagan fit anyone's conception of a Southern belle. The picture she made now, galloping across the soggy meadow astride Laughter, was typical. Since childhood, she had kept in the stable a cache of boys' clothing that she had begged from the young grooms and which she had changed into unfailingly each day.

Meagan's parents had always reveled in a world of foxhunts, horsebreeding, cockfights, dancing, card-playing, and travel. She had seldom seen them, and when she did, they merely patted her on the head while passing in the hall. Early on she had put their inattention to good use, growing up a free spirit who rode with the skill and daring of any man, her raven hair flying freely like a banner. She eluded her governesses, choosing to take books from the library, and spent her afternoons reading under a pecan tree in the meadow.

The past summer had been like all the rest. Russell and Melanie Sayers had sailed to France to cavort at Versailles and Paris, but their daughter had pleaded to remain at home. With guilty sighs of relief, they agreed, for Meagan fought them every step of the way in their intermittent efforts to civilize her.

Now, galloping out into the waterlogged meadow, Meagan's mind returned to the October afternoon when she had learned of the shipwreck. James Wade, a lifelong neighbor, had ridden over to break the news of her parents' deaths and she had found herself reacting more strongly to his repellent, "brotherly" embraces than to the tragedy of losing both mother and father in one blow. Over and over, she had waited for the grief process to begin, but it never really had. Meagan felt a tenseness in her breast at the realization that she had not loved her parents enough to mourn their deaths. And yet, her intuitive common sense told her that affection must be earned, and it was not for her to feel guilty because they had not known how to love anyone but themselves.

A voice was calling from the shelter of the pecan trees, and reluctantly Meagan reined in Laughter, turning him back toward the house. She found one of the stableboys waiting for her.

"The Wades are in the big house, ma'am."

Meagan made a face, but knowing they would sit and drink tea until she arrived, decided to get it over with. Sliding from Laughter's back, she handed the reins to the stableboy and ran off toward the imposing Georgian brick house.

Flora, the large black cook, frowned as Meagan came into the kitchen but refrained from scolding. The girl was disheveled, her breeches grimy and her jet-black hair loose and windblown. Yet, who could

3

resist her? Petite in stature, Meagan exuded energy and good health with glowing cheeks, an impudent, winning smile, and sparkling eyes of deep violet. She marched right through the kitchen, down the hall into the parlor where four generations of Wades and Sayerses had shared tea.

Priscilla and James were years beyond surprise at the sight of Meagan's scuffed figure in the doorway. They had known her all their lives, and despite the efforts of her mother, she had rarely been seen in a proper gown in all her seventeen years.

"Well! I see you are taken care of!" Meagan exclaimed, noting James's generous portion of brandy.

The Wade siblings, ever proper, smiled at their hostess, who dropped into a wing chair.

Slinging a slim booted leg over the rose velvet arm, she grinned. "To what do I owe this honor?"

James, dark-haired and pudgy, squirmed slightly. "Meagan, you act as if nothing has changed. We have been worried about you and only wish to be reassured concerning your state of mind . . ."

Meagan softened somewhat; her violet gaze traveled from the lecherous James to his willowy, auburn-haired sister. The two girls had been incompatible friends since infancy, yet Meagan's heart warmed maternally toward Priscilla.

"I don't mean to seem flippant, but you two certainly are aware that my existence doesn't depend on Mother and Father! After all—"

"Meagan!" warned Priscilla. "You must learn to show respect—"

"Oh, pooh!" she broke in, resisting the desire to use a stronger word. "I happen to feel that honesty is a better virtue. Priscilla, you know perfectly well that you and I have never agreed on anything. I cannot believe that you could continue to preach to me now! I have thought at length about Mother and Father, and I feel satisfied with the answers I have reached. I need no advice from you!" Meagan had lifted herself partway out of the chair and James's beady eyes watched her firm breasts strain against the boy's jacket she wore.

A servant appeared with the teapot and a fresh cup and saucer for Meagan, giving the room's occupants a chance to cool down.

"Have you heard any news concerning your father's estate?" asked James when the girl had gone.

"Nothing very encouraging. Mr. Bumpstock, our attorney, has written to me saying that Father appears to have been in debt. Of course, he insists on keeping me in suspense. The final word will hopefully arrive before the end of the month, but knowing Mr. Bumpstock's tendency to putter . . ."

James was downing his brandy—rather piggishly, Meagan thought—and licked his lips, savoring the last drop.

"Meagan, dear, I do hate to rush off, but there are some matters I should attend to. I am traveling North to Philadelphia tomorrow, but I simply could not depart without seeing you again to be certain you are well." He stood up and crossed to her side, bringing his face so close that Meagan wrinkled her nose at the odor of brandy that enveloped her when he spoke. "If you should need me before tomorrow, I would gladly rush to your side at any hour."

"I will keep that in mind, James dear, but don't lose sleep waiting for my summons." These words were delivered with her sweetest smile, a tactic that never failed to confuse the recipients of her sarcasm.

James cleared his throat foolishly. "I'll be going then. I am sure you two have a great deal to chat about, so I'll send the carriages back later. Good day!"

When he was gone, Meagan looked curiously in Priscilla's direction. "Philadelphia! What takes your charming brother there?"

"As a matter of fact, he's going on my behalf. He hopes to arrange a match for me."

"Oh? Do go on. The suspense in excruciating!"

Priscilla preened. "If all goes well, I should be the wife of a wealthy man by spring. Isn't it exciting? Me —one of Philadelphia's social leaders!"

5

"Well, for Heaven's sake, you goose, James hasn't even left yet! Do you imagine he can simply go into a shop and pick out a wealthy husband for you?" Meagan's voice sharpened with irritation as she jumped up to pace the thick Oriental rug. She fumed silently at James Wade. Priscilla was too frivolous to realize it, but Meagan knew that James had been squandering the Wade fortune ever since their own father died. He had drunk and gambled and traveled to excess, somehow believing that West Hills could run itself. And now, Meagan could clearly see that he intended to sell his sister the way he had already sold paintings, horses, and precious land.

"Goodness, Meagan, you should know that James would do anything for me. He says that I should have a position in life to equal my beauty. Isn't that sweet?"

"Sweeter than I can stomach," Meagan muttered, then turned to look straight into her friend's emerald eyes. "Are you truly happy about this? Do you wish to marry a *stranger?*"

"James wouldn't pick someone substandard, and after all, there are more important considerations than *love*. I wasn't aware that you were particularly romantic." She eyed Meagan's breeches and riotous curls. "I wouldn't be surprised if you are jealous. I don't seem to recall any marriage proposals coming your way lately."

Meagan tensed, like a kitten ready to pounce, glaring at Priscilla through narrowed, sooty-lashed eyes. "I could answer that in a dozen different ways that would doubtless send you into a faint, but from years of experience, I know that nothing reaches through that *lovely* coiffure of yours. Sometimes I think your head is stuffed with auburn curls!"

Priscilla, an automatic loser in these verbal duels, answered warily, "I will forgive your rudeness. It is probably due to the strain of your grief. Speaking of which . . . people are wondering what you intend to do now that your mama and papa are . . . gone." She sighed and shook her head mournfully.

Refilling her own teacup, Meagan dropped back

into the wing chair. "What is that supposed to mean?"

"Well, certainly you are aware that you cannot stay here . . . alone—"

"As a matter of fact, I am not aware of any such thing! I've been alone here most of my life. Besides, 'alone' is a rather academic word since there are more servants than I can count. Furthermore—" she gestured angrily with a tiny hand "—it happens to be no one's business but mine!"

"Meagan, you are so silly. Do you expect everyone to just ignore you? A seventeen-year-old girl?"

"Yes!"

"Well, they won't. For your own good! You must begin to think of your future—a husband—"

"Mind your own business!"

"Meagan!" Priscilla's lovely face was flushed. "Even James has been worrying about you. He's suggested that you might come to West Hills after I am gone—"

"No!" Meagan exploded, jumping up again. She could feel the elegant paneled walls closing in and frustration choked her. "Why can't everyone just leave me alone? Just because I have different ideas about life and happiness, I'm labeled a misfit, a crazy person!"

Priscilla was startled to see tears sparkle in her friend's amethyst eyes, and though she hadn't the faintest notion what Meagan was saying, she was impressed.

"I'm sorry. I know that I'm a miserable hostess, but this room drives me mad. I've got to have another ride before the sun goes down." Her anger had evaporated, but she emanated a brilliant energy as she impulsively leaned down to kiss Priscilla's cheek. "I'll have Flora send you some more tea and some cakes. Wish James a—successful trip."

With that, Meagan darted off to the kitchen, where she passed along the tea instructions to Flora. The old cook followed behind to the door, wiping her rough hands on the white length of her apron as she watched Meagan run across the garden.

"That chile is roundin' the corner," Flora muttered

to herself. "I been afraid of what would happen when she's forced to grow up. My little laughin' baby . . . Is those tears of hers 'cause she's findin' out there's no place for her in this ugly world?"

Chapter Two

FRANKLIN COURT, LIKE the rest of Philadelphia in late January, was veiled by plump, wet snowflakes. A half-dozen inches had accumulated on the ground with no end in sight, but inside the new three-story library wing, all was cozy. Benjamin Franklin was feeling better today and, having dressed, was sharing a cup of tea with his daughter.

The library reflected his personality even more than the rest of the house, serving as a showcase for his inventions, most of which were in constant use. Clean, even warmth beamed out from the latest Franklin fireplace; the arm-extender lay where it had been put just minutes before, used by the Doctor to reach a book on the top shelf.

At eighty-three, he looked frail and thin yet as alert and confident as ever. The constant pain from his bladderstones had driven him to take large doses of laudanum, even opium, but he remained in control of his spirits. They were higher than ever today.

"Ah, Sally, this tea is just the thing! Be sure to have a full pot when Lion arrives. He'll need some warming up!"

"Tea?" Sally echoed doubtfully.

Her father laughed. "Gad, you are right! Is there brandy?"

"Waiting on a tray downstairs, Father."

"Good, good." He sipped his tea in silence for a

moment, gazing intently at his middle-aged daughter. Children and hard work had aged her, but the white mobcap and fuzzy gray curls framed a face as kind and warm as any Franklin had known.

"You seem thoughtful," she commented. "You aren't in pain, are you? Do you want to lie down?"

"No, no! I was just thinking—about Lion. Do you remember the first night he came here?"

"Why . . . yes. Summer before last, wasn't it? I recall that it was raining and very warm and you were upstairs pedaling that treadle-fan——"

"Naked as a baby!" he supplied happily. "I'll never forget Lion's expression! You know, that was the first day of the Constitutional Convention. The thunderstorm kept me at home and Lion came along that night with the delegates who reported to me."

"That's right! I remember now that he became a delegate of sorts after that. It seemed odd at the time . . ."

"He had just returned from the Orient with a magnificent cargo. I really slipped him into that Convention before he knew what had happened, but it certainly turned out well. With my illness, he became an extra set of eyes and ears for me on the days I couldn't be there, and I'd wager that the experience had a lasting effect on him."

"Lion Hampshire?" Sally scoffed, rising to her feet. "Certainly the man is bewitching, but it has always been my impression that his interests lay more along the lines of adventure, women, and money!"

A cynical voice answered her from the doorway.

"My dear Mrs. Bache, I am devastated to hear your description of my character!"

Sally spun around, her rosy cheeks deepening to scarlet. "Lion, I—meant that in the best way——"

The man's looks were enough to tongue-tie any female, and Sally Bache was no exception. He seemed taller than ever, his shoulders broader, his skin more deeply tanned, and his hair as gold as fire. When he smiled, white teeth flashed and ocean-blue eyes sparkled. Sally watched him cross the room, the epitome of

9

powerful grace, and her plump hand went cold as he lifted it to his lips.

"Mrs. Bache, I admire a woman with opinions. Do not back down now!"

She gulped. "Why, Lion, you know how fond we all are of you. It's wonderful to see you again. I hope your voyage was a success! I hope you have been eating. It looks as though you've lost weight . . ."

"The farther my ship got from Cathay, the less appealing that stored food became. However, I'm certain the problem could be corrected with a few of your celebrated meals."

Sally blushed again and Dr. Franklin spoke up from his chair, "Is my daughter so entrancing that you can spare neither a glance nor word for her sick old father?"

Lion laughed and Sally exclaimed, "I think I heard the children calling! I'll be back in a moment with your refreshment."

She hurried out of the library and Lion settled into a cozy red chair across from Franklin's. Leaning forward, he grasped the frail hands of his mentor and declared, "I can't tell you how wonderful it feels to be home again and to see you up and about. How are you?"

It had been more than a year since Lion had left for Cathay and he was alarmed by Franklin's apparent deterioration. The wispy fringe of hair that brushed his shoulders was visibly thinner. So was the Doctor himself. His back was bent, and chronic pain had etched hundreds of new lines in that famous face, but the warmth in his smile and dark eyes was undimmed.

"Right to the point, as always, eh? Well, I've been better. My body may be withering away, but I find that the energy in my mind remains undiminished. The conflict which ensues between my mental and physical abilities is mighty frustrating!" He paused as though to rest. "I can see how *you* are! You're looking splendid; the sea air must agree with you."

They conversed at length about Lion's experiences in China and the latest developments in America until

Sally Bache returned with Lion's brandy. Apparently, there was some crisis involving Franklin's grandson Benny that she wished to discuss with her father, so Lion leaned back in his chair and let his thoughts wander.

Sipping the brandy reminded him of the enormous amount of the stuff he had bitterly consumed since his return to Philadelphia three days ago. How was he to tell Dr. Franklin what was *really* on his mind? It was the old man's fault, after all! Persuading him to attend the Constitutional Convention on a permanent basis . . . including him in the elite group that met almost nightly in the dining room at Franklin Court. Washington, Madison, Robert Morris, not to mention Franklin himself. It had turned out to be the sort of experience that left Lion with a craving for more, a burning desire to be one of these men whose brilliant minds and courage were shaping the new, idealistic nation of America. Day after day in the stiflingly hot East Room of the State House, Lion had been unaware of the changes taking place inside himself; he only knew that he loved every moment of debate, even the longest, most pompous speeches.

There had been no choice in his mind when the time came that autumn to return to the Orient. It never occurred to him that his experience that summer would have any permanent effect. He had always loved the sea. After fighting in the Revolution and receiving a degree at Harvard, he had chosen the new China trade as a means to amass a fortune and lead an adventurous life at the same time. Where other ships seemed continually plagued by hostile men-of-war and destructive storms, he had found that as a captain he led a charmed life. Now, at thirty-two years of age, he was both wealthy and successful.

And satisfied . . . until this last voyage.

Taking a large swallow of the brandy, Lion looked up to find that Mrs. Bache had gone, and Dr. Franklin was watching him with an uncomfortably penetrating gaze.

"You seem pensive," the old statesman commented

11

casually. "Is something bothering you? A woman?"

"God, no!" Lion replied vehemently. "Would that it were so simple! Do you really want to know? Are you certain?"

Franklin was taken aback by this outburst from a man who was usually so cool and cynical.

"Why, of course, if—"

"Then I'll tell you, and you can have a good laugh! I ran into a storm off Macao on my way home that delayed me so much that I missed the elections for the First Congress!"

Totally bewildered by now, Franklin inquired, "Should I understand what that means?"

"It means that I intended to return in time because I hoped for a seat in the Congress!"

"Am I hearing correctly? I could have sworn that you said "

"Yes! It's all your fault, you know. I became addicted during the Convention! After a few months at sea, I was a man obsessed. Lord, how I longed to be back at the State House, listening to Madison discuss the Virginia Plan. I tell you, it's in my blood and now I've missed my chance! What the hell are you going to do about it?" Lion was leaning forward, his shoulder muscles outlined against his tailored coat, blue eyes blazing.

"I?" Franklin echoed. "My dear boy, I do hope you have not directed all your ferocious rage in *my* direction! I am an old man and very weak . . ." His eyes were twinkling, and Lion relaxed in spite of himself.

"God damnit, I've got to blame someone," he muttered, repressing a smile.

"That's better. You know, this is quite a shock, though I must admit I suspected your interest even then. I did not, however, dream that it would reach such proportions!"

"Neither did I," Lion growled.

"At any rate, your frustration is not necessary. You would never have been elected anyway. That is not to say that the men who will make up the Congress are any better than you, for they are generally a sorry lot.

12

I am simply afraid that you have too many strikes against you at this point in your life."

Lion's amazing blue eyes flashed. "Such as?"

"A well-known temper," he returned with bland amusement, lifting his eyebrows for emphasis. "Your age, your background, your marital status, your reputation as a womanizer and an adventurer—even your looks."

Lion raised a hand to his cheekbone. "My looks? What the hell is wrong with my looks?"

"Absolutely nothing, and that is the problem. You look too spectacular to have any serious intelligence."

"That's absurd!" he exploded, coming halfway out of his chair.

Franklin held up a veined hand, smiling. "I never said that I subscribe to the theory, my boy. Yet I fear that it is quite widely held. In your case, however, I would say that the other points I mentioned are more important. If you are serious about being a member of Congress, Lion, you will have to put in some time and build a name for yourself. Not that you don't have a name of sorts now, but . . ." He smiled at him, eyes dancing behind the gold-rimmed spectacles.

Lion sat back in his chair, raking a hand through his burnished hair. "I'm not used to playing waiting games," he sighed at last.

"It is not a simple thing to turn one's whole lifestyle around overnight. I realize that you are used to getting what you want, but perhaps you have reached a point where you will have to compromise. My advice to you is to cultivate some patience and lay your plans carefully. However . . . there is one thing you might do to speed up the process of achieving respectability."

"What's that?"

"Get married."

Lion looked as if he'd been struck. For a moment, speech failed him, but finally he managed to choke, "What? You say that as if it is in the same category as ordering a new coat from the tailor!"

"It can be."

"Are you mad? A wife? *Me?*"

Franklin merely reached for his teacup, arching a faded eyebrow in a way that told Lion he had never been more lucid.

Chapter Three

MORNING SUNSHINE STREAMED into the dining room where Lion was sharing a late, leisurely breakfast with his host, Dr. Elisha Dick. The two men had not seen each other for thirteen years, since their days together at the Academy of Philadelphia, and were pleased to find their friendship intact. Dr. Dick had chosen the quieter life of a dedicated physician and family man, but was not surprised to hear that, for his devil-may-care friend, the intervening years had been crammed with adventure.

"I can't tell you how happy I am that you searched me out last night!" he repeated for the dozenth time. "It's amazing that you remembered I was here! I am especially pleased since I am sure James Wade must have been most anxious to have you stay at West Hills."

Smiling, Lion lit a cheroot. "That is putting it mildly! It was all I could do to persuade him to travel on to Virginia ahead of me. He wanted to wait and show me the way. I was afraid that if I stayed at his plantation he might chain me to his sister! Besides, I couldn't pass up an opportunity to look you up. I had a feeling you would not have strayed far from your family homestead." He paused to sample the fresh coffee. "Good friends are rare these days. I'm sure that we would never have lost touch if the war hadn't turned our lives upside down."

14

"Lion . . . I know that you have plans to ride out to West Hills this morning, and I don't want to make you late, but—" The doctor's sensitive face reflected his search for the right words. "I don't mean to pry, but I know the Wades quite well, and this news concerning you and Priscilla comes as quite a shock!"

Lion's smile was wry. "Because I've never met the girl?"

"Well, of course . . . and then there is the matter of Priscilla herself!"

"Don't tell me she's ugly! Her brother described her beauty to me until, to my great relief, the port he was swilling did him in for the evening."

"No, no, she's a lovely creature—well-bred and all—but supremely shallow and narcissistic. I am simply at a loss to understand how all this came about! For God's sake, Lion, I expected you to marry the most charming, delightful female on earth . . . and Priscilla is less than endearing."

"Shallow, you say? Splendid. Perfect." Lion grinned enigmatically, white teeth flashing against bronzed skin, before taking pity on the curious Dr. Dick. "Don't worry so, Elisha; this entire affair is my idea. James Wade just happened to arrive in Philadelphia a month ago at the moment when I needed him most. We met at the Indian Head Tavern; he learned that I was, ah—eligible, and proceeded to make me an offer that was tailor made to my current need."

"Which is?" Dick prompted, his courage mounting.

"An ornamental wife. You needn't look so baffled! My motive is quite simple—and timeless. Ambition. I intend to become a congressman, or even a senator, within the next few years, and in my case a wife seems to be one of the prime prerequisites. You see, it *suits* me that the arrangement not be complicated by the question of love. Meeting James Wade was a stroke of luck, for it seems that Priscilla would use me as impersonally as I am using her. She will gain wealth and position in Philadelphia; I will gain the well-bred, beautiful wife that I need."

15

Hannah Dick appeared at that moment to ask if the men needed more coffee.

"No, thank you," Lion replied, grinding out his cheroot as he stood up. "The breakfast was delicious, but I must be going now. I wouldn't want to keep my bride-to-be waiting!"

Hannah beamed at his words, but Elisha was all too aware of the mocking glint in Lion's blue eyes. He felt stirrings of the old worry that had characterized his feelings toward Lion when they were young, but he forced himself to stifle them. After all, Lion was a grown man and so far, for all his recklessness, had never met with anything but success. Right now, illuminated by a soft, yellow beam of sunlight, he seemed larger than life and quite invincible.

"I cannot believe your capacity for immobility!" Meagan exclaimed as she pulled aside the wine and rose brocade bed-hangings. Priscilla opened one large green eye and moaned convincingly. Sunlight flooded the cold room when Meagan opened the heavy curtains, turning back to the bed with a frown. "It is past ten o'clock, you dolt, and your fiancé arrives today!"

"Well, I want to look my best, don't I? Sleep is a very important part of beauty."

"If that is the case, then you must be the most spectacular woman alive!"

Priscilla failed to hear the sarcasm in her voice and merely smoothed her auburn curls with a pleased smile. "Why, thank you, Meagan. You know, you could stand some beauty sleep yourself, if you don't mind my saying so. You look altogether wild!"

Meagan tossed her glossy black hair irritably as she threw herself down on the window seat. "My looks are of no importance to me whatever, Priscilla. Some of us have more pressing worries than the color in our cheeks."

"How tedious," the other girl yawned, critically taking in Meagan's tangled curls and mud-spattered breeches and coat. "I can't imagine why you persist in

16

wearing those horrid boy's clothes. It's not as if you didn't have any gowns."

Meagan dismissed her words with a wave of her tiny hand, which she then thrust down the front of her waistcoat, withdrawing a crumpled sheet of parchment. "I received this letter yesterday from Mr. Bumpstock."

"Who?"

"Father's attorney!" Her voice took on a desperate note. "It's all been settled. The plantation and all the slaves, furniture, everything, will be sold to pay the debts and I'm to be packed off to Boston."

"Boston? Whatever for?"

"Mother's maiden aunt Agatha lives there. As I'm underage I shall have to live with her. Mr. Bumpstock informs me I have no choice!" Meagan shuddered and scrambled to her feet, pacing across the carpet. "I only met her once; she was shriveled and deaf and smelled of musty air. I shall go out of my mind!"

She was realizing today just how unprepared she had been for the reality of her father's financial position, even after the trail of hints dropped by Mr. Bumpstock since the shipwreck. Growing up at Pecan Grove, in a lavishly furnished mansion, Meagan had never questioned her family's wealth. However, the attorney's letter had shown her the truth in transcripts from those frustrating ledgers; Sayers had overextended himself repeatedly. Although the profits from the plantation had been sizable, they were far exceeded by the cost of her parents' extravagant lifestyle. Meagan thought back with bewildered horror to the sumptuous dinners and balls, her mother's silk and satin gowns, the expensive furniture, and the custom-made wigs. Her bitterness left little room for forgiveness, especially when it became clear that everything would have to be sold to meet the debts, leaving her homeless.

The crowning blow was the news that she would be moving to Boston and Aunt Agatha; Meagan's mind rebelled at the injustice of her fate. Her violet eyes smoldering with defiant resentment, she paced at the foot of Priscilla's four-poster bed.

"I don't know . . ." Priscilla remarked as she accepted a cup of chocolate from her maid Lily, "Boston might be just the thing, Meagan. If your aunt is rich, you will doubtless be exposed to some *very* prominent men. Actually, your opportunities would probably be better there than here in Virginia where all the boys know you are—that is—"

"Oh, do be quiet, Priscilla. I've got to think of some way out of this mess."

The spindly Negro maid was scurrying around the bedchamber, pouring water and laying out clothes, so Meagan retreated to the window seat. She casually pulled her knees up to her chest, ignoring the dust her shoes left on the cushions, and gazed outside.

January and half of February had gone the way of the two previous months, depressingly wet, but last week had brought a tremendous thaw, and a heavy dose of sunshine. The vast lawns of West Hills were brown, the ground soggy and black beneath, but the sky was clear blue and mild at last and Meagan sensed that the horrible winter was behind them. Soon the roads would be fit for travel and she would be on her way to Boston. Sheer misery overtook her momentarily and one crystal tear escaped, clinging to her thick lashes.

"I wonder what he'll be like?" Priscilla asked her reflection as she sat at her dressing table. Lily brushed the long auburn curls until they shot sparks in the sunlight and her mistress closed her eyes, letting her head drop back slightly.

"You mean your fiancé?" Meagan stressed the last word with meaningful irony.

Priscilla's eyelids fluttered, a smile curving her lush red lips. "Isn't it a lovely word? James says he's dreadfully handsome and *so* well off. Imagine him wanting to marry me with all those beauties in Philadelphia!"

"Yes," Meagan murmured dryly. "Imagine that!"

"Life will be so exciting there! James says the assemblies never end!"

Meagan sat forward suddenly on her knees, pressing her little nose against the glass. "Priscilla, I don't mean to interrupt your dreams, but I do believe your prince is arriving!"

A horse and rider had appeared between the huge oak trees that bordered the road leading to West Hills. It was the reflection of the sun against the man's gold hair that caught Meagan's eye, and she found herself staring at him in fascination.

His blond hair was caught neatly back at his neck, revealing a bronzed, obviously handsome face. He rode well, carrying himself with easy grace in spite of his size.

"Why is he riding a horse?" Priscilla fretted as she joined Meagan at the window. "I thought he would surely have a carriage! Oh, but do look at his coat. Such handsome green velvet, and so well tailored!"

Meagan rolled her eyes hopelessly, then turned back to watch as Lion Hampshire drew up to the mansion, handing over the gleaming chestnut roan to a stableboy. He smiled at the slave and slipped him a coin, then started up the broad steps to the front door.

Priscilla was moving faster now than Meagan ever imagined she could. With Lily's help, expensive gauze petticoats were layered over her long legs, followed by stylishly simple beige muslin skirts sprigged with green and orange flowers. The colors made a subtle backdrop for her rich auburn hair, ivory skin, and huge green eyes.

While Lily skillfully applied rouge to her mistress's high cheekbones, Meagan pulled up a slender rosewood chair and tried to get her attention.

"Priscilla, I think I'd better be getting home. I do have to begin packing, and I know it would be embarrassing for you to have to explain me to Mr. Hampshire."

"Meagan, dear, would I be overdoing it if I wore my emerald necklace?"

Meagan got to her feet, throwing up her hands in

exasperation. "I can't believe that my opinion would matter to you." A loud knock interrupted her and she turned to answer it, adding, "Why not ask your brother? He's an authority on everything, after all. Good luck, Priscilla. How long will it be before you leave for Philadelphia?"

"Four days."

"Well, I'll be over again to say good-bye."

She opened the door to admit James Wade, whose close-set green eyes glowed with triumph over his coup.

At the sight of Meagan, his corpulent face split into a broad smile. "What a pleasant surprise, my dear. May I say that you are the loveliest little ragamuffin I have ever encountered? That smudge on your nose is particularly enchanting!" A perfumed handkerchief floated from his breast pocket and when she saw it coming toward her nose, Meagan ducked under his outstretched arm.

"Wonderful to see you as always, James!" she sang a trifle too sweetly and scampered down the hallway. Reaching the oaken banister, she leaned over the top to make certain her escape route was clear, then hurried down the broad stairway. Her speed was such that when she touched the last step and Lion Hampshire emerged from the parlor, it was impossible for Meagan to stop. Only Hampshire's surefootedness saved them from falling to the floor on impact, and Meagan found her face buried in the clean-smelling frill of his shirtfront. She was horrified to find her breath stuck in her lungs; even worse, she was trembling under his strong, sure grip.

"Egad!" he laughed. "Are you all right, young—ah—lady?" The last word was uncertain, the abundant raven curls winning out over the male attire in his mind.

Meagan looked up into sparkling blue eyes far above her. When his hands left her arms, she felt her confidence flow back through her veins.

"Excuse me, sir. My behavior is absolutely atro-

20

cious, isn't it!" Instinctively, she returned his grin, feeling him scrutinize her.

Lion was interested and curious at the sight of the tiny, scuffed girl with her amethyst eyes and sooty lashes. The face, with its small, tilted nose and dimpled smile was deceptively childish. He had a feeling that she was older and more clever than she looked.

"You aren't Priscilla by any chance, are you?" he queried in a vaguely hopeful voice.

"Goodness, no! What a terrible shock that would be for you! I am—I am—merely a servant," she blurted without thinking, then paused, wondering why. After a moment, she decided the situation would only be more embarrassing if she stopped to explain and continued, "I must be running along! Again, my apologies, sir!"

She was gone as speedily as she had appeared, leaving Lion standing alone in the marble entry hall, scratching his blond head in perplexed amusement.

Long rays of iridescent moonlight slanted across the dark parlor, spilling into silvery pools on the needlework carpet. Meagan sat with her elbows propped up on the polished block-front desk, palms cupping her chin as she stared miserably at the shadowy miniature of Aunt Agatha. In the hallway, the tall-case clock struck twelve.

Getting to her feet, Meagan pulled the sash of her Chinese silk robe more closely around her waist and walked out onto the flagstone terrace. The rush of chilly night air refreshed and fortified her.

"Lord," she whispered, gazing up into the inky, star-strewn sky, "this time, could you please lend me some assistance? I have a feeling I am going to need help to carry this off!"

With a rueful smile, she turned back into the empty house, dark and quiet after more than twenty years of gaiety and light. Her candle stood on a table in the stair hall, the flame struggling weakly in a pool of liquid tallow. Picking up the brass candlestick, and shielding the flame with her hand, Meagan ran up the stairway and down the hall to her spacious bedcham-

21

ber. She pulled on a pair of clean, fraying breeches, a rough woolen shirt, and a warm gray coat. After turning up the cuffs until her hands showed, she found a ribbon with which to tie back her hair.

The back stairs that led to the kitchen were cold and winding, and Meagan slid her hands along the damp walls to feel her way down through the darkness. Her buckled shoes sat next to the kitchen door, and after slipping them on, she went outside to the stables. Her own gelding was in the first stall. She was accustomed to saddling Laughter herself and only minutes later she sat astride his back as they trotted out to the road.

Moonlight cast eerie shadows as it filtered through the trees, but Meagan had no time for midnight fears. The ride to West Hills took less than half an hour, and when she gained sight of the plantation house, Meagan slowed the horse to a walk. Hopping to the ground, she led Laughter into a grove of fruit trees and tied his lead to a low-hanging branch. In her breeches, the run to the mansion was easily accomplished, despite the muddy ground. The servants' entrance was as familiar to her as her own, and Meagan slipped in silently, pulling off her shoes. It took less than a minute for her to reach Priscilla's room and she lost no time waking her friend, who immediately opened her mouth to scream.

"Priscilla, don't do anything foolish!" Meagan commanded, pressing her hand over the red lips. "It is I! I have to talk to you!"

Priscilla pushed herself up against the lace-edged pillows, her eyes wide with disbelief. "Meagan! What are you doing now? I declare, you are the most startling person—"

"I had to talk to you when I was certain Mr. Hampshire wouldn't be around. I have arrived at the perfect solution to all our problems!"

22

Chapter Four

THE HIGH YELLOW wheels appeared slender to the point of fragility, and Dr. Dick eyed the post-chariot dubiously. A cool, sunny breeze ruffled his dark hair as he turned to speak to Lion Hampshire. "Are you certain that this contraption is strong enough to support the weight of human beings?"

Lion laughed out loud, his blond head bent as he finished strapping his valise to the carriage. "Elisha, you are entirely too skeptical! I assure you that not only is it strong enough, but it is also one of the fastest vehicles on the road." He came around then to clasp his friend's outstretched hand. "I thank you for providing me with such fine accommodations these past few days. It has been wonderful to see you again and to meet Hannah at last."

"The pleasure has been entirely ours! You are welcome in our home at any time." Dr. Dick paused, frowning slightly. "Are you certain that this marriage to Priscilla Wade will go according to your plans?"

"Well," Lion smiled dryly, "I'll admit that her brother may have oversold her to me, but I believe she'll do. Priscilla's shallow beauty should suit my purposes quite well."

Elisha raised an eyebrow and started to say something, then seemed to think better of it. "I suppose farewells are in order. Again, thank you for coming to me; it's been wonderful catching up on each other's lives. I hope, after all you've told me, that your problems with Marcus Reems can somehow be resolved. It seems such a shame . . . Perhaps your marriage might help—"

"I don't lose sleep over Marcus, and haven't for fifteen years," Lion replied laconically. "His bitterness goes too deep to allow room for hope of mending matters between us. I cannot enjoy knowing that any man would name himself my enemy, but at least I am assured that the fault lies in Marcus, not in me."

Elisha Dick sighed, his face puckered with sadness, not only because of what Lion had said, but also because of the tone of his voice. The gregarious, magnetic youth he had known so well at the Academy had a new, diamond-hard facet to his personality; cool, determined, and apparently lacking in sentimentality. Was it possible for him to have hardened so, or could this attitude be a defense? Blinking, Dr. Dick extended his hand. "Good fortune to you, Lion. Give my regards to our old friends in Philadelphia and keep in touch. If you should change your mind—if your plans don't work out—we should be delighted to see you settle here. Alexandria is destined to become a great seaport, you know!"

Lion grinned, white teeth contrasting with his tanned face. "I appreciate that, Elisha, but I intend that my future will be all that I desire."

He called to Joshua, his coachman, who hopped onto the carriage perch, and then Lion mounted his own chestnut roan. Hair shining in the sunlight, he waved to Elisha and to Hannah, who had appeared in the doorway, then rode away down Cameron Street.

It was still early when the white columns of West Hills appeared on the horizon, rising over the bare treetops. The yellow carriage was right behind him as he galloped down the drive, scattering a shower of mud against the sky.

Priscilla stood on the veranda, looking attractively nervous. The robe of her emerald green silk gown was parted to reveal a pale muslin underskirt tiered with narrow ruffles, while her lovely breasts curved above the low, round neckline. Only a woven shawl protected her from the crisp February air and she took care that it was held open across her bodice. As Lion came toward her she smiled at him coquettishly, dropping her eyes when he raised her soft white hand to his lips.

"You are looking exceedingly lovely this morning, Miss Wade. I am honored by this personal welcome!"

His eyes lingered on her bosom in a way that made her blush, her long lashes sweeping her cheeks. "You are too kind, Mr. Hampshire . . . but now that we're betrothed, won't you call me Priscilla?"

He grinned. "Nothing would please me more. Now —are you ready to leave? Where are your things?"

Flustered, she hurried past him into the marble entry hall. A large assortment of trunks and boxes filled the area, and Lion let out a low whistle at the sight.

"Ah—Priscilla, I was not able to bring an extra wagon for the baggage due to the weather, and I fear that if we attempt to load all of these onto my carriage, the wheels would sink out of sight in the mud!"

Her expression was horrified. "Sir, I hope you are not suggesting that we leave any of my possessions behind! I was given to understand that I could bring whatever I wished!"

Lion raised an eyebrow coldly, deciding that his fiancée was beginning to resemble a petulant child. "That, my charmer, was before I realized that you owned more possessions than even one of my ships could carry!"

"How insufferably rude you are!" she shrilled.

"Perhaps you had better become accustomed to it or else cease your spoiled tirades. Now, if you still want to travel to Philadelphia, I suggest that you choose two of those trunks and one bandbox. Anything else you need I will purchase for you after we arrive."

She bit off her next complaint as a vision of the fashionable dress shops in America's largest city flashed in her mind. Suddenly her face was sweet and lovely again as she edged closer to Lion until he could smell the heady scent of magnolia that clung to her. "I really must apologize for my behavior, Mr. Hampshire. Why, if Mama were alive, she'd thrash me for

25

speaking that way to you! I can't imagine what came over me. I certainly wouldn't want you to get the wrong impression of your future wife!"

"Don't worry," he replied with an ironic smile, "I'm sure I won't form any inaccurate opinions."

Her lush crimson lips were turned up to him and Lion took his cue, lightly tipping her chin back with a brown finger. Priscilla closed her eyes, waiting, and was surprised to feel his mouth touch hers so lightly that for a moment she thought she had imagined it. Hesitantly she peeked out from under long lashes and found Lion smiling down at her in an odd way. There was an icy, bitter frost in his blue eyes that confused and vaguely frightened her.

Removing his hand from her chin, he inquired, "Where is your brother? We really ought to be saying our farewells and getting on our way."

Priscilla flushed hotly, stammering in a false, high voice, "Well, it is quite the most peculiar thing! He seems to have eaten something at breakfast which did not agree with him and he has been forced to take to his bed!"

Lion watched her closely, raising an eyebrow. "It is fortunate that you were not similarly afflicted."

"Yes!" She glanced around agitatedly, half expecting James to recover from his sabotaged meal and appear on the stairs to find her out.

"Where is your maid? Call her so that we may take our leave."

He went outside to call the coachman to help with the trunks and Meagan popped out from behind the highboy in the parlor. She wore a demure gray dress with a mauve pelisse, giggling softly with excitement as she pulled the hood over her black curls. "What a marvelous adventure this is! I am looking forward to practicing this small deception on your self-assured fiancé!"

Priscilla was wild-eyed. "It will never work! He will know—"

"Not if you can manage to collect your wits and

stop acting so guilty! Besides, what does it matter to him who your *maid* is so long as you have one?"

Lion came through the door then and Meagan immediately stared at her feet, assuming an attitude of meek subservience.

"I thought I told you to call your maid," he said sharply, frowning at Priscilla. "What trunks have you decided on?"

In her panic Priscilla pointed to two of them at random, then hurried over to Meagan's side. For a moment Meagan feared she might attempt to hide behind her. Lion stared at the two of them while the coachman carried out the cowhide trunks.

"What the hell is going on here? Where is your maid?"

"H-here," Priscilla gasped and Meagan wanted to pinch her.

He strode across the floor to peer at her, then pulled off the hood on her pelisse. The long black hair spilled down her back and recognition sparked in Lion's eyes.

"It's you!" He turned to Priscilla then, who shrank back against the paneled wall. "I've seen your maid this past week and I distinctly recall that her skin was a radically different color," he said caustically. Meagan could see that her friend was on the verge of a teary confession so she impulsively stepped between them and smiled sweetly at Lion.

"Lily has lived at West Hills all her life, Mr. Hampshire. Her family is here and Miss Wade is far too kindhearted to separate her from them. Whereas I—" she attempted a forlorn expression, "I am merely a waif who knows no life but service to my betters. Also, Mr. Wade thought that I might provide some small female companionship for Miss Wade. We are nearly the same age and it is sure to be difficult for her, moving North and beginning a new life among strangers . . ."

She knew that her speech had been overdone; no servant would ever be so bold, but since Priscilla was obviously incapable of acting her part, Meagan had no choice but to act it for her.

Lion was eyeing her suspiciously, but finally he let

27

out an exasperated sigh and declared, "Something isn't right here, but I have neither the time nor the interest to figure out what it is. Half this day is wasted and we have a long journey ahead."

Once inside the richly upholstered carriage and with her fiancé riding outside, Priscilla seemed to relax.

Meagan was grinning as she bubbled inside with relief and her sense of victory. "Don't worry so, Priscilla," she laughed, "it will get easier from now on. Just try to keep your head!"

"I don't know why I ever let you talk me into this," she replied miserably. "He's going to find out and then we'll both be sent home! James will murder me and you'll be forced to go to Boston in the end and—"

"Oh, do stop it. No such thing will happen. You may believe that your Mr. Hampshire is somehow superior to ordinary people, but I have complete confidence in my ability to outwit him. Besides, after we reach Philadelphia I'm sure I'll hit on a new course of action. I certainly do not intend to pass the rest of my days as your maid, you goose."

"But what about James? What will happen when he discovers that Lily hasn't come with me and the news of your disappearance reaches him?" Priscilla began to panic anew at this latest thought.

"I told Lily to inform James that Mr. Hampshire decided there was not enough room for her and promised to find you a new maid in Philadelphia. As for me—no one would expect me to sit by and accept my fate in Boston, but James certainly would never guess that we could outmaneuver this blond nonpareil you are betrothed to." A fresh burst of laughter escaped Meagan's impish mouth, but Priscilla was not amused.

Barely an hour later Meagan's own confidence suffered its first shock when she realized that their carriage was approaching Mount Vernon. They ascended the hills on which the mansion stood and Priscilla gazed out the small window to admire the view. The entrance to the circular drive looked out over miles of surrounding countryside including the majestic two-mile-wide Potomac River which divided

Virginia from Maryland. The water was still and bright in the afternoon sun, while all around were woods, cliffs, meadows, and neighboring plantations.

"Isn't it beautiful?" she sighed, turning to find a panic-stricken Meagan pulling at the loose tendrils of hair around her face.

"Dear God, Priscilla, you are both frightened and blissful at the wrong moments! Now is the time to be wild with terror, you ninny! He's taking us to Mount Vernon!"

Priscilla gazed back at her blankly. "Why, I shall be very pleased to see General and Mrs. Washington. After all, he is going to be the President soon—everyone says so. Perhaps Lion intends that we should lodge here tonight!"

"How can you be so dense?" Meagan cried, violet eyes glistening with alarm. "The Washingtons *know* me! They have known me since I was a child! They were at my house just this past Christmas to offer their sympathies! What will I do?"

The question was purely rhetorical, for any advice Priscilla might offer would be worse than useless. As the carriage rolled up the long drive, Meagan decided she would be ill and suspected there would be no problem convincing Lion of this. Her face was chalk white and the look in her eyes could easily have been interpreted as pain. When Lion opened the door to the carriage, waiting for the coachman to put up the steps, he looked her over critically. Privately he thought that her conversion to female attire had done little to alter her disheveled appearance.

"Miss—ah—"

"Meagan!" Priscilla supplied immediately. Meagan felt like choking her again, for she had told her a dozen times that her new name was to be Eliza.

"Yes, well, Meagan, if you don't mind I'm going to ask that you remain in the carriage due to your—ah—state of disarray. We shouldn't be long, for I cannot spare much time this day. We shall pay our respects as speedily as possible."

Meagan watched as Lion helped Priscilla down the

few steps to the ground, her heart thudding with relief. She noticed absently that they made a handsome couple; even the colors of their clothes, complexions, and hair were complementary. There was another coach ahead of theirs on the drive and Meagan recognized it as James Madison's. She had visited Montpelier many times with her parents and felt a fresh chill at the thought of his presence here.

By the time they had been inside over half an hour, Meagan's uneasiness began to lessen. Mount Vernon in itself had a quieting effect on her, for there was an indefinable air of peacefulness about the plantation. She knew that the Washingtons were contented in their home, and their love for it was reflected everywhere. Meagan was personally quite partial to the house, for it lacked the overt luxury of her parents' mansion. The perfect simplicity of the huge, white, red-roofed dwelling lent it an elegance that excessive ornamentation could never achieve, while the network of shops and small houses which fanned out from the mansion had a clean charm all their own. She had spent many happy hours in her youth walking in the hanging wood which grew down to the river and riding through the surrounding meadows. It was common knowledge in Fairfax County that General Washington was heartsick at the thought of becoming President, and Meagan pitied him for having to leave his home again for the service of his country. "It is a shame," she mused, "that one man should be forced to take on so many burdens. It is sad and unfair."

Her thoughts skipped back to Lion Hampshire and she wondered idly why a sea captain should be so interested in paying his respects to the future President, especially when the day was so far advanced. She vaguely recalled James Wade saying that Hampshire had been a delegate to the Constitutional Convention over which Meagan knew General Washington had presided. That seemed a partial answer, but she was still mulling it over curiously when the red front door opened and Nelly Custis appeared. Laughing, she tossed her brown curls and called to Washington, her younger brother, who followed her outside. At ten and eight years of age, Martha Washington's grandchildren were delicately attractive and likable. As they ran onto the lawn, Meagan repressed an impulse to call to them and pulled her hood up around her face, sliding farther down into the seat. She watched, stomach knotting, as Martha Washington came through the door, arm in arm with Priscilla. The General's lady was several inches shorter than her companion, but her highly dressed white hair covered by a Belgian lace mobcap gave her added stature. She was wearing a simple pearl-gray silk gown with a large folded kerchief covering her shoulders and bosom, and the smile on her face was unquestionably sincere.

Several minutes passed before the men appeared, talking and gesturing enthusiastically. Meagan was astonished to see the animation in Lion Hampshire's expression; he appeared nearly spellbound by his companions. She was also surprised to see that he was slightly taller than the General, for all her life she had seen Washington tower over other men. Now there was a look of sad resignation in Washington's deepset, gray-blue eyes and Meagan guessed they were discussing the Presidency. The gentle, black-clad James Madison had to tip his head back to see the faces of the other men as they talked, but in spite of his diminutive appearance and soft voice there was an aura of power about him, wielded by his superb mind. For years he had been part of the backbone of Virginia politics, but had only recently won the respect and fame due him by creating the structure of America's new Constitution with his Virginia Plan.

As the group neared the carriage, Meagan hunched over and pretended to search for something near her feet. Voices came right through the window to her and she felt sick with fear. At last the farewells were said, the sound of the well-known childhood voices sending a wave of melancholy over her that blotted out all other emotions. Pressing her face into the folds of her skirt, Meagan fought tears as she realized for the first time the upheaval her life was about to undergo. It

31

was too late to turn back, but sadder still was the knowledge that there was nothing to turn back to.

The door beside her was pulled open then and Lion handed Priscilla in, eyeing Meagan in perplexity.

From her vantage point she could see all of their feet as they stood clustered on the drive: Martha's silk toes showing from under her skirts, Washington's high black boots, and Madison's silver-buckled shoes. In the distance, the children called to each other in high, happy voices. The door was pushed shut and there was a chorus of good-byes as the carriage rolled away toward the Potomac.

Chapter Five

IT TOOK SEVERAL hours for the yellow post-chariot to travel the nine miles from Mount Vernon to Alexandria. The road was in terrible condition—an omen of worse things to come. They jounced over the rutted, muddy thoroughfare, stopping constantly to open and then close the gates which had been built to regulate the local pigs and cows.

Meagan said a prayer for the concealing darkness as they drew up outside the familiar Wise's Tavern. Lion was in poor humor over their progress and took it out on the tavern keeper, providing Meagan with the ideal distraction to slip away to her room. Priscilla joined Lion downstairs for supper, pleading illness as Meagan's excuse. After her fiancé disappeared into the barroom to smoke and drink with the other men, she went back to the kitchens to procure a tray of hot food for Meagan. Both girls were too tired to talk or worry and slept side by side in the feather bed until Lion rapped on the door the next morning.

"Get up!" he ordered angrily. "Dress as hurriedly as you can. It will be a long day and we need an early start."

Meagan wondered at the harsh tone of his voice as she rubbed her eyes in the darkness and stumbled out of the deep, warm bed. Pausing at the window to see if the sunrise had begun, she found the reason for his ill humor. It was sleeting. Large, wet frost flakes were falling thick and fast through the night sky, while the barest suspicion of light illuminated the rooftops of Alexandria's handsome brick houses. Meagan felt ill at the prospect of the day's travel ahead, and worse yet when she remembered Priscilla's childlike fear of bad weather. With a sigh she padded around to the other side of the bed and shook her awake, steeling herself for the long hours of fretful whining that lay ahead.

Several times during the few days that passed before they reached Baltimore, Meagan expected Lion to kill Priscilla with his bare hands. If the truth were known, she came close to doing it herself more than once.

Either snow or rain fell the entire way, and because of it Lion insisted on traveling from dawn to dusk in an effort to regain a portion of their lost hours. As it was, they had lost a full day by the time they reached Spurrier Tavern.

Even Meagan, who had known and tolerated Priscilla's childishness all her life, could scarcely believe that she could behave so badly. She worried and complained every mile of the way in a shrill voice that grated unbearably on Meagan's nerves and whimpered pitifully every time someone spoke sharply to her. The situation wouldn't have grown so serious if Priscilla could have followed Meagan's suggestion to exert some control over her emotions in Lion's presence, but she seemed to be even worse when he was within earshot.

One incident in particular had occurred which seemed to set the mood for the remainder of the journey, and in Meagan's eyes formed the basis for the relationship between Lion and Priscilla. Ever since the day less than a month before when James Wade had returned home from Philadelphia bearing the news of the marriage he had arranged for his sister, Meagan had been skeptical. Only Priscilla's excitement over her future and her inherent lack of sensitivity had prevented Meagan from speaking out. Since Lion Hampshire's arrival on the scene she had been too preoccupied to worry much over Priscilla's situation; also, she made an effort *not* to think about it, for she realized that any conclusions she might arrive at would be far from cheerful or optimistic. However, hour by hour, Priscilla was growing more nervous and agitated, and Meagan sensed that it was due not only to the wild weather but also to the lack of attention she was receiving from her traveling companions. She had been pampered and catered to all her life, and Lion Hampshire's attitude toward his fiancée was far from solicitous.

The tenuous hold he had exerted over his patience finally snapped as they were being ferried across the Potomac to Georgetown, Maryland. The storm-filled winter had combined with the latest onslaught of snow and rain to transform the river into a swollen, swirling tide which made even the usually fearless Meagan a trifle uneasy. Since they had left Alexandria a few hours earlier, Lion had ridden his horse in spite of the chill, blustery weather. Now, as the ferry tipped out onto the Potomac and Priscilla began to wail with fear, he opened the carriage door and climbed in. His clothes were sodden, and the air grew frosty with his presence as he leaned back in the narrow seat across from the girls and pulled off his bicorne hat. Priscilla was momentarily surprised into silence and Meagan, who could read the fatigue in Lion's expression, prayed that she would hold her tongue.

However, no sooner had he reclined against the cushions and closed his eyes than Priscilla practically screamed, "How can you be so rude and inconsiderate? Have you no concern for my feelings at a time like this? This is a nightmare!" The pitch of her voice rose so high that Meagan expected the glass beside them to shatter. "I am your fiancée, and I am frightened out of my wits by this ordeal that you have subjected me to! I demand—"

Lion's voice, menacingly quiet, cut her off. "My dear Miss Wade, if you say one more word I shall toss you into the river."

Meagan stared at him with reluctant admiration, believing he actually meant it. Priscilla's pretty chin dropped, and for one long, blessed minute she was speechless. Under them the ferry lurched wildly, sending a wave of icy water against the carriage, and suddenly Priscilla burst into tears. Meagan was horrified. This was a ploy she had seen her friend utilize countless times over the years when she failed to get her own way, but this time Meagan could scarcely believe that she would dare it. A quick glance at Lion told her that the situation had grown dangerous, for his square jaw was set and she saw his strong brown hands clench warningly. When she met his electric blue eyes and saw the look in them, she knew she had to act. With one hand, she grabbed Priscilla's left arm and with the other she slapped her full across the face. "For God's sake, you imbecile, shut up!"

Spurrier Tavern provided a welcome haven for the edgy, exhausted travelers. Their journey from Mount Vernon to Baltimore, which usually was easily accomplished in two days, had taken three very long ones. Since the episode on the ferry, any pretense of amity which had existed between Lion and Priscilla had disappeared. She seemed to take pleasure in irritating him and he responded with a coldness bordering on disgust. Meagan, caught between them in this non-relationship, was feeling rather miserable herself.

When their carriage bumped up the muddy road to Spurrier Tavern, the prosperous appearance of the inn caused her to sigh a little in relief. The gray, cloud-laden sky was darkening quickly as night approached, and Meagan was painfully hungry.

The greeting they received from the jovial tavern keeper led Meagan to believe that Lion had probably stayed there on his way to Virginia. As Joshua, the coachman, brought in their baggage, the man declared that they were the first travelers he had seen all day. "I've been looking for Mr. Madison!" he boomed. "Hope nothing's happened to him! After all, Congress convenes in barely a week—"

Lion, with little patience for small talk, started toward the stairs. "Mr. Madison has decided to remain at Mount Vernon a while since it seems the weather will delay everyone's arrival in New York. Now—if we might see our rooms?"

Lion barely paused long enough at Meagan and Priscilla's door to set a time for supper before disappearing down the hall. Meagan absently watched his retreating back, surprised to feel an odd prick in her breast when he put a brown hand up to rub the knotted muscles in his neck. Hastily she turned away, closing the door, and surveyed this latest lodging place.

The room was lovely. There were two beds with matching red and white printed coverlets as well as a large dressing table and two Windsor arm chairs. Everything looked clean and fresh, a welcome contrast to their lodgings of the night before.

A serving-girl arrived with fresh water and a taper with which she lit the candles around the room. As Meagan pulled the pins out of her hair, she observed Priscilla sitting on the edge of one of the beds. Her full lower lip was thrust out sulkily, and Meagan realized that she had scarcely spoken during the past hour. It was odd deportment.

"Priscilla, you had better hurry and wash. At this point we can't afford to keep Mr. Hampshire waiting!"

"As far as I am concerned, that man could wait all night for me and I wouldn't be a bit sorry for him!" she said spitefully.

Meagan was unable to repress a small smile. "Somehow, I cannot imagine him keeping an all-night vigil. More likely, he will go off to supper and leave us here if we are not downstairs at the assigned minute!"

Priscilla squirmed peevishly. "I shouldn't doubt it! He is the rudest man I have ever met. I detest him."

"Well, why ever are you going with him to Philadelphia? Why not return home?"

"Because I want to live in Philadelphia! Everyone says it's going to be the capital city after General Washington becomes President—the center of the social world! I could be a great hostess—"

"But what about your marriage?"

"He'll come around once he realizes how many other men want me," Priscilla replied, waving a slim white hand. "In any case, I don't really care a fig if I marry Lion Hampshire or not. I'll vow that there are plenty of rich, influential *gentlemen* in Philadelphia who would be simply honored to call me their wife."

Meagan could think of no polite reply to her companion's immodest speech and she was tired of haggling with her. "It's your life, Priscilla, and I daresay that Lion Hampshire is old enough to know what he is doing. Do hurry now; I am famished."

Priscilla affected an attitude of nonchalance as she lay back on her bed and replied, "Hurry yourself. I am not going."

Meagan froze in the midst of washing her face and turned around slowly. "I'm sure you don't mean that. You must realize that I cannot sup with Mr. Hampshire alone, Priscilla."

"So what. Go and eat in the kitchen with the rest of the servants."

Meagan held her breath until she gained control of her temper, realizing that Priscilla was obviously still bitter about the slap on the ferry.

"Whatever you say, dear," she said in the sweetest voice she could muster. Quickly she changed into her last clean gown, a lilac muslin quite unsuited to the climate. Brushing her long raven hair until it shone, she pinned it so that a cluster of loose curls fell down her back, then appraised herself in the undulating mirror which hung over the dressing table. The girl who looked back at her had all the charm of a gamine on the brink of womanhood, and she smiled a little, wondering at the glow in her large violet eyes.

"Have an enjoyable evening," she called to a frowning Priscilla and went into the hallway feeling oddly elated. She realized she was alone for the first time in three days and wondered how she could spend the evening.

If only I could find someone to have a card game with! I wish men weren't so stuffy! she thought as she fluffed out her skirts and ran down the stairway. When she rounded the corner at the bottom, she nearly fell over Lion Hampshire, who sat in a wing chair against the wall. He looked impossibly immaculate; his gray suit was neatly pressed, his cravat pure white against his tanned face, and his hair like burnished gold in the candlelight. He was smoking a cigar, which he now placed in a dish as he reached out to steady her.

"Always in a hurry, aren't you? I knew when I heard that clatter on the stairs that it had to be you." There was a sparkle in his blue eyes that Meagan dared to believe was the beginning of a smile. "Dressing up like a female hasn't altered your behavior a bit!"

Meagan swallowed an inappropriate retort, dropping her eyes instead. "I beg your pardon, sir."

Now he laughed in reality, and she stole a glance at his handsome face. His laughter was rich with an irrepressible humor that Meagan had not seen since the day she had run into him in the entry hall at West Hills. His features were transformed from cool perfection to irresistible splendor.

"You really chafe under that subservient act, don't you?" he said at last, meeting her eyes. "You would love to tell me off." He reached for his cigar and inquired, "Well, where is the queen? Her court awaits her and is damned hungry."

"Miss Wade is not coming," Meagan said bluntly, unable to bring herself to make excuses.

Lion's eyes narrowed a fraction, then he smiled

suddenly and stood up, his broad shoulders even with the top of her head. "That's the best news I've heard in days. Let's go."

When he put his hand around her elbow, Meagan's protests died on her lips and she found herself running along to match his long strides as they crossed into a private dining room adjacent to the large public one. Cream-colored walls were bathed in the yellow light given off from the paneled fireplace, and Meagan saw that covered dishes of food were already being set on the table by two well-scrubbed serving-girls.

When the tavern keeper appeared with a bottle of red wine, Lion told him, "Miss Wade will not be joining us. You may remove the third setting."

As if by magic, Priscilla's place disappeared along with the servants, and Meagan realized that she was quite alone with Lion Hampshire. Shyness suffocated her and she wondered at it.

Lion reached across the table to pour her wine, his mouth curving in silent amusement. Blood rushed up Meagan's cheeks, and as she stared down at her napkin, she mentally shook herself. When she raised her chin to look at him, her shoulders were squared and her eyes sparkled like amethysts in the soft light.

Casually Lion began to lift the covers from the dishes, allowing their heady aromas to escape and enrich the stale air. Meagan forgot everything, including her manners, as she arched across her plate to get a better view.

A serving-girl appeared from the kitchen to ladle out the steaming okra soup, and silently, eagerly, Meagan began to eat. Each spoonful was crowded with tomatoes, okra, corn, rice, and lima beans, and flavored with bacon, vinegar, and fresh pepper. Meagan was in ecstasy as she rolled her tongue around the rich broth while Lion watched her with detached amusement.

"I gather this dish must be a delicacy compared with the fare served in the Wade kitchen," he remarked at last.

Meagan looked up in surprise, the wide silver spoon poised near her open mouth. She had almost forgotten his presence; now she was confused by his words. As the meaning became clear, she let her spoon descend back into the bowl and her impish mouth turned up. The irony was laughable to Meagan as she recalled only too well the sumptuous, excessive meals of her past life. Memories of heavy creamed soups and spinach soufflés came back to her and she laughed out loud.

"I'll admit, sir, that this dish is an improvement over what I'm used to. The flavor is simply splendid! I'm particularly fond of okra."

Lion lifted one slashing golden brow.

"Well, perhaps you'll have an opportunity to sample some more sophisticated foods in the future."

"I rather hope not," Meagan returned, striving to repress a giggle.

Lion leaned closer in the candlelight. He had the distinct feeling that she was not the least bit impressed with him; worse, he feared that she was on the verge of laughter. Meagan dropped her eyes before his scrutiny and turned her attention back to the now lukewarm soup. Lion watched her eat, frankly curious. Sipping his wine, he thought back over the past three days. His preoccupation with the weather and their progress had coupled with his extreme irritation with Priscilla, leaving him little time to notice Meagan. Now he remembered clearly the way she had slapped her mistress that day on the ferry. Thinking back, it seemed now that she had done a great deal to keep Priscilla going. Lion could recall seeing Meagan leading her by the arm, her eyes conveying a stern message. Now, as the serving-girl filled their plates with molasses-cured ham, mashed carrots and parsnips, and hot potato rolls, Lion said, "I gather that you have been with Priscilla for a long time."

Meagan met his sharp blue gaze, her own eyes smoky in the firelight. "Yes."

"You seem to know how to handle her."

Meagan took a sip of wine, measuring him. Suddenly

she smiled. "It is an acquired art, sir, and one that is impossible to perfect." Her smile widened enigmatically before she turned to her dinner.

Lion continued to watch her as they ate, wondering. Her speech patterns were distinctly refined and her delicate, intelligent features had an aristocratic quality.

"Have you always been a servant?" Lion asked suddenly, surprising himself.

Meagan stared at him in astonishment, and for a brief moment he thought she looked alarmed. "I can't imagine why you should ask such a question, Mr. Hampshire. But since you have—the answer is no."

"Would you tell me the reason?"

"My parents died."

The burnished brows drew together, shading his eyes in the half-light. "I'm sorry. I shouldn't be prying into your affairs. I know how irritating that can be." He leaned back in his chair, staring off into space as he sipped his wine.

Meagan watched him as she ate, glancing out from under her long lashes. There was a hard, bitter cut to his handsome profile as he gazed into the fireplace. Meagan saw the pain flickering in his icy blue eyes and for the first time since she had seen him outside West Hills she felt prepared to be his friend.

Chapter Six

THE REMAINDER OF their journey North took nearly ten days, and Meagan wondered frequently if it would ever end. Or, more to the point, if they would live through it. The weather grew worse the farther they traveled, and Lion's mood darkened with the ominous clouds that dogged their progress.

The night at Spurrier Tavern had formed an odd, unspoken alliance between Meagan and her friend's fiancé. He came to realize that she could keep Priscilla's tantrums in check, while she managed to convey to him that the less he was seen the fewer scenes there would be. To Lion, the silent bargain was a good one, for his daily battles with the elements were exhausting enough; he had no desire to take on his whining bride-to-be as well.

The master and servant learned to communicate with their eyes behind Priscilla's back as Meagan reassured him that she had everything under control. There was little opportunity for further conversation. The days were long and tiring and Meagan began to eat her nightly meals in her room with the pouting Priscilla. She regretted her unguarded behavior during her dinner with Lion Hampshire and had no wish for a repeat performance to further arouse his curiosity. Her performance that night had been unskilled; she had committed the clumsy blunder of dropping her guard and showing him herself. She knew that he had been intrigued by her and now she was panicky at the thought of getting herself in any deeper. So she played the role of lady's maid to the hilt, staying out of Lion's way and dropping her eyes with proper subservience when he came near. She could feel his mocking smile as he watched her, making her cheeks burn with the indignity of her position. But she refused to let down her guard again. The thought of his finding out the truth and sending her home to Virginia in his anger caused her scalp to chill and prickle with unaccustomed fear.

When she wasn't preoccupied or worried about Lion or Priscilla, Meagan found herself actually enjoying the long hours of travel. The country was new to her and she longed to see it in the rich verdant garb of spring. Baltimore was a lovely surprise. Half the size of Philadelphia, it was a quaint, charming town perched on a hill that sloped down to Chesapeake Bay. Meagan tried to visualize the spacious streets under blue skies and sunshine, with the numerous dovecotes filled with singing birds. Lion told them that the townspeople believed the doves and swallows would bring prosperity, but none were in evidence as the carriage clattered down the sleet-swept streets.

Maryland's rolling countryside charmed Meagan even as it frustrated her. The roads were poor, seeming to grow muddier with every mile. Each hill became a frightening challenge as the horses struggled to bring the yellow post-chariot to the summit. Through the rain, Meagan could see the farmhouses and stone barns standing desolately under the frozen gray sky. Flocks of sheep huddled together, nibbling at the dry, brown stubble that poked through the frosty ground. Meagan consoled herself with the knowledge that soon enough the fields would be moist and warm and filled with flax, with the sheep happily roaming the lush hillsides.

Luck favored them the day they ferried the Susquehanna River, for though it was dangerously swollen, the weather was unusually peaceful and mild. There were no frightening winds or sudden lurches during the crossing, and Meagan managed to keep Priscilla from becoming agitated.

The next few days took them across the head of the Elk River and on into Delaware. The journey to Newcastle, which was usually accomplished in one day, took them two. Meagan could see that Lion was becoming less tense, however, as they neared the Pennsylvania border. The next day they left Newcastle and followed the majestic three-mile-wide Delaware River northward.

When they drew up outside a remote tavern that evening, Lion helped the girls down with an irresistible grin. "Ladies, this is our last stop, God willing. This time tomorrow night I hope to be deep into a bottle of Bingham's brandy!"

Meagan felt herself smile back at him, caught in his high spirits and her own excited anticipation of the future.

Priscilla, on the other hand, managed to sniff

loudly while looking the other way. "I must say, it is about time! I can't imagine enduring a more terrible ordeal than the last fortnight has been for me. My upbringing certainly did not prepare me—"

Lion's eyes had hardened to sapphire ice as he regarded her with distaste. "It is evident that your upbringing neglected to prepare you for anything worthwhile."

Priscilla's lower lip trembled with rage as she sought a retort. Failing that, she turned and flounced into the inn, her lovely head erect on its long, white neck.

Meagan thought privately that the entire effect of her profile was spoiled by that willful lower lip. Shrugging tiredly, she started after Priscilla, Lion at her side. Meagan ventured a tentative glance in his direction, expecting rage and finding instead an expression of rueful amusement. One side of his mouth curved cynically as he rolled his blue eyes at her, and for a moment Meagan feared he might chuckle aloud. Priscilla was as testy and volatile as a little child, growing worse by the day, and Meagan had no desire to endure another of her scenes.

Once upstairs in their room, Priscilla calmed herself with a glass of wine. Two more were consumed before their supper arrived, by which time Priscilla was stretched out across the narrow bed in her chemise. While she rambled about her plans for the future, Meagan busied herself by scrubbing with cold water and a rough cloth, trying to ignore her. When the innkeeper's wife arrived with their supper, the two girls sat down facing each other, sharing the wobbly table between the beds. The stew held more barley than beef and seemed to have cooled down considerably during the trip upstairs. Priscilla pushed around in the bowl with her spoon, searching for meat and smiling strangely to herself.

"What do you look so pleased about?" Meagan demanded.

"I was just wondering where I'll be dining tomorrow night . . . I'll wager that I'll be living like a queen by then. Did you hear Lion mention the name Bingham?

Do you suppose he knows them? I've heard such tales from James about their house! It's supposed to be modeled after the Duke of Manchester's, only Anne Bingham wanted it grander—"

"If I were you I'd tread a little more cautiously," Meagan broke in curtly, "If you don't use more discretion in your dealings with Mr. Hampshire, you may find yourself eating with me in the kitchen!"

Priscilla wrinkled her nose and stuck out her tongue, a gesture which ended in a huge yawn. Stretching like a cat, she lay back on her bed and was fast asleep, the empty wine glass dangling from her slender fingers.

Meagan sighed as she leaned over to remove it and spread a quilt across her friend. By now the stew was cold. The fresh decanter of wine beckoned to her, and after pouring a large glass, she leaned back against the feather pillows to feel sorry for herself. Dusk had darkened into night by the time she finished the wine and ceased her brooding. On an impulse, Meagan decided to venture downstairs. There was a longing inside her for honest human contact, a craving for laughter.

An oil lamp had been lit in the paneled hallway, throwing elongated shadows down the steps. Meagan descended quietly, listening to the muffled voices that drifted up from the kitchen and the taproom. Although she had been hoping to run across the friendly wife or daughter of some fellow traveler, the first person she saw in the taproom was Lion Hampshire. The room was not empty. A handful of men were gathered around a large gate-leg table arguing over a sheaf of papers, two more were hunched across a game table, and one lone fellow snored against the wall near the fireplace. Lion sat not far away, scowling at a newspaper while taking long drinks of brandy from a stoneware jug. His gilded hair was as bright as the nearby fire, while his skin seemed more bronzed than ever in the evening light.

The wine gave Meagan courage to venture in among the men, and she walked up to Lion and peeked over the top of the paper. "Hello."

He turned his chin a fraction as he observed her, squaring his jaw. Meagan noticed the blond hair that showed above the open collar of his shirt, curling against his honey-brown neck. She felt alarmed at the sudden pounding of her heart.

"Ahh, Meagan. Is anything wrong? Has Her Highness made a proclamation?" He smiled a little, in spite of himself, showing a flash of white teeth. Meagan's own mouth twitched helplessly.

"No, as a matter of fact, she's asleep."

"Then, why—?"

"I'm bored silly, and that dark room was driving me to distraction." She glanced longingly at the chair next to his. "Would you mind very much if I sat down for just a few minutes?"

"Please! Be my guest. I apologize for not offering you a seat sooner."

Meagan sank down, spreading her skirts.

"Let me get you a glass of wine," Lion said, gesturing to the tavern keeper. From behind his cage-topped bar, the burly man poured the glass and brought it across the room, eyeing them knowingly. Lion managed to ignore him as he grinned at Meagan. "I can see why you might feel a little berserk after an evening shut up with Priscilla."

Meagan was startled by his comment. Suddenly she decided to speak her mind. "Pardon me for saying so, but I think that's a rather odd attitude for a man to hold about his fiancée!"

"You're absolutely right."

"You admit it?" she exclaimed incredulously.

"I fear I must. I have no talent for deception." He smiled slightly as though he were making fun of her, but there was an unmistakable bitterness in his expression.

Meagan stared at him hard before she spoke again. "I know this is unpardonably rude of me, but I simply cannot help myself! Why ever are you marrying Pris—that is, Miss Wade? Is it for money? I didn't think that they had so awfully much on hand."

A voice in the back of her mind told her that she

46

was way out of place as a servant, but she took another gulp of wine to silence it. Lion Hampshire was leaning back in his chair, looking at her with the same interested curiosity she had seen in his eyes the night they had dined together in Baltimore. He grinned, and Meagan felt as though a fire had been lit inside her. It was the kind of dazzling smile she had left her room in search of, and she responded to it instinctively.

"There is something very suspicious about you." Lion attempted to sound stern. "I sensed it that first day when you ran me down in the entryway at West Hills. The trouble is, I can't put my finger on it. And the other problem is, I like you. I don't trust you —but I like you. And I appreciate your efforts to make this journey as bearable as possible—not to mention as safe as possible for your mistress. If I'd been alone with her she'd probably be at the bottom of the Potomac right now." There was a glint of laughter in his eyes as he raised the mug. "Am I right in assuming that we are allies of a sort?"

Meagan strove for a dumb expression. His bluntness took her by surprise, and she knew that any good lady's maid would never show any disloyalty to her mistress. Valiantly she attempted to take Priscilla's side, but when she met his eyes, she felt her cheeks grow hot and the words died on her lips.

Lion grinned triumphantly. "I knew it!" He leaned close to her blushing face, and Meagan felt faint as she breathed in the scent of him. "We are friends, aren't we? I don't suppose you'd care to reveal the solution to your mystery . . . ?"

I must never talk to him alone again, Meagan thought wildly, her violet eyes widening. Aloud, she stammered, "No! That is, there is no mystery! It is all in your mind."

Lion shook his head with amusement as he leaned across the table to light a cheroot on the guttering candle.

"Whatever you say, little one. For my part, I also

deny any ulterior motives . . . save the more noble one of true love."

Meagan cast a dubious glance at his dancing blue eyes. "I don't believe you."

"Neither do I believe you." His smile flashed in the shadows. "You are an enigma. I am sure that solving the mystery will provide an entertaining winter diversion."

"Don't trouble yourself," Meagan murmured darkly under her breath. Across the room, the three men rolled up the sheaf of papers and got to their feet, chairs grating harshly on the planked floor.

"Careful," Lion taunted. "Let's not be insolent. I shouldn't like to be forced to dismiss you."

"You—" Meagan began, rising to the bait. Her teeth bit her tongue as she stopped herself.

"Ah, that's more like it." Leaning closer, he grazed her neck with his mouth.

For a frightened moment, Meagan was unable to exhale, then recovering her senses, she glared at him with smoldering violet eyes. "You behave strangely for a man overcome by true love," she commented.

Lion laughed out loud at this and reached out to catch her wrist. "What unbelievable nerve! You are the one behaving strangely, my dear lady's maid!"

Meagan snatched her hand away just as a magnolia-scented shadow fell across the table, and they both looked up to find Priscilla standing there.

Immaculately gowned, she smiled at them with narrowed green eyes. "My, what a cozy twosome you make," she purred. "I don't recall giving you permission to leave the room tonight, Meagan."

Meagan's knuckles went white as she gripped the edge of the table, all too conscious of Lion's interested eyes watching them.

"I'm sorry, ma'am. You were asleep, and I felt the need for some fresh air."

"It seems to me that this air is decidedly smoky," Priscilla returned sweetly. "Why don't you run along now, dear? I'm sure you have bored Mr. Hampshire

48

quite long enough with your chatter. From now on, I suggest that you remember your place."

Meagan stood up, cheeks crimson, her eyes drawn to Lion's by some magnetic force she couldn't control. While Priscilla took over her chair and proceeded to link arms with Lion, he winked at Meagan quite deliberately. Meagan dragged her eyes away and murmured with cold effort, "I beg your pardon, Miss Wade, Mr. Hampshire. It won't happen again."

Blood pounded in her head as she turned toward the doorway, but it couldn't drown out their voices.

"I hope you won't think me too forward, Lion, but I've decided that it's time you and I became friends," Priscilla was saying in a sugary voice. "I'm afraid I haven't behaved very well these past two weeks, but I'm hoping you'll forgive me and we can start afresh."

"My dear, you have read my mind. Those are my thoughts and desires exactly."

Chapter Seven

DARKNESS AND SILENCE stretched the minutes out in Meagan's imagination as she lay in her narrow bed, waiting. The room grew starkly cold. At last she forced herself up, hurrying across the frozen floor to agitate the embers in the fireplace. She was turning the hot brick at the foot of her bed when Priscilla came in wearing a satisfied smile that doubled Meagan's rage.

"Meagan, are you still awake? I would have thought you'd be asleep ages ago!"

Meagan regarded her angrily in the darkness, thinking that Priscilla's pieces no longer fit together so predictably. The empty-headed stare was gone; a new shrewdness lurked behind her innocent expression. Meagan's keenest instinct warned her to speak with care, but her temper had raced beyond caution. "Don't you put on airs with me, Priscilla Margaret Wade! I am so mad at you I could spit! How could you speak to me the way you did tonight?"

Priscilla, unhooking the front of her gown, widened her eyes in an effective imitation of incomprehension. "I can't think why you're so angry! I was only trying to act my part, Meagan! You've lectured me so often about being a bad actress, and now you're doing the same thing when I'm good! I thought I was supposed to treat you like a servant!"

Her pretty chin trembled in the shadows, but Meagan warned herself not to be taken in

"I know better than that, Priscilla. You loved that scene downstairs! You really enjoyed acting high and mighty with me."

"I think that's a hateful thing to say, Meagan Sayers!" Loud sobs were heard as she lifted her dress over her head, but when her face came back into view it was dry. "Besides, maybe it's my turn. You've been bossing me around ever since we were tiny children."

"That's ridiculous. All I've ever done is prod you into action occasionally. If you had had your way, you'd have spent your life lying in bed, having your hair brushed, and taking baths!"

"At least I wouldn't be in the scrapes you're always in!" Buttoning her bedgown, she went on. "Look at you now. You could be living in society in Boston, but you've chosen to reduce yourself to a servant. I realized tonight that it really isn't such a masquerade, Meagan. I mean, you really are dependent on me now. Whom else do you have?"

Meagan was stunned by her words. It was obvious that Priscilla was taking her new thoughts very seriously. Tiny hairs rose on her arms and legs in the chilly night air; slowly she crept into bed.

The silence stretched between them, finally broken

by Priscilla, sweetly imploring, "Meagan, don't misunderstand now. You'll always be my best friend, no matter how high I go on Society Hill. You know, that's what James says they call the rich part of Philadelphia. Anyway, I won't desert you."

"You're too good," Meagan said sarcastically.

"Just don't you embarrass me with one of your little pranks! Oh, Meagan, I want to thank you for bringing me to my senses tonight—about Lion, I mean." She pulled up her quilt to her chin and sighed meaningfully. "I'm going to make him love me, you'll see. I wouldn't be surprised if he does already! I declare, he can look so attractive when he turns on that dazzling smile of his!"

The final day of their journey put Priscilla's new determination to the fullest test.

The three travelers rose before dawn. In his single-minded desire to reach Philadelphia, Lion was distant and brusque toward both girls, saving his attention for the horses and the roads.

As it turned out, the sun never had a chance to make an appearance, for as they moved northward, a band of black clouds began to climb on the horizon. Inside the carriage, Meagan had little to say to Priscilla, transferring her attention to the blurred little window beside her. Through it she could see the clouds stacked across the sky like fat, clinging puffs of smoke. Lion cantered nearby on his chestnut roan, his tanned face set like stone as he watched the storm gathering strength. The air was eerily still. Finally the rain began and the wind rose up to join it so that the heavy droplets shot from the black sky like bullets.

Meagan clearly saw the old terror in Priscilla's eyes, but felt disinclined to reassure her, and for once Priscilla's pride kept her silent. Barely a minute passed before the carriage came to a stop at the bottom of a hill, and Meagan saw Lion tethering his roan to the rest of the team. When he came around to the side and pulled open the door, the assault from outside had the impact of a tidal wave. By the time Lion and

Joshua had climbed in, the girls were nearly as wet as the men.

Meagan managed a bemused smile as she ran a hand over her rain-splashed face and pushed back her hair. The coachman sat next to Priscilla, looking very young and pale. Then Meagan felt Lion Hampshire beside her, felt his sodden cape soaking her skirts. The seat was small, joining them together like Siamese twins. Meagan's heart began to pound.

"Damnation!" Lion ejaculated, pulling off his hat to run a brown hand through lustrous hair. "I swear that nature has conspired against me to prevent this journey from being completed!"

The pair across from him stared back, speechless, but Meagan heard herself rejoin blithely, "What hellish luck!"

She could have hit herself once it was out. Priscilla looked faint; Joshua stunned.

However, after barely a moment's pause, Lion gave a shout of laughter. "Good Lord, what a delight you are!"

Meagan was blushing and examining the seam of her pelisse when the post-chariot was rattled by a sudden onslaught of hailstones. The horses whinnied and stamped helplessly.

"Won't they run, poor things?" Meagan asked anxiously.

"No, ma'am," came the coachman's quiet voice. "I tells them to stay."

Lion grinned. "Joshua has a talent with animals. Those horses understand every word he says and never disobey him."

The four passengers were jostled from side to side as the lead pair of horses reared up against the storm outside. Meagan's heart ached for them. Across from her, Priscilla's face was as bloodless as Joshua's, but she seemed determined not to give way to her usual bout of hysterics.

They all sat together for over an hour, waiting for the wind and rain to abate. Little was said; the atmosphere did not lend itself to small talk. Meagan stiffened beside Lion, feeling the hard muscles in his arms and legs pressing against her own body through her thin cloak and dress. Every one of her nerves was painfully aware of his presence, and Meagan hated her body for its instinctive reactions.

Lion, however, seemed unconcerned with her or anyone else. His damp head was turned toward the window, eyes serious as he stared at the gray sky and the dead, dark fields. It was depressing for him to see the land looking so bleak, for he knew it best in the spring, when clover, grain, and flax abounded, followed by miles of orchards and elegant villas, each with a garden more beautiful than the last.

Alert to the silence outside, he looked over to Joshua. The rain had tapered off and stopped; now Lion threw open the door. The air that rushed in was pure, fresh, and cold.

He and Joshua leaped to the ground and closed the door.

"Do you imagine that he likes you?" Priscilla asked bluntly, catching Meagan off guard.

Hot blood stained her cheeks before she could summon up a semblance of composure. "Why, I suppose he does. What of it?"

"Don't think you can steal him from me, Meagan. I've heard plenty of stories from James about the things men do with their servants. There is only one way he would ever like you."

"How dare you say such a thing? Or suggest that I would invite that kind of—"

"I've seen you with him at night! I know the way you look at him. I'm not so simple-minded as you seem to believe!" Her green eyes sparkled with jealousy.

Meagan was shocked to see her display so much emotion over Lion Hampshire.

"All I'm saying is that you should stay away from him. If you want me to remain your friend—and if you want to avoid a proposition from Lion—just keep away!" Her voice caught, choking near tears.

Before Meagan could respond, the door flew open and Lion was framed in the opening.

"How are you ladies doing?" His smile was tight, troubled. "Are you prepared for more? Our back wheels are deep in mud. We were on a slight downhill slope when we stopped, but the horses moved during the storm to the very bottom. There's nothing ahead of us but another hill, and I'm afraid it will be one hell of a task getting us going and on our way up."

Priscilla reached for his hand protectively. "What does this mean?"

"It means that you'll both have to get out and walk. Prepare yourselves for a lot of mud."

Priscilla managed to moderate her cringing expression when she saw Meagan silently put a hand on Lion's shoulder and hop to the ground. Priscilla struck the perfect balance between femininity and bravery as she bent, poised in the doorway. Lion lifted her down gently, blue eyes flickering with surprise as she smiled up at him courageously.

The slender yellow wheels were half-swallowed by the mud. Both girls stood on the side of the road, a clean, chilly wind catching the hems of their pelisses, causing them to billow out like sails. Neither of them spoke as they watched the efforts to free the carriage. The five horses strained up in front while the men pushed from behind. In moments, both Lion and Joshua were showered with black mud and the wheels were still mired under. This went on for several minutes, Priscilla covering her face in horror as Lion was sprayed again and again by the spinning wheels. At last they seemed poised on success, but their strength gave out just as it seemed the carriage would roll free. Lion swore softly when the wheels dropped back into the deep ruts, tightening his dirty jaw. When they repositioned themselves before Joshua called the order to the horses, Meagan found herself rushing forward to stand between them.

"Let me help, too. I'm really quite strong."

Lion grinned caustically. "What the hell—come on and put your back into it." He looked over to Priscilla who seemed both panicky and angry. "Why don't you come over and lend a hand, too?"

Priscilla was speechless as she hesitated, then lifted her skirts and ventured forward. After shooting one furious look at Meagan, she put her hands against the carriage, closing her mouth and eyes tightly.

When Joshua gave a shout to the horses, everyone began to push, the men grunting loudly. The wheels spun, showering them with frosty black mud, and Meagan could feel her silk-encased feet being forced deeper into the bog the harder she pushed. Suddenly the carriage broke out of the rut, rolling away from them. Priscilla, her eyes closed and her face screwed up in a grimace, fell forward abruptly, landing full in the quagmire. The other three were so happy to have freed the wheels that the sight of her lying there was too much to endure. Lion and Meagan clung to each other, laughing helplessly until they cried. Finally, Lion reached out with Joshua to lift his fiancée to her feet, offering a large handkerchief to wipe her mud-smeared face.

Priscilla gingerly opened her eyes and promptly burst into a torrent of tears.

Along the banks of the icy Delaware River the ships were huddled close together, their sails furled tightly along the skeletal masts. Philadelphia's docks were empty; even the wide, wet thoroughfares were nearly deserted. Meagan leaned forward to stare out the window as the horses clopped noisily through the puddles along Front Street. The outline of the city was barely visible now; the sky was rapidly shading toward complete darkness. The post-chariot turned onto Spruce Street, following the hill up from the waterfront until a cheerful-looking inn came into view. The horses stopped in front of a sign that read "A Man Full of Trouble." Above the legend a man and his wife were pictured, carrying between them a parrot, a monkey, and a bandbox.

Lion pulled the door open and helped the girls down to the wet cobbled pavement. Even in the misty darkness the tired lines were apparent on his face. "Well, Priscilla, you may clean up here. I'm in no mood to wait very long, though."

She said nothing. She intended to nurse her grudge against both Lion and Meagan until it suited her purposes to forgive them. The hour of furious crying that had followed her fall into the mud that afternoon had done little to soothe her injured pride, particularly since her companions had ignored her.

The three of them went silently into the clean, redbrick tavern. A few crusty-looking sailors sat drinking in the bar and most of them called hasty greetings to Lion. The respect was evident in their voices, a fact that surprised Meagan since all the men appeared older than him.

He took a pewter mug from the tavern keeper and dropped into a bow-back Windsor chair in the midst of the other seamen. His sudden smile was astonishing.

A plump woman wearing a starched white apron and mobcap came forward to lead the two girls upstairs to a warm, cozy chamber where a basin was already filled with steaming water.

Meagan scrubbed hurriedly, but Priscilla took her time, clearly making an effort to provoke her fiancé. Meagan hated the silence that had been growing more oppressive with each hour that had passed since the incident in the road, and looked up with relief when Lion's loud knock hit the door.

"Let's go!" The tone of his voice brooked no argument.

Hastily Priscilla pushed the remaining pins into her hair and they were on their way again.

While they were in the tavern, lamps had been lit along the wide streets, their flames now flickering against the inky night. Meagan shivered in her corner of the carriage as they rolled up Spruce Street, slowing down just two blocks west of A Man Full of Trouble. Both girls peered out the window, only to see yellow lamplight dancing up a high, painted fence that was so long its end was swallowed up by the darkness. The post-chariot drew up before a towering ornamental gate immediately opened by a watchman. Lion rode ahead along the circular driveway which led to the impressive Mansion House of William and Anne Bingham. Lights blazed on all three floors, shining a welcome through the fanlights and pouring out both gleaming light and liveried servants through the double doors.

Priscilla's pout disappeared. "It's the Binghams', Meagan!" she exclaimed, her face glowing with excitement. "The most magnificent house in America! The stories I've heard James tell about this place . . . I just can't believe that I'm a part of this world now. Isn't it wonderful?"

"Wonderful," her companion agreed dryly.

When a satin-clad footman rushed forward to open the carriage door, Priscilla stepped down wearing her most brilliant smile. Lion took her elbow, eyeing her cynically. As Meagan climbed down behind them, William and Anne Bingham appeared in the doorway, and even she allowed herself to feel impressed. Meagan watched as greetings were exchanged and Priscilla was introduced, following the group at a distance as they turned into the house.

The entryway took her breath away, for it was far more magnificent than anything she had seen in all the great mansions of Virginia. The floor was an incredible mosaic of priceless marble which ran up to a wide, white central staircase also built of marble. Ahead of Meagan, Priscilla was chattering gaily as she took in her surroundings with darting emerald eyes. Meagan had to admire her composure; she hadn't even gasped.

A thin, austere man clad in black satin crossed over to her. "Miss, my name is Wickham and I am the butler here. I gather that you attend Mistress Wade?"

"Uh—yes!" Meagan stared at him, astonished by his haughty manner until she realized that in the class system of servants he ranked far above her. "My name is Meagan, Wickham." He raised thick black eyebrows, waiting. "Meagan . . . South." What imagination, she thought sarcastically.

"Well, South, the head housekeeper will be here momentarily to show you your room and Mistress Wade's suite."

"We're staying here?"

"Of course. Until Master Hampshire and Mistress Wade are married." He nodded slightly and disappeared around a corner.

Meagan stood against the wall, suddenly very conscious of her grimy appearance as she watched the two couples who stood in the parlor which opened off to the left of the entry hall.

A servant was moving among them distributing glasses of wine, and Meagan found her eyes drawn to Anne Bingham, watching as she lifted the crystal goblet to her lips. Her beauty was undeniable. She wore an exquisite gown of amber silk, rich in its very simplicity. Her hair was lightly powdered, the soft brown curls pinned up around her face while a cluster of long ringlets escaped to fall over one white shoulder. Even from a distance the elegant bone structure was unmistakable: high cheekbones, long graceful neck, willowy figure combining with her innate gracefulness to make her unforgettable. She was laughing now, and everyone's eyes were on her. William Bingham watched her proudly, confident that his newest guest was properly dazzled by Anne. His reason for living was the accumulation of wealth and beauty, and Anne was the most splendid of all his possessions, outshining even the sumptuous Mansion House.

Meagan found Bingham far less impressive than his young wife. Ruddy-cheeked and stocky, his manner seemed affected to her. Lion's presence made him look even worse.

She let her gaze slide over Priscilla to Lion and was startled to find him staring boldly back at her. Blushing hotly, she was grateful to Anne Bingham for finding just the right words to reclaim his attention. "Lion, you will never guess who is back from sea!" she exclaimed with an innocent enthusiasm that rang false. "Marcus Reems! If I didn't know better, I would swear he was following you . . ."

Lion's entire body tensed, the muscles showing in his shoulders and neck, his eyes alert. Priscilla, oblivious to his reaction, had no use for names unknown to her and promptly changed the subject.

Her eyes on Lion, Meagan failed to notice when someone stopped next to her. A throat was cleared discreetly. Startled, she turned around, running smack into the tiny woman who was about to tap her on the shoulder.

"Oh my! I beg your pardon! I didn't know—"

"That's all right, dear. No damage done." The other woman was quite young, thirty perhaps, and no taller than Meagan. She wore a neat gray cotton dress and a lace mobcap over her powdered curls. Her hazel eyes were as warm and friendly as her smile, set off by the roundest, rosiest cheeks Meagan had ever seen. "My name is Smith. I'm the housekeeper here. I want to welcome you to Mansion House."

"Thank you, Smith. Will you call me Meagan? I'm afraid the names Smith and South might get a bit confusing!"

Smith laughed softly. "Perhaps they would at that. Let me take you to your room now. The servants' quarters are right this way."

Servants' quarters! Meagan thought. What have I gotten myself into?

Chapter Eight

WILLIAM BINGHAM OBSERVED Lion over his glass of port, wondering at the tired, distracted look he wore. Finally, he cleared his throat and remarked, "I paid a visit to Dr. Franklin last week."

"How does he fare? Better than a month has passed since I last saw him."

"His spirits are good, but physically he is unchanged. We discussed the next meeting of that newest political society of his and the progress of the Philosophical Hall. He told me frankly that he doubts he will ever attend a meeting there once it is completed."

"Aren't you a vice-president of this Society for Political Enquiries? What's it all about?"

"Yes, I am, along with George Clymer," Bingham admitted a trifle pompously. "We still meet fortnightly at Dr. Franklin's house. There are only fifty of us and we just discuss politics. Of course, that is quite a topic these days and the Doctor is full of ideas and opinions. It is great entertainment for him, but God only knows how much longer he'll be able to get downstairs to the large room."

"I'd better make a point to see him tomorrow."

William Bingham puffed on his long, slender pipe, watching Lion across the shadowy study as he stared into the fire. He had been unusually quiet all evening, in spite of Anne and Priscilla's attempts to make him laugh during supper. It was not the dashing Lion Hampshire of months past.

"Confound it, man, aren't you going to ask me about Reems?"

Lion looked up, appearing rather bored, but amused by Bingham's consternation. "By all means, do give me the news before you burst with it."

"Ahem!" He scowled, puffing on his pipe. "The fact is, things did not go well for him, though at least the ship returned intact this time. The man simply lacks talent as a sea captain, I fear. The crews he chooses are inept and untrustworthy, and he makes bad bargains in the Orient. I suppose I needn't spell it out for you. If I didn't know better, I would think the man simply doesn't give a damn, but you should have seen his face when I told him I'd not give my backing again!"

Lion lifted gilded eyebrows. "You went that far?"

He smiled cryptically. "I can well imagine Marcus's reaction."

"Well, it's made cursed unpleasant by Anne's regard for the man. She claims to find him charming—'mysterious'—and invites him here even yet. I could swear that she enjoys having him about simply because the situation is so uncomfortable!"

Mockery infected Lion's smile. "Why don't you tell her you won't allow it?"

The other man choked on his port. "For God's sake, don't you think I've tried? You're a fine one to be giving advice on wife-management. Wait and see a few months from now!" However, watching Lion's cool, lean face, he doubted whether any woman would cross him—even a wife. Such men were hard to come by, and with a qualm, Bingham remembered his recent conversation with Benjamin Franklin.

"I have been told that you may not take a ship this spring," he blurted, coming to the point.

Lion looked up, his eyes like blue flames. "How does that set with you?" he inquired bluntly.

"Naturally, as your backer, I'm disappointed. Mordecai and I have two magnificent ships almost finished at the Kensington shipyard and I was counting on you to captain one of them. No one else has your spirit, your quality of leadership, your competence. You are so at home on the sea, and the men sense it—" The flowery compliments died on his lips when he realized that Lion had withdrawn. "Listen to me. More than disappointment, I feel curiosity. What are you doing? Why this sudden marriage? And why don't you want to sail? Is it because of Priscilla Wade? As your friend, I am concerned—"

Lion laughed so bitterly that Bingham stared in surprise and puzzlement.

"Come on, William. We both know that my prime qualification for your friendship is my ability to line your pockets with gold when I sail your ships home up the Delaware! As to my current plans, I really don't feel like discussing them now. The whole affair is getting too damn complicated and all I want to do

61

is go home and sleep. I'd be gratified to wake up tomorrow and find all my problems solved." He paused and sighed, closing his eyes. The firelight mingled with his golden hair and softened the hard lines of his brown face.

William Bingham wavered between sympathy and frustration, his basically selfish nature winning out. "Damn it all, you can't dismiss me so easily! I have backed you for more than three years now, making it possible for you to acquire a tidy fortune and majority ownership of two fine vessels. I have offered to shelter some unknown southern girl just because you asked me to—no questions asked. I believe, however, that I am *owed* some answers! I will not have you deposit some featherbrained chit on my doorstep and then proceed to tell me you don't wish to take my ship this spring without some clarification. You owe me—"

Tired of watching William's face redden and swell, Lion shifted his eyes to watch the shadows leap over the carved cornices and across the decorated ceiling.

"Really, William, I do wish you'd spare me this tirade," he interjected coolly. "If you continue at this rate, you'll be struck with an apoplectic seizure and I shouldn't like that on my conscience. I'll tell you this much. I am considering a career in this new government and *that* is why I am marrying, and why I don't wish to sail this spring."

The hot blood drained rapidly from Bingham's face. "Or ever?"

Lion studied his frilled cuff, straightening it with tanned fingers. "That remains to be seen."

"How can you do this to me? What about your ships? I can't believe you're saying this!"

"You needn't doubt my veracity, William. And don't worry, I won't leave you and Mordecai so cold-bloodedly. I'll still be down at the waterfront, and I flatter myself on having an eye for a competent seaman. You can count on me for anything except my presence on board when those ships sail next month.

As for my own craft . . . I'll have to think about that."

The note of finality in his voice was unmistakable, and Bingham knew that the subject was closed for the time being. Feeling ill, he took a long drink of port and muttered bleakly, "Your audacity is quite incredible. But, I suppose I must forgive you."

Lion's mouth twitched in an instinctive grin. "Imagine my relief!" Bingham flushed and drained his glass while Lion continued suavely, "Will you still find space in your magnanimous heart—and house —for my fiancée? I realize the imposition—"

"My word is good. I said she could stay here, and so she shall."

"If you'll excuse me," Lion said, getting to his feet, "I believe I'll be going home myself. For the past ten days I have dreamt of this evening—of drinking your fine brandy before this fire. But now that I am here, the pleasure seems empty somehow . . ." His eyes were fixed on the clock above the mantel; then he shook his head, laughing softly. "No offense intended, William. I suppose I am tired after all."

"I don't suppose there's a chance your thinking will change after a good night's sleep?"

"If it does, we'll know that God has heard your prayers."

They came into the brightly lit marble entry hall, their steps echoing through the silent house. At the door, Lion paused as Wickham approached with his cloak and hat, both dry and spotless.

"There is one thing I'd like to ask, William."

"Yes?"

"It's my fiancée's maid. She's no ordinary servant—"

Bingham blinked in confusion and spluttered, "Have you taken leave of your senses? What will you say next? First you tell me—"

"Don't begin again, William," Lion broke in tiredly. "I only want to ask that you have a care with Meagan—that's the girl's name. You can't ignore her. She's tiny with coal-black hair, and incredible eyes

63

like amethysts. And, if I know you . . ." Out of the corner of his eye, he saw Wickham incline his head in their direction. "She's no ordinary servant, that's all. Not common, if you take my meaning. If I find that she's been mistreated, by *anyone*—"

"You'll *what?*" William asked in total bewilderment. When it became apparent that Lion did not intend to answer, he demanded plaintively, "What in God's name is going on around here?"

The rustle of expensive silk announced the approach of Anne Bingham more eloquently than words, and both girls froze, waiting. The swish of her skirts stopped outside the bedchamber; then there was a delicate tap. Meagan left the dressing table to open the door, taking care to curtsy and lower her eyes.

"Good morning, madame," she murmured, clenching one fist in silent defiance.

Anne nodded ever so slightly in her direction before sweeping forward to greet her guest.

"How did you sleep, my dear? Well, I trust?"

Priscilla met her halfway across the plush flowered carpet, eyes shining with admiration and envy. Meagan was instantly aware that Mrs. Bingham had become her friend's idol and model. Her breath escaped in a disgusted sigh.

"My eyes did not open once the entire night!" Priscilla was exclaiming. "It would be impossible not to sleep well in such a beautiful bed, especially after the ones I have had to suffer this past fortnight during our journey here."

Anne smiled proudly at the massive Hepplewhite and rich gold draperies.

"I'm so happy that you like it, Priscilla. After all, you'll be staying here for several weeks and your comfort is most important to us."

Priscilla was dazzled, blinded. "You're too kind, Mrs. Bingham!"

"Do call me Anne! I thought we settled that last night! After all, I'm not so much older than you. In a few years, you'll have a house just like this and two little children just as beautiful as mine."

Oh, *really,* thought Meagan, rolling her eyes.

"I hope you're right—Anne," Priscilla giggled in her most honeyed Southern accent.

"Of course I am. Now you hurry and get dressed. After breakfast you and I are going shopping!"

"Oh!" The green eyes lit up, then clouded. "But Lion said he was coming over—"

"My dear girl, I can see you have a lot to learn about men. That is precisely why you must hurry; so we can leave before he arrives! Constant mystery is the key to keeping a man intrigued. That was the most important lesson I learned in France! You have to keep the chase interesting for him!"

At that moment, only two streets away, Lion Hampshire was standing near his bedroom window, shaving. The sun was warm on his bare back and shoulders, and the blond hair that covered his chest glinted as it reflected the light. Lion shaved with clean, long strokes, trying to force himself into a more amiable frame of mind. First he concentrated on the weather, leaning toward the window to observe the dark clouds breaking up as they receded over the Delaware River. To the west, the sky was an incredible, vivid blue, as blue as his eyes. For a moment he just stood there, absorbing the welcome sunshine. Then, as he dipped his razor in the basin of hot water and continued shaving, he made himself think of Priscilla. Determinedly, he added up her good qualities, pushing away the faults that intruded on his consciousness. His mind lingered on the memory of her lovely eyes, the magnolia scent of her white skin, the perfect curves of her figure.

By the time he had dressed in a well-cut dark brown suit, a brocade waistcoat, and a frilled pale-yellow shirt, he had almost convinced himself that he was anxious to see her. The intoxicating weather prompted him to dismiss his waiting carriage and walk the two blocks to Mansion House.

The area of Philadelphia in which Lion and the

Binghams lived was universally known as Society Hill. The houses were elegant, most of them built of red brick and trimmed in white. Row houses stretched down the block ahead of Lion, each dwelling three stories tall with one or two gabled dormer windows jutting out from a sloping roof. People were venturing out to sit on the benches before each front door for the first time in weeks, watching the sky suspiciously. Lion nodded to his neighbors, although he knew few of them by name. Young ladies opened their fans to hide blushes while their mothers curiously eyed Lion's wide shoulders and light, gleaming hair as he continued down the street.

The sun had already dried the long wet brick footpaths, and even the wooden gutters were emptying at last. Open carriages appeared on the broad streets holding ladies in unbuttoned pelisses and hatless men. Everyone was smiling.

Lion turned onto Third Street and caught sight of Mansion House's numerous chimneys in the distance, expelling pale gray smoke into the blue sky. As he approached, he could see the people clustered outside the fence, hoping for a glimpse of Philadelphia's unofficial queen.

Brown, the coachman, hurried down the drive when he spotted the tall, golden-haired man at the gate.

Lion grinned at the familiar face, waiting as Brown relocked the ornate doors behind them. "How have you been?" he inquired as they walked down the circular drive. "Still impressing all the tavern wenches with this prestigious job?"

"Laugh if you like, sir," Brown retorted, his dark eyes twinkling, "but it's better than spending the rest o' me life as your cabin boy!"

"Is that intended as an insult?"

"Only to the sea, sir. Those long months staring at the endless water and a crew of bearded ruffians were too much punishment for a bloke like me."

"It did seem sad to deprive womankind of your presence," Lion agreed with mock gravity.

"Now you've got it, Captain!"

"Well, it's good to know that one of us is content with his new pursuits."

Brown glanced up at the taller man quizzically, noting the distant look that came into his eyes. At sea, those eyes had been the identical color of the ocean on a cloudless, breezy day; no one who met Lion Hampshire ever forgot his eyes. Now Brown wondered idly if it was possible for the color to have muted and paled, then chided himself, deciding that the difference must have been due to the absence of the brilliant water as a backdrop.

"Is Bingham at home today?" Lion inquired, breaking into Brown's wandering thoughts.

"No, sir. I drove him to a meeting with Mr. Gilmor and Mr. Lewis better than an hour ago. He was planning to be away all day. Matter of fact, come to realize, you won't find much of anyone here now. The two ladies left not more than a quarter-hour ago, bound for the dress shops in Mrs. Bingham's new landau."

Lion came to dead halt, sun-bleached brows meeting over azure eyes that suddenly came to life.

"What? Are you saying that Priscilla Wade has left the house?"

"Why, yes sir! Can't think why I didn't mention it to you right off." He paused, recognizing the look on Lion's face all too well. "Are you mad, sir?"

"Damn right I'm mad! The wench knew I was going to be here!"

"Per'aps she forgot?" Brown suggested hopefully, only to be rewarded with Lion's most withering stare.

Meanwhile, upstairs in Mansion House, Meagan was busy unpacking Priscilla's trunks. The sound of a familiar voice being raised outside brought her to a standstill, then she carelessly tossed aside the velvet gown she had been holding and hurried to the window. Her palms went cold and damp, her fingers clumsy, as she pushed open the heavy casement. Lion was standing far below on the drive, engaged in what appeared to be a one-sided argument with the young

67

coachman. How handsome he looked! His clothes fit to perfection, setting off his broad shoulders, narrow hips, and long well-muscled legs, while the sunlight seemed to strike sparks against the blond hair tied back at his neck. Meagan read the curse on his lips and guessed the reason for his anger. Deciding that it would be wise to stay out of the way, she turned from the window just as Lion glanced up and caught sight of her glossy black hair.

"Meagan!" he shouted. "Is that you? Come down here!"

She hesitated only a moment before she ran across the bedchamber and out into the hall, relishing the sudden taste of excitement.

Lion was waiting in the entry hall when she came rushing down the wide stairway and he smiled suddenly at the sight of her, skirts raised incautiously to reveal slender ankles and lacy petticoats. He was shocked by the sudden stab of enchantment he felt at the sight of her, accompanied by a hot wave of desire to lift her dress and explore the delights hinted at by those charming ankles. It took his entire reserve of discipline to remember that his wild, reckless days must now be ended. She is a mere lady's maid, he thought fiercely, and I am betrothed to the lady she serves!

Meagan was halfway down the stairs when her mind finally caught up to her feet, causing her to slow her pace and lower her skirts. Her cheeks were hot as she met his eyes from the bottom step, and Lion could feel his resolve melting under her blush.

"I seem to forget myself, sir," she murmured.

"Invariably," he agreed, his voice full of laughter. "Predictably. Delightfully."

Her blush deepened so that she put her hands up to her face, hoping to cool her burning cheeks. Lion reached out for one of them, his own hand dry and strong.

"You are so easily embarrassed that I cannot resist the temptation to bait you. Only do not hide that charming blush; it is most becoming."

Brown was standing in the background, watching the scene with high interest.

The news of Captain Hampshire's betrothal had come as a stunning surprise to Brown; one which was compounded by his first glimpse of Priscilla Wade stepping out of her carriage the night before. Physically, she was beautiful, but there was an artificial quality about her. Brown had always believed that if the captain ever married, the girl would have to be the embodiment of every feminine virtue, but this Wade female seemed common enough in a city filled with shallow beauties, all of whom went limp at the mere mention of Lion Hampshire's name.

Brown had seen the girl now standing with Lion when he had first glimpsed Priscilla Wade. Even from a distance in the misty darkness she had appeared piquantly lovely. Then, this morning, as he drove Mr. Bingham to the office of Mordecai Lewis, his employer had warned him against making brash advances to the new maid. Brown had been perplexed, wondering if Mr. Bingham had designs on the girl himself, but now he was totally baffled.

He had a feeling that these mysteries were all pieces of an intricate jigsaw puzzle which he now attempted to assemble mentally: Captain Hampshire's puzzling engagement; the warning from a man who generally couldn't tell the serving-girls apart; finally, the scene unfolding before him now, the mysterious maid blushing prettily before the bantering captain. Brown shook his head, realizing that the combination of the riddles only served to worsen the tangle. So, in his usual brash way, he decided to join in the drama. Peering around the taller man's shoulder, he grinned at Meagan and cleared his throat.

Lion glanced down, exasperation and affection mingling in his expression. "Are you trying to tell me something, Brown?"

"Pardon me, sir! I just remembered that I ain't had the pleasure yet of meetin' Miss—"

Meagan smiled back, feeling very friendly. "South. But do call me Meagan, Mr.—"

"Brown!" Lion snapped. "This questionable character was my cabin boy during the last two years; so that accounts for his excessive nerve in my presence. He's the coachman here now; so you'd better watch out for him. His reputation with women is decidedly unsavory."

Meagan regarded the small, wiry young man who stepped out from behind Lion to reveal the Bingham livery. He wore a curled white wig, but slashing black brows and merry dark eyes betrayed his coloring.

"I'm pleased to meet you, Brown, and I promise not to judge you on the basis of anything Mr. Hampshire has said!"

Before Brown could reply, Lion turned to him and said, "Why don't you go dust the wheels or something so I can find out what's going on around here?"

One blond brow was arched in a way that Brown had come to recognize and respect. Quickly he flashed his brightest smile at Meagan, bade her good morning, and scurried back outside.

"Isn't he delightful!" she laughed when the door swung shut.

"Not particularly," Lion replied dryly. "Let us go into one of the parlors. I want to talk to you."

"I couldn't! Mrs. Bingham would faint if she saw me in one of her Gobelin chairs!"

Lion realized that this was probably true, so he drew her over to sit down on the stairway.

"Now, tell me where Priscilla has gone and why she went out when she knew I would be arriving before noon."

Meagan avoided his sharp blue gaze. "I know that she and Mrs. Bingham went shopping for her new wardrobe, but as to the other . . ."

"Meagan, look at me and don't play the idiot. You wouldn't lie to me, would you?"

Her heart thumped against her breastbone and in her memory she heard his voice laughing, "We *are* friends, aren't we!" She had been furious and disgusted with Priscilla earlier, and now she thought, at least *he* hasn't ignored me now that we're in Philadelphia and my status as a servant is so clear. He treats me more fairly than my supposed friend who even knows the truth about my breeding!

She looked up to meet his eyes and said hotly, "No, I wouldn't lie, and certainly not for such a dishonest cause! She went out *purposely,* at Anne— that is, Mrs. Bingham's urging. They feel that this is some sort of clever game to increase your interest."

Lion raked a hand through his pale gold hair and let out a low whistle. "Leave it to Anne to play on all of Priscilla's weaknesses. So, they expect me to run this obstacle course with a smile on my face?"

"Apparently. I tried to make Priscilla see how horridly she was behaving, but I don't seem to have much influence with her these days."

"A pity. I was counting on a large quantity of that from you."

"I'm afraid that Priscilla is only listening to Mrs. Bingham right now. She's quite impressed."

"She would be. The ideal wife—a carbon copy of Anne Bingham," he muttered sarcastically.

They were silent for a long minute, then Meagan began, "Mr. Hampshire, I really should go back to work. I have to finish unpacking the trunks—"

"The hell you do." He reached out to catch her wrist, pulling her back down beside him. "Neither of us is going to be used today. You'll take your mistress's place and come out with me."

"I couldn't! No! I have so much work—"

"Let her do it herself. Have you forgotten who pays your wages? I am your employer and I am ordering you to go and change your dress. The sun is out and we're going to enjoy it!"

Chapter Nine

THERE WAS A dreamlike quality about the entire day for Meagan; in her heart she was Meagan Sayers again, the winsome, fun-loving daughter of a wealthy Virginia planter. All her life she had dreamed of the excitement she felt at this moment, walking along Third Street and listening to Lion Hampshire laugh. During the entire two weeks of her masquerade as Meagan South, lady's maid, she had never had more difficulty remembering her new name and station; for, in truth, she longed to forget. Just a few hours, she thought recklessly, wondering if Lion were part of her dream. Could he forget, too? Would he allow her to?

Meagan would have been surprised to know Lion's own thoughts, for they were remarkably similar to hers. He could not recall the last time he had felt so relaxed. He had been startled by Meagan's appearance. She looked absolutely exquisite and had managed to achieve this transformation in barely fifteen minutes. She chose her least drab gown—the same lilac muslin she had worn the night they had dined together in Spurrier Tavern. The color made her skin look creamy and brought out the darker violet of her black-lashed eyes. Lion studied her delicate, animated features in the bright sunlight and found himself charmed. There was a contagious excitement that showed not only in her rosy cheeks and sparkling eyes, but in her voice and the energetic way she walked.

"Do you always take your servants out for a daytime promenade?" she inquired now, revealing dimples when she smiled.

"I've been known to," he laughed. "Unfortunately,

most of my employees are men, so it doesn't happen very often."

Meagan cast him a sidelong glance, liking the way the smile lingered on his mouth and the way the lines crinkled out from his sea-blue eyes when he laughed. It was a beautiful day.

"You know, I've never been to Philadelphia before," she remarked.

"That's hardly surprising. It's a good distance from Virginia. Have you even been out of the state before this?"

"Oh, yes," Meagan smothered a giggle, thinking of the journeys she had made with her parents to Boston, New York, London, and Paris since the end of the war.

Lion decided to let her answer go, turning his attention to the sights around them. A pleasant-faced man emerging from a small two-story row house nearby called a greeting.

"Good day, Mr. Hampshire! How are you this fine spring day? Allow me to offer my best wishes on the news of your impending marriage."

William Wister beamed at Meagan politely, waiting. She eyed Lion from under her thick lashes and noticed that he looked more irritated than panicky.

"Thank you, Mr. Wister. Is there any news from Grumblethorpe?"

"All is well. If this fine weather continues, I shall journey there within the next few days."

"Give my regards to your brother. I shall convey your greetings to my fiancée. Good day, Mr. Wister!"

Meagan could feel the other man's eyes on them as they continued on along the footpath.

Lion was grinning. "I probably just created the potential for a large problem there, but right now the expression on his face was worth it! Ha! Wait until he sees Priscilla and finds out that *she* is my fiancée!"

Meagan glanced at him in puzzlement. "I don't understand . . ."

It took him a moment to remember their situation. Briefly, he had allowed himself simply to exist and en-

73

joy the company of this refreshing gamine, but now he was conscious once again of his position—and hers.

"I didn't intend for you to understand," Lion said coolly. "Just keep smiling."

They walked on in silence, Meagan lifting her chin into the cool, sun-washed air to inhale angrily. Well! He had certainly put her in her place! Why didn't he make up his mind? Was she to be friend and ally or docile slave?

Lion stole a glance at Meagan, his sense of humor returning at the sight of her striding along beside him. Her black, gleaming curls ruffled back in the breeze, fully revealing the stubborn, indignant expression on her face. Lion noted the fiery sparkle in her purple eyes and the decided flare of her slender nostrils. He saw his chance to break the silence that lengthened between them when the cupola atop St. Peter's Church came into view.

"Well!" he exclaimed. "Here is our famous St. Peter's Church! As a newcomer to Philadelphia, I'm sure you're suitably impressed?"

Meagan looked at the handsome red brick structure, then turned suspicious eyes on Lion. "It's nice enough," she allowed.

"Nice enough!" he gasped dramatically, pressing his hand to his shirtfront as if wounded. "This church is a masterpiece and the pride of Society Hill! You insult it at your own risk, for the residents nearby will not take it lying down!"

"Oh, all right!" Meagan burst out, trying to sound more exasperated than amused. "It's a splendid building. I am speechless with admiration."

"That's better." He stared at her until she looked up to meet his eyes. "Truce?"

"It's not that easy, Mr. Hampshire. You went to great lengths to wear me down, convincing me to forget my role as a servant in your company. I won't let you use my position in life to suit your purposes—ignoring it and recognizing it at will."

Lion stopped in front of the red brick wall that ringed St. Peter's Church, reaching for her hand. When he touched her, Meagan's skin burned and the nerves tingled all the way up her arm. Common sense warned her to pull away, but she seemed frozen.

"You are right, Meagan. I'll grant you that. I promise never to patronize you again. Although, it's very obvious you don't approve of my actions, I must ask you to refrain from meddling in my private affairs."

More angry words rose in her throat, but she was unable to find her voice. Sheer panic overtook her when he lifted her palm and pressed his mouth against it.

"You have lovely hands," he murmured. "Soft."

To hide her recurring blush, Meagan pulled away and turned to look at the church, thankful for the wind that blew shielding curls across her cheek.

"This really *is* a handsome church. Do you attend here?"

He was grinning, his teeth white against tanned skin. "Very infrequently in the past. I imagine that the sabbaths ahead will find me in my pew, however."

"Tell me, why do they call this Society Hill? Because of the rich people who live here?"

"It seems so now, but I understand that the name originally was derived from the Free Society of Traders. A century ago it was formed and set up its warehouse and office over on the west side of Front Street—not too far from our Man Full of Trouble Inn. At any rate, the name stuck and eventually became quite appropriate. Even this church was built for the comfort of these affluent residents who grew tired of the muddy trek up to Christ Church on High Street. Wouldn't want anyone to get tired!"

Meagan's face cooled down as he spoke and she looked back at him, laughing softly. "Heaven forbid!" As they began to walk again, she asked hesitantly, "Who was that man we met?"

"William Wister? Nobody exceptional, but he's important enough, merely by virtue of his family name. The Wisters are well-respected in Philadelphia; they've been here seventy-five years at least. Daniel Wister, the other brother, owns a fine place north of here in

Germantown that's called Grumblethorpe. Are you familiar with the flowering purple wistaria?" Meagan wrinkled her brow, then nodded. "It was named in honor of the family."

Lion stopped in front of an L-shaped brick house, smiling at Meagan. She waited.

"This is my home. Do you like it?"

She was impressed but tried not to show it. Easily the handsomest house on the block, there was an aura of quiet elegance about it that lent it character. It was very large—three stories topped by three dormer windows and numerous chimneys. The first two rows of windows were bordered with clean white shutters; even the paint on the front door looked fresh. While Lion used the footscraper, she studied the two fire-marks that flanked a third-story window.

"Those are the marks of the Green Tree and Hand-in-Hand fire-insurance companies," Lion explained, following her eyes upward. Meagan caught sight of a white marble stone under the eaves which read "1787."

"So that's why the paint looks so new!" she teased. Lion smiled as he opened the door for her.

"I bought the house less than a year after it was built. It's still almost unused, for I have spent little time in residence."

The narrow entrance hall where they stood ran straight through to the garden behind the house. Meagan could see it through the arched doorway leading outside. "There is something about this place," she mused, "that puts Mansion House in the shade for all its opulence." Sunlight streamed through the fanlight over the front door, throwing triangular patterns across the paneled floor that led up to the stairway. At that moment, soft, quick footsteps were heard overhead, growing closer. A tiny, odd-looking man appeared on the landing.

"Missa Lion, I so solly!"

Meagan couldn't have been more startled by the appearance of Lion's butler. The man was more than a foot shorter than his employer, with distinctly Oriental features and yellowish skin set off incongruously by a curled white wig. There was nothing Oriental about his dress either, for he wore a plainly cut black broadcloth suit, a black-and-white striped silk waistcoat, a white stock, white silk knee stockings, and black shoes with gold buckles. Shiny teeth dominated his angular face as he grinned up at her.

"Missy Priscilla, I so *happy* to make yoh acquaintance!"

"Wong!" Lion broke in. "This is not Priscilla. This young lady is a new maid in my employ—presently in Miss Wade's service. Her name is Meagan South. Meagan, this is Wong Washington, my butler, who manages to meddle in affairs of mine that have nothing to do with the management of this house."

Meagan could not restrain herself. "Wong *Washington?*"

"I want to be American!" Wong declared, smiling. "So I choose new second name."

"Well, that's certainly American!" she laughed.

"Wong sailed over from China last year," Lion explained. "He attached himself to me when we were in port and Brown was ill. So I gained an extra valet whom I have been unable to lose since, despite valiant efforts on my part!"

"He love me," Wong whispered loudly in Meagan's ear. "He lost without me!"

Lion made no move to deny this, merely smiling over Wong's head at her.

"Listen, Wong, I would like to discuss a luncheon menu with you. Meagan, why don't you wait in the library? Pour yourself a glass of wine and I'll join you in a moment." He gestured toward a door near the stairway, then turned in the direction of the kitchen, one arm draped across Wong's narrow shoulders.

Meagan was feeling rather giddy with good spirits as she opened the paneled door to the library. Inside she was faced with a long wall of books, the red and earth-toned bindings glittering with gold letters. Oh, she thought, I could lose myself in this room! I could bury myself for days. Her eyes searched for a likely daybed or chair in which to hide, and it was then that she spotted the other girl. Afterward, Meagan would wonder how she could have stood there so long without noticing her, for her golden hair was as bright and shining as Lion's. Until the girl spoke, Meagan thought for a moment that she was not real, so complete was her physical perfection. Her face, framed by the sunny curls, was exquisite with its large, soft, sky-blue eyes, tiny nose, and rosebud mouth. Her complexion was peaches and cream, her neck graceful, and lovely, firm breasts swelled over the lacy neckline of her dress. Suddenly she moved, and Meagan could see the huge eyes pool with tears.

"Are—are you—the girl? The one he's going to marry?"

"Me? Oh, no. My name is Meagan. I'm just one of the servants." The faintest hint of amusement touched her voice. "Actually, I'm lady's maid to Miss Wade."

Crystal droplets rolled out to the ends of the beautiful girl's long lashes, flickering off onto her cheeks. "So —so—it's true!" Now she began to weep in earnest, but Meagan noticed with envy that her eyes did not puff up and her face remained pink and white.

Meagan went over and gingerly perched on the edge of a chair across from her, wondering how to handle the situation. She was spared a decision, however, for at that moment the door opened and Lion entered, his blue eyes stormy.

"Damn Wong! If his head weren't attached, he'd have lost it by now! Trust him to let me send you in here with Clarissa already—" His voice broke off as he became aware of Clarissa Claussen's ladylike sobbing. "What the hell! What's going on here?"

Meagan watched with a twinge as Clarissa got up and hurried into Lion's arms. She saw all too clearly the way he held her to him, whispering against the wet pink cheek and gently caressing her flaxen curls. Meagan wished she could climb out the window.

"Oh, Lion," Clarissa wept, "how could you do this to me? When I heard the news, I just wouldn't believe it, but I saw *her* today with Anne Bingham. I mean,

I just assumed! I was on Second Street and I didn't even wait for my carriage . . . I ran all the way here. And then—then—Wong even admitted—"

Lion glanced sharply at Meagan. "Wait for me in the parlor across the hall."

She scrambled up and hurried past them, catching a glimpse of Clarissa straining upward to find and cling to Lion's mouth. There was a pain near her heart like the twist of a knife, but Meagan managed to convince herself that it was due to simple hunger.

The parlor was utterly charming and elegant. Meagan moved around the room, touching the rich upholstery and warm, polished wood of the furniture. Lion's taste was flawless, if indeed he had decorated the room. The quietly elegant pieces were interspersed with priceless treasures from the Orient and Europe, but the total effect was never overpowering. Meagan paused before the handsome mantelpiece faced with gleaming marble, wondering what was happening in the library.

Then she heard the sound of a door opening across the hall and she caught a glimpse of two golden heads passing. More quiet sobbing, interrupted by Lion's firm voice. Meagan couldn't resist peeking out the window to watch them walking to the carriage he had ordered for Clarissa, but she dashed back across the room when he started back up the walk. His brown face was further darkened by a frightening scowl as he strode into the parlor. Silently he crossed the room and stopped beside her at the fireplace, slamming his fist down on the mantel. The force of the blow caused Meagan to jump involuntarily, her violet eyes like saucers, and suddenly Lion's mouth twitched. Laughter followed as he turned to look at her, but she was too confused and startled to join in.

"Meagan," he choked at last, touching her cheek, "you are invaluable. I find it impossible to remain in a bad mood when you are nearby. I wish you could have seen your face!" More laughter. "Did you think I would gobble you up? Do I really appear to be such an ogre?"

"Well . . ."

"I have an idea that you would be perfectly capable of defending yourself if the need were to arise."

The smile lingered at the corners of his mouth as he moved to fill two glasses—one with brandy and one with wine. After handing the latter to Meagan, Lion locked eyes with her and proposed a toast.

"To the most refreshing female I have encountered in years." His expression was typically sardonic, but Meagan sensed a note behind the amusement in his voice that turned her knees to water.

"It is a pity that Miss Wade isn't here to accept that compliment in person," she retorted, hoping that she sounded sufficiently prim.

Lion laughed with frank delight. "Perhaps this day has possibilities after all, in spite of Clarissa's interruption."

Meagan thought to follow him over to the settee but sat down in a large chair some distance away. A heady gulp of wine bolstered her courage.

"She was certainly a lovely girl. If you'll pardon me for saying so, I can't imagine why you'd traipse all the way to Virginia to propose marriage to Priscilla Wade when that girl was right here and obviously willing—"

"I had my reasons," he said shortly. For a long moment he stared at Meagan, unaccountably angered by the penetrating intelligence of the gaze she returned. Suddenly he heard himself shout, "Since you persist in prying into my affairs, I suppose I may as well tell you the reason for this marriage, if only to shut you up! I want a seat in Congress by the next election and it seems that because of my scandalous past, it is necessary that I acquire a wife."

Meagan's eyes were huge with surprise at his announcement and outrage at his groundless anger. The sheer loveliness of her expression only inflamed him further.

"Shocked, are you? I suppose that you think me a cold-blooded villain! Let me remind you that your mistress was just as cold-blooded in choosing her husband, so we should suit well, don't you think?"

"But—why—"

"My future plans do not allow great portions of time for a lovesick bride. If love and beauty were all I wanted, let me assure you that there are more ladies in my life than just Clarissa who would fit the bill. So, part of it was the fact that I didn't *want* a clinging woman at my elbow all the time—"

"And?" Meagan prompted in a tiny voice.

Lion scowled at her. "And I wanted a wife with an impeccable family background—one that would make up for my lack. Virginia is the seat of respectability these days."

"Well, I must say, you laid your plans well!"

"My dear, you are absolutely right."

"And is there no room for human emotion or error—?"

"That is what I must avoid at all costs."

"No matter whom you hurt? Even Clarissa?"

"Clarissa is by no means the angel of purity that she appears," Lion shot back with a brief, bitter laugh. "She knows she will always have a place in my bed. She'll come to me when desire has overcome her hurt pride."

Meagan hoped that her face did not reflect the shock she felt. "I think you are quite awful. What about your own human emotions? Do you intend to avoid those, too?"

"Your conversation is quite unique for a servant," he observed harshly. "I suggest that you save your clever insights into human nature for the cook or the butler."

Meagan jumped to her feet and paced back and forth in front of him, her violet eyes snapping angrily. "I feel rather stifled suddenly! And I feel an overpowering desire to say a lot of things that would get me into terrible trouble with my employer!" She stressed the word sarcastically. "So, if you will excuse me, Mr. Hampshire, I believe I'll be on my way now."

Lion stood up and caught her wrists. Meagan stared up at him with open contempt, but his own expression was one of delighted amusement.

Meagan fought the effect that his nearness worked on her; she was furious as she felt her cheeks heat up so predictably.

"Let go of me! I want to go home!"

"Damn, what a wildcat you are!" His grin was tantalizing and dazzling all at once, and Meagan's skin tingled against his strong brown hands.

"I would rather be a wildcat than the low form of life that you are, sir!"

His loud laughter brought a new rush of blood into her face and she struggled to break the grip on her wrists only to have him transfer his hands to her back. In one easy movement he encircled her with arms that were as unyielding as iron, and Meagan felt her heart leap into her throat as she inhaled the masculine scent of his starched shirtfront. She forgot to fight when he tipped her chin up, forcing her to meet his flashing blue eyes.

Meagan had never been kissed in earnest before. There had been a few boys who had attempted clumsy embraces, but she had never had much trouble putting them in their places. Besides, her breeches and renegade personality had not served to make her the belle of Fairfax County, so she had little in her past to prepare her for this headlong plunge into womanhood.

Lion's kiss was lazy and insistent at the same time, his practiced lips driving all thoughts from Meagan's usually energetic mind. Totally intoxicated, she stood on tiptoe and responded ardently when he parted her lips to explore the sweetness beyond.

Chapter Ten

BUTTERY YELLOW LIGHT outlined the figure of Sally Bache as she stood in the narrow doorway, waving. Meagan turned before Lion could help her into the carriage, looking back over her shoulder at the older woman, then up to the candlelit second-floor window. Once seated against the familiar leather upholstery, she shivered and sighed at the same time. Lion pulled the door shut, dropping down beside her, but to her relief he did not speak. The inside of the carriage was all inky blackness, broken only by the orange ember of Lion's cheroot, flickering as they clattered off down Oriana Street.

The long eventful day had left Meagan little time for reflection or consideration, and she was anxious now to sort out her feelings. A soft, wine-induced haze clouded her brain, but she attempted to dispel it.

How tangled her life had become in such a short time! All the years she had passed reading novels under the pecan tree in the meadow had not prepared her for so much living all at once. Of course, the issues were complicated by the fact that she was no longer Meagan Sayers; the entire day she had just passed had only occurred because Lion Hampshire had the power to direct her actions. A small voice taunted her: what if he had ordered her to share his bed? Meagan's conscience shouted back that she would never have acceded, that the forfeit of her position and security would be far preferable to the loss of her virginity and self-respect. Even as she reassured herself, the memory of that incredible kiss flooded her with an involuntary, liquidlike warmth that was almost frightening.

She stole a sidelong glance at the man beside her. His dark profile was sporadically illumined by an occasional street lamp, his clear-cut features seeming harder and more enigmatic than ever. His eyes were narrowed thoughtfully as he smoked, and Meagan wondered for the dozenth time why he had decided to take her to meet Benjamin Franklin.

After the infamous kiss—which he had ended with startling abruptness that left her humiliated—Lion had more than one drink, apparently deciding to pretend it had never happened. They had lunched together, Meagan's confusion and reserve diffused by wine, while they talked about safe subjects—the city, politics, China and sea trade. It was nearly dusk when Lion announced that they would pay a visit to Dr. Franklin, telling her that the appointment had already been made and assuring her that one female would do as well as another.

Actually, the evening had gone remarkably well. Dr. Franklin was confined to his bed and feeling the effects of the pain-dulling opium. Meagan, warm and brave with wine, charmed him instantly. They talked together for more than two hours while Lion and Mrs. Bache looked on in wondering delight at the improvement in the old statesman's mood.

Meagan had watched the two men together as well and had recognized the same animation in Lion's face that she had seen when he was at Mount Vernon, conversing with Washington and Madison. The interest that had sparkled in his eyes when Franklin discussed the upcoming inauguration and proposed Bill of Rights gave Meagan an insight into the motive behind the impending marriage. Perhaps, she mused, he isn't as unfeeling as he pretends, even though it is the new government and not Priscilla that he cares about.

Next to her, Lion sat brooding in the shadows, wondering why he had not been able to find the opportunity, or the heart, to tell either of the Franklins that Meagan was not his new fiancée. He was angry at himself for being fool enough to take her, a servant, to that house, but also at both Meagan and Priscilla. People were getting in the way of everything, and no one was cooperating with his plans.

Abruptly, his ice-blue eyes sought her out, discovering her own scrutiny of him.

"What are you looking at?" he demanded harshly.

Stung, Meagan managed to lift her chin. "As a matter of fact, I was admiring that handsome watchman we just passed."

The barest gleam of humor flashed in Lion's eyes and Meagan caught a glimpse of white teeth in the darkness.

"Tired of me so soon, my dear?" he inquired, his tone amused yet laced with an undercurrent of bitter sarcasm. One strong hand found her waist, closing the space between them, and Meagan's nostrils were filled with the aromas of brandy and tobacco. His breath was warm on her forehead when he spoke. "How fickle is woman! I was under the distinct impression this afternoon that you rather liked me!"

Meagan summoned all her resources. "You are a cad!" she gasped, her shortness of breath caused solely by the intensity of her attraction to him. "Take your hands off me! I'll not be used again, you unfeeling brute!"

"Ah," he laughed softly, pulling her slender, wriggling body nearer, "so you were actually repelled by our earlier encounter! Strange that I should have misinterpreted your response so completely. Perhaps I'd better repeat the test—just so there will be no question . . ."

A barely audible sob escaped from Meagan, for she knew that all her strength was about to dissolve into jelly. A struggle would be pointless and too brief to be noticed. Lion caught her delicate chin with his free hand, bringing his mouth down over hers almost savagely. There was no slow expertise in this kiss, which drove the breath from Meagan's lungs even as it flooded her with an intense tide of sensation even stronger than the whirlpool that had sucked her under in the parlor earlier that day. Her hands went up to touch his hard cheekbones and the rich texture of his burnished hair; she longed to lose herself in him, she could not get close enough. Lion broke the kiss then, leaving her gasping, but it was not the end. Meagan melted against the muscles of his arm as he bent her head back and buried his face in her scented hair. The pulse in her neck beat wildly under his hard, burning mouth, and Meagan could sense that he was venting some sort of impersonal rage on her; yet she was powerless to stop him.

He had unfastened her pelisse without a wasted motion, his lips and hands finding the warm, sweet breasts beneath. Meagan was conscious of nothing except his touch and the fire that grew in her loins, spreading its warmth through every nerve in her body.

Suddenly, Lion's voice shattered the spell and brought her crashing down to earth. "We're here."

Meagan blinked in confusion, her breasts heaving as she finally recognized the blazing windows of Mansion House. Even as a footman approached to open the carriage door, Lion tilted her chin back and kissed her savagely until she felt close to tears. Then he pulled her hood up to cover her disorderly curls and straightened his own cravat with steady, cool hands. Silently, impersonally, he handed her down, and together they walked toward the huge double doors.

Wickham's expression was politely quizzical as he greeted them in the entry hall, and Meagan felt sick with humiliation. Her eyes stung at the sound of the querulous voices approaching from the parlor. Turning, she looked into Priscilla's frantic, confused eyes, sensing at the same time Lion's satisfaction.

She heard him saying smoothly, "My dear, I'm sure you were far too busy today to notice or mind Meagan's absence since you were plainly too preoccupied to remember our engagement. There were a few services that she was able to perform for me."

Even in her horror, Meagan was quick-witted enough to think, if I blush, they'll be sure that he took me to his bed and everyone will label me a prostitute.

By sheer force of will she managed to remain expressionless while murmuring in a distantly courteous voice, "I was pleased to lend a hand during your maid's illness."

One of Lion's eyebrows went up as he glanced at her in surprise. Anne and William Bingham looked foolishly relieved while Priscilla continued to stare at her fiancé and her maid. Meagan was on the verge of taking her leave of them when she caught sight of an unfamiliar figure moving forward from the shadowy parlor.

Although he was as tall as Lion and nearly as broad through the shoulders, any resemblance between the two men ended there, for Marcus Reems had hair as black as the starless night, shrewd amber eyes, and a prominent hawklike nose. His wide mouth was twisted into the oddest smile Meagan had ever seen.

"Hello, Lion. Welcome home. I've been keeping the lovely Miss Wade entertained in your absence. I trust that you have no objections?"

When Lion spoke, his surface cordiality had a dangerously sharp edge to it. Watching the two men, Meagan felt a cold chill go down her spine.

"Well, Marcus, I did not expect to meet you here tonight," he was saying with a smile. "It has been many months since—where was it? Whampoa?"

"Your memory is faultless, my friend."

Priscilla's wits returned to her at this point as she beamed and stepped between the tall men, apparently oblivious to the darker undercurrent in their polite conversation.

"I declare, I do believe I am in the company of the handsomest men in Philadelphia! Lion, why didn't you tell me about Mr. Reems?"

"I can't imagine how it could have slipped my mind, Priscilla dear," he replied with an ironic smile.

Meanwhile, Anne Bingham was shooting disapproving looks at Meagan, who finally saw her chance to take the hint.

"Do excuse me," she whispered, dropping a quick curtsy. As she hurried away toward the servants' quarters, her face was hot with shame, for Lion Hampshire had not even troubled to nod in her direction.

The blackest of moods had enveloped Lion by the end of that evening; no amount of Bingham's brandy could dispel it. Ordinarily, the very presence of Marcus Reems set his teeth on edge, but this situation was intolerable, and he couldn't believe he was being forced to endure it in silence. For two hours he sat in a stuffy parlor in the company of four of the people he liked least. Anne Bingham's flawless charm grated on his nerves, and he found himself longing to hear her laugh or even scold as artlessly as Meagan had that day. William seemed more pompous than usual, dropping names into every sentence. Neither of the Binghams, however, caused him a fraction of the irritation that he felt whenever he looked at Priscilla. His future wife. Tonight she was oozing with Southern sweetness, obviously confident that Lion and Marcus both craved her attention. She sat between them, giggling and fluttering her long lashes until Lion felt like strangling her.

Marcus was clearly enjoying the situation, positive that Lion's own hatred for him was being compounded by jealousy. He flirted continuously with the willing Priscilla, misinterpreting Lion's black expression for that of a possessive lover.

The tall-case clock in the corner was striking eleven, but Priscilla's laughter rose above it.

"Mr. Reems, how you do run on! Have a care or you'll turn my head!"

A dove in a nearby gilded cage cooed unhappily, and Lion suddenly felt he would go berserk if he did not get some air. Standing up, he filled his glass to the brim and left the room without a word.

A footman stood patiently in the softly lit hallway, but Lion passed by without his usual friendly greeting. The expansive, lush grounds beckoned to him. Once outside the rear door, he closed his eyes and inhaled deeply, savoring the moist, chilly night air. Crickets chirped in celebration of the spring while, overhead, clouds shifted to reveal a profusion of stars against the ebony sky.

The three-acre garden was still quite bleak after the long winter, but Lion could detect the scent of new green life beginning. In the darkness, the large assortment of rare trees and shrubs was budding again, and he found himself smiling at the prospect of that garden in full flower.

He strolled out over the damp lawn, soothed by the cool, pure breeze. Finally, Lion paused and leaned against one of the new Lombardy poplars, regarding the back of the mansion and trying not to think about his problems. Most of the lights were out by this time. Single, muted candles burned upstairs in the yet unoccupied bedchambers of the Binghams and Priscilla, while the ground-floor servants' wing was completely dark. Lion did not find that surprising in view of the strict hours kept by the domestic staff, but his curiosity was aroused by the ghostly white fluttering at one of the windows. Welcoming the diversion, he decided to investigate. As he approached, Lion saw that the sash was thrown open and the specter was actually a voluminous white bedgown. Shadows from the trees blocked the moonlight, so he was only a few feet away when he realized the identity of his ghost. It was Meagan.

Common sense told him to turn back before it was too late; another confrontation with her would do his nerves little good. And, in the back of his mind, hidden by his other worries, a seed of guilt had been taking root. Guilt over his recent treatment of the girl. Lion was not accustomed to dealing with his conscience, and he had no desire to begin at this stage of his life.

Indecision made him pause while he temporarily drowned the unwelcome guilt with expensive brandy. Silently, he and Meagan regarded each other. Hair unbound and body swimming in the white, calico bedgown, she appeared more diminutive than ever. There was nothing childish about her expression, however, for her smoldering, dark purple eyes communicated a womanlike rage. Lion instinctively accepted the challenge.

"Well," he laughed softly, "if it isn't my favorite little maid!"

Meagan balled her hands into tight fists, biting her lips as she glared at him.

"You look tense, dear child," he continued in mock anxiety. "Do not tell me that your day was not sufficiently tiring?" He reached the open window and dropped his voice conspiratorially. "Or were you waiting for me?"

Meagan pushed at his chest with all her strength, but he was as solid as a stone wall. "You are odious!" she cried in a half-whisper. "I am awake because I had to finish the work you took me away from this morning!"

Lion's eyes danced with merriment. "Don't go on, Meagan. These effusive thanks are not necessary; I know that you are grateful."

"I do not find you amusing, Mr. Hampshire. In fact, I find you hateful! And I don't care if you discharge me for saying so! I never want you to come near me again." She paused for a gulp of air. "What happened today was the most degrading experience of my life!"

His eyes were serious now, holding hers like intense blue magnets. "You only feel degraded because you enjoyed it so much."

"That is a lie! You were a monster! You urged me all these weeks to trust you, to be your friend. In my naïveté, I believed you—and then you betrayed me so horribly. You used me as if I were a common whore!"

"Now, Meagan, I wouldn't go that far—and I didn't! Let's keep this in perspective!" Lion was smiling again, and now he lifted both brows. "By the way, where in the world did an innocent like you acquire that word?"

"From books, I assure you. Certainly not from personal experience!"

"Shh," he admonished, laying a brown finger across her lips. "You will make me laugh and then we'll be caught."

90

"You deserve it!"

"I'll not argue that. The question is—do you?"

Impulsively he reached across the sill for Meagan's hands and kissed the small, cold palms. Even in the darkness her ready flush was not lost on him. Belatedly, she pulled her hands from his.

"You must be deaf, sir! I have asked you most plainly not to touch me again! If you and Priscilla Wade choose to ruin your own lives that is your affair, but I'll not be drawn into your games. Perhaps Clarissa and all your other dimwitted females don't mind being made fools of, but I do. Goodnight!"

Leaning forward, she grasped the casement with both hands and pulled it shut so forcefully that Lion had to jump aside to avoid being hit. Even after the white-gowned figure had disappeared from his view, he remained there under the chestnut tree, rubbing his jaw and wearing a bemused smile.

Chapter Eleven

DELICIOUS COOKING SMELLS filled the roomy, well-equipped kitchen and Meagan lifted her head to inhale them from time to time, smiling dreamily. Three plump chickens were roasting on a spit over the fire, turned by a vacant-eyed serving-girl, while the aroma of baking bread wafted out of the oven.

Meagan sat at the sturdy table with Wickham, Smith, and the long-limbed loose-tongued cook, Bramble. Three of the servants were polishing the Bingham silver, while Bramble simultaneously directed the activity of the rest of the kitchen help and sliced potatoes with amazing speed. She was also a self-righteous gossip, keeping up a nonstop dialogue punctuated only by the sizzle of chicken fat dripping into the fire.

Smith and Wickham sat together on one side of the table, letting their hands touch from time to time. Meagan had guessed their feelings for one another the first time she saw Smith look at Wickham. There was a radiance in her gentle hazel eyes that was unmistakable. They said little except to each other so Bramble directed most of her conversation at Meagan.

"If you were to ask me, I'd say it's a disgrace!" she exclaimed, and Meagan glanced up quizzically.

"What's that, ma'am?"

Bramble leaned closer, pursing her narrow lips.

"The theater!" she hissed. "I'm told the Assembly passed the bill two days ago, making it legal here again. 'Tis a sin! This city has been known for its purity of spirit, but this be the first step to its ruin. Mark my words!"

Meagan attempted to change the subject. "My, those chickens smell wonderful. I do so admire your ability in the kitchen."

" 'Tis only hard work," she sniffed. "I believe in it. Not like some people hereabouts. There are times when my conscience cries at me for working for people like *these*."

"The Binghams?"

"What other? They are bad enough, for there is no condition worse than that of quality people letting themselves fall away from virtuous lives. I am truly sickened, however, by the class that is beginning to make itself at home here . . ." Her knife paused for only a moment before she resumed the rapid slicing. "I do not believe in spreading tales, but of course, it be common knowledge in any case."

"Pardon me?"

"Marcus Reems. A despicable, godless man. I only say this with the hope that as her maid, you may be able to help Mistress Wade."

Meagan had the feeling that some portion of the conversation had escaped her. Marcus Reems and Priscilla? Was this woman unbalanced? Two days had passed since Lion Hampshire had taken her away from Mansion House. Since then, she had become painfully aware of the realities of her new life; all the excitement had gone from the masquerade. She was a common servant, working from dawn to dusk and on into the night, with no time or opportunity to discover the latest news from Priscilla. In any case, her former friend showed no inclination to confide in her. Meagan was beginning to believe that Priscilla had forgotten they were ever sisterly companions, for Priscilla's attitude toward her had become as condescending as Anne Bingham's.

Contributing to Meagan's flagging spirits was the fact that she had not had so much as a passing glimpse of Lion Hampshire since their late night conversation at the garden window. Was it possible that he was taking her at her word? Meagan told herself that she was delighted to be rid of him, reminding herself that she found him insolent and presumptuous. Still . . . all her senses remained alerted to some signal of his presence —his step in the hallway, his scent in the air, the sound of his amused, dry voice, or the sight of his bright golden hair. Worst of all, when she slept, Meagan could feel his arms holding her and his mouth against hers. The dream would continue until she reached the limits of her endurance, then she would awaken, feverish and consumed with a strange longing that she was learning to despise.

From snatches of Priscilla's conversation and that of the other household members, Meagan was aware that Priscilla was seeing much more of Lion. Perhaps he had fallen in love with her after all?

"Bramble, whatever does my mistress have to do with Marcus Reems? Surely you know that she is betrothed to Mr. Hampshire?"

Bramble laughed humorlessly, showing long teeth.

" 'Tis of no consequence to people like these. I *saw* her with that Reems man today. Arm in arm they were, and Mr. Hampshire weren't so much as on the grounds."

"I don't understand!"

"What be there to understand? 'Tis a breed apart, South. Fidelity and righteousness mean nothing to these people!"

Meagan turned her eyes on Wickham and Smith. "Is this true? Is Miss Wade carrying on with Mr. Reems?"

Smith flushed a little, exchanging looks with Wickham. "It is true that he was here today . . . and Miss Wade entertained him. As far as anything else—"

"It be only a matter of time!" Bramble declared. "Marcus Reems be a hard man—a cruel one to my mind. And he has but one ambition in life."

"What's that?"

"To eclipse Mr. Hampshire."

Meagan let the spoon she was polishing fall to the table. Again she looked to Smith.

"I am so confused! Can you tell me what she's talking about? What an odd word to use—eclipse!"

"I shouldn't," Smith began with a sigh, "but Bramble may be right. Perhaps you could offer Miss Wade some advice. Of course, she has no way of knowing, but Mr. Reems and Mr. Hampshire have been rivals—perhaps enemies—for a long time now."

"Mr. Hampshire despises Mr. Reems with good cause," Wickham said tersely.

"We aren't certain of the reason," Smith continued in her soft voice, "but there have been some general, obvious causes. Marcus Reems is quite a nasty man, and somehow he got it into his head that he didn't like Mr. Hampshire."

"Jealous," grunted Wickham, and Bramble nodded in emphatic agreement.

"Perhaps it began over a woman—who knows? But ever since, Mr. Reems has been trying to outshine Mr. Hampshire in every way. Unfortunately, it has grown worse since the China trade began. Mr. Hampshire has done so well and Mr. Reems wrecked his first ship —dashed it to pieces. Mr. Bingham won't give him the backing he gives Mr. Hampshire, so the bad feelings have increased. At any rate, his appearances here the other night and today seem to be signs of trouble ahead. Worse, Mrs. Bingham is charmed by the man and has given him an open invitation."

"In that case, Miss Wade must also find him charming," Meagan said dryly.

Wickham brought his black brows together. "That is what we all fear."

At that moment one of the downstairs maids burst into the room. "There's a guest for tea!"

"Heaven's upon us," muttered Bramble. "I'll prepare the cart." She jabbed a bony finger at Meagan. "Change that apron and you can serve."

Surprised, Meagan dashed along a back corridor to her bedchamber where she hurriedly discarded her gray-smudged apron, replacing it with a fresh one of stiff taffeta. She tucked rebellious black curls back under her mobcap while retracing her steps to the kitchen. Miraculously, Bramble had assembled an assortment of cakes on the tea cart, along with a steaming china pot and matching cups.

"Off with you," she scolded, "before the mistress arrives to see what's become of us."

Meagan pushed the cart out the door and along the hallway toward the east parlor. Her mind was so occupied with the clattering dishes that she was totally unprepared for the eyes that met hers as she came through the door.

It might have been a different Clarissa who sat there between Priscilla and Anne Bingham, so cool and composed was this girl. Only the faintest glimmer of recognition showed in her frosty blue eyes as she watched Meagan approach with the tea cart. Anne Bingham smiled coolly.

"Thank you . . ." she paused, reaching for the name and finding it with a note of triumph. "South. I will pour and you may serve."

Meagan waited, venturing a look at Priscilla, who acted as though she were a stranger. Meagan felt her cheeks redden with indignation—an emotion she found common these days.

In spite of her anger, it was impossible for her not to be aware of the combined beauty of the three women seated together. Priscilla was looking more and more like Anne Bingham, imitating her coiffure, her gestures and even her speech. The two of them flanked Clarissa like perfect bookends, the girl seeming even more exquisite than Meagan remembered. Her gown was fashioned of sky-blue velvet, setting off her creamy ivory skin and golden curls.

Why is she here? Meagan wondered at last, suddenly puzzled. After serving the tea and cakes she was dismissed, but she could not resist stopping in the hallway. The conversation she heard left her more bewildered than ever, for Clarissa was impeccably gracious, declaring that she was certain she and Priscilla would be the best of friends.

Lion's name was never mentioned.

Meagan made several false starts at counseling Priscilla during the next two days. It was difficult to find her alone, even in the morning, for Anne Bingham fluttered near her like a butterfly. Finally, an opportunity presented itself when Priscilla sent for her after a noon meal. Priscilla had an engagement to go riding in Marcus's new carriage and was alone.

Meagan found her seated at her dressing table, clad in a lace chemise, and staring into the mirror.

"Oh, Meagan, it's you," she murmured distractedly, not bothering to look up. "I am certain I can see a spot here. Look."

Meagan rolled her eyes and bent closer. Priscilla was pointing to a pink blemish the size of a pinprick located above her right eyebrow.

"Your vision is exceptional," she remarked. As usual, the perfectly proper words were underlaid with sarcasm that went undetected by Priscilla. "I am certain no one else could possibly see it."

"Well, perhaps if you add some extra powder . . ."

"Priscilla—" Meagan bit her lip as she pulled a footstool around to sit on. She leaned nearer in an effort to catch her eye. "We have known each other a long time, and even though circumstances have altered, I still care about you."

Priscilla yawned, critically examining her lacquered fingernails. "I will be glad when you master the art of the manicure," she commented.

"Are you listening to me?"

"I don't have time to think about the past, Meagan. As I've said before, you made the choice to change your position in life, and I find matters much simpler if I refrain from dwelling on other days."

"I'm not asking you to 'dwell on other days'! I have no wish to discuss *my* situation. You are the one I am worried about! I have heard things about Marcus Reems—"

"Meagan, if you stop this right now, I will try to forget your outburst." Priscilla was looking into the mirror again, her lovely mouth set stubbornly. "I do not need advice from my maid—especially when she is openly trying to entice my fiancé!"

Meagan bolted from the stool, cheeks burning furiously. "Priscilla! How can you think—"

"I'm certain you don't mean to use such a familiar form of address, Meagan. Now, do fetch my bronze silk. Marcus will be arriving any moment now, and I am so anxious to see his new carriage!"

Meagan backed up toward the armoire, staring at her one-time friend in angry, stunned disbelief. You pretentious goose! she raged silently. You deserve to make a mess of your life!

Her teeth were clenched against the words that threatened to spill out; instead, she turned to pull the silk gown from the armoire. An hour later, Priscilla was being assisted into Marcus's carriage, along with Anne, cast in the role of chaperone.

By the third afternoon, the carriage rides had become a part of Priscilla and Anne's schedule, and Meagan was hearing Marcus Reems's name spoken more often than Lion's.

One day in early March, Priscilla and Anne left the house for a full day of dress fittings. Many delegates to the new Congress had arrived in town by this time and the Binghams were planning a party for later in the month. The bad weather had managed to delay the start of Congress in New York indefinitely and no one was in a hurry to get there anymore. There was a festive, holiday mood through the town, heightened by the now-legal theater. The *Gazette* was announcing a performance of *The Roman Father,* a hornpipe by Durang, and a "celebration over the victory of the theater." For the fist time in fifteen years in Philadelphia, the American Company published its cast for the evening "By Authority." Meagan heard the excited plans being made for attendance, aching inside to be able to participate in the fun.

Smith seemed to sense Meagan's despondency and took pity on her, perhaps because of her own happiness in love. The day that the women were away for their fittings, Smith found her ironing Priscilla's chemises in a corner of the kitchen.

"Not a very cheerful task on a pretty day like this," she offered.

Meagan tried to smile. "Well, that's the price of being a working girl, hmm?"

"Perhaps, but there should be more to life than just work. You look a bit washed out to me."

Meagan said nothing.

"As the head housekeeper, I'm in charge in Mrs. Bingham's absence, you know."

"What are you saying?"

"I'm saying that I've decided it would benefit your health and performance if you would get away from the house for the afternoon. The sun is shining; why don't you go out and tell Brown to give you a horse."

The excitement that rose in Meagan's heart almost overwhelmed her; she looked at Smith with adoring eyes. Impulsively, she leaned over the hot iron and hugged her.

"You are a wonderful person!"

"Well, hurry up, then! Just be back here before the mistress returns for tea!"

Anne Bingham had regally christened the winding

98

alley which led into the grounds and to the spacious stables beyond "Bingham Court." Meagan ran along it now, skirts lifted, radiant with the long overdue dose of sunshine and fresh air and smiling at the sight of the two fawns that grazed on the lawn. When she spotted Brown, she waved, laughing, and watched his eyes light up at the sight of her.

"I thought that Mrs. Bingham had rather overdone it with all those live birds she keeps throughout the house," Meagan told him when she drew near enough to be heard, "but I do believe that these fawns are the topper!"

Brown pushed back his bicorne hat, wiping his forehead with a handkerchief as he grinned at her.

"Truth to tell, Jacob Reads brought those to her from South Carolina not so long ago. People know that anything exotic will pleasure Mrs. Bingham, I'll wager. See those greenhouses over there? Right now they are filled with rows of orange and lemon trees that the gardener keeps in tubs. When warm weather settles in, they'll all be put out onto the lawn. And that's but a sample of the rare sorts o' shrubbery you'll see hereabouts in a few weeks."

Meagan laughed. "Well, if all these strange luxuries make them happy, I suppose that's fine."

"What sort of bloke wouldn't be? I'll swear I would!"

"You might be surprised, Brown."

He shrugged amiably. "Tell me now, sweetheart, what brings you outside today?"

"Smith has told me that I may have a few hours of freedom. I have permission to go riding! Have you a horse that I may use?"

"Ain't you the lucky one! Wish I didn't have such a lot o' work to finish today or I'd go along with you." His eyes met hers, more serious than she remembered them. He wasn't wearing a wig this time, and his hair was very dark and thick, fastened untidily over his collar. "Do you know your way? Just ride out Spruce here and you'll reach the countryside. The road that runs south from there will take you out to

Gray's Gardens. You'd find that a pretty ride, I'll wager."

Meagan beamed as he disappeared into the stables and returned leading a horse out into the sunlight. It was a beautiful spotted mare with soft eyes.

"Oh, Brown, thank you! She's wonderful!"

He put a sidesaddle onto the horse's back, then helped her up.

"Victoria, you behave yourself with this pretty lady. Hope you two have a nice ride."

His hand brushed Meagan's quite purposely and as he watched Victoria trot down Bingham Court, Brown remembered Mr. Bingham's warning. What made this little serving-girl so special that one of the most important men in America gave her his protection? What was his interest in her, or was Captain Hampshire the one who actually held the claim to her? A natural lover of all womankind, Brown was definitely intrigued by Meagan South.

Meagan could feel his eyes on her as she rode Victoria to the end of the Court, turning onto Fourth Street. Her discomfort vanished soon enough in the open air, however, for there was no space inside her for any emotion other than pure enjoyment. She felt more lighthearted than she had for weeks; since before her parents had been killed.

The streets were fairly crowded with other horses and vehicles; so for several blocks Meagan rode along slowly behind an open landau. Since it was her first view of the western sector of Philadelphia, she was quite content to take her time and look around. The farther she got from the center of town, the fewer houses there were and the worse the roads got. After she passed the Pennsylvania Hospital at Eighth and Spruce Streets, the city dissolved completely into countryside. Gently rolling fields and orchards were spread out on all sides, lovely in spite of the fact that the trees were starkly bare and the grass still withered and brown. Overhead, the sky was a bright azure blue and a sweet, friendly breeze ruffled Victoria's dark mane. The horse broke into a sedate canter and

Meagan closed her eyes, smiling against the wind and feeling as though they were alone in the world.

Across the hillsides an occasional rooftop came into view, surrounded by a thick collar of trees. Twisting, ribbonlike roads broke off from the main thoroughfare to lead to the country estates, and Meagan was tempted to follow one of them.

Reality made a sudden intrusion when Meagan became aware of the muffled sound of a horse's hooves approaching from behind. A quick glance over her shoulder gave her cause for mild alarm, for the animal and rider were both massively built and bearing down on her with suspicious speed. Meagan was horribly conscious of the total isolation of the area and of Victoria's ladylike nature. When a man's voice shouted to her, panic overcame all else and she veered off onto a side road, pressing her heels into Victoria's flanks to urge her into a gallop. Leafless trees bent over the trail, one branch reaching out like a gnarled hand to rip Meagan's hat from her head. She could feel her heart pounding in her stomach and throat at the same time and her hands went cold with sweat at the sound of twigs snapping behind her. Victoria had no racing skill, but Meagan begged her in a near scream to go faster, her voice dying completely as the other horse's shadow fell across her shoulder and she felt fingers like iron reach out to grip her forearm.

"For God's sake, Meagan, what the hell is wrong with you? Have you lost your mind?"

Sheer relief made her head spin as she looked up into Lion Hampshire's chiseled face, shadowy under the brim of his hat. She laughed shakily.

"I—I had no idea—I didn't recognize you . . ."

"Did you think I was some ruthless highwayman out to rob you of your virtue?"

The wry laughter in his voice made her see the humor in the situation though her heart continued to pound with emotion.

"I'm not sure what I thought. It was my first time out alone in a strange place. It sounds so silly now,

101

but all I saw was this huge horse and rider, chasing me . . ."

"I suppose I simply never thought to see you panic!"

"Perhaps if I had been at home, in Virginia—on my own horse . . . This mare is so well mannered!"

"You used to have your own horse?" he asked a trifle incredulously.

"In a way. At any rate, that is all past. Now that I've gotten my exercise, I think I'll be going back. Somehow the fun has gone out of it . . ."

Her eyes were averted, seeking a ray of light to mark the main road through the dense trees. Lion caught her chin with a brown hand, turning her face up to his. Helplessly, Meagan felt the hot blush stain her cheeks.

"Have I truly ruined your day?" he inquired, obviously unrepentant. Meagan clearly saw his blue eyes dancing as he watched her. "I could not go on with such a sin on my conscience. I insist on making amends."

His mere presence stimulated her beyond belief and she hated herself for feeling so giddy when he touched her. Her common sense told her to say a cool good-bye and ride away, but it was impossible.

"You're absolutely right, you know. You scared me out of my wits!" Meagan felt herself smiling back at him. "You deserve to provide recompense for my suffering. Shall I name the price?"

Lion flashed a white grin, arching an eyebrow. "That's an interesting idea, but not what I had in mind. I was thinking of doubling as your guide and bodyguard—since you are so unfamiliar with the area and so chickenhearted in the bargain. Now, Meagan, sheathe those claws! You see, I was out to inspect a country estate that is for sale and thought you might like to accompany me. It should be a rather interesting place and perhaps you will know if it is to Priscilla's taste."

The last words stung Meagan unaccountably, but she attempted a casual shrug. "Why not? After all, how often do I get to escape from Mansion House? I suppose that even an afternoon with you is better than that indoor drudgery."

She wheeled Victoria around toward the road before Lion could reply, biting her lip to keep from smiling.

PART II

If the heart of a man is deprest with
    Cares
The mist is dispell'd when a Woman
    appears;
Like the notes of a Fiddle, she sweetly,
    sweetly
Raises the Spirits and charms our Ears,
Roses and Lilies her Cheeks disclose,
But her ripe Lips are more sweet than
    those.
        Press her,
        Caress her,
        With Blisses,
        Her Kisses
Dissolve us in Pleasure, and soft Repose.
          —JOHN GAY
            The Beggar's Opera
            (1728)

Chapter Twelve

THE APPROACH TO Markwood Villa was badly neglected. Wild grass had grown over much of the rutted road, but Lion's roan seemed sure of his footing and Victoria did well by following him. Since turning off the main road, neither Lion nor Meagan had spoken. Meagan reviewed in her mind the half-hour ride south, warming when she remembered the way he had laughed so frequently and with such obvious enjoyment. They had talked and teased, but no mention was made of their past physical encounters, and she was grateful to him for that.

Rounding the crest of a hill, they suddenly came into a large, open circular drive which led to the villa itself. Lion stopped, looking back at Meagan.

"What do you think?"

The house was much larger than anything she had seen in Philadelphia, yet different from the country mansions of Virginia. Its design was predictably Georgian, but instead of red brick it was a muted gray, its grooved stuccoed surface simulating stone masonry. There were handsome Palladian windows across the front, while the white doorway stood out, complete with pilaster, a fanlight, and a large pediment at the top. Yet, the shrubs which grew around the drive were in sad need of trimming and the house itself seemed shabby in spite of its magnificence.

"It's a wonderful place . . . but who lives here?"

Lion threw back his head, laughing in delight. Sunlight illuminated his handsome features and Meagan felt a familiar tingle run through her at the sight of his dazzling, magnetic grin.

"Ah, Meagan," he choked, wiping a tear from one eye, "you are the most novel female!"

She began to feel rather foolish and raised her chin at him. "Didn't anyone ever tell you that it is rude to make fun of people? If I had a fan, I would swat you with it."

Lion appeared to be on the verge of a fresh burst of laughter, but for her sake, he managed to restrain himself. His blue eyes sparkled with merciless merriment as he met her indignant violet ones. Meagan saw an odd warmth infuse his expression, and when he spoke, his tone was gentler.

"I humbly beg your forgiveness for my discourteous behavior, Miss South. And I am sorry that you do not have a fan. I doubtless deserve to be swatted." One side of his mouth quirked slightly. "It is all my fault for not explaining earlier—about the villa. It has been empty for several years now—abandoned and untended. The owner, Andrew Markwood, was a British Loyalist. When the English were in occupation in Philadelphia, Markwood invited some officers to lodge here. Unfortunately, a neighbor returned home after Yorktown; a man who happened to be fanatically loyal to the American cause. At that time, the Loyalists were badly persecuted, but this fellow rather overdid his part. He and Markwood argued several times and it all ended in a duel. Markwood was killed and his family took the money that remained and booked passage to England with a group of British soldiers who were on their way home. Markwood Villa was confiscated by the government and has been empty ever since, while the superstitions have grown around its past as fast as the weeds in its garden. Now, there's not a woman in Philadelphia would permit her husband to buy it."

The horses had reached the front steps and Lion drew in on his reins and swung lightly to the ground. Meagan went tense when his strong hands encircled her waist to lift her down.

"Why are you interested in this house, then?" she

asked, glad for the diversion. "It looks like it would take a great deal of work to restore it."

After tying the horses to a large oak tree, Lion started up the steps to the front door.

"That's what I'm here to decide—exactly how much work would be involved. This was a showplace a dozen years ago, and I think it's a crime to let it decay because of a lot of ridiculous, wild tales."

Meagan leaned around his elbow as he tried the door. "What sort of wild tales?"

"Oh, people are convinced that Markwood's spirit is still in this house. Every now and then someone claims to have seen him," he replied in an offhand tone.

The door swung open with a long creak and Lion stepped inside, only to feel Meagan pull at his sleeve. Her feet were rooted to the doorsill.

"People have seen him?" she echoed in a high voice.

"Meagan! I thought you were too intelligent to believe such nonsense! I was teasing you when I said that you were chickenhearted, but perhaps—"

"Oh, all right! I suppose you can protect me if we should encounter Mr. Markwood."

"That's the spirit." He put an arm around her shoulder. "You must take an oath not to tell Priscilla about these tales if I should decide to buy the house. I have a feeling she would adapt easily to the role of the hysterical wife."

"I won't say a word to her, but I cannot make promises for Anne Bingham."

Lion wasn't listening. His keen eyes were scanning the entry hall and Meagan followed his gaze. Mouse and bird droppings were scattered across the patterned brick floor, and the furnishings that had been left behind were covered with a layer of gray dust. The air was pungent with must.

Still, Markwood Villa's innate elegance shone through. Meagan held on to Lion's arm as they toured the house, never quite losing her uneasiness although Lion was clearly ebullient. He was obviously pleased with what he saw and Meagan, in spite of everything, was inclined to agree with him.

The walls were beautifully paneled, while above them ran intricately decorated stucco ceilings, works of art in themselves. A stunning, though dirty, Turkey carpet covered the parlor floor and a tile-faced fireplace dominated the east wall of the room.

Meagan was speechless at the sight of the staircase, which consisted of an elaborate, amazing arrangement of trellises, once painted white but now yellowed and peeling. Lion told her that the style was called Chinese Chippendale and Meagan declared that she had never seen such a thing in Virginia.

Upstairs, the rooms continued the pattern of basic loveliness with handsome woodwork and ceilings and well-designed bedchambers, each with its own painted floorcloth. Meagan trailed along as Lion examined every corner of the house; then, finally, they went outside to explore the grounds. The sun shone so brightly overhead that Meagan felt silly to have worried about encountering a spirit. The gardens were badly overgrown, the boxwood borders choked by weeds and vines. Still, there was a kind of beauty about the place that was undeniably appealing.

"Well?" Lion asked abruptly. He had not dropped Meagan's hand and she was suddenly very conscious of his touch.

"I love it. I honestly do! I must say, it's a far cry from the classic simplicity of Southern homes, but it has a certain quality . . ."

"Charm. Personality. I am totally in favor of this new style that Washington is bringing with him to the North, but I am not particularly worried about following the current mode myself. Once the house is finished, it will be a warm and inviting place to be."

"Your home in Philadelphia already fits that description. Why do you need this place?"

"It is the accepted thing to do! All the upper class have summer homes where they can escape the 'horrid crush' of the city. I must do what is expected of creditable men these days, you know!"

Meagan glanced up at the bitterly cynical tone in his voice. "I do not understand you."

"It is not your place to understand," he returned brusquely.

"But, if you are so eager to do what is correct, why choose *this* estate? Certainly you could find a more acceptable—"

"I know. And there's the rub. I know that I have to do a lot of things that I despise, so to keep a fraction of my self-respect, I cannot resist rebelling just a bit. The whole affair has become an absurd sham. The only thing that keeps me going is that goal . . ." His expression softened. "When I feel like telling everyone to go to hell, I force myself to remember that summer in the Constitutional Convention. I truly believe that if I can have that every day, I will be able to endure all the rest."

"It's a shame," Meagan said softly, her eyes on the brick walkway.

"What is that supposed to mean?"

"I think it is a shame that you should be forced to become a hypocrite just to have a career that is supposed to be so moral and honest. It doesn't make sense."

"Well, perhaps the day will come when my status will be such that I can do as I please without fear of retribution. But, for now, this is the only way I can get into Congress *soon*. My reputation is in sad repair and it will take a great deal of redemption on my part to mend it."

Meagan stopped and looked up at him. "You won't like my saying this, but I don't think this act of yours will work. I believe that your character is too strong for you to play it out. Someone like William Bingham or James Wade, perhaps, but not you."

"I happen to take the opposite view," he shot back. "I am counting on my strong will to carry me through. Are you finished now with these wise observations?"

Meagan saw his jawline harden, but he met her

brave gaze with eyes that held a gleam of admiration along with the glitter of anger.

After a long moment, he spoke again. "Your nerve is excessive. It irritates the hell out of me, but at the same time, I do rather appreciate your honesty." He paused, allowing a slight smile to flicker at his lips. "Just don't get carried away. You wouldn't want to make me mad. I tend to lose all reason when I get angry enough."

Meagan relaxed at the sight of his indulgent smile, forgetting herself as she stared at his handsome face. She thought it incredibly attractive, almost too appealing to be real. Never had she seen such a contrast between hair and skin as this; in the sunlight his hair was blindingly gold against the deep tan of his face. His eyes were more than a vivid sea-blue, and they seemed to sparkle with a life all their own, while his sculpted features radiated vitality and strength. Right now, his expression was one of wry amusement.

"Meagan, what can you be staring at so assiduously? Is there a wart forming on my nose?"

She flushed with embarrassment, dropping her eyes until her thick lashes brushed pink cheeks. "You are tactless, sir," she murmured at last.

Lion laughed out at that, lifting her hand to his mouth and kissing her tiny fingers.

"What a statement! To coin a phrase of Doctor Franklin's, the pot is calling the kettle black!"

His laughter only deepened Meagan's blush, while her hand burned under the pressure of his lips. Suddenly flooded by panic, she pulled away from him and stumbled on into the overgrown garden. Why do I always go to pieces when he is near? she thought in frightened bewilderment. Why did I ever agree to come with him today when I told him only a few nights ago that I wanted nothing to do with him?

The garden gave way to uncleared land, mostly oak and elm trees which grew close together. Meagan welcomed their shelter, for her breath burned in her throat and her eyes stung. Unexpectedly, a thick gray root which had burst its cover of dirt caught her foot and sent her reeling sideways against the nearest tree trunk. Her hands grasped at the ragged bark and she regained her balance, but a sharp pain twisted up her leg when she tried the injured foot.

"Oh, dear God," Meagan choked, her voice hovering near a sob, "what next?"

Lion came into view then, his eyes unreadable as he drew near. Wretchedly, she covered her face to hide tear-filled eyes. Lean, gentle fingers cupped her trembling chin and through a blur she saw a half-smile playing about his lips.

"Have I said something amiss? My only intent was to amuse you, sweeting, but you have surely shaken my confidence in my wit!"

In spite of herself, Meagan felt a bubble of laughter rise in her throat. Forgetting her ankle she reached out to cuff his arm and suddenly gasped in pain. Lion's arms went around her back, holding her up, as Meagan dissolved into gulping sobs and pressed her wet face against his fawn coat.

"My ankle!" she cried at last, though it was but a part of her distress. Relief showed on Lion's face, for he was infinitely more comfortable dealing with physical pain than the emotional sort. Slipping an arm under her knees, he lifted her effortlessly off the ground and carried her through the trees until they gained sight of a charming gazebo-like schoolroom which stood in a clearing.

Inside there were wide benches circling the window-lined wall, muslin sheets protecting the plush velvet cushions beneath from light and dust. Three writing tables had been pushed against the far wall, collectively draped with another thin white coverlet.

Lion sat down on the bench and Meagan found herself on his lap. She could feel the hard muscles in his thighs through her pelisse before he shifted her onto the cushions so that her legs rested over his. Without a word, he lifted her skirts and surveyed her ankles, softly turning the right one until she bit her lip to keep from crying out.

"It's not broken," he reassured her. "In fact, I doubt that it will swell any more than this. It's painful, I know, but I'll wager that you'll be much improved by morning."

"Thank you, Doctor Hampshire," she said with a weak smile and was rewarded by his quick, flashing grin.

"I wouldn't overdo the sarcasm, my girl," he admonished playfully. "You and your ankle are rather dependent on my good nature right now!"

She was suddenly acutely conscious of his large, sun-darkened hand resting on her bare leg, and her mouth went dry. Silence grew between them and Lion watched her face until she slowly raised her eyes to meet his own. His gaze caressed her, lingering over gleaming raven curls, black-lashed violet eyes, rose-hued cheeks, and finally moving irresistibly down the delicate line of her alabaster neck and throat. Meagan felt naked under his brilliant ocean-blue eyes as they seemed to strip away the lavender muslin from her swelling breasts. Reality receded, replaced by some heady magic that wove its spell around them until Meagan felt nothing but Lion's presence, his warm touch against her leg, his mesmerizing stare holding her willing prisoner.

Lion's lean fingers slid up her satiny leg and Meagan's breath caught in a gasp as a throbbing heat spread where her thighs joined. Strong hands caught her waist and then she was against him, drinking in the feel of his firm, brown skin pressed to her cheek and the scent of tobacco and maleness that was so much a part of him. Long fingers laced through her hair, lifting her face, and Meagan's temples pulsed against his palms as their mouths came together. She was suffused with a terrible yearning as his tongue touched hers with fire; her arms twined about his sturdy neck while she felt his own like steel across her back.

It's like drowning, she thought fuzzily, her will and strength sucked under in the tide of their passion. Lion's warm, hard mouth traveled over her

113

face and neck, tracing her fragile bone structure, while his fingers removed her open pelisse and unfastened her gown with skillful ease.

Somehow, her dress and chemise came away from her shoulders and his blond head bent, inhaling the lilac fragrance of her silky hair, then scorching her petal-smooth skin with his lips. When they touched her breasts, Meagan cried out softly. His tongue and lips and teeth lingered there until she flushed hot and cold, tingling with the sensations he aroused in her. Lion shifted, leaning her across the muscles of his arm, and she felt the hard, bold manliness that strained against his buckskin breeches.

Suddenly the velvet cushions were uncovered and strewn across the floor; strong arms laid her lightly down, and through a haze, Meagan saw Lion strip away his clothes. Spun sunlight poured through the windows, silhouetting him in a golden luster that added to her dreamlike state of mind. His body was more magnificent than she could have ever dreamed —bronzed, with taut muscles that flexed and rippled with every movement. His broad shoulders and chest tapered down into lean hips and long, powerful legs. Silently, with the grace of a jungle cat, he knelt beside her and slipped her own garments over her hips and down her legs. Meagan's violet eyes were liquid with desire and her loins ached with a need she could not name. She flinched as their bodies first came together, then shivered in his arms, poignantly conscious of the difference between them. His manhood pressed against her belly and she arched her hips by instinct while melting under the heat of his kiss. His mouth devoured her fragrant, soft body, lingering over her newly aroused breasts until they strained against his lips and Meagan gripped his shining blond hair, moaning aloud. He slid back up to find the secret places on her neck and throat, kissing her nape where baby-down curls grew along the hairline and teasing her pink ears with his tongue. Then their mouths came together again, passion building until kiss followed kiss, each one sweeter and deeper than the one before. Meagan's hands ran along his ribs, then down to the lean, narrow hips. She could feel the muscles contract when she touched the firm surface of his buttocks and, beneath him, she burned against his hardness.

Neither of them could have formed one lucid thought at that moment, for fate would win out, as it was meant to. The last kiss ended slowly, Meagan clinging to him as her need washed over her in hot waves of nearly unbearable sensation.

"Oh, Lion, please . . ." she whispered brokenly, opening her thighs to welcome him. Gently, he went into her, probing deeply until he felt her respond. His strong hands turned her hips so that she panted with mixed pain and pleasure, finding his rhythm and meeting him at each thrust. He groaned then, white teeth clenched, and as he drove far up inside her, Meagan's own frustrating ache gave way to a flood of pleasurable relief that swept up her belly and down her legs.

Corded veins stood out on Lion's forearms as he braced himself above Meagan, slowly lowering his head to taste her moist lips. After moving to lie beside her, he drew her against him and she pressed her cheek against the light matting of golden hair covering his broad, dark chest. The drumming of his heart slowed as she listened until at last it was regular. For herself, mindless passion and hunger had been replaced by a creeping glow of contentment. His arms about her felt right and she sensed that they had communicated more in those minutes of prelude and union than they could have in hours of honest verbal conversation.

"Meagan?"

She drew her face away from his warm, well-muscled chest with reluctance and looked up to find him staring at her intently, his eyes full of wonderment, questions, and contradictions. Her own were calm and guileless as she gave him a blissful smile.

"Yes?"

"I—" He dropped his gaze from hers, already

feeling the prick of guilt, wondering what to say. He was well-versed in the art of casual love, skilled in the subtleties of conquest, bedding, and adroit elusion of the inevitable marital trap. None of his rules fit Meagan, and what had passed between them had been something unknown to him. Was such—such *magic* possible, or could it have been the sun . . . ? Perhaps his mind had been playing tricks. Eyes fixed on the curve of her hip, he sought words to ease his predicament, already wishing he had avoided this situation, for some instinct warned him that unheard-of complexities would arise and weave themselves about him in the future. The first one showed itself as he noticed the smear of crimson on her thigh. Blood. Lion groaned as softly as possible.

"Oh, Meagan," he implored, meeting her eyes again, "tell me you weren't a virgin!"

"I could say it . . . but it would be a lie," she replied frankly, seemingly undisturbed by her plight.

Lion pressed a hand to his forehead and closed his eyes, displaying thick tawny lashes. "Oh, Meagan . . . How could you let me?"

She giggled lightly in spite of herself. "Must the responsibility lie with me?" Reassuringly, she ran a finger along the lean line of his jaw. "I do not blame you, though, for I cannot think that a crime has been committed. Rather I would give you credit for bringing me as near to heaven as a mortal could come."

Abruptly he let her go, turning away and sitting up. A long arm stretched out to hook his fawn jacket, while Meagan felt a corner of her dream crumble to dust as she sensed reality's invasion. His hand sought a handkerchief in the pocket of his coat, but she was distracted, looking past him as a movement outside caught her attention. A slender blond figure was just disappearing into the trees and Meagan's heart froze with instinctive recognition.

"Lion?" she asked as he turned back, holding out the snowy linen for her to use.

"Hmm?" His eyes avoided hers. "Are you—that is, you aren't in any pain?"

116

"No, no. Lion, what did Mr. Markwood look like?"

His mind spun. "Markwood? Why, he was quite tall, I believe. Heavy-set, brown hair. What a question at such a moment! Don't tell me you've seen him too?"

He was clearly amused, relieved by the distraction, but Meagan's worried eyes were fixed on the clearing outside. The alarm and perplexity she felt chilled the last of her radiance.

"No—I'm afraid I haven't."

Chapter Thirteen

MEAGAN FORGOT ALL about the figure in the garden during their ride back to Philadelphia as her preoccupation with Lion's behavior grew. She had waited while they dressed for him to tell her that he loved her—that he would break his engagement to Priscilla immediately. Deep inside she knew it wouldn't happen. Hadn't he told her that his goal of a career in Congress must override every other facet of his life? Still, she pushed their past conversations from her mind and continued to hope. As they cantered along the country road in the deepening twilight chill, Meagan tried to keep her voice light, her face smiling, but in truth, a sick feeling was spreading through her body. Now that the spell was broken, she wondered if it had ever been at all. Her ears rang when she thought of what she had done—of what she had become to Lion. How many girls had gone before her?

He, however, seemed relaxed; his manner toward her was affectionate, if slightly bemused. Meagan cast him sidelong glances out of the corners of her eyes as they rode along. His profile was dark against the flame-colored sky, perfectly drawn and completely inscrutable.

After they passed the Pennsylvania Hospital, Lion drew his roan off to the side of the road and Meagan followed.

"I think we should part here," he said gently. "After the other day, it wouldn't do either of us any good to be seen together."

Meagan could see the harsh truth of the matter and the feeling of vague nausea gave way to a flood of shame and humiliation. When she tried to meet his gaze with cool, unfeeling eyes, they filled up with hot tears. She longed to disappear, but it was impossible. Instead, she turned her head away and wiped her eyes with the edge of her pelisse.

"Meagan," he said quietly.

"What?" Her own voice was husky, yet defiant. She despised him.

"Don't do this. Don't disappoint me."

Her eyes sparkled with tears, lilac against the magenta sky. "How dare you speak of *your* disappointment?"

"I never thought I would see you cry. You knew how I felt! Did you think I would give it all up? You *knew,* Meagan, so don't look at me that way! You wanted it as much as I did." His eyes darkened meaningfully, yet there was an undercurrent of defensiveness in his voice as though he sought to convince himself. "If the truth were known, your need may well have been greater than mine."

Angrily she turned away, intending to leave him, but he caught her hand before Victoria could start toward the road.

"Listen to me, little one. You mustn't hate me, but at the same time, I wouldn't want to mislead you. And I do not feel that I have so far. Why don't you take my view? I believe that we must reach out for happiness when and where we can find it." He cupped her delicate chin in his now familiar way, tipping it up so that she was forced to meet his eyes. "I found a great

118

deal of happiness today with you. I know you felt the same way. Don't make the mistake of losing those good memories under a heavy load of guilt. Because —make no mistake—the woman in you has no regrets."

With that he leaned over and kissed her with bittersweet tenderness, and when he drew away from her, Meagan was certain that she saw pain in the cerulean-blue eyes.

"Rest easy, my lady," he whispered, then gave a sharp tug on the reins and cantered off down the street.

Meagan was numb. She watched until his broad shoulders and golden hair were blocked by a phaeton, then, somehow she remembered Mansion House: Teatime! Only a thin tangerine crescent of sun crowned the chimney-topped roofs of the city, while behind it, the sky was layered in deepening shades of orange and pink. Certain that she was late, Meagan jerked at the reins with uncommon force and Victoria trotted out onto Spruce Street.

The air had the cold edge of evening in it now. Meagan could feel tears rolling down her cheeks, chilling and drying there as Victoria twisted through the crush of horses and carriages. Men returning home from their businesses, home to cozy parlors, hot meals, and loving families. As Meagan turned Victoria off onto Bingham Court, she felt more disconsolate than at any other moment in her life.

At that moment, Anne and Priscilla were seated in the landau, its top up to protect them from the chilly evening air. The day's dress fittings had taken far longer than Anne had anticipated, and now they were caught in the mass of vehicles making their way home along High Street.

"I am exhausted!" Priscilla exclaimed, yawning with elaborate delicacy.

"Well, there are tedious days like this, but the evenings will make up for them. Especially when you receive the finished gowns and are able to enjoy them!"

"I suppose . . ." She was watching the other carriages and pedestrians with languid green eyes. "Didn't you say that Clarissa Claussen lived on High Street?"

"Yes!" Anne leaned forward to look outside. "There is the house—the third one!"

"It looks as though it needs paint" was Priscilla's acid observation.

"Probably. Edgar Claussen was once one of Philadelphia's most prominent citizens, one of the early leaders in sea trade. He had five daughters older than Clarissa and his wife died giving birth to her. He is seventy or more now and has had a hard time of it, what with the war, raising his daughters and finding husbands for them, and then losing two ships when the China trade opened up. He has little money left and I think he is just waiting to die . . . Clarissa is the only child left at home and is poorly supervised, as one might guess."

Anne's voice trailed off as they both caught sight of a familiar dark head descending from the perch of a black and green phaeton.

"Driver!" called Anne. "Stop!"

Marcus Reems had just started up the Claussens' front steps when he heard Anne's greeting. Momentarily, he considered ignoring it, but then Priscilla joined in. He turned back reluctantly. In the heavy, rose-hued twilight, the two faces in the landau looked nearly identical and utterly lovely.

"Ladies! What a pleasure it is to see you both; it is just the refreshment I needed after a tiring day."

At that moment, the front door flew open to reveal Clarissa, oddly flushed and agitated. "Marcus! I thought you would never get here! Wait until you hear—"

"Miss Claussen, I am equally anxious to learn what your father has to say to me. Please tell him that I shall be in as soon as I bid these lovely ladies good evening."

Her huge, sky-blue eyes shifted in confusion to follow Marcus's gesturing hand. From the covered lan-

120

dau, Priscilla and Anne met her gaze with raised eyebrows.

"I'm sorry . . . I didn't mean to interrupt, Mr. Reems." She smiled and nodded at the landau. "Mrs. Bingham, Miss Wade . . ."

Hastily the door was closed. Marcus looked back in some relief, giving Priscilla his best debonair smile. "Such an excitable girl. One would think her father ruled the world!"

"Are you certain your business is with Mr. Claussen and not his daughter?" Priscilla queried archly.

Marcus flinched imperceptibly, recovering his wits in the space of a deep breath. His sharp instincts told him that Priscilla was only jealous, and his first stab of panic was lost under a wave of euphoria. He moved toward the carriage, reaching in to take her hand. She colored prettily.

"Miss Wade, do I detect a possessive note in your voice?" He kept his own tone light and properly teasing. "You must know that no man with eyes and a heart could notice any woman but you."

"I wish that were true, Mr. Reems," Priscilla responded, faintly tragic.

"For *me*, it is." He kissed her fingertips, then carefully repeated the gesture with Anne Bingham's hand. "I fear I must bid you ladies adieu. Mr. Claussen must be most impatient."

"We must be going as well," said Anne. "William and Mr. Hampshire will be waiting for us."

"Oh?"

"We are having an early supper; then the men are taking us to Southwark Theater for the first performance of *The Roman Father*."

"More irony! I am planning to attend myself. Alone . . ." He turned sad gold eyes on Priscilla.

"Perhaps we shall see you there," she said reassuringly.

"I shall retain that hope. Until then . . ." Marcus closed the door and stood back as the landau rolled back onto High Street. The women waved, and as he watched the carriage turning right at Third Street, his expression changed from forlorn to slyly confident.

Some stray remnant of good fortune saw Meagan home before the return of Anne and Priscilla. Smith greeted her in the servants' hall with a gasp of relief, setting down the taper which she was using to light the house's candles.

"Meagan! I've been frantic! I couldn't imagine you purposely letting yourself be missed, so I was convinced that some harm had come to you. I should never have let you go off alone!"

In spite of herself, Meagan smiled. "I'm sorry if I worried you. Truly. I didn't mean to be late . . . I just went out too far and I suppose I misjudged the time."

Smith inclined her head, eyeing the disheveled girl quizzically. "Well, did you enjoy yourself? Where did you go?"

Ignoring the first question, Meagan answered simply, "Out to Markwood Villa. I must go now and tidy myself before Miss Wade returns. I can't imagine what has kept them out so long."

After she had gone, Smith continued along down the paneled hallway, lighting the candles and wondering how Meagan had learned the name of Markwood Villa.

In her room, Meagan poured tepid water into her basin and woodenly began to wash. When she slipped her gown off, she stood before the hazy mirror that hung over the washstand and stared at her bare arms and shoulders. It seemed impossible that only an hour before, Lion's mouth and skin had been touching hers. Slowly she pulled the pins from her tumbled hair and watched, hypnotized, as she brushed it, welcoming the painful pull of each tangle. Finally she began to twist the gleaming jet-colored stream of hair, fastening it atop her head. Then she saw it. A faint, rose colored bruise below the downy base of her hairline, a few inches from the nape of her neck. The color of a kiss, if such existed. Meagan's heart began to race, her chin trembled, and she closed her eyes against the scalding tears even as she put her fingers over the mark Lion had left. The memory of him engulfed her—the hard yet gentle touch of his hands, the intoxicating scent of his golden skin, the pressure of his lips that set her afire, and the remarkable, magical feeling of being held in his arms, of lying against, fusing with his lean, warm, muscular body . . .

Meagan let the tears come, and with them came an exquisite, agonizing pain that seemed to begin in her breast and spread to every corner of her body. She was conscious for the first time of a burning ache between her legs which reminded her of her plight more eloquently than any words.

Finally, her tears were spent and Meagan felt somewhat revived. The numbness had left her brain and she got up to look into the mirror again, searching her reflection. Slowly she felt her innate, headstrong determination infuse her being. When in my life have I ever allowed another person to hurt me? she thought almost incredulously. Even Mother and Father. . . . Since I was little, I've learned not to rely on anyone else for my happiness. Is there any reason to allow a—a barbarian like Lion Hampshire to cause me such anguish now? The strength came to her in a heady rush and soon she was dressing hurriedly. I have made a terrible mistake and have made a fool of myself, but that is no reason to go on this way! From now on, I shall do just as I've always done—look out for myself. I don't need anything from him, or from Priscilla either!

Her eyes sparkled like amethysts and her hair shone in the lamplight as she tied a crisp apron over her black dress. Her creamy skin was glowing, two smudges of rosy emotion brushed across her cheekbones.

I will simply leave this town and go elsewhere. A fresh start is what I need! As soon as I can save—

A sharp knock sounded at the door as Meagan was reaching for her mobcap. Instead, she hurried over to see who it was. A tall, starched kitchen maid stood in the hallway, her bony hand poised to knock again.

"Is Miss Wade back?" Meagan asked her.

123

"Yes, South, but they've gone straight to dinner, no time to change clothes, and she didn't request you until now. You're to go directly to the green parlor. They're having their wine, and—"

Closing the door, Meagan joined her in the hall and rushed on alone, only limping slightly, toward the front of the house.

At that moment, in the green parlor, Lion Hampshire was standing by the fireplace, one elbow propped against the elegantly carved mantel. Lazily, his clear blue eyes flickered across the room, resting on William, Anne, and finally Priscilla. She was looking particularly beautiful in an emerald-green striped gown, its bosom fashionably puffed out to accentuate her tiny waist. A green collarette encircled her long neck, while her auburn curls were dressed in the latest style, full on the sides, with a looped-up queue in back. The excessive coiffure only served to make her lovely face seem more fragile, her green eyes larger.

Out of the corner of one of those eyes, Priscilla perceived that Lion was watching her. Attempting a coquettish smile, she tipped her head slightly so that her best profile was visible to him.

Lion sighed inwardly as she finally started across the room after waiting in vain for him to make the first move. In spite of her physical beauty, which was now perilously near Anne Bingham's own, there was something about Priscilla that repelled him. She was affected, so shallow and vain . . . Lion took a long drink from his glass of brandy and looked down into the swirling umber liquid. Unbidden, Meagan's piquant face filled his mind and he felt a sharp twinge of longing, mingled with the now familiar guilt. She didn't deserve the treatment he had given her although until the moment he had seen that telltale blood on her leg he had not realized she was in over her head. Who had ever heard of a serving-girl as pretty and personable as Meagan staying a virgin? He couldn't imagine James Wade letting her escape his bed. Still . . . it was a relief. He knew he had no business feeling relief or any other emotion for an ordinary maid, especially in his position now. Yet, how uncommon she was! The stinging guilt returned as he remembered her ever-hopeful, strained expression that day in the twilight, the bright tears that shone in her eyes. *I led her out into deep water, right over her head, and then I left her there,* he thought bitterly, taking another drink of brandy. *But, damn—how was I to know she'd never been swimming before?* The analogy brought a grim twist to his lips.

"I declare, Lion Hampshire, you must be a million miles away!" Priscilla was at his elbow, her voice petulant. "I've been standing right here for a full minute!"

"Not a full minute! Milady, I humbly beg your pardon." The tone of his voice belied his words and Priscilla looked at him suspiciously.

"You are a puzzle to me, Lion. I never know what to think—"

"My dear, I am exactly what I seem. Do not invent mysteries where none exist." He sipped his brandy, glancing up to see Meagan come into the room. No longer the pale, tearful girl to whom he had said good-bye at the edge of town, she was now defiantly radiant. Seeing the naked emotion flash in Lion's eyes, Priscilla turned her head to follow his gaze.

For Meagan, the shock of seeing him there affected her like a hard slap in the face, and for a brief moment she faltered. He had never looked more handsome, and as always, he emanated an intangible charisma that made his mere presence in a room stimulating. Snowy white breeches fit against his muscular thighs and narrow hips, above which he wore a rich, dark turquoise velvet coat that emphasized his wide shoulders. Meagan saw the pleated frill of his cuff, so white against the sienna hand which held his drink. On his other hand, which rested on the mantel, a plain gold signet ring glinted in the candlelight.

She took a deep breath and looked into his eyes. Her cheeks burned, but in her expression there was no trace of the vulnerability she had shown earlier. Her eyes were a smoldering violet, flashing with hostility, and Lion raised a sun-bleached brow in surprise. Obviously the minx had too much spirit to drown on his account!

Meagan ignored him from that moment until she left the parlor. She addressed herself only to Priscilla, who informed her that they were attending the theater later in the evening and she wanted her apricot satin gown to be aired. "You may attend me in my chamber at half after eight," she finished, her tone completely remote. One of Meagan's delicate eyebrows lifted slightly in silent revolt as she curtsied, bobbing her head mindlessly. Lion found himself grinning at her retreating figure, unaware of Anne Bingham's watchful eyes across the room.

Meagan stopped in the shadowy hallway, leaning against the wall until the trembling subsided. The powerful yearning to touch Lion, to press her face against his wide, hard chest and feel his arms around her, was something that she could neither control nor fathom. Tears sprang into her eyes as she thought, he takes his pleasure with me in the afternoon and pauses only long enough to change into his finest clothes before dining with his fiancée and escorting *her* to the theater! She fought back the tears and straightened her back, clenching her fists until her nails bit into her palms. Blackhearted cur! I won't let him win! I shall fight whatever demon has taken possession of my emotions; Lion Hampshire can have his precious Priscilla, but he can't have me. His friend! What a silly fool I have been!

When she turned toward the kitchen, she saw Brown's slight, dark-haired form coming around the corner. His puckish grin warmed and relaxed her and she found herself welcoming the distraction he provided.

"Hello, Brown! What are you looking so cheerful about?" She was surprised to see him blush in the dim amber light.

"The prospect o' seein' you, miss. Might I say that you are lookin' rare beauteous tonight?"

"Why, thank you. I don't believe you, but it's a

126

lovely compliment all the same. And you mustn't call me 'miss' as though I live rather than work here! My name is Meagan."

"I'd be pleased to call you Meagan. If you'll pardon me again, you seem better bred than the richest women I've met." He flashed his disarming grin, black eyes dancing. "I'm famous for tellin' the truth, so you're obligated to believe me."

Meagan laughed, delighting in the lessening of the bitter pain in her breast. "You are too kind."

"I'd be honored if you would call me by my Christian name—Kevin."

"Kevin! The name suits you."

" 'Tis a long while since I've heard it."

"Not if the stories I've heard about you are true! I understand you have a bevy of girls."

They were walking slowly toward the kitchen and Brown halted at her words, clasping a hand against his chest with an elaborate grimace.

"Untrue! You see before ye a lonely man! Who has spread such slander?"

"Did you forget? It was—" The name died on her lips along with her smile, and Brown glimpsed raw suffering in her eyes. Quickly, in bewilderment, he fumbled for a new subject.

"Tell me, how went your ride today?"

Her face was a mask of pain, but she managed to speak in a husky whisper. "I would like a cup of tea."

Perplexed and alarmed, Brown steered a weak-kneed Meagan into the kitchen where she sank into a ladderback chair near the hearth. For a long minute she sat there like a statue, her face paper-white; then slowly Brown could see the sparks kindling in her eyes and the color returning to her cheeks. Relieved, he went to fetch a cup of tea from Bramble, who was none too pleased to be bothered in the midst of supper preparations. By the time he returned to Meagan's chair, he found her holding her hands out toward the fire and smiling quite cheerfully.

"Thank you, Kevin," she said, accepting the cup

127

with fingers that shook slightly. "I am so sorry. I don't know what took hold of me. Suddenly I felt so very cold . . ."

Brown had enough sense to stay clear of the subject of Lion Hampshire and Meagan's ride that day, whether or not they had anything to do with her sudden change in behavior. Instead, he coaxed her into a corner of the servants' dining hall where they sat down in facing Windsor chairs.

"Now," he began with forced gaiety, "I want to know if you have asked for a day or a night free yet, and I'm not talkin' about what time Smith lets you slip by with!"

"Well . . ."

"Aha! I thought not! Well, it's time you did. Your mistress comes and goes; to assemblies, balls, to the dressmakers and milliners, to the theater. I should know, I'm the coachman! So, you deserve a bit o' relaxation yourself. I happen to know that there is goin' to be a reception tomorrow afternoon at Mayor Powel's that will take the Binghams and Miss Wade out of the house. Bein' as that's next door, I'll not be needed to drive them and I'll have the time free. I'd be pleased if you would ask for the afternoon off as well."

Meagan was thinking, she'll be with him at the theater tonight and at the Powels' tomorrow! While I sit at home with nothing but a twisted ankle and a pain where my maidenhead once was! Her eyes flashed as she answered, "What did you have in mind?"

Brown smiled, confident of his charm. "Bein' as you are new to this city, I thought you might enjoy seein' Peale's Museum. Would you of heard of it?"

Meagan's expression was a trifle smug. "We Virginians are not entirely ignorant. I have not only heard of it, I happen to know that General Washington has sent Mr. Peale the French pheasants given him by the Marquis de Lafayette—one by one as they died." By now she sounded not only smug but snobbish—a trait Brown was unused to in his peers. His merry grin faded as she spoke, and Meagan hated herself. I

128

sounded like Anne Bingham, she thought. Must I be so defensive?

At this point, Brown was as curious about her background as Lion. He leaned closer, searching her face before inquiring with a weak chuckle, "Are you certain you're the lady's maid? You sound like the lady to me!"

"Oh, Kevin, forgive me—" She broke off at the sound of a bell pealing outside. "What's that? Surely not a church?"

" 'Tis the butter bell! They ring it the night before market days—twice weekly. Ah, Meagan, Philadelphia's market is a sight, enough to cause a person to wish for wealth!"

"Oh, dear . . . I had completely forgotten. I am supposed to go along with Smith and Bramble tomorrow!"

Brown gave a laugh. "You'll need to retire early, then, for Bramble rises before five o'clock on market days. The stalls open at dawn."

Meagan groaned. "Perhaps I had better be on my way to Miss Wade's chamber, then. I should be airing that gown for tonight and she's expecting me to attend her at half after eight."

He put a hand on her arm. "Wait! I had best come more directly to the point before you slip away. It would please me if you would promise to accompany me to the Peale Museum tomorrow afternoon. 'Tis truly a rare spot—full of strange bones and stuffed animals of every description—even a waxwork statue of Peale himself. What d'ye say?"

His earnest expression made her smile. "I would like to go, and it's kind of you to ask me . . . but I wonder if I'll be allowed?"

Brown let out a snort of laughter. "I'll tell you this much, 'tis my belief that you'd be allowed most anything were you to but ask. Mister Bingham has given strict orders that you're to be treated gently." He watched her closely, but her surprise seemed genuine.

"Whatever do you mean?"

"Truth to tell, Meagan, I was hopin' you could tell *me!* That's all I know; he told me right off that no one

129

was to make 'brash advances' toward you or mistreat you in any way. 'Twas strange, for serving-girls and maids have come and gone by the dozen just since I came to work here but two months past, yet Mister Bingham never even remarked on any of them."

"But I don't even know the man! He's not so much as spoken to me!"

Brown looked surprised and bit his lower lip before suggesting, "Perhaps it could be Captain Hampshire's doing?"

All the color drained from Meagan's face as she quickly dropped her eyes, studying the hooked rug on the oaken floor. When she raised her head to meet Brown's penetrating gaze, her skin was revealingly flushed. "That's even more absurd," she protested shakily. "I'm inclined to believe it's all some sort of mistake."

"Must've been," Brown agreed, producing a broad grin that eased the tension in the air. "Mistake or not, I'll wager you get the night off if you ask. Only, wait till you can put your request to Mister Bingham himself."

"All right," Meagan replied absently, seething inside as she realized how Lion had tried to prevent the men at Mansion House from approaching her. The part that puzzled her most was the fact that he had done it when she first arrived, at a time when she had thought their relationship to be quite casual. "Kevin," she said aloud, "aren't you asking for trouble by attempting to be my friend?"

He laughed gaily. "So far, sweetheart, I'm hopin' I am safe. Am I guilty of advancin' brashly or mistreatin' you?"

Meagan returned his grin, her own somewhat ironic as she thought, Lion is the only man guilty of those things. Brown lifted her hand to his lips and she let him, but then her face and heart froze as the sound of laughter drifted in from the hallway. The voices were mingled, but she could not mistake Lion's. He sounded horribly happy, and suddenly Meagan felt nauseous, her skin prickling with a sickening chill that swept her body. When it passed, Brown was still holding her hand, but the only thought in her mind was the realization that there was no fire, no magic in his touch . . .

Chapter Fourteen

AT DAWN, BRAMBLE, Smith, and Meagan set out on foot for the High Street Market, accompanied by a young stableboy driving the cart which would later carry their purchases home. Bramble set a brisk pace, striding up Third Street to the narrow alley called Pear Street which would bring them out at the market. To the west, the sky was still midnight blue, but they walked toward the sunrise and it was a sight to behold. Through the houses, Meagan glimpsed the reflection of the blushing sky on the wide Delaware River, the water shimmering under the fiery new sun. The air was cool and sweet, holding a hint of dewy moisture, and she breathed deeply of it, welcoming its curative powers.

As they emerged on Second Street, she realized that her thinking that the three of them were the only people awake in the city had definitely been an illusion. Sleepy-looking women, bundled into their pelisses, were hurrying up the brick footpaths, each hoping to have first choice in the market. Vehicles and horses crammed the wide street, all heading northward, many of the wagons filled with goods and animals and driven by the German farmers who lived in the Pennsylvania countryside.

Bramble's sharp eyes were busily darting all about as she marched up the street and she rarely spoke, but Smith sensed Meagan's curiosity and took the time to explain the market to her.

131

"It really is quite a place. I do love to come in spite of having to rise in the middle of the night!" She pointed to the long market shed which consisted of brick piers supporting an arched, plastered ceiling and gabled roof. "Those are the permanent stalls. The entire structure is known as the 'shambles', but don't ask me why! The farmers who have stands under the eaves pay three pounds for the privilege."

Meagan looked questioningly at the carts and baskets that had been set up alongside the curb just ahead of them and Smith answered her before she could speak.

"These farmers come from New Jersey. They don't have to pay a fee, but they are continually risking the elements."

By this time, they were at the edge of the brick 'shambles' and Smith extracted a long list from her reticule. She and Bramble compared notes for a moment; then the gaunt cook turned back to speak to Meagan for the first time.

"Ye need not help this day, South. 'Tis task enough to learn your way about." And with that, she set off into the crowd.

Meagan stayed close to Smith most of the time, watching her as she chose items, then bargained with the farmers and merchants with a forcefulness that surprised Meagan. First they inspected the fish, sold in single rows alongside the market. There was something for everyone, fresh and salted fish of every variety. Meagan was astonished to hear Smith click her tongue as she looked it over.

"It's not anyone's fault, of course," she explained after paying for her purchases. "Winter makes it hard for everyone. Wait a few months and you'll see such a change! The vegetables and fruits right now are almost nonexistent; most of them have been raised in greeneries."

The butchers were in the marketplace proper and the display of beef and pork in their stalls was magnificent.

Smith was smiling now. "You know," she said in a

132

pleased undertone, "it's said that Philadelphia beef is the finest in the world, and I am inclined to believe it."

Bramble came up then and Meagan watched the two of them exclaim over the meat before turning her head to look around. What a wonderful place, she thought in delight. There was an overwhelming feeling of vitality in the air, of sheer, elemental life. The smells of fish, herbs, meat, oranges, animals, dairy products, and hard-living people assailed her nostrils, while her eyes were full of the patchwork color of the goods and the men and women who bought and sold them. Voices mingled together in wild confusion, spiced with the shouts of the bargaining arguments. This is the best experience I have had as a servant, Meagan told herself with a grin. Meagan Sayers would still be in bed asleep just like Priscilla and Anne Bingham are right now. Let them have their stuffy old theater and assemblies!

Smith had led her over to the produce stalls where they were inspecting the roots, herbs, and garden seed when Meagan spotted little, black-clad Wong Washington. He carried an oversized basket and wore a bicorne hat that seemed to cover half his head, but there was no mistaking his voice as he screamed at one of the largest butchers.

"I not pay so much! You trying to lob me, missa!"

They continued to quarrel until finally the butcher gave a resigned sigh and said something to Wong in a low voice. The tiny Chinaman grinned gleefully and the exchange of money for beef was made.

Meagan could not resist the impulse to speak to him. She edged her way through the crowd until she was near enough to touch Wong's sleeve and he looked back, meeting her eyes which happened to be level with his own.

"You want me, missy?" he asked impatiently; then recognition dawned. "Hello, Missy Meagan! I so glad to see you!"

"Wong, I'm happy that you remember me!"

His smile widened, displaying dozens of teeth. "I tell

133

truth—most Missa Lion's ladies I forget. But you special."

Meagan felt her face grow hot. "Don't be silly. I'm only a servant—an ordinary lady's maid."

He shrugged amiably, but not without a surreptitious wink at her. "Maybe so . . . but if you ordinary, Missa Lion never bring you to his house. Or laugh so happy when you alone with him."

Meagan wished she had never approached Wong. Her high spirits were crushed and she felt the familiar constriction around her heart. "You are talking nonsense. Mr. Hampshire is engaged to be married—to a real lady." The last words were forced out between clenched teeth as she thought of her own venerable lineage.

"You know what they say here in Amelica, missy. There more than one way to skin cat!"

Meagan had an uneasy feeling she was being insulted, good-naturedly or not. "I think that is a terrible expression!"

She turned and made her way back to Smith, who was heading toward the north shambles to look over the eggs and butter. Suddenly the crowds of people made her head ache. Not until Bramble had joined them and they were out in the open air and sunshine having the cart loaded did Meagan begin to relax. This entire tangle is no one's fault but my own. I can't expect people to treat me with the respect afforded a lady when I have chosen to leave the ranks of the upper class. I never felt comfortable in it anyway—and if I feel cheap now—well, I could have gone to Aunt Agatha . . . She shuddered, the thought of her alternative making her situation seem better. At least I'm living life instead of stagnating in Aunt's musty, dark house in Boston! I'll figure out some sort of solution. All I need to do is save some money and get away.

The adventure was fading quickly from her masquerade and for the first time Meagan began to contemplate the idea of finding some old friend who would take her in without alerting her aunt of her

134

whereabouts. The well-loved faces of George and Martha Washington flashed across her mind and as she realized how ludicrous that thought was she chuckled out loud.

Smith eyed her speculatively. "Well, that's better. You looked positively ill for a while at the market."

Meagan gave her a rueful smile. "Don't mind me. I seem to be having my ups and downs these days, but I never stay down for long."

"Good for you. You know, you ought to ask for some real time off. Perhaps you've been working too hard."

"I'm going to. Kevin Brown has asked me to visit Peale's Museum with him this afternoon. I gather everyone will be away at some reception—"

"Oh, yes! The Powels'." Smith's hazel eyes twinkled above her pink cheeks. "Hmm . . . Kevin, is it? He seems like a nice fellow—if a bit roguish."

Meagan sighed softly. "Yes, and he makes me laugh, which is no small accomplishment these days. As for the roguish part—you needn't worry about that, for I am in no danger of losing my heart to him."

They were approaching Mansion House and Smith slowed her walk, searching Meagan's face in hopes that she would reveal more.

"Wouldn't you like to talk about whatever is bothering you, Meagan?"

She blushed and looked away, fixing her eyes on a nearby strong post. "I can't. But it's nothing that can't be resolved with a bit of time and determination. I can be very determined!"

Smith put a smooth hand on her cheek. "I wish you luck. And, if you ever need a friend—"

"I'll remember. Thank you."

Bramble was turning down Bingham's Court toward the back entrance. "Be quick!" she called sharply over her shoulder.

Smith grimaced, whispering, "You'd think *she* was head housekeeper!" She paused, trying to decide whether or not to say more and finally gave in to temptation. "I shouldn't mention this, and indeed I do not mean to gossip, but I'm sure I can trust you not to repeat this confidence."

"Of course you can."

"Well, Wickham and I have been told that Bramble is to be replaced before the month is out."

"You must be joking! She is a wonderful cook!"

"That is neither here nor there. Apparently Mrs. Bingham has gotten her hands on an available French chef. The mistress is very enamored of all things French and this cook will be a status symbol whether he has any talent in the kitchen or not!"

"Oh, dear! Has Bramble been told?"

"No."

"It will destroy her!"

"I'm well aware of that. The question now is whether or not her pride will allow her to stay on in second place—taking orders in the kitchen from someone else."

Meagan looked ahead to the stiff, self-righteous woman who was striding past the orangerie and shivered as she imagined Bramble's reaction to this turn of events.

Meagan arrived just in time to assist Priscilla in her preparations for the reception at Mayor Powel's. It was being given in honor of the many members of the new Congress who had arrived in town that week, stopping over on their way to New York. Word had reached them that their business in the new capital could not begin for at least two weeks so they lingered in Philadelphia to enjoy its lively social whirl. Priscilla had heard at the theater that James Madison was now in town as well, his arrival delayed by the week he had spent at Mount Vernon. Apparently, he had been joined there by John Page, where the two of them had encountered Robert Bland Lee from Alexandria. Meagan was all too well acquainted with each member of that trio and she panicked anew at the prospect of meeting one—or all—of them in Mansion House or on the street. This town is probably teeming with people who have met me in Virginia, she thought with a groan.

Priscilla had chosen one of her finest new gowns for the reception. Fashioned of ivory silk, it was embroidered with a scattered repeat pattern in blue and green. The tight, elbow-length sleeves were edged in rich lace as was the round-necked bodice and the petticoat that showed behind the open skirt. Meagan helped her dress, arranging the *cul de Paris,* a little cushion attached to the underskirt, which was placed on the buttocks. There was a special corset, designed to make the breasts more prominent, which was lined with a piece of triangular wire, curved and padded. Over all of this went the gown itself, finished off by a handkerchief, knotted like a fichu, which covered the neckline. It was held up so stiffly by the 'pigeon's breast' that it almost reached Priscilla's chin. Still, in spite of all the false curves and stiffness, the final effect was quite striking. Priscilla's waist looked tiny, her neck long, and her face lovely. Anne Bingham's abigail had taught Meagan to apply special French cosmetics —rice powder, lip salve, and rouge—so skillfully that they were almost impossible to detect. Around her neck, Priscilla wore a green velvet ribbon from which hung a pearl droplet as well as a long gold chain with an enameled watch at its end. Meagan dressed her auburn hair so that it was full at the sides, with soft curls falling over her shoulders, then topped the coiffure with a large Florentine straw hat, tied under her pretty chin with a green satin ribbon. Cologne water, imported from France, was the finishing touch. Meagan had already laid out a fan made of embroidered silk that matched the gown's material and a little pearl-encrusted box called a *nécessaire,* holding such indispensable items as perfume, a watch key, tiny scissors, ear and nail cleaners, a pencil, and a little ivory plate on which to make notes.

As she helped Priscilla dress, Meagan listened with unwilling interest to her extravagant tales of her night at the Southwark Theater.

"There was a marvelous dance. I believe it was called a hornpipe, performed by a man named Darlang, or—"

"Durang," Meagan corrected.

Priscilla narrowed her eyes briefly. "Yes. Well, he was dressed like a sailor with a lovely red vest. The amazing part was that he seemed to *fly* onto the stage. Lion said he had jumped from a trampoline though I'm not quite sure what that is . . ."

Priscilla went on to describe the performance of *The Roman Father* in sadly sketchy terms that only added to Meagan's suspicion that her mind had been more on her surroundings than the play. Apparently, the Binghams had obtained seats befitting the wealthiest family in America, and Marcus Reems had accepted Anne's invitation to share their box. Meagan imagined that it must have been an exhilarating evening for Priscilla to be seen by all of Philadelphia society in the company of the Binghams and to be sitting with not only a handsome fiancé but his attractive rival as well.

Priscilla took one last look in the mirror before slipping into the blue pelisse that Meagan held for her. She smiled at her reflection in a way that made Meagan's stomach turn, then went out into the hallway to join the Binghams. Only William was waiting there, his face looking more flushed than usual.

"Ah, Priscilla dear! You are looking splendid as always. Lion will be a proud man today with you by his side! Anne is still dressing. I do hope she will be ready soon, for the hour grows late . . ."

Meagan approached him, feeling unusually shy. "Mr. Bingham, could I have a word with you?"

Hearing the refined, softly melodious voice behind him, he turned to find the little black-haired maid about whom Lion had spoken. Since that first night, he had meant to have a closer look at her in an effort to discover what his friend was about, but he had seldom seen her at close range. There was undoubtedly something odd about the girl, for neither her face nor her voice were those of a common servant. Her features were delicately made, her skin as translucent as a pink and ivory shell, and when she looked up at him—

what amazing eyes! He had never known that such a true violet color was possible.

"Most certainly, Miss—"

"South, sir."

"Of course. Do pardon my memory." He gave her a hearty smile. Bingham was a man confident of his charm, for what he lacked in physical attributes he made up for by the aura he exuded of power and wealth. Anne was truly his better half, for she brought her dazzling beauty and versatile charm to unite with his shrewd intelligence and unlimited wealth. In his mind, the resulting combination was matchless. Anne emerged at that moment from her suite of rooms, looking as breathtaking as always.

"I am ready, William. Let us go."

Beaming, he tucked her hand through the crook of his arm. "Momentarily, my dear. Miss South desires a word with me."

Anne lifted an eyebrow at Meagan, who met her gaze unflinchingly. "Do tell," she said coolly.

"Yes. I only wanted to ask Mr. Bingham if I might have the afternoon free."

William laughed good-naturedly. "Why, I certainly have no objections, but perhaps you should be asking Mr. Hampshire. After all, he is your actual employer. He'll be here any minute if he's not downstairs right now, and . . ."

Anne broke in quickly. "Now, William, we needn't waste Lion's time. I'm sure he would be agreeable to this if you are." She turned her beautiful eyes on Meagan. "Do behave yourself, South. You'll be expected home to attend Miss Wade before dinner."

With that, she turned and swept away down the hall, her saffron silk skirts rustling. Bingham gave Meagan one last distracted smile before going after her, Priscilla at his side.

It was a long way down to the end of the stairway, but after a minute, Meagan could hear Anne's vivacious greeting for Lion Hampshire. The sound of his voice, typically dry and amused, drew Meagan to the top of the stairs like a magnet. She allowed herself one

139

quick glimpse of his gold hair and bronzed face, which appeared to be smiling down at Priscilla, before forcing her feet to back away. As she made her way toward the rear stairway, Meagan determined that she would make a success of the afternoon she was about to spend with Kevin Brown.

Chapter Fifteen

BROWN'S PLAN TO take Meagan to Peale's Museum proved to be inspired, for she was utterly delighted with the place. Having grown up outdoors in the meadows and woods of Virginia, riding and walking in her breeches and making friends with every animal in sight, she felt right at home with this stuffed menagerie, set in recreations of their natural habitats.

"I had heard that he had done wonders . . ." Meagan murmured, her face flushed with pleasure, "but I never dreamed . . ."

The entire seventy-foot museum had been built onto the back of Charles Wilson Peale's home, located on Lombard Street, directly south of Mansion House. Meagan learned that it had begun as a picture gallery to display his famous portraits of Washington and the other notables he had known during the war. Apparently, it did not take long for Peale's interest in nature to intrude; the first additions were sketches of mammoth bones found in a New York swamp. His notorious enthusiasm was soon at a fever pitch. He began badgering friends and acquaintances from far and wide for items like alligator skins, wild ducks, and silk grass . . . even approaching Benjamin Franklin for the body of his dead French Angora cat. Much experimenting had to be done before a suitable technique was arrived at for preserving, skinning, and stuffing the carcasses; but the results were amazing.

During her tour of the museum, Meagan found herself forgetting that the animals were dead. Peale had constructed a mound covered with trees, as well as a thicket, a rocky grotto, an artificial pond made from mirrors, and a beach. Animals of every description were posed against this natural background, including bears, tigers, a variety of snakes, fish, exotic birds, deer, and even a mongoose. Brown laughingly told Meagan that the latest rumor was that Peale had acquired a swarm of East Indian insects.

"Nothing is too absurd to be believed where Mr. Peale's museum is concerned," he chuckled.

"It is a splendid project," Meagan replied earnestly.

They had already been there two hours, determined to get their shilling's worth, and finally Meagan left the animals to examine the portraits. At the upper end of the room hung a life-size portrait of George Washington that took Meagan's breath away.

"It's a perfect likeness," she said softly, and Brown gave her a curious glance.

" 'Tis a fine specimen of a man, indeed."

After looking over the other paintings, most of which were of heroes from the Revolution, many of whom Meagan readily recognized, Brown led her over to a rather bizarre display.

"Wasn't sure if you'd enjoy this, but you don't strike me as a swooner!"

She gave him a grin, which changed into an expression of revulsion at the sight of several Indian scalps. The next exhibit was a set of rattlesnake fangs mounted under a magnifying glass.

"You were right to save the worst for last!" Meagan told Brown with a weak laugh. "It makes it easier for me to take my leave."

Brown set a leisurely pace for their walk back to Mansion House, despite Meagan's attempts to go faster. Ever fearful of encountering someone who knew her, she pulled the hood of her pelisse up so that it covered as much of her face as possible.

"You wouldn't be cold?" Brown inquired with surprise. The late afternoon air was barely cool and the sun still shone cheerfully.

"Not really, but I've felt a slight case of the ague coming on and I'm rather afraid of making it worse out in this open air."

She avoided looking at him directly, focusing on the coaches passing them on Third Street. A striking black and green phaeton pulled by a pair of ebony horses turned off Spruce Street and came clattering toward them. Fascinated, Meagan's eyes were on the handsome horses, their glossy dark manes flying in the spring breeze. As they passed, she saw the passengers —Marcus Reems, looking lawless in a fluttering black cape, and the fashionably-garbed Clarissa. They sat close together, so deep in conversation that they saw neither her nor Brown.

Meagan's mind was spinning as Brown guided her across Spruce Street. Why were the two of them together? What could it mean?

Brown, meanwhile, observed the troubled expression on her face and wished he could read her thoughts. From any other girl, the ague explanation would have easily satisfied him, but somehow it rang false when she gave it.

As they neared Mansion House, the elegant home of Mayor Powel loomed before them where the reception for the visiting congressmen was being held. Brown's sharp eyes had no trouble spotting Lion Hampshire leaning against a strong post at the edge of the brick footpath. Looking coolly elegant, even from a distance, he was smoking a cheroot and conversing with two men. Brown recognized William Maclay, but the slight, plainly dressed man standing with them was unknown to him.

"Good afternoon to you, Captain Hampshire," he called cheerfully. Ordinarily, Brown would never have been so bold as to greet publicly someone as far removed in social class from himself as Lion Hampshire, but the captain had never been a man who placed any importance on such distinctions.

Meagan stiffened with cold, chilling fear. What could she do? Lion looked down the street, the sweep of hair caught back at his neck as bright as molten gold in the sunlight. Meagan was unnervingly conscious of him but the bulk of her attention was riveted on the smaller figure of James Madison.

Lion straightened up as he recognized the couple standing near the gates to Mansion House. His companions were engaged in a lively debate on their future roles in the new government, so he decided to walk down and speak to Brown and Meagan. He was uncomfortably curious to learn what they were doing together.

Meagan saw him speak to Madison and Maclay, then start toward them, an odd spark in his blue eyes. Then, as Madison paused in mid-sentence to look toward Brown and Meagan, she dropped her eyes and whispered hoarsely to Brown, "I am ill." Keeping her head turned so that her hood shielded her face, she ran past the gates and up the drive.

Brown, utterly stupefied, stared after her.

An hour later, Meagan was beginning to relax. She had given an explanation to Brown which seemed to satisfy him and had been kept so busy herself that the hard knot of panic in the pit of her stomach finally began to ease.

There had barely been time for her to wash and change into her formal black dress and white apron before being notified that her mistress had returned from the Powels'.

The women planned to rest in their rooms before dinner, and Meagan was ordered to take tea on a silver tray up to Priscilla. At first, she looked around nervously, frightened of meeting Lion—or one of the Sayers's family friends—in the hallways, but when she passed the library on her way upstairs, the sound of male voices and laughter rang out from behind a heavy oak door. With a sigh of relief, she hurried up the marble steps and down the hallway to Priscilla's darkened room. There, she helped her undress, listening anxiously to the names of their mutual friends who had been present at the reception.

"You know," Priscilla told her as she sat back against her satin pillows and accepted the tea cup held out to her, "most of them will be leaving after the dinner at Dr. Shippen's house tomorrow night. I know for a fact that Mr. Madison plans to be on his way then, so perhaps you can stop dashing around looking so rattled." She gave a large yawn, which made her breasts swell above her thin chemise. "Why don't you run along now? You might take a moment to do something with your hair. You have all sorts of stray curls."

Priscilla closed her eyes and Meagan left, but not before putting her hands on her hips and clicking her tongue in disgust.

Descending the back stairway, she suddenly felt drained and decided that after returning the serving tray to the kitchen she would try to steal a few minutes' rest. As she rounded the corner next to the great stone hearth, Meagan pulled off her mobcap, letting her raven hair fall down her back. Oh . . . she thought, how wonderful that feels. She set the tray on the long wooden table and extended her fingers, running them through her hair with a loud sigh.

"You appear tired, my dear," a deep voice said from across the room. Meagan's back stiffened instinctively before she turned her head to seek him out. As always, the sight of him in a room made her breath catch and the strength went from her legs.

Lion sat half-veiled in shadows, with his sturdy bow-back chair tipped against the wall, gleaming boots propped negligently on a stool. Meagan saw that he was smoking, and he looked so much at ease that a stranger would have thought he belonged here in the kitchen.

She twisted her mobcap until it was taut. "What are you doing here?" Her voice was a hiss.

Lion's teeth flashed white from the dimly lit corner. "Certainly you can do better than that, sweeting," he chided mockingly. "Anyone would think you were not glad to see me!"

Reminded of the public nature of the room, Meagan glanced over her shoulder hastily, then made her way across to him.

"Sit down," he offered genially, indicating the chair to his right.

"Thank you, no," she replied stiffly. Lion grinned again, obviously enjoying himself, and Meagan felt an unsettling current of warmth as she met those twinkling azure eyes.

"Now, Meagan, I can't believe that you would intentionally disobey your employer. Especially when he is so kind and charming."

"Goodness! When did this radical change in his personality take place?" she retorted sarcastically. Just to be on the safe side, she did drop into the chair, but not without murmuring, "I do seem to be a bit tired."

Lion caught her hand lightly, rubbing his thumb absently across the palm. "My, my, but we are certainly cutting today," he smiled.

"Are we? We didn't intend to be."

"Meagan, I get the distinct impression that you don't like me anymore! Tell me I'm mistaken."

"I'm not a very adept liar, but since you insist . . . sir, you are mistaken." The last words were spoken in her best wooden voice.

Lion was laughing, his head tipped back and his chest shook. "God, Meagan, how I love these conversations—the verbal duels—with you!" he choked at last. "You are just delightful! That little face of yours is so animated and I love the way you put me in my place. How fed up I am with flattering females."

"I'll agree that is one thing I'm not," she replied dryly while attempting to disengage her fingers from his. Lion merely tightened his grip.

"I know you'd be content to sit here with me all evening, sweetheart, but I do have a limited amount of time, so I must get to the point." He grinned as she shot him a withering look. "Wong seems to have the idea that he might have offended you at the market today, so I have come bearing his apologies."

He was watching Meagan closely, noticing the way she swallowed twice and dropped her eyes.

"Never mind," she replied. "It's of no consequence, and besides, I should not have expected civilized behavior from a man in your employ."

His blond eyebrows went up. "Hmm . . . Wong must have really put his foot in his mouth! But Meagan, you mustn't be angry. He meant no harm. I realize that *both* of us can be quite unchivalrous, but our intentions are the best."

She looked up to find him regarding her tenderly, his eyes warm and penetrating. "Oh, Lion," she whispered and let out a long, gusty sigh.

He gave her a heart-melting smile. "That's much better." Bringing her hand up, he pressed his warm, firm lips against her palm, then against the pulse that fluttered at her wrist. "Just to be sure I've softened you up completely, I brought you a peace offering. From both Wong and me . . . to show you how sorry we are if we've hurt you." His expression was serious now and Meagan felt her face grow warm under his gaze.

With his free hand, Lion reached over on the far side of his chair to produce a neatly wrapped bundle.

Meagan was totally undone by this time, incapable of coherent thought or speech. "But . . ." she faltered.

"Open it!" he smiled, putting the package on her lap. When he freed her hand, Meagan felt some of her composure return.

Before she could untie the string, the door at the far end of the room swung open and Bramble strode in. When she spotted them, her eyes narrowed and her lips tightened. "Excuse *me*."

Meagan's face was burning, but Lion merely nodded politely at the cook.

"I don't suppose that whatever it was you had to do could wait?" he inquired. "Miss South and I were just discussing Mistress Wade's impending birthday."

"Supper will not wait, sir," she told him imperiously and Lion met her disapproving stare with a grin.

"Well, perhaps there is somewhere else we could converse. Meagan?"

She could not look at Bramble as they got up and went into the hall. "How embarrassing!" she whispered heatedly.

Lion chuckled, "Don't let that old hawk intimidate you, little one. She's not your mother—or mine!"

He found a small storeroom and Meagan reluctantly allowed him to lead her inside. An assortment of odd chairs was crowded against the far wall; Lion pulled two of them around, dusting off the seat of one for her.

"Now then," he began cheerfully, "where were we?"

"You were trying to win back my friendship, and I was resisting all your efforts," she said firmly.

Lion arched an eyebrow appreciatively. "I don't remember it that way at all! As a matter of fact, I thought I had worn you down quite effectively!"

Meagan studied a wrinkle in her apron. "Obviously, you were mistaken."

"Well, we'll see. In any event, *all* my 'efforts' have not been put to the test yet."

Meagan looked up automatically, blushing, to meet his dancing eyes.

"My dear, your thoughts do me a grave injustice! I was referring to this package."

Back it went onto Meagan's lap, and this time she was able to undo the wrapping without being interrupted. The paper fell away to reveal yards and yards of beautiful white silk material sprigged with tiny embroidered violets.

"Oh!" Meagan gasped, her eyes so wide that the lashes seemed to touch her eyebrows.

"Do you like it?"

"Like it? Why, Lion, it is exquisite! But—"

He relaxed against the back of his chair. "Good. I'll admit that it may not make the most practical gown, but you deserve something really beautiful. I would have had it made for you, but it was impossible

147

without you along to be measured." He smiled. "I didn't imagine you'd consent to that!"

"Oh, Lion . . ." she had found the delicate Belgian lace and pearl buttons that had been concealed within the folds of the material.

"I hope you'll let me see the finished product."

"But, I don't see how I can accept this. Don't you understand? It wouldn't be at all proper."

"Proper?" He laughed derisively. "You'd be a good deal happier, Meagan, if you'd forget propriety. Besides . . . if you won't take it, I'll be forced to offer your gift to Priscilla."

He spoke with studied nonchalance, watching her out of the corner of one keen blue eye.

Meagan automatically held the violet-sprigged silk against her breasts, her forehead puckering at his words. After a moment, she capitulated. "Blackmailer," she accused him, but a smile tugged at the corners of her pretty mouth.

"True." He reached for one of her hands, tracing the outline of her fingers with one of his own. "Tell me, what were you and Brown doing on the street today?"

"He was kind enough to show me Peale's Museum," she replied cheerfully, failing to notice the edge of steel in his voice. Instead, she was thinking of Clarissa and Marcus Reems and was feeling mellow enough toward Lion to speak to him about her uneasiness.

"Now that you mention my outing," she began, "something happened while we were walking back that gave me cause for worry."

"Goddamn that Brown! What did he do?"

"Brown? Why, nothing. Lion, don't be silly." She laughed a little at the stormy expression on his face. "I'm talking about something I *saw*. It was your friend Clarissa. She was riding with Marcus Reems in his phaeton. Are they well-acquainted?"

"Not as far as I know, but I couldn't say for sure. They are both capable of most anything. What are you worried about?"

"I'm not certain . . . It's really more a feeling that I have." She couldn't bring herself to tell him about the figure outside the schoolroom at Markwood Villa. "I'm just afraid that Clarissa may be up to no good."

"Little one, I appreciate your concern, but I'm confident of my ability to handle Clarissa. At any rate, it's probably your imagination. You should confine your worrying to Kevin Brown."

Stung, Meagan lifted her chin. "Oh, really? Do you think he might take advantage of me? Besmirch my reputation—such as it is?"

Caught off guard, Lion felt a stab of raw guilt. "Meagan—"

She stood up. "Mr. Hampshire, I've said this before, but you seem to be rather slow to catch on. Stay out of my life!" Eyes flashing, she thrust the mass of silk and lace at him and ran out of the room.

Chapter Sixteen

HARD BROWN FINGERS made quick work of the starched white cravat while, higher up, Lion Hampshire appraised his own handiwork in the mirror. It would have been impossible to find fault with his appearance. Clad in ivory breeches, a blue-and-gray brocade vest, and a smoky-blue velvet coat, he was looking impeccably splendid. The snowy cravat made his face seem tanner, his eyes more vividly blue, while his unpowdered hair shone like polished gold in the candlelight.

Wong appeared in the doorway and grinned appreciatively. "You looking velly fine, Missa Lion."

"Spencer did an excellent job with this coat. It's the first one in months that hasn't been too small through the shoulders. I only hope the rest of them fit as well."

"You want cape now?"

"No. I believe I'll have a brandy in the library before I leave. I could use one before facing the crowds again." Silently, he added, And another evening with Priscilla.

They went downstairs together, Wong inquiring about the Powels' reception of the day before.

"I enjoyed seeing the new congressmen and was lucky enough to have a conversation with James Madison. Do you know who he is?"

"Father of Constitution!" replied a proud, beaming Wong.

"That's right! Wong, you really have been studying!" Lion exclaimed in surprise. "Well, Mr. Madison is currently working on a plan for a Bill of Rights—amendments to the Constitution. Understand?" They were entering the library and Lion looked over his shoulder to see that Wong appeared confused. He smiled, splashing brandy into a glass, and turned back to the Chinaman.

"The additions would spell out clearly what rights the American people are entitled to. Some men don't think they are necessary, but Madison makes an excellent case. In the *Federalist Papers,* he writes that the amendments will 'fortify the rights of the people against the encroachments of the government.' " Lion was looking past Wong as he spoke, his eyes flashing yet soft. "Beautiful words, aren't they? Splendid plans—"

"What would lights be?" asked Wong hesitantly.

"Oh, God—rights more precious than diamonds. Freedom of speech and the press, the right to a speedy and public trial, the right of peaceable assembly, prohibition of cruel and unusual punishments. Do you get the idea?"

Wong nodded, entranced.

"That's only the beginning. Madison is already hard at work on the list; after the inauguration, he'll present the plan to the House of Representatives."

"And they vote yes?"

Lion laughed at this earnest question. "I wish it were that painless, but no one ever agrees so easily in America. That's why I wish I were going to New York now, as a representative! Christ, how I long to add my voice to such a vital agreement." He had moved to the window, staring out over the dark garden. "To me, the cause of American liberty and rights is sacred—almost holy. Can you understand that?" His voice had dropped to a near whisper; he seemed to be talking to himself, or to someone else Wong could not see.

"Yes, Missa Lion, I understand."

A long minute of silence stretched out. Wong finally turned, intending to slip away, but Lion spoke up.

"Wait! I meant to tell you . . . I had an encounter with Meagan South yesterday. You were right. She *is* irked with you! I relayed your apologies, but I fear you'll have to prove yourself to her. The sooner you realize that your usual serving hall repartee does not find favor with her, the safer you'll be."

"She some strange maid, Missa Lion!"

"Would that they all were as strange!" He started to pour himself another drink, but stopped in mid-air, smiling ruefully. "No, for once I must recant. If all the serving-girls were like Meagan, the American aristocracy would be lost."

As he thought of her, his eyes took on a newly familiar expression of mingled amusement, bewilderment, and pain.

In her room at Mansion House, Meagan was working furiously on her new gown. She somehow hoped that if she forced all her concentration on her sewing, the nagging thoughts of Lion could be kept at bay.

She was humiliated and angry with herself for keeping the gift he had brought her, yet every time she decided to relinquish it, her fingers would caress the rich silk and her eyes would drink in the perfectly embroidered flowers. Her conscience was beaten. All her life she had shunned the beautiful clothes which filled

151

her armoire in brilliant profusion, but now that she had none . . .

Meagan reached for the scissors to clip a thread and then sat back in her chair for a moment, allowing her thoughts to take her. But it wasn't the fine silk that lured me back to the storeroom yesterday, she mused. It was my own curiosity—to know if he had left it there for me after all. Her lovely mouth turned down. If the rogue had brought me burlap, I doubt if it could mean any less.

She began to rethread the needle, anxious to escape from the reality which pursued her, afraid to turn and face it. As the needle flew in and out of the silk, Meagan remembered Smith's expression the evening before when she had shown her the contents of the bundle, asking her to help with the measurements and cutting. She had explained it as a gift from the lady at a neighboring plantation in Virginia, given as a remembrance when Meagan left for Pennsylvania. "I nursed her through an illness," she had lied, cheeks burning, and added, "There has been no opportunity before now to begin a gown." Smith had seemed somewhat perplexed by the situation, but accepted Meagan's explanation and cheerfully agreed to help. She even brought out a box of patterns for her to choose from and supplied all manner of sewing necessities.

Oh, Meagan groaned inwardly, to what have I reduced myself? First I become a servant, to Priscilla Wade of all people, then I allow myself to be used like a common tavern slut by the man engaged to marry her! Finally, I accept expensive gifts from the same man and to cover my tracks, I have begun telling lies! Desperate tears sprang up in her eyes, but she wiped them away as a knock sounded at her door.

"Who is it?"

" 'Tis only me, my lady. Kevin."

Meagan hurriedly stuffed the white silk into her bureau drawer before opening the door.

"Have I disturbed you?" he inquired politely, his black eyes taking in her drawn face.

"No, not really. What—"

152

Encouraged, he relaxed into an easy smile. " 'Tis bold of me to ask it, since you gave me your afternoon just a day ago, but I wondered if you might share some refreshment with me."

Her expression softened. "I think that might be just what I need. Thank you." She turned back to blow out the candles which burned near her sewing chair. "I mustn't remain long, for I have a great deal of . . . mending that must be done."

Brown made idle, cheerful conversation as they walked toward the serving hall. Tentatively, he offered her a glass of wine that she accepted immediately, taking a chair near the hearth as he left the room to procure the bottle and glasses. Her eyes burned from the long hours she had spent laboring with needle and thread and she closed them now, soaking up the enveloping warmth of the fire.

"Heavens! I am so relieved to have found you!"

Meagan's eyelids fluttered open, almost unwilling to see the person who had entered the room. It was Clarissa. She was wrapped in an elegant robin's-egg-blue pelisse which was trimmed lavishly with silver fox. That perfect oval face was framed by the fur, the only part of her that was visible, for even her hands were concealed inside a huge fox muff.

Speechless, Meagan stood up, and Clarissa hurried over to her. Her large blue eyes were sparkling with some emotion that Meagan could not put a name to.

"Miss South, I am asking—*begging*—for your assistance!"

"Whatever for? I don't understand—"

"There is an emergency. I have desperate need of Lion Hampshire and I want you to take a message to him immediately."

"Me? But—"

"No time can be spared for explanations. Suffice it to say that I trust you—and know that you alone can persuade him to meet me." Momentarily, her eyes narrowed almost malevolently, but it passed so quickly that Meagan wondered if it were her imagination. "By

153

that, of course, I mean that Lion trusts you also," Clarissa finished hastily.

"Well . . ."

"Thank you! This means so very much to me. Go now to Dr. Shippen's house and instruct Lion that he must meet me at once, at our usual spot."

Meagan flinched slightly at the words, but for some undefinable reason she felt compelled to do Clarissa's bidding. "As you say, ma'am. But, where does Dr. Shippen live?"

"His house stands on the corner of Fourth and Locust Streets, barely a square away. The side presented to the street will seem to be four stories tall, for it is the chimney end. Now, do fetch your wrap and make haste!"

Polished silver outlcry clattered against fine Queensware china as, up and down the long table, well-known dinner guests divided their attention between the sumptuous meal and high-spirited discussion. Few houses in the world could have boasted such an assemblage; the dining room nearly burst with stimulations for any mind and eye. Such handsome people! Their clothing was the finest, the richest to be found, their faces were among those best known in America, and all lesser citizens longed to be privy to conversations such as were taking place among them.

Lion smothered a yawn and knitted his blond eyebrows as he listened to the familiar sound of William Bingham's voice reaching its fever pitch.

"Would you, my dear Mr. Madison, demean our highest office before the rest of the world? All other countries have *kings!* Would you lessen their respect for our own supreme leader by giving him such a plain, common title?"

Across the table, Chief Justice Thomas McKuan gave a snort of agreement. "Mr. President, indeed!"

James Madison remained unruffled as the target of their arguments. His clear, intelligent eyes held the hint of a smile as he replied evenly, "My good friends, have we not agreed before this day that what we seek

154

is a new direction? We fought a long and bloody war to free ourselves of a king and all the pompous posturings that the word implies. I am certain that more careful consideration will bring you to the realization that the simple title of 'Mr. President' will lend that new office a purity of strength and dignity." He coaxed them gently. "In any case, we are all aware that mere words are not important in comparison with the spirit of the young government and the man who will head it. Might we now toast him together, uniting in our common hope for a bright future as free Americans?"

Lion warmed under Madison's prose, silently renewing the strength of his own ambition to someday work beside such a man.

Fragile, cut-crystal goblets were raised, catching the glittering rays of light from the chandelier, and voices rang out in spirited unison. "Long live our President!"

Lion grinned at William Shippen, who sat at an angle from him, and took a long drink of wine. A tap on his shoulder interrupted that pleasure and he set down the goblet, turning his head curiously.

Cyrus, the family's Negro butler, stood there looking somewhat uncomfortable. "Mister Hampshire, there is someone in the hallway who insisted I fetch you. I hope I've done right."

In the entryway, Meagan waited nervously. There were more possibilities for discovery here than she dared count. Even Mrs. Shippen loomed as a potential traitor, for she was originally a Lee from Virginia, sister to Richard Henry and Frances Lightfoot, two of the state's most illustrious citizens. The Lees had visited at her own home often, and she had met Alice Shippen at the Lees' Stratford Hall more than once.

At any moment someone could come into the hall . . . Meagan jumped, violet eyes wide, as a tall figure strode through the arched doorway. "Lion!" she gasped in relief.

Bathed in the golden luster from the lantern-like chandelier overhead, he towered above her like some great bronzed god. As she gathered her wits, Meagan perceived that an amused smile tugged at the corner of his handsome mouth and when he spoke, laughter infected his voice.

"My sweet, yesterday you struck a powerful blow to my confidence with your cruel words and actions, but to know that you have missed me so sorely as to seek me out *here* lightens my heart more than I can say."

As his words sank in, Meagan's eyes narrowed and she set her hands upon her hips. "You conceited fool, the day that I can destroy your confidence will give me much cause to rejoice!" Taking a step away from the powerful force of his attraction, she admonished, "Now be serious. I have not come here to trade quips with you!"

"I accept your apology," he grinned, white teeth gleaming against his dark face. "You may explain this happy visit."

With an effort, she repressed an urge to put him in his place, but his last words returned the worried frown to her brow.

"I had a visit tonight from Clarissa." She cast an uneasy glance toward the dining room entrance as a chorus of laughter swelled from within. "Could we talk outside? I shouldn't like the Binghams to see me here—"

"Of course. I am as anxious for a moment alone in the moonlight as you are."

Warningly, she swatted his arm lightly as he opened the front door, and Lion chuckled aloud.

"What a dull evening it was till you appeared, my minx!"

The house opened onto Locust Street, and Lion drew her over against the iron railing which ran around to the garden gate. Meagan was noticing his handsome garb, admiring the rich smoky velvet and the way it flattered him. She saw that he watched her, one brow lifted as though he read her mind, and she snatched her hands from his and scolded, "I am not your minx!"

"My mistake," he grinned, folding his arms across his chest. "Well?"

156

She backed against the Flemish bond bricks of the house, plucking nervously at the English ivy which clung there.

"Your dear Clarissa bade me fetch you to your 'usual spot'," her eyes were purple with venom. "She made a great show of distress, but Lion, I only took her message in the hope that I might dissuade you from going."

"As jealous as that?"

"Do stop! I am serious! I have a feeling—and you may laugh at my instincts at your own risk, sir! She means you harm."

In her desire to make him listen, she came out of the shadows to lay her hand on his arm. He put his own over it, caressing its softness with his thumb.

"Meagan, do you doubt my ability to defend myself against some righteous female who imagines herself scorned? You must not judge me much of a man!"

She sighed in frustration. "It is not that—"

"I think it is time this mystery you have concocted around Clarissa was solved. I would not have you spending sleepless nights worrying over my safety!" He brushed a dark curl from her temple and Meagan went weak at his touch. "I will let you know that I am well. I will come to your window at midnight."

She longed to deny her concern, but the words would not come. Instead, she implored, "Please, don't go."

For a moment, the world was forgotten as their eyes met and held. The quarter moon slid from behind a luminous cloud, recasting the spell in stardust.

Meagan somehow pulled her eyes from his brilliant blue gaze, but relented to her heart enough to touch slender fingers against his cheekbone. "Take care."

A reckless grin spread across his face, gleaming in the darkness, and he turned against her hand so that his mouth grazed its tender palm.

"So, little one, you would not have me gone so far from your life as that?"

She blushed at the reminder of her words spoken the day before. "I would never wish you harm, sir."

" 'Sir' is it now?" He laughed low, then assumed an expression of perplexed concern. "It seems that barely a minute has passed since you named me a conceited fool. You have an enchanting facility for stationing yourself above or below me at will!"

She found herself smiling after him as he moved away from her toward the street, soon swallowed by the inky darkness.

"Until midnight . . . ," he called softly, and she had no wish to argue.

Meagan had no intention of returning meekly to Mansion House to await Lion's pleasure. Alone again on the footpath, her nagging suspicions returned to plague her twofold, for Lion's unworried, casual mien added to her apprehension.

His direction was southward, and Meagan lagged behind, watching the bright gleam of his hair to mark his progress. Luckily, there were lamps lit where Fourth Street met Pine so that his change of route was readily apparent to her. His pace was quick and quiet and Meagan found herself lifting her skirts, nearly running to keep him in sight. At the corner, she crept up near a house to stay out of the lamplight. Searching, she saw Lion down the square, crossing the street near St. Peter's Church.

Then his shining gold hair disappeared from sight.

Fearful, Meagan came out of the shadows and pulled her hood closer about her face before following. Upon reaching the high brick wall that ringed St. Peter's churchyard, she stopped to listen, hoping to catch the sound and direction of his footsteps. Instead, she heard voices.

"What dire emergency has caused you to interrupt my dinner at Dr. Shippen's?" Lion's voice was low, but had a steel edge of anger. "Pray explain your reason for appointing Meagan as your messenger. Have your parents' servants all taken ill?"

Meagan could scarcely credit that their place of rendezvous could be a graveyard, but, peering around the brick wall at the entrance, she could see them standing among the ghostly white markers. In the darkness, the silver fox which trimmed Clarissa's pelisse fairly glowed.

"Lion, Lion," she was saying in a honeyed whisper, "do not berate me. I am a woman in love and we are a breed that needs no excuse for our actions."

"The hell you are! You had better have a damned good reason for your actions tonight and I want to hear it *now!*"

He gripped her arm and for a moment, Meagan ignored their argument as she bent over and tiptoed inside the churchyard. She slipped from behind one gravestone to the next until Lion and Clarissa were only a few feet away.

"I was hoping you might be aware of your error by now and be ready to admit it without any help from me, but I can see that your pride has blinded you," Clarissa was saying in a cold voice. "Men are so obtuse. In the future you will thank me for taking matters into my own hands. Wait and see . . . I'll make you happy."

"For God's sake, what are you babbling about?"

"You're going to have to marry *me*, Lion. If you don't, I'll see your name become a joke in Philadelphia."

He gave a snort of derisive laughter. "Have you taken leave of your senses?"

"Hardly, darling. As a matter of fact, I have sharpened them these past days keeping pace with you, your fiancée, and your little paramour."

"I tire of these word games. Show your hand."

"I *saw* you with that little harlot; naked, in broad daylight, in the schoolroom at Markwood Villa. You both made me sick!" She made a show of revulsion, but her voice was acid with jealousy. "You thought me a fool, telling me you were in love and betrothed, then betraying me not once but twice!"

"You bitch! You had no hold on me! And I never pretended otherwise!"

"Well, I have a hold on you now, darling. I hear that you have bought Markwood Villa . . . Do you suppose that your precious Priscilla would marry you and live there if she knew what had gone on? If you do not break with her and marry me, I shall see that the whole town knows that you bed your fiancée's serving-girl!"

Lion laughed out harshly and Meagan could see confusion flicker across Clarissa's face. "Were you planning to run an advertisement in the *Packet*, or perhaps the *Gazette*? Your silly threats do not move me."

Clarissa's soft lower lip went out as she stared at him bitterly. "We shall see, darling. Would it move you to learn that your little black-haired whore has been, shall we say, *removed* until you marry me? You wondered my reason for choosing her to walk the streets tonight on my errand. Even now, she is on her way out of the city and her captor awaits my word on her fate."

Meagan was so surprised at her words that she almost exclaimed aloud. Peeping over the headstone, she saw that Lion had gripped Clarissa's shoulders and now he shook her so hard that it seemed her neck would snap.

Meagan saw Clarissa's right hand find its way inside the suspicious muff she carried and then silver flashed in the darkness.

"Unhand me, Lion! You see, I have outwitted you at every turn!"

The knife was held near his throat. Wildly, Meagan searched for a weapon and desperately grabbed a long stick. Jumping to her feet, she leaped forward and pressed the broken branch into the back of Clarissa's pelisse.

"Not quite," Meagan told her sternly, her voice sounding almost comically deep. "You have one of William Bingham's dueling pistols at your back so I would suggest that you surrender your weapon."

With an effort, Lion managed to suppress his amused disbelief at the scene being played out. He was ready to take Clarissa's knife and go home for a drink when she suddenly gave the screech of a wounded animal and turned on Meagan. Violet eyes big as saucers, the smaller girl tried to beat away the threatening knife with her stick. Lion got ahold of Clarissa's wrist and wrested the weapon from her hand, but not before she locked her elbow, bringing the blade up in a wide arc that left a jagged slash across the side of Meagan's cloak.

"You demented witch!" Meagan railed. "I am bleeding!"

Chapter Seventeen

THROUGH A WARM amber haze, Meagan perceived a figure sitting near her. White stockings, close-fitting white breeches on lean, well-muscled legs outstretched with casual nonchalance toward the fire. White linen shirt, open to reveal a wide brown chest covered with gilt hair. White lace falling over dark, strong hands, one of which held a snifter of sorrel-hued brandy. Her eyelids dropped languorously before she could inspect the man's face and Meagan drifted back down into the comforting embrace of her dreams.

She was sixteen again, spending the summer of 1787 in Paris with her mother and father. They had mingled with Jefferson and John and Abigail Adams; William and Anne Bingham were in France as well, but Meagan barely glimpsed them. Her parents, as usual, left her to her own devices, so while they were seeking the company of the beautiful, celebrated Mrs. Bingham, Meagan was off on her own. Other girls her age were learning the stilted social graces, hovering about the fringes of the court at Versailles in hopes of snaring a rich, handsome husband. The only dashing Frenchman Meagan met that summer, or at least the only one who intrigued her, was a fencing instructor. Carefree and young, Michel was the possessor of a blinding smile, and he dressed all in white when he fenced. Meagan thought it a magnificent divertissement and persuaded him to teach her. She used her allowance to pay for her lessons, which she took wearing neat white breeches; her hair was pinned under a cap and she became "Marcel." The adventure, for Meagan, far surpassed any visit she paid to Versailles during that summer.

Her thick, coal-black lashes fluttered again and she became aware of a hot pain along her left arm, near the shoulder. The white-clad figure leaned nearer and she smelled cognac.

"Michel?" she ventured groggily.

"Drink a bit of this, Meagan."

Obediently she parted her lips and tasted the liquor. Then more of it came into her mouth and she felt it burn her throat. Her arm felt hotter, but the pain numbed. She shook off the tendrils of her dreams, opening her eyes completely and straining to focus them.

Lion was smiling at her, his face just inches away, charismatically handsome in the burnished glow of the fire. Blond hair gleamed against his tanned face and at the base of his throat where his shirt was open. Meagan's eyes lingered on his exposed, well-remembered chest, then moved curiously to the source of her pain. Gauze was wrapped around her arm, covering almost the entire area between elbow and shoulder. Flecks of red showed against the white bandage.

"Goodness!" she murmured, managing a crooked smile.

"You lost some blood, but you'll be fine. Dr. Rush has taken excellent care of the wound, and luckily it was not deep."

"Did I . . . faint?"

"Hard to believe, isn't it? Truth to tell, I think it was due as much to excitement and an overdose of temper on your part as it was to this." A long brown finger indicated the injured arm and Meagan saw that he was doing a poor job of hiding his amusement.

"Well, I'm relieved to see that you are not prostrate with worry. You conceal your anxiety most admirably, Mr. Hampshire."

Lion grinned, ivory teeth flashing in the firelight, then gave way to muffled laughter. Meagan glared at him until he finally gasped, "Sweetheart, you are my greatest delight! Only you could produce such well-aimed barbs at a time like this!" He touched his fingers against her neck, curving his hand around the small, satiny column. Meagan trembled beneath his touch but managed to continue giving him what she felt was a cool stare.

"I only strive to emulate your unconcern."

Lion watched her silently for a moment and when he spoke again, his voice was softer, deeper. "Do you imagine that I could laugh if you were seriously hurt? Only when I was assured that you were not in danger did my sense of humor return, and, believe me, all my amusement is born of affection. You were inimitably Meagan tonight, so endearingly comical—"

"Comical?" she echoed frostily, trying to ignore the sensuous caress of his hand against her neck.

"I'll admit that if I hadn't known better, I'd have sworn the whole episode was staged by Hallam and Henry's acting troop!" He could not repress a fresh guffaw, but managed to stifle it as Meagan narrowed her amethyst eyes warningly. "All those dramatics of Clarissa's were ludicrous enough, but then *you* appeared out of nowhere, brandishing that silly stick!" He mimicked her voice. " 'You have one of William Bingham's dueling pistols at your back!' " Laughing again, he choked helplessly and Meagan told him, "I hope you strangle."

"Now, now, little one, there's been enough blood let tonight."

"Oh, yes—it's so easy to see the humor in a situation when you emerge unscathed!"

"I only wish you could have seen yourself—so tiny—flailing around with that cursed stick of yours! You couldn't have been more shocked when Clarissa mounted her attack!"

"It was fortunate that I was there to defend you," she commented bitingly, hoping to prick him. Lion gave her a leisurely smile, eyes a-twinkle, and replied, "It was fortunate that you couldn't wait until midnight to see me, my love! If you hadn't been so eager for my company, Marcus Reems would have easily abducted you before you ever reached Mansion House!"

"Eager for your company! You churlish jackanapes!" She ignored the sunbleached eyebrows flying up over dancing azure eyes. "I only followed you because I knew you were so puffed up with your own consequence that you would make a ridiculously easy target for sweet Clarissa. But would you thank me? I risked my life for you, you ingrate—"

Suddenly his face was perilously close to hers, his breath warm on her lips. "So you do care, fondling!" he murmured, eyes gleaming devilishly. "As for my ingratitude—never say that I am so puffed up with my own consequence that I could not manage to express my appreciation."

Strong arms enfolded her and Meagan felt her breasts press against his warm, broad chest before his lips found hers. Carefully, he avoided touching her bandaged arm as he kissed her, tasting the sweetness of her mouth as it opened beneath his own. Her heart beat wildly against him, then he felt her sigh deep inside and her tongue searched for his while her bare lithe arms went up over his shoulders and around his neck.

A searing flash of pain withered Meagan's passion and she drew back sharply, moaning aloud. Lion was already bringing her arm down with gentle skill, looking for fresh blood. One or two more dots of crimson appeared against the bandage, but nothing more.

"Silly minx," he chided, and Meagan blushed with shame at her heedless abandon.

Dropping her eyes from his keen regard, she was aware for the first time of her lack of attire. She wore only her chemise and petticoats, and unfortunately the undergarment that covered her chest was one of her oldest. The batiste was still fresh, though sheer by its very nature, but the bodice was made for a sixteen-year-old form. Her breasts, flushed soft pink in the firelight, swelled above the lace trim, yearning to be free. Glossy ebony curls had slipped from their pins, lying in vivid contrast against her creamy neck and shoulders.

"What colossal nerve you have!" Meagan accused him, her arm forgotten again. "You could have at least put something around me for modesty's sake!"

"But I did!" He reached behind her, pulling a satin quilt over her shoulders. "You kept pushing it off while you slept and I finally decided to let you have your way."

Meagan pressed the down-filled comforter against her breasts and tried, with small success, to inch away from Lion. The settee they shared was designed for cozy intimacy.

"What has become of your loving Clarissa?" she inquired, gladly producing a diversion. "I gather that you must have managed to subdue her."

Lion leaned over to retrieve his brandy, taking a slow drink before replying, "I let her go. She was crying—quite humiliated and beaten—and I felt that it was safe to send her home. I gave her some quick but well-chosen warnings, and I think she is ready to accept defeat."

"Just like that? You ever play the trusting fool, sir!"

"I could not see that I had much choice, Meagan. Am I to broadcast the story of this night to the entire town? The scandal would wreak havoc on a score of lives; Clarissa's parents, Priscilla's, . . . yours, and mine."

She knew that he was right, but the injustice of the situation galled her.

"And Marcus Reems? I noticed that you mentioned him as her accomplice and my would-be abductor. Did she admit as much to you?"

"She did not speak his name, neither did she deny

it when I put it to her. But, you see, Clarissa's word on this means little to me, for I never doubted his complicity." He turned his profile to her, staring pensively into the fire. "Marcus has long been a thorn in my side and I must deal with him in my own way. I don't anticipate any further trouble from Clarissa, but Marcus will never give up."

"Would he try to . . . harm you?"

Lion heard the emotion in her voice and turned his head quickly, scanning her face before she could mask her expression. "Your tone betrays you, lover," he said with a small smile. His eyes were like the leaping blue flames that punctuated the orange and yellow fire, melting Meagan's resolve as they burned through to her soul. "Worry not," he told her softly. "There are bonds between Marcus and me that prevent him from resorting to murder. His methods are more subtle . . . Thus far, I have been able to outmaneuver him."

Meagan wondered briefly at those cryptic words before she gave herself to his kiss. Longing for his touch overcame all else and soon she was caught under heady waves of euphoria, conscious of nothing but Lion and their need for one another.

Renewed pain from her injured arm finally pulled Meagan back down to earth, bringing with it a terrible misery of the spirit. Suddenly, she could see the two of them in her mind's eye as though from a distance—gold hair against spilling ebony, hard bronzed limbs entwined with her own of cream and rose, and her mouth: soft, eager, moaning beneath his . . .

It took all her strength to cut through the powerful attraction she felt for him, but somehow Meagan managed to turn her face away and force a tiny hand between them. She tried with all her might to push his chest from her naked breasts, but she could not budge him.

"What's amiss?" he inquired gently, growing used to her quicksilver moods. "Are you in pain?"

"Yes!" Her voice broke on a sob. "Get off, you oaf!"

Lightly he drew back, surveying her with casual bemusement. "Could it be that your pain is not confined to your arm?" He reached out a hand to aid her in her struggle to sit up, for she was frantically pulling at her displaced bodice with her left hand.

"Yes! Can't you see that you have hurt me mightily —repeatedly? You use me and you tamper with my feelings, which happen to be important to me."

"And to me."

"Oh?" Her voice rose testily. "Then why do you treat me so? Your Clarissa was right to label me harlot and whore, for I am no better. Each time I see you, each time I let you touch me and I yield to you, my wounds deepen along with my shame. Only more hurt can come from this—this—relationship, can't you see that? If my feelings matter even a jot to you, you would stop—stop—" Bright tears filled her amethyst eyes and spilled down her cheeks and onto the first curve of her breasts.

"Stop caring? It is not that easy, Meagan. Do you think I sought this any more than you did? If I thought either of us could find happiness apart, I would heed your wishes." He drew her into the curve of his arm so that her head rested against his hard chest, her tears blotted by his white linen shirt. "I have been thinking, more and more these past few days, of a solution to our dilemma. I believe I have found it."

Meagan's heart beat so loudly that she felt it would burst. Hope swelled in her even as she fought against it.

"I want to take care of you, sweetheart. I want to take you away from the kind of life you have now and give you the love and happiness you deserve. A fine home, beautiful clothes, horses," he smiled, "and me, of course."

Meagan raised her eyes to his, hesitantly. Her throat was so constricted that she could scarcely breathe, let alone speak. "Lion . . . what are you saying? Do you want to marry me?"

He held her more tightly even as he felt her stiffen.

"Meagan, if it were possible . . . I would give anything if that could be. But, don't you see—"

She was on fire. Frantically she pushed his arms from her and bolted from the settee, backing away. Her hair, her eyes, her gestures were wild. "Don't come near me! I hate you! I don't want to hear another word, you despicable cad! You are worse than a dog! You are—"

At that moment, the library door opened and Kevin Brown stood there, framed against the candlelit hallway. Wong appeared in the background, peering anxiously around the other man's shoulder.

"Missa Lion, I try to stop him—" he called, but Brown cut him off.

"Meagan, what the devil! I've been lookin' all over for you! What's happened?"

He crossed the room, his black eyes taking in her half-dressed figure, finally resting on the bandaged arm, now bright with blood. Lion was on his feet, wrapping Meagan in the satin quilt and positioning himself between her and Brown.

"Since when have Miss South's activities been your concern?" he inquired coolly, staring down at the smaller man with hard-cut sapphire eyes.

"Since she promised to spend the evenin' with me! I left the room to get us a bit o' wine and when I came back she were gone! I waited for a long spell, then started to look for her, but she wasn't in all the house! Scared the wits out o' me, it did! Finally, after these long hours passed, I decided to go and search her out. Captain Hampshire, I went to Dr. Shippen's house to ask your help since I knew you felt friendly toward Meagan—and Cyrus tells me you left there with a little chit who sounded for all the world like Meagan herself!" He craned his neck to peer around Lion's shoulders in an effort to confront her. "Ain't somebody goin' to explain? And where's your clothes? What happened to your arm?"

Lion interrupted him. "Brown, your noisy ranting begins to wear on my patience. I'm afraid that your curiosity will have to go unsatisfied. All I can tell you is that Meagan got tricked into an ill-fated errand, but all is well now. There was a small accident—"

"Kevin," Meagan called in a tired voice, "I want to go home. Someone find my pelisse . . . It will at least cover me."

Encouraged, Brown immediately fled to search out Wong. As soon as he had left the room, Lion turned questioning eyes on her. "Your arm—"

"Devil take my arm! I don't want your concern." Her eyes were dark purple in her small, pale face. "Remember this, Mr. Hampshire, when you toy with the thought of bothering me in the future. I will never *settle* for your terms. I cannot be bought, like a country estate, for your pleasure. If you have even a shred of decency left buried under that growth of conceit and ambition, you will *leave me alone.*"

Brown rushed back in then, carrying the torn pelisse, and wrapped it around her protectively. Meagan took his arm, suddenly weary, and left the room without a backward glance.

Even as Brown and Meagan walked out the front door of Lion's house, a black and green phaeton came around the corner just in time to spot them.

"Well, at least you can take comfort in the fact that the chit's been rescued by the coachman and isn't occupying your place in Lion's bed," one of the occupants commented sardonically.

"Don't patronize me, Marcus!" shrieked his companion. "I've been made a fool of tonight and it's all your fault!"

"I don't think it is fair to lay *all* the blame at my feet, but, gentleman that I am, I shall accept it." His gold eyes glittered with irony and something else that sent chills down Clarissa's spine. "Don't fret, my dear. I have no intention of giving up so easily."

169

Chapter Eighteen

ALL THE SERVANTS at Mansion House had been up since dawn, preparing for the Binghams' first spring party, while Anne and Priscilla slept until nearly noon in anticipation of the long night ahead. Bramble grumbled about the indolence of the rich as she prepared a breakfast tray for her mistress, but Meagan was so preoccupied with her own thoughts that she scarcely heard the cook. The silver tray handed her was heavy with a double load of hot chocolate and pastries, for Priscilla was breakfasting with Anne in the state bedroom.

Nearly a week had passed since the Shippens' dinner and Lion's proposition. The days had moved by in a blur of soothing sameness; Meagan managed to avoid Lion completely and was kept distractedly busy as complex preparations were made for the party. Now, as she carried the tray up the long stairway, her nearly healed arm began to throb, reminding her of the night she so desperately yearned to forget. At first, she had been so filled with outrage and raw pain that there was no room for any other emotion. The last few nights, though, she had lain in bed and let herself remember the joy of his touch, his kiss, of merely listening to his voice and watching his face. It was self-indulgent, she knew, and only led to more pain in the long run, but the simple, sweet bliss of her memories made even the ache that followed them seem worthwhile.

Meagan passed several pedestals topped with busts and bronze figures, counting them off silently. Anne Bingham's door was next to the seventh statue, and once there, Meagan hesitated slightly. She had managed to hide the flesh wound on her arm from everyone except Brown and Smith until last night. She had been changing the dressing herself with Smith's help, but apparently Lion did not trust her, for he sent Dr. Rush over to check on her recovery. When the prominent doctor had appeared at the front door, a curious Anne Bingham had personally led him back to the serving hall in search of Meagan.

Dr. Rush was diplomatic and tactful, managing to deflect all of Anne's cleverly probing questions. Once he left, however, she was not so discreet. Meagan possessed none of the feelings of inferiority that marked her fellow servants and was not the least bit intimidated by Anne Bingham's manner. She had met her gaze boldly, refusing to reveal the story behind her wound and unwilling to lie just to satisfy the mistress's curiosity. Priscilla had called Meagan away at the crucial moment and since then, there had been no chance for further conversation.

Now, as she paused outside the door with the breakfast tray, Meagan hoped without much conviction that Anne would have forgotten the matter amidst her preparations for the party.

When she knocked, the conversation inside ceased and a voice called, "Do come in. We are simply famished!"

Meagan was stunned at her first sight of Anne Bingham's state bedroom though she thought afterward that she should have realized it would be even grander than the rest of the house. As her personal chamber, it would have to stand out, even surrounded by rooms filled with sumptuous beauty, just as Anne herself stood out in a crowd of magnificent women.

Decorated in white satin and varying shades of blue, the main chamber was enormous, dominated by a fantastic seven-foot bed hung with rich sapphire-hued curtains. An open door led to a spacious boudoir where Mrs. Bingham's abigail was sorting through an ocean of stylish gowns.

Anne herself looked slender and delicate in the

171

huge bed. She wore a beige satin wrapper edged with frothy lace and was reclining against plump pillows which were also fashioned of satin and lace, but tinted a soft pastel blue. It was the first time Meagan had ever seen Anne Bingham with her hair both unpowdered and undressed. Long, light brown curls lay against her shoulders, softening the elegant line of her neck and making her beautiful face seem younger and more vulnerable.

Near the tall windows, one of the familiar Japanned dove cages had been hung. In it, three pure white birds were perched, gazing longingly at the sunny blue sky outside. Between the windows and the bed, Priscilla struck a languid pose on a blue-and-silver brocade daybed, but Meagan managed to more or less ignore her.

A pie-crust tea table had been set up beside the bed and Meagan gratefully set the tray down there. She was anxious to escape, worried that Anne Bingham would pursue the matter of her cut arm and the reason why the town's most celebrated physician happened to be attending a common lady's maid. Anne's keen eyes were on her as she poured the chocolate; in fact, she seemed to be intent on memorizing every detail of her face and figure. The conversation consisted of only the most usual, murmured amenities, however, and Meagan soon dropped the two women a curtsy and fled with a sigh of relief.

"These pastries are not as fresh as usual," Priscilla commented through a mouthful of cream.

Her breakfast companion made no response; her large eyes were fixed on the door that had just closed behind Meagan's retreating figure.

Priscilla tried again. "I suppose the confectioner is busy making things for tonight."

Anne thoughtfully tapped a long, polished fingernail against her cheek. "Hmm?"

" 'Twas nothing important. Dare I ask what has distracted you?"

"To be frank, I was rather wondering about your little maid. She seems quite—unique."

"Yes," Priscilla agreed, almost grudgingly.

"Where did she come from, do you know? Was she with your family from birth? How long has she been your personal abigail?"

"Why—uhm—" Priscilla flushed as her mind groped awkwardly for a plausible lie. Anne, however, was a master at reading others' expressions, even at detecting telling inflections in the voices of her partners in conversation.

"There *is* something unusual about her, isn't there!" she declared triumphantly. "I insist that you tell me all, Priscilla dear. And do not fret. There is no one more trustworthy than I."

In a way, it was a relief for Priscilla to expose the masquerade to Anne Bingham, for she had never become adept at her part in it. Haltingly, she pieced together the story, careful to point out the fact that Meagan had masterminded the entire scheme from the start.

"She always was a bit wild," she concluded to an amazed, attentive Anne. "I never really understood her even though I suppose we were best friends all our lives. That is, if Meagan could have a best friend. She spent what I considered a depressingly huge amount of time by herself. Most of the time in breeches, riding her horse astride like a boy. I declare, talking about it now, it sounds like some wild tale I am making up . . ."

"Oh, I believe you, though I confess that she must be a bit touched to have thrown away a position in Boston society in favor of becoming a servant!"

"Oh, I agree! The day she brought over the letter from her father's solicitor, saying that she would have to go to her aunt, I told her that her opportunities to find a good husband would undoubtedly increase in Boston. All she needed to do was start behaving like a proper lady! Meagan always was stubborn, though, and unmanageable even when her parents were alive. At first, I think she expected this to be a lark . . . Now I'll wager she's changed her mind."

A thin smile curved Anne's mouth. "No doubt. I

wonder that she hasn't given up the deception and gone to her aunt."

"Oh, you don't know Meagan. She'll never give up. She'll probably surprise us all in the end—find some way to bring it all off in her favor. My brother used to say that she reminded him of a kitten, the way she always landed on her feet."

Anne nibbled at a pastry, carefully framing her next question. "Strange you should say that, Priscilla. I was wondering, figuratively speaking of course, if you think Meagan could have any interest in Lion. Do you take my meaning?"

"Well, I'll confess I've had my worries in that respect," Priscilla replied airily. "No more, though. After all, as far as he knows, she is only a mere serving-girl. Secondly, Meagan has never been particularly interested in men. She wouldn't begin to know how to flirt with Lion and I don't think she'd care to. Lastly, I have the impression that your coachman is keeping her occupied and out of trouble. 'Tis strange to think of aristocratic Meagan Sayers from one of the grandest plantations in Virginia carrying on with a servant, but I don't doubt that she may be more at home with that rowdy type."

"I'm sure you are right. Sayers, hmm? I have an idea that I was acquainted with her parents. In France, I believe."

"No doubt. They were there often." Priscilla leaned forward anxiously then. "You will promise never to breathe a word of this? Why, poor Meagan lives in absolute terror of being discovered and sent off to that old aunt in Boston. I did give my word . . ."

"And I give you mine, dear Priscilla. Absolutely nothing could persuade me to divulge the truth about Meagan's past to *anyone!*"

"You are going to be in trouble if you aren't down-stairs before the guests begin to arrive," Meagan warned. "Can't you just choose one? Must you try every patch in the box?"

Priscilla pouted prettily. Her winged eyebrows had

been darkened with burnt cloves and she seemed to be enjoying watching herself in the mirror, lifting first one brow and then the other. Meagan personally thought that her blackened eyebrows and rouged cheeks and lips looked absurd, but she knew any advice from her would be ignored.

"I simply cannot decide between *la passionée*," she pressed a star-shaped black patch near her left eye, "and *la coquette*." The second speck of silk was heart-shaped, carefully positioned on Priscilla's upper lip.

Meagan winced at Priscilla's French accent and the expression froze on her face as she studied the two appliqués and overdone makeup. "Oh, do wear them both. The total effect is simply indescribable!"

Priscilla flashed her brightest smile, closed her patch box, and stood up. "I should hurry along. Anne did stress punctuality."

Meagan straightened the folds of her mistress's elaborate watered-silk gown, arranged the powdered curls around her shoulder, and forced a smile. "Your looks will be—unequalled."

"Why, thank you, Meagan," Priscilla murmured, her voice honeyed with condescension.

Emeralds gleaming against her white throat, she swept from the room just as Wickham's voice rumbled below, "Senator William Maclay!"

Meagan set about putting Priscilla's boudoir in order. As she gathered up discarded undergarments and organized the clutter of cosmetics on the dressing table, she tried to ignore the cheerful voices and swells of laughter from downstairs. A heavy loneliness stole over her heart, and before she could force it back, a vision filled her mind of Lion and Priscilla dancing, smiling, touching . . .

Bitter tears pooled in her violet eyes, clinging like stars to the thick lashes. She opened the *semanier* to borrow one of Priscilla's handkerchiefs and it was then that she noticed the fan which Priscilla had forgotten.

Priscilla had conceived the notion herself of wearing combs in her hair with miniatures of Washington painted on them and having a silk fan embroidered to

175

match with a scene showing him at Mount Vernon. A little gold chain was attached to the fan so that it might be clasped about her waist.

Meagan thought the scheme was typical of Priscilla's taste, but she also knew that once the fan was missed she would be the one to hear of it for days to come. With a sigh, she picked it up and set off for the back stairway.

Minutes later, she stood in the darkness of a hall which joined the brightly lit drawing room. Only a few richly garbed figures were already there, while the crowd in the entry hall grew even as she watched. William, Anne, and Priscilla stood together in a row at the doorway, greeting the guests as Wickham announced them and Smith and other maids took their wraps.

Meagan was acutely conscious of her disheveled appearance. All the other servants who moved among the guests were models of starched perfection, while her own apron was smudged with rouge and burnt cloves, wayward black wisps of hair curled against her neck and forehead, and her mobcap was somewhat askew. All the men wore the Bingham livery and curled white wigs, and the maids had carefully powdered their hair.

Oh, well, Meagan thought with a sigh, brushing back some of the stray curls. She smoothed her skirts and went out into the brilliantly lit drawing room which Anne had taken particular pains to decorate impressively. There were folding doors covered with mirrors that reflected over and over the fashionable Gobelin chairs from Seddon's in London. The rosewood chair-backs were shaped like lyres and trimmed with festoons of crimson and yellow silk, as were the curtains. The carpet was one of Moore's most expensive patterns, while the wallpaper was distinctly French. All around, people were exclaiming over the beauty of the room and its furnishings, but Meagan personally was less than overcome. Increasingly, Mansion House and the life-style of its inhabitants reminded her of everything that she had abhorred about her own youth in Virginia.

Coming up behind the Binghams and Priscilla, Meagan wondered how to transfer the fan without attracting attention. It occurred to her that she might be able to fasten the gold chain around Priscilla's slim waist without anyone even noticing. Robert Morris's wife Mary was greeting Priscilla vivaciously as Meagan surreptitiously tossed one end of the chain and caught it at Priscilla's other hip, smiling a bit at her own skill. The fan dropped to the side as she felt for the clasp, and at that moment her composure withered as Wickham announced, "Captain Lion Hampshire!"

Against her will, Meagan's eyes sought him, watching as he pulled off soft doeskin gloves and a camel-colored greatcoat. Is it possible, she wondered in agony, that a man's looks could improve each day? His hair shone in golden contrast to tawny skin, while his eyes and teeth flashed as he laughed at something whispered in his ear by Eliza Powel. Her gaze hungrily devoured every detail of his appearance, for his clothes were flawlessly elegant as always. He wore an indigo blue suit over a waistcoat of gold and blue brocade. His shirt was a light, dull gold color, making a perfect foil for the simple, well-cut coat, and the narrow ruffled cuffs were warm against his tan hands. Unlike the other men, Lion made no great display of jewels or military decorations; he wore only the plain signet ring and a gold watch, the small chain of which glinted against the brocade of his waistcoat.

Meagan fumbled frantically with the clasp as he approached the receiving line. Priscilla felt her by this time and cast a wondering, irritated glance over one shoulder.

"The fan!" Meagan hissed, near tears.

Priscilla tightened her lips and sought to ignore the commotion at her waist.

Of course, Lion saw Meagan immediately; in truth as soon as he turned from Eliza Powel. Little more than a wilted mobcap and some rebellious black curls were visible behind his fiancée, but he seemed to sense her presence even before identification was made. When Meagan met those dancing sea-blue eyes, all her remaining coordination vanished. Lion made short work of the greeting line, coming around beside her with a roguish look. She blushed rosily under his knowing, laughing eyes, wishing fervently that the drawing-room floor would open and swallow her up.

"Allow me, Miss South."

His long, tan fingers brushed against her hands as he promptly fastened the clasp. Meagan shivered.

"Thank you," she whispered, her tone void of gratitude.

"It is my pleasure to serve in any small way that I can." Sparkling blue eyes mocked her and Meagan longed to slap him; instead she dropped a curtsy and turned to leave.

"Goodnight, Mr. Hampshire."

Lion watched with a smile as she hurried off toward the serving hall, the lace edge of her petticoats showing in her haste.

Someone else was watching as well, while handing his cape and ivory-handled walking stick to Smith. His eyes remained on her bouncing sable curls until Wickham called out, "Major Henry Gardner!" and the man turned toward his host and hostess, florid face beaming.

Chapter Nineteen

BOTH KITCHENS WERE frenzies of activity, and Meagan found herself pressed against a wall to keep from being run down. Through it all, Bramble was organized, issuing orders to her regiment of servants as they dashed to and fro. The sideboards were heaped with every sort of delicacy as well as dozens of bottles of wine and brandy, all imported from France, while a team of perspiring cooks still labored over their bowls and pots.

Meagan was ready to seek escape back to Priscilla's chamber when Smith's welcome face appeared at her side.

"It is quite a production, is it not?" she asked with a smile.

"Quite!" Meagan agreed, laughing. "I rather fear for my life!"

"Well, when the Binghams give a party, they do it in a grand way. To tell the truth, I was on my way for a bit of air. Won't you join me?"

Meagan grinned her assent and they hurried off together toward the cool night air of the garden. It proved to be a rare, mild evening for March, and Meagan felt herself relax as they collapsed side by side on a stone bench.

"Soon enough the guests will find their way out here," Smith said softly, "but for now, we're safe."

"How did you get away?"

"The initial crush is past. The other maids can cope with the latecomers." She paused, breathing in the sweet, cool air. "That's the glory of being house-keeper. I can dismiss myself!"

Meagan smiled and closed her eyes for a few moments, comfortable in their friendly silence. After a time, she asked, "Do you ever envy them?"

Smith turned her hazel eyes, scanning Meagan's face. "I never thought to. Do you?"

"No. I suppose I do rather long for the gaiety, but I wouldn't take the place of any woman there." She laughed, and the sound was like music in the dark garden. "The patches and paint—ugh! If they could only realize how silly it is."

Smith nodded. "Miss Wade and Mistress Bingham are mild in comparison, too. Did you see some of those women? They've taken to wearing some horrid white paint on their faces. Dr. Rush told the mistress

179

that the paint has lead in it—quite dangerous! Apparently it has been ruining teeth and causing the eyes to swell, and heaven knows what else."

Meagan made a face, but bit off her reply when she spied a liveried figure coming toward them across the grounds.

"Good evenin', ladies!" Brown called merrily. "I thought I recognized my Meagan's sweet laughter!"

When he stopped before them, grinning, Meagan knew the reason for his boldness. The odor of Madeira assaulted them.

"Kevin, should you be roaming about tonight? And drinking?"

He sought to straighten his wig. "My stableboys have matters well in hand. As for the drink—I've barely gotten a taste!"

Smith stood up, apparently much less perturbed than Meagan. "Now that the party is under way, I suggest that you seek a bit of amusement as well, Meagan dear. Go and put on your beautiful new dress for Brown and have a glass of wine. Miss Wade won't be needing you for hours, if at all. These affairs frequently go on all night!"

Meagan was horrified by this suggestion, but Smith seemed cheerfully unaware of her reaction as she waved to them and started back toward the house.

Alone at last with his lady love, Brown did not waste a moment.

"Perhaps," he coaxed, "you'd enjoy a look at the party—see how the other side lives! It might change your mind about the dress." Even in his state of near intoxication, he sensed that more subtle tactics were in order. Meagan was not a girl to be pushed.

"Well . . ."

He did not wait for her to seize on an excuse. Promptly taking her arm, he led her across the dark lawn toward the drawing room's French doors. The light that poured from within was like white-hot fire, and as they drew closer, vibrant strains of music filled their ears. Brown had to tug a bit at Meagan's elbow to bring her up to the windows, but when they peeked in he smirked triumphantly to himself. What a stroke of luck! There, in plain sight, under the magnificent crystal chandelier, were Captain Hampshire and Priscilla Wade. They were performing an elegant, complex minuet, moving in perfect harmony. The picture they made was that of an ardent engaged couple, and Brown could feel Meagan stiffen when their eyes met in a shared smile.

"They make a handsome pair," he commented casually.

Meagan turned away from the French doors, inhaling deeply of the cool night air.

"I believe you and Smith may be right after all," she murmured huskily. "A bit of amusement is in order. I'll go and dress. After all, I may not get another chance to wear the gown!"

Henry Gardner finally found a moment alone with Anne Bingham when she paused between minuets for a glass of champagne.

"Ah, my dear Mrs. Bingham. May I compliment you on a lovely party? The beauty of your home is only exceeded by that of its mistress."

Anne recoiled from the foulness of his breath, but managed to force a bright smile. "Major Gardner, you are too kind. But I shall accept your compliment with some humility, for I understand that your own new home is quite a showplace in its own right!"

Gardner's ruddy cheeks puffed out in a wide smile. "I am proud of it. I hope that you will honor me with your presence very soon, for I plan to host a number of festive gatherings over the coming months and years."

"Your importing business is doing well, then?"

"Confidentially, yes! The demand for wine seems to be on the rise." He could see her beautiful eyes begin to wander and knew that he would have to come to the point before she slipped away. "You know, with the size of my new residence, I find that I seem to need more servants each day."

Anne laughed politely. " 'Tis a problem I am well acquainted with!" At that moment, Samuel Powel stepped forward to claim her for a cotillion, and she gave Gardner a relieved smile in parting. "So nice to see you, Major!"

Disgruntled by the interruption, he looked around to see Marcus Reems standing nearby, his brilliant tiger eyes fastened on the figure of Priscilla Wade who swirled in the arms of her fiancé. Gardner stamped over to him, blustering under his breath.

With a look of sardonic distaste, Marcus politely acknowledged the major's presence, then returned his attention to the willowy Miss Wade.

"Cursed difficult to carry on a conversation, what with people hopping out to dance all the time!" Marcus inclined his head in a gesture that fell somewhere between a nod and a shrug.

"Do you know this household well, Reems?" Gardner pursued, determined to speak his mind to someone.

"I may."

"Any of the servants?"

"A few."

Maddened by the man's cool indifference, Gardner burst out, "The fact is, I am in sore need of help in my new home, and I've taken a fancy to a serving-girl I saw here tonight. Gad, what a winsome little beauty! Black hair, great violet eyes . . ."

Suddenly, Marcus was alert, but like a panther, showed his interest only in the slight movement of his head and the flickering of his amber eyes. "I know the girl you mean," he said in a bored tone. "Unfortunately, it will do you no good to make inquiries to Anne, for Captain Hampshire is the girl's actual employer. She is lady's maid to his fiancée. I doubt whether he would let the chit go since she accompanied Miss Wade from Virginia."

Marcus Reems's attitude was so discouraging that Gardner fell silent, deciding not to approach Anne about the maid again. The cotillion had ended and she was standing nearby with Mayor Powel and his wife Eliza.

Anne narrowed her pretty eyes as Marcus asked

Priscilla for the next dance—a scandalous act in itself. However, Lion only served to inflame the situation. Moodily sipping brandy, he seemed unconcerned by this breech of etiquette, and when Marcus and Priscilla moved onto the dance floor, he picked up his glass and sauntered off toward one of the other parlors.

"It's the best party we've seen in months!" Eliza exclaimed. She had to repeat herself three times before Anne heard.

Lion was bored. The strain of playing the enamored, attentive fiancé had given him a headache and he knew that he would never last the night without a respite. It angered him that he could not summon the strength to carry off one sustained performance in this new role he had chosen. There would be talk about his leaving her alone to dance with Marcus, for the popular custom demanded that the same partners stay together throughout the evening, yet he could not care.

All the parlors on the ground floor were ablaze with lights, but he headed straight for the extensive conservatory which opened off one of them. It offered much needed quiet, solitude, and darkness. Lion longed to loosen his cravat as he moved between the rows of greenery and flowers toward the windows. Leaning against the cold glass, he took a long drink of brandy and felt the tense muscles in his back and shoulders relax.

"It's Priscilla," he mumbled bitterly. "If I cannot abide her now, how shall it be when we are married?" His thoughts spun back in time to the day he and Meagan had strolled together in Markwood Villa's overgrown garden. Lion could hear her voice in his mind, predicting that his act would never work, and he let out a harsh sigh. "She may well turn out to be right. In my blind arrogance, I have probably blundered—"

A movement outside in the trees caught his eye. When he could distinguish the two figures dancing slowly on the velvety lawn, he gave it little thought, assuming that they were errant party guests. His brandy was gone before he glanced out again, and this time a spark of recognition kindled in his mind. There was something familiar about that diminutive, raven-haired girl—then Lion recalled that every woman in the drawing room had powdered hair. A cloud moved obligingly to unmask the moon and in the silvery light, he could see that the man was clad in the Bingham livery.

Cold rage flooded him, turning his eyes to blue ice. Even as he stared at them, the far-off melody from the drawing room drew to a close and the lone dancers stopped. When Brown did not release Meagan, but pulled her nearer and began kissing her, Lion was transformed into a jungle cat infused with a killing instinct. His hard fingers clenched his glass until it popped and broke into splintery pieces, then he moved toward the garden door.

Out on the lawn, Meagan was nearly as angry. She cursed herself for putting on the violet-sprigged gown and dancing alone like this with Brown, for it was obvious that drink gave him courage. Sober, he was impulsive but manageable, but now he was like a slobbering fool. Meagan was horrified when he began to hug her clumsily, then totally revolted by his intimate embrace. She tried to push him away, but he only intensified his assault, devouring her like a starving man who has suddenly found food. Her hands struggled free to find his face as she attempted to force his lips from her; when that failed she dug her nails into his cheeks mercilessly, for her revulsion was giving way to real fear.

Suddenly, it was as though a great wind had lifted him into the air, and she stumbled back against a tree. Through a haze she recognized Lion, and she watched as he hit Brown with such raw force that she thought the smaller man's neck must be broken. Even in her own overwrought state and in spite of the darkness, she could see that Lion had become a person she had never known before. He was the embodiment of a real lion, his tan face fierce with absolute fury, his lean, hard-muscled body moving with all the instinctive grace and power of a wild animal. Certainly no man had ever looked like this.

Meagan was so mesmerized by the sight of him that she forgot to be afraid. When Brown lay unconscious, sprawled across the lawn, Lion turned to move toward her and she stared up at his face in wonderment.

Blazing eyes seared her and steely fingers gripped her arm. "Bitch!" he spat, a muscle moving in his jaw as he sought some control. "Whore! Would you like to see him dead? Dead because of desire for you?"

"But, Lion—"

"Don't try to work your charms on me. I could snap these bones with little provocation right now." The pressure on her soft forearm increased to the point where she blinked back tears. "You are no better than the scheming females in that drawing room. Look at you! In that dress! What the hell were you up to?"

Meagan felt a reassuring surge of indignation and she raised her tiny chin. "Don't you take that tone with me! I saw you dancing with your precious Priscilla, mooning over her like a lovesick calf! You don't own me. In fact, I thought I made it quite clear last week that there are to be no ties between us whatever—"

"Damn you! Would you have me ignore the sight of you in *his* arms? Did you want that?"

Meagan was suddenly weak, almost faint, and she swayed against his wide chest.

"Oh, Lion, don't be a fool. Just look at his cheeks. I assure you that no tide of passion caused me to leave those marks."

"Well then, what are you yelling at me about?" The soft suppleness of her body against his cooled his rage considerably. "Did I imagine it or have you just admitted that you got yourself into this mess because you were jealous of Priscilla and me?"

Meagan almost smiled at the note of elation in his voice. "I am too upset to talk sense. Perhaps I was delirious."

A grin flashed in the darkness as he drew her closer.

"Ah, Meagan, you silly minx. How can you think that I could care for Priscilla, let alone enjoy myself with her?" His eyes moved down to take in her dress, which had turned out perfectly. Skillfully sewn, it accentuated her coloring, the smallness of her figure, and all its sweet curves. Meagan had arranged her hair in loose curls atop her head, leaving a cluster of luxuriant ringlets to tumble down her back.

"You look lovely. Enchanting." His dark fingers grazed the gentle swell of her breasts above the low neckline. "For God's sake, how could you let him see you like this? Hold you like this?"

When his arms encircled her back, Meagan melted with light-headed longing. All the turbulent emotions that swirled within her broke in a flood, and she clung to Lion's shoulders for support. The armor of anger and bitterness that she had built around herself during the past week was destroyed.

Hard, insistent lips came down to cover her own and they kissed with a fierce hunger that neither of them thought to question any longer. Meagan could feel all his muscles tauten where their bodies touched and as he held her ever closer, her feet left the ground.

"Well, well," a sharp voice broke in, only a few feet away. "This is all very interesting."

Over the top of Lion's broad shoulder, Meagan made out the figure of Anne Bingham, tapping an Alençon lace fan against her ball gown.

Chapter Twenty

IF LION WAS shaken by Anne's sudden appearance, he hid it well. Unhurriedly, he set Meagan on her feet, turning to face the other woman with one blond brow arched.

"We seem to be found out," he told Meagan in a stage whisper.

"So you are," Anne declared, frowning at his nonchalance.

"Would you have me quake with fear? Surely you are not innocent to such situations, dear Anne. It cannot have escaped your attention that I bear little love for my intended."

"I am not your mother, Lion, if that is what you are trying to say. But I must consider Priscilla's welfare. She is still so naïve, so filled with romantic ideals! It would truly destroy her—"

Lion laughed caustically. "Pray halt!" he mocked. "Poor, darling Priscilla—how could I have been so heartless? I am overcome with guilt: I repent!"

"This is not a joke! And, incidentally, what has happened to poor Brown?"

"Poor Brown, poor Priscilla—all victims of a cruel scoundrel!" His expression sobered then as he caught sight of William Bingham approaching across the lawn, and he leaned down to speak to a dazed Meagan. "You had better be off to your room before a crowd gathers, little one. Worry not. I shall take care of everything."

Usually she would have balked at being sent away in the midst of such excitement, but this time she was relieved to escape. Her leg muscles were weak as she lifted her silk skirts and ran across the grounds toward the servants' entrance. Once in her room, Meagan dashed to the window, straining to view the drama on the lawn. Panic swept her each time she remembered that first sound of Anne's icy voice, but she could not doubt Lion's ability to settle the matter somehow.

William, Anne, and Lion stood together talking for a few minutes, and then Priscilla and Marcus Reems came strolling across the lawn to join them. Through it all, Lion appeared supremely relaxed, even laughing from time to time. Before long, the group dispersed. Lion slung Brown over his shoulder and carried him off toward the coach house, with William walking along at his side. Anne returned directly to the draw-

187

ing room, while Marcus and Priscilla took a more leisurely route. Meagan noticed that he kept his hand at her elbow or waist through it all, even in Lion's presence. What a strange world they live in! she thought. And I am sunk right in the middle of the scandal and intrigue!

As she exchanged the violet-sprigged dress for her cambric bedgown, she vowed for the hundredth time to stay away from Lion Hampshire. He may have pacified Anne Bingham once, but Meagan knew that lady was not to be underestimated.

Marcus sat in Anne Bingham's boudoir, waiting curiously for the lady to make an appearance. It was past two in the morning, but there were still plenty of guests downstairs.

Marcus wondered what could be on Anne's mind that wouldn't wait until tomorrow; something serious enough for her to risk his presence in her private boudoir. The elegant room adjoined her bedchamber and served as an ultra-intimate sitting room. Propriety dictated that no man save her husband should venture within, so when Anne had told Marcus to wait for her here, he was more than a little intrigued.

White doves continued to coo sleepily in the Japanned which were liberally scattered around the pale blue and white room. Marcus thought the furniture looked too fragile to support his weight and expected the gilt chair to snap beneath him at any moment.

Anne came in as silent as a thief, closing the door noiselessly behind her. Marcus decided that she looked as cool and stunning now as at the beginning of the evening and wasted no time in telling her so.

"Spare me your flattery, Marcus," she said briskly, spreading her brocade skirts as she sat down opposite him. "I am not seeking a lover—this time—only a friend whose sly mind I value."

Marcus gave her a sardonic glance. "At your service, madame."

"Good." Without wasting a word, Anne explained

the situation that existed between Lion and Meagan, omitting the tale of Meagan's true background she had learned just recently. She stressed the need to protect poor Priscilla's interests, finishing, "You can see, I'm sure, that after what I witnessed tonight, that wench must not remain in this house."

"I gather that this is where I fit in?" Marcus inquired with cynical amusement. Beneath his smile, his mind was busy. Anne is truly amusing! he thought. She is so self-absorbed that she cannot see that my interest in Priscilla is personal. She thinks I use the girl as an excuse to be near *her* and will do anything to win the favor of my goddess! His smile twisted slightly. "You must let me think about this."

"Fine. I trust you to find a solution, but we must work quickly! I should go now, before someone begins to worry. Do be careful when you leave."

She bestowed her most brilliant smile on him before making her exit, and Marcus sat back to let his thoughts circulate.

Of course, the last thing he really wanted was to remove Lion's little lovebird, for she had proved to be a perfect wedge between the engaged couple. Certainly there was no possibility of Lion marrying the chit, but the little affair left Priscilla ideally vulnerable.

On the other hand, if the serving-girl were removed, it might clear a path for Clarissa who was still fuming at Marcus about last week's fiasco. If he were to count on her continued help, he must do something to cheer her up and this certainly seemed a made-to-order opportunity.

Lastly, he could not afford to cross Anne. She was his ticket to Priscilla and if she closed Mansion House's doors, God himself could not get him back inside.

So, it seemed there was no choice . . . for the moment.

It did not take Marcus long to remember his earlier conversation with Henry Gardner and he grinned wolfishly at the thought of the black-haired wench in the clutches of that gentleman.

Morning came shortly after the last of the guests had departed. The sun was shining and a chorus of birds could be heard even indoors. The help at Mansion House was as busy as it had been the day before, undoing all that had been so carefully prepared. Every servant worked at top speed, cleaning furiously, until at noon it seemed impossible that a party had gone on in the house just a few hours before.

For Meagan everything appeared uneasily normal. No one mentioned the altercation which had taken place on the lawn; indeed, everyone seemed unaware of it, though Smith commented quite casually that Brown was "indisposed." Laughing, she whispered to Meagan, "He undoubtedly imbibed a bit too freely!"

There was plenty to keep her busy all morning while Priscilla and the Binghams slept. It seemed that all would go on as before, but in the back of her mind she worried and was curious to know how the affair had ended. How had it been explained to Priscilla?

When she took a breakfast tray up to Priscilla's darkened bedchamber at noon, she seemed to be her normal self. Surprisingly, she displayed no irritation with Meagan for leaving her clean-up chores half done the night before. She prattled on excitedly about the party, relating conversations she had had with the celebrated guests and remarking more than once on the charm and good looks of Marcus Reems. Apparently, the episode in the garden had been explained to her complete satisfaction.

Meagan was beginning to believe that all was well as she hurried back to the kitchen with her tray. There was little time to spare for her own lunch before she must prepare Priscilla's bath and help her dress.

In the kitchen a fragrant pepper pot bubbled over the fire, and she felt her appetite return as she breathed in the aroma.

"Oh, I am hungry! That smells delicious!" she exclaimed to Bramble. Setting down the silver tray, she reached for a bowl and spoon, but the cook put out a bony hand to stop her.

"Before ye eat, I'm told the mistress would see ye. In the library, as I recall."

Meagan's heart turned over. A vague nausea replaced the ravenous appetite of moments before, and it was with a feeling of dread that she made her way through the maze of paneled hallways to the library. Her hesitant knock brought an immediate response from within.

"You may enter, South."

Meagan took a deep breath and opened the door. At first, she was struck by the walls of books, but her attention was immediately diverted by the sight of Anne Bingham, who sat before a mahogany secretary. Sipping tea, she appeared erect and cool to the point of frostiness. In a wing chair facing hers sat a man Meagan had never seen before. His size was enormous and was emphasized by a startling crimson velvet coat and emerald green silk vest. The stockings which covered his fleshy calves were lavishly embroidered with clocks, while jewels sparkled on his stubby hands and in his stock.

"Well, well," he leered, his florid face ballooning in a smile that made Meagan cringe, "you have come at last."

"Don't just stand there," Anne ordered crisply. "I want a word with you."

Meagan had a feeling that she was walking to her death as she crossed the room. "Yes, madame?"

"This is Major Henry Gardner, the famous import merchant. Major, this is Meagan South, Mistress Wade's abigail."

Closer up, he was even more repulsive. His large teeth were stained, his eyes bulged, and his entire red face was glazed with sweat. An unpleasant odor surrounded his chair and Meagan thought that the ugly white wig he wore looked rather fusty.

"How do you do?" she murmured, dropping a curtsy, then turned keenly questioning eyes on Mrs. Bingham.

"I suppose you are wondering what this is about? Well, I shall come directly to the point. After last

191

night, I do not see any future for you in this house. For everyone's sake it is imperative that you go, and I have taken the liberty of securing a new position for you with Major Gardner. He has purchased a truly grand home nearby and has desperate need of qualified servants."

"Indeed I do!" he agreed heartily, his bloodshot eyes roaming over the length of Meagan's figure.

She was aghast. "Mrs. Bingham, I am in the employ of Mr. Hampshire! You have no right—"

"I am merely relieving him of this unpleasant task, South. He has seen where his duty lies."

"I don't believe you!"

Anne's face was as cold and perfect as a piece of sculpture. "You have little choice. Have you forgotten your station in life?"

Oh God, thought Meagan, she knows.

Chapter Twenty-one

HENRY GARDNER'S NEW house was magnificent and he knew it. Even Meagan allowed herself a moment's admiration for the huge, leaded-glass fanlight which crowned the double front doors.

Gardner had escorted her himself, waiting at Mansion House as she freshened up and gathered a few belongings. Anne had promised sweetly that she would have her remaining clothes and possessions sent over immediately, then hurried the two of them out the door with an audible sigh of relief. Meagan was not even allowed a moment to say good-bye to Priscilla or Smith; even as she closed the door to her room for the last time, one of the other serving-girls was on her way upstairs to prepare Miss Wade's bath.

During the quarter-mile walk to the Gardner house, Meagan's mind was working hard and fast. What was she going to do? Of one thing she was certain: she would not stay with this lecherous man who ogled her in broad daylight as they walked up South Fourth Street. At one point, feeling his bloodshot eyes on her breasts, she had given him the most angry, indignant look she could muster.

Gardner had appeared momentarily surprised before letting out a delighted guffaw. "I believe that we shall deal well together, missy!" he chuckled.

"Then you delude yourself, Major Gardner."

They came to his house then and he waved her inside with a flourish. A silent, stone-faced butler approached to take their wraps, disappearing almost immediately. Meagan was looking around the marble-tiled entry hall and into the first parlor when Gardner took her arm and began to lead her up the wide staircase.

"What do you think you are doing?" she inquired coldly.

Gardner was perspiring. "I thought I would—ah—show you your new chamber, and we can—uh—discuss your duties here."

Meagan pulled back, grasping the mahogany rail with her free hand. "I am going to sleep *upstairs?*"

"But of course, my little mouse. You are to be my head housekeeper! Since I am unmarried, you will be in charge of *everything,* and I want you to have a chamber befitting your position."

His grip tightened painfully as he continued to mount the stairs. Meagan reluctantly let go of the rail and trailed along. When he opened the door to her new room, she stepped inside and gasped.

The chamber was nearly the size of Anne Bingham's state bedroom and decorated so vulgarly that Meagan wondered briefly if it were a joke. A brightly patterned Kuba rug covered the yellow pine floor and on it stood a giant Hepplewhite bed. Its high posts were carved with serpents that peeked around the folds of the scarlet brocade drapes. Numerous chairs with heart-shaped backs were placed against the walls though their bright red-and-yellow striped seats appeared unused. There was an ornate armoire in one corner, flanked by an Adamesque looking glass and one of the new tambour desks.

"How do you like it? It is very current."

Meagan wrinkled her nose. "I think it is quite *garish.*"

The meaning of this word escaped him. "Ah, so you do like it!" Pleased, he hooked fat thumbs in his emerald silk waistcoat and rocked back on his heels.

Meagan spun around in exasperation. *"No,* I do not like it! I think it is flashy and vulgar and—and—obscene!" Her violet eyes flickered around the room, resting on a door in the far wall. "What is that?" she demanded suspiciously, but did not wait for the stunned Henry Gardner to answer. Crossing the floor, she pulled the golden knob open and stamped on into a dressing room and the suite of rooms beyond. Seconds later, she reappeared, her cheeks bright with color.

"Odious lecher! Think you that I would accede to this so docilely?" She spat upon his buckled shoes. "Think again!"

By now, Gardner's utter astonishment at her behavior was wearing off and he felt a surge of rage.

"Listen here, missy! Just who do you think you are? You are mine, understand? My *servant,* and you'll *accede* to anything I say!" His red ham of a hand gripped her arm around the nearly healed knife wound and Meagan let out a gasp of pain. Gardner's lip curled in a sneer. "Not so high and mighty now, are ye? You'll do well to remember my power, missy, and be thankful that I've seen fit to give you such a fine room and high position in my house! If you cooperate and keep your place, you'll be paid handsomely. Now, this time, I will forgive you for your insolence, but if you ever show me such discourtesy again, you'll regret it."

Meagan heard the heavy threat in his words, but she burned with an outrage that could not be cooled.

"Greasy swine," she hissed, violet eyes smoldering with contempt, "I would die before letting you use me."

Gardner's face grew so red that Meagan wondered if he might explode. His eyes bulged grotesquely and a bit of yellowish foam bubbled to his thick lips. Still holding her arm in a punishing grip, he brought his other hand up to strike her full across the face.

Meagan felt her neck snap backward and her ears began to ring from the force of the blow. At first, the entire side of her head seemed numb; then it began to throb and burn so that scalding tears stung her eyelids. Through a blur, she tried to focus on the huge form in front of her, raising her chin a notch and straightening her shoulders. "Such treatment serves only to reinforce my opinion of you."

"You little baggage! You forget yourself! I'll see you humbled yet. You'll be begging to do my bidding and share my bed before I am through!" His eyes began to glow as he ranted on, but Meagan was too furious to feel any fear or apprehension.

"Never!" she vowed through clenched teeth. "You will have to kill me and bed my corpse."

His obese face swollen with hot blood, Gardner pulled her against his foul-smelling body and bent to kiss the lips that so tempted him. Meagan angrily brought her knee up sharply to his stiffening groin, smiling with satisfaction when his hands dropped away and he fell backward against the doorjamb.

Henry Gardner held himself, whimpering as he rocked to and fro. Meagan was not quite sure what she had done to cause him such agony, but she had once seen a stableboy quickly dispatch a quarrelsome young footman with just such a tactic.

Intent on escape, she made for the dressing-room door, thinking to exit from the other end of the hall. However, Gardner's pain was apparently more intense than prolonged, for he caught her as she came dashing out the door of his adjoining suite.

"Vixen, you shall rue this day," he choked, inflamed with a consuming rage.

"I rue the day you were born, you repulsive pig!" she told him audaciously.

As he hauled her roughly back down the stairs, Gardner growled under his wheezing breath. Meagan resisted him, dragging her feet and clutching at the fancy mahogany balusters and an occasional piece of heavy furniture. They passed through the opulent parlors with their carved marble mantelpieces, crossed a deserted kitchen, and finally reached the pantry and its attached storeroom. A door broke the wall between the rooms and Gardner flung it open.

Damp, musty air assailed Meagan's nostrils and, wrinkling her nose, she peered into bottomless, inky darkness.

"Charming spot, isn't it?" he sneered, pleased with her instinctive reaction. "Certainly not flashy, or—what was it? Garish? Oh no, it's not garish in the least down there!" He laughed at his own wit, then thrust her onto the wet stone steps.

"At the bottom, you'll find my dungeon. Every now and then I have cause to punish some of my seamen, for they can be as stubborn in resisting my authority as you have been. A day or two down there usually brings them around; they decide that even I am preferable to hungry rats!" His laughter sent a chill down her spine. "As it happens, there are a half-dozen being brought in tonight, so you are in for a double treat, missy! You'll get your fill of the damp, the darkness, the rats and the spiders down there and —after a few hours—the sailors will be along to amuse themselves with you." Slowly, he was closing the door, leering maliciously. "Who knows? They may never want to come out!"

The door clicked shut and Meagan was engulfed in total darkness. Suddenly it opened again, letting in a thin ray of white light and the rank smell of Gardner's breath.

"Listen, missy, I am going to prove to you that you've misjudged me. I'll allow you to come out and start fresh with me, whenever you call. Take a few minutes to think about that rich chamber waiting upstairs—and the seamen who will be arriving soon to join you. I'll be waiting."

With that, he slammed the door in her face and Meagan heard the bolt slide across.

Gardner's lumbering footsteps receded as she shouted, "Loathsome vermin! Odious gargoyle! Noxious, slimy scum!"

If she could have thought of any more epithets, she would have employed them. The sound of his retreat had ended by the time she fell silent and now all Meagan could hear was a steady dripping in the dungeon below, accompanied by an odd squeaking from time to time.

Rats, she thought in revulsion. Ugh!

There was no light whatever and even after several minutes passed on the step, her sight had barely improved. She could make out the gray outline of stone walls and steep, wet stairs that curved downward into more blackness.

Meagan was afraid to sit down or lean against the slimy walls, imagining that great hordes of rodents or spiders would swarm over her. The air was cold, its chill increased by the dampness. Through her black dress, Meagan's skin prickled, and after a short time she grew stiff. She waited tensely for the arrival of the seamen, all hardened criminals—murderers perhaps—in her imagination. At length, she decided that some course of action was called for. Summoning every ounce of courage from within, she descended haltingly to explore the dungeon below in hopes of discovering either a hiding place or an effective weapon.

Once on the cobbled floor, the sound of scurrying rats intensified. When one nibbled at the toe of her slipper, Meagan thought she would die of fright and revulsion. Convulsively, she kicked out, feeling stiff wet fur brush across her foot before the rat came loose and flew against the far wall with a dull thud.

"Dear, merciful God!" she whispered, her voice barely audible above the hammering of her heart. "That Gardner monster was right. He does begin to look good next to this place!"

But Meagan knew she would never give in to him. Since the day she had left Fairfax County, she had been forced to compromise her standards again and again until her once fierce self-respect and pride were badly eroded. She knew now that this was the one time she would have to stand firm, for if she submitted to Gardner she would despise herself even more than she despised him.

Feeling more determined, Meagan began to move slowly through the dungeon. She discovered chains and shackles bolted to the stone walls and shuddered as she thought of the poor men at Gardner's mercy who had suffered here.

There were no tiny storerooms or closets for her to hide in, but she did discover another huge room annexed to the dungeon. It was filled with wooden crates and barrels which were packed with wine and liquor. Meagan was elated. She decided she could stave off a dozen men with the bottles, using them full as clubs or empty and broken to stab her attackers. She chose two hefty quarts of burgundy and perched atop a barrel to wait.

As luck would have it, barely an hour passed before she heard the door creak, followed by footsteps on the stone staircase. There was low, indistinct conversation, and then, as the men drew nearer, Meagan recognized the bluff voice of Henry Gardner.

"Where could the little she-wolf have gotten to?" he wondered, then called out, "Missy, show yourself!"

They approached the door and Meagan stationed herself, bottles poised and heart pounding, around the corner from it. As the first man came into view, she brought the quart of burgundy crashing down over his head and he crumpled to the floor at her feet.

Chapter Twenty-two

THERE WAS NO time for shock. Meagan disposed of the dripping, splintered bottleneck and instantly grasped the second one with both hands. Even as she raised it, peering in the darkness for her next target, a steely hand caught her wrist. Pressure was applied until Meagan exclaimed aloud in pain and her fingers opened to surrender the heavy instrument. However, if her attacker thought that she would be a willing captive, he was in for a surprise. As powerful arms held her fast, drawing her near, she began to kick, wriggle and claw the air in search of his cheeks.

A familiar, dry chuckle broke the tension. Meagan's eyes went wide as she drew back, trying to confirm the man's identity. Through the inky blackness she perceived the glint of fair hair and flash of ivory teeth and wondered how she had not recognized those warm strong hands, arms that had held her so many times before.

"My little vixen!" he laughed softly, enfolding her in an embrace that Meagan willingly accepted. "How fortunate for both of us that I chose to allow Major Gardner to lead the way!"

Her bones seemed to melt as she sobbed, "Oh, Lion!" and pressed her face against the clean-smelling starched expanse of his chest. "Please take me away! Do not force me to remain here—I simply will not! I refuse!"

Suddenly she shuddered, swept by a cold, prickling chill, and huddled closer to his muscular frame.

Lion lifted her off the ground so that he might study her face in the gray light; he found it filled with the warring emotions of anxious fright and rebellious determination.

"Meagan, what could make you imagine that I would force you to remain in this place? Why do you think I am here? To pay a social call on the ingratiating Major Gardner?"

"B—but—Mrs. Bingham told me you agreed that I should work here—"

"Don't be a fool!" he broke in, his voice hard. "You know me better than that. I came to take you away as soon as I learned what she had done."

Meagan's shuddering subsided into a few last tremors of pure relief as Lion scooped her up like a child and moved confidently through the darkness toward the curving stone steps.

"You can see in the dark!" she accused him happily. "Like a cat! A lion!" Boldly, she snuggled her face against his neck, the collar of his fine linen shirt and touched his gleaming blond hair. "Thank you for rescuing me, though I should have managed myself somehow."

Lion was grinning as they came into the brightly lit pantry and he set her on her feet.

"That I can believe! And Major Gardner will have the swollen head to prove it."

She held fast to his arm during their brief tour of the house to retrieve her belongings and inform the butler of his master's whereabouts. Lion laughed out in great amusement when they entered the vulgar red bedchamber.

"I can see that the good major had high hopes for you! I gather that you preferred the accommodations belowstairs?"

"You seem to find much humor in my troubles, Mr. Hampshire," Meagan retorted, blushing hotly. "You might not laugh so, were you in my position."

He gave her one of his dazzling smiles, sea-blue eyes sparkling, as he replied, "It is only that you get into trouble so frequently and with such irresistible charm—"

"The last time I believe you described me as 'comical.'"

Lion tried to appear thoughtful. "Yes . . . well, on that occasion I was privileged to witness the performance. This time . . ." He gestured with a dark hand to indicate the ostentatious bedchamber, "I can only use my imagination."

"There is little to imagine," she replied in a scathing tone. "I simply made my position known and Major Gardner hoped that a stay in that hideous dungeon might change my mind. But I should make it clear that rats could have eaten me alive and I would not have given in to that swine."

"Egad!" Lion exclaimed. "What courage! What fortitude! I am only glad to have spared Major Gardner such an agonizingly endless wait."

Meagan bit off a tart rejoinder when she saw the affection in his eyes. Instinct told her that his mocking banter masked a fair amount of admiration.

As they started toward the stairway, Lion hooked an arm around her tiny waist and commented, "You know, little firebrand, it occurs to me that I seem to be greatly occupied with your safety and welfare of late. Snatching you from the jaws of death, so to speak."

"So to speak," she repeated in a voice heavy with irony.

Lion allowed her a half-smile before continuing, "This may come as a tremendous shock to you, but I do have other things to do besides check on you and tend your various battle wounds."

"This may come as a shock to *you*, but I could look out for myself! I never asked for your protection. I could have easily done without that unique cure that you administered when I twisted my ankle at Markwood Villa! You seem to think—"

A hand came around to cover her mouth and Meagan glared up at him. Lion arched a gold eyebrow in seeming disbelief. "Didn't anyone ever teach you that women are supposed to keep quiet when a man speaks?" His eyes were sparkling, but he managed to keep a stern expression. "When I desire your opinion, I will ask for it. Understood?"

Meagan jerked the hand down. "Certainly not! And you stop making a jest of every word I utter!"

They came out of the house and into the sunlight. Lion let her march along down Fourth Street, breathing with heated passion.

At last she demanded, "Where are we going?"

"I thought you would never ask! Home, fondling. You are going to remain where I can keep an eye on you and see that you stay out of trouble—at least for as long as that is possible!"

It was not an arrangement that Meagan could pretend to approve of, but secretly, within her deepest self, she was excited. Living in Lion's house! Seeing him every day and doubtless spending a fair amount of time in his company . . . When she pondered that, Meagan felt all her hard-won pride dissolve. It irked her to realize how her heart sped merely at the thought of spending her days surrounded by his things, eating at his table, breathing the air that he breathed which held the intoxicating scent of him even after he had long departed from a room. On the surface, it seemed enough, but Meagan knew that the giddy pleasure she felt now would go sour before long.

Lion had enough sense to give her a room downstairs. In fact, he took great care not to insult or offend her, for he knew that her pride was vulnerable. Now, as she folded some chemises into a drawer of the polished maple armoire, Meagan smiled. It was not something she would have let Lion see, but she was not above admitting to herself that he held a powerful, tantalizing attraction for her.

A voice broke her reverie then. "Well, I see that you are feathering your nest."

Meagan spun around to find Lion lounging in the doorway and smoking a thin cheroot. He had shed his coat and vest and now wore only ecru-colored breeches, topped by his snowy linen shirt. It was open to reveal the familiar sienna chest with its mat of golden hair. Bits of lace fell across the backs of his dark hands.

Meagan stamped a tiny foot in exasperation. "You could knock! Am I to have no measure of privacy?"

Lion seemed to be enjoying himself. Strong teeth showed in a disarming smile as he answered, "I offer my humble apologies, milady." Straightening, he backed away and closed the door. A second later, there was a knock. "May I have your permission to enter?"

"Oh, you are truly a witty knave!" Meagan retorted sarcastically, her cheeks flushed from his mockery.

Lion opened the door a fraction and blue eyes peered inside. "Have I won your favor?"

"Kindly cease these vagaries and come inside."

He grinned wickedly. "With pleasure, sweeting."

Meagan had no way of knowing how lovely she appeared to him. As usual, her curls were untidy, the gleaming jet-colored tendrils framing her rose and cream face. Her violet eyes were large and sparkling with life, her cheeks were stained with color, and her mobile pink mouth showed her displeasure. Lion glanced warmly at her petite, temptingly molded form, noticing the way her breasts strained against the black silk of her dress as anger quickened her breath.

When she saw the way his eyes lingered there, Meagan turned away to finish unpacking the few belongings she had brought from Mansion House.

Lion sat back on his heels before the fireplace and arranged the wood inside, then lit a taper from his cheroot and touched it to the slender logs.

"It is nearly dark," he commented, settling into a nearby wing chair. Meagan did not reply, so Lion smiled at her back and surveyed the rest of the room.

He had forgotten how lovely it was; so perfect for this exquisite little gamine. The walls were papered in a pattern of lacy white stripes on a buff background which blended well with the polished maple furniture. There was a stunning field bed, its high curved canopy draped generously with light, unbleached muslin while the feather tick was covered by a glazed wool spread exactly the same shade of pale yellow as the stitching in the yellow and ivory brocade wing chairs which flanked the fireplace. There was a Queen Anne dressing table, a blanket chest, and, finally, the handsome armoire where Meagan stood.

"Do you like the room?" Lion inquired. "Is there anything you require?"

"That is supposed to be *my* question," Meagan said tartly, but she softened at the sight of him. "Actually, the room is charming. Far too lovely for me, as you well know."

Lion tried to sound gruff, studying his cheroot as he smoked it. "You shall earn it, Meagan. Believe it or not, I truly need you here. This house is far from being a home and I expect you to change that."

"What do you mean? What shall my position be?"

"I hesitate to define it, but I suppose it would be housekeeper. I want you to oversee the cooking, meal plans, the furniture. Any additions or rearranging will be up to you. See that things run smoothly, but add a touch of—warmth. I would like to see flowers about, that sort of thing."

"What about Wong? Won't he be offended if I interfere?"

"Wong should have enough to do as butler and now he can look after my personal needs more efficiently. I will let you two divide the labor as you wish, but I don't want any quarrels; I refuse to act as mediator between you."

Meagan made a face. "Tell that to Wong! I cannot believe that he will appreciate my arrival."

"Wong works for me. He must learn to adjust. I have warned him that my staff would need to be expanded, and besides, he chronically complains of overwork."

"Have you considered Pris—Miss Wade? You know perfectly well that she will want to choose her own servants. I suspect that she would not cast me in this role, and to be honest, I doubt that we would deal well together at all."

"Come over here."

Meagan eyed him suspiciously, but Lion put his cheroot between his teeth and tapped a muscular thigh.

"I promise to behave. Please, let me hold you near for just a moment."

Her heart turned over and she went to him, perching on his lap stiffly at first, then softening as his arm encircled her waist. With a loud sigh, she leaned her cheek against his burnished hair while every nerve in her body tingled pleasurably.

"Why can't you relax this way more often?" He ground out his cheroot in a candy dish. "Must you fight me continually as though we were at war?"

"I should," she whispered huskily. "And you know why. I have told you often enough, and if you truly cared for me at all you would not test me this way. I do not have the energy to fight endlessly."

"How fortunate for me." He was rubbing her small, tense back, his lean hands moving over it until delicious chills ran up and down her spine.

"You are as lecherous as Major Gardner."

"Out of the frying pan and into the fire?"

"How aptly you put it! By the way, you have avoided my question about my position here after Miss Wade becomes . . . Mrs. Hampshire. I can see, even if you cannot, that it is impossible for me to remain here."

"Why?"

"Must I spell it out?" she cried brokenly. "Would you have me admit my weakness?"

"For me?" He pretended astonishment. "I am honored, sweetheart."

She heard only too well the tender note in his voice and tried to resist its effect on her, while Lion traced the baby hair along her hairline with a tan finger.

"You may not believe it of this self-centered villain, but I have taken your feelings into account. I would not ask you to remain in the same house with Priscilla after our marriage."

"Oh, Lion, what a relief to hear you say so! I have been thinking more and more lately—especially today during my exile in the dungeon—that the best solution would be for me to leave Philadelphia. I had hoped to save the money myself, but now I fear there will not be time. Since you feel as you do, could you possibly make me a loan? I swear that I would pay you back, every penny—"

"Meagan," he interrupted, "slow down and retreat. I have no intention of letting you vanish from my life so easily! If that is your choice, however, I will help you in any way I can—after you have made a compromise with me."

"A compromise?" she echoed, wide-eyed. Lion thought her lashes looked as long and soft as sooty feathers.

"Of course. You see how civilized and reasonable I can be? Now it is your wish to leave Philadelphia and you would like me to finance the journey—"

"As a loan!"

"Shh." He laid a brown finger over her lips. "Hear me out, for I have another side to present—mine. As you know, it is my heartfelt desire that you should stay with me, let me take care—" She started to bolt from his lap, and he pulled her back down. "I'm sure you know what I was going to say! At any rate, this is my compromise. I propose that you remain here as my housekeeper, on a strictly platonic basis, if that is your wish, until my marriage to Priscilla. I am speaking in terms of a period of three or four weeks. At that time, you may decide whether or not you wish to leave me. If you do, I will finance your relocation completely, as a gift. Or, you may remain in Philadelphia—as my lover. Despite what you believe, I know that I could make you happy. Do we have a bargain?"

Meagan's eyes were amethysts, narrowed as she regarded him.

"You are a cad," she muttered at last. Lion laughed out at that and she finally pinched him hard to make him stop. When he composed himself enough to speak, his smile was inscrutable.

"That is what I love most about you, sweeting. You

are so quick with compliments; I feel like a new man when we are together."

"Let us hope he is an improvement over the old one!"

Suddenly Meagan could see that Lion was tired of their constant badinage. The laughter went out of his brilliant azure eyes as he pulled her down into the curve of one arm, bringing the other firmly around her back. A thrill ran through her body and she had no heart for a struggle; warmly she accepted his kiss, lost in its magic.

When at last he drew away slightly to let her catch her breath, Meagan managed to gulp, "I will never say yes. I shall meet your bargain since I have little choice, but Lion, you'll never see me settle for anyone's leftover love. Not even yours!"

Chapter Twenty-three

LION PLAYED HIS cards very carefully. He made himself scarce for three days until Meagan found herself positively yearning for the sight of his smile turned upon her or the sound of one of his clever quips.

She had been correct in her suspicion that Wong would not appreciate her presence, or more exactly, her interference. Lion spoke plainly to him at the outset, but it was difficult for Wong to relinquish any of his responsibilities to a newcomer. To Meagan, it seemed that he was constantly hovering in her wake, waiting for her to make a mistake.

None were made. Without Lion's distracting presence, she threw herself into her new role with gusto, infusing the house with her own taste and personality. Meagan turned to Wong for advice whenever possible, but limited her dependence only to asking where she might find what she desired. With his help, she acquired, among other things, greenery-grown flowers of every variety and hue which she coordinated with the color schemes in each room of the house. Lion realized that he had truly been taken at his word when he discovered a small vase of purple hyacinths in his dressing room.

Meagan quizzed Wong about Lion's taste in food and drew up imaginative menus for those few meals he took at home. However, the cook was not nearly as skilled as she would have wished and it was concerning this issue that she first approached Lion for a conversation. He had been taking care to greet her very perfunctorily, and Meagan was only too well aware that he intended to hold out until she made the first move. Although she passed each day nervously listening—hoping—for his arrival, she convinced herself now that it was merely business which brought her to approach him.

She looked for an opportunity for two days, but Lion was out of the house most of the time. When he was at home, he worked or read in the library, frequently taking his meals there at the commodious knee-hole desk. When he did eat, hurriedly, in the dining room, Meagan stubbornly stayed away from him in hopes that he might invite her to join him. On the third night, however, she decided that her business could not wait, and she sought Lion out in his bedchamber as he dressed for a night at the theater.

He had requested that a tray be sent up with a few slices of roast chicken, a buttered muffin, and a decanter of brandy. Meagan decided to deliver it, waiting until Wong reported that Lion was long out of his bath. Her pulse raced and her palms grew moist as she stood outside the paneled oak door. Finally, she lifted her hand, rapping so softly that she could barely hear it herself.

"For God's sake," Lion barked, "get that food in here! I am famished!"

Meagan balanced the tray against one hip and

turned the knob. Afraid that he might be only partially dressed, she peeked around the door hesitantly.

His scowl vanished at the sight of her enormous violet eyes and riotous curls.

"Meagan! Come in!"

She could not repress a smile, so euphoric did she feel under his warm gaze.

"I brought your tray."

"So I see. Did Wong break a leg?" His eyes glinted like the ocean under an April sun.

Meagan blushed. "No—sir. I wished to discuss a matter of business with you, and since you are so seldom home, it seemed prudent to take this opportunity."

"Oh, yes,—ma'am," he mocked, grinning at her knowingly. He stood in the doorway of the dressing room, clad in stockinged feet, spotless white breeches, and a fine linen shirt which was unbuttoned to reveal the chest that Meagan ached to touch. His hair was freshly washed, gleaming gold, swept and tied in back with casual neatness. "I have meant to inquire about how you've been getting along. I am sorry that you were driven to—"

"Beard the lion in his den?" she supplied with a winning smile.

Lion laughed at the pun and came out to take the tray. He set it on a bow-front chest of drawers, immediately removing the decanter's stopper and pouring a small amount of brandy into a glass.

"Do you always drink before you go out?" Meagan asked bluntly as she watched him drain the glass and refill it.

"If you want me to admit that I can only tolerate Priscilla with my senses dulled, then I suppose I must."

She clicked her tongue. "Will she have a drunkard for a husband?"

"Perhaps not if that husband has someone else to supply what his wife lacks."

Meagan turned away from his keen gaze and paced across the room, stopping short before the handsome testered bed. Hurriedly, she retraced her steps, but kept her distance from him.

"I had better come to the point before it is time for you to leave. This matter is quite important to me."

"You have my undivided attention," he assured her, even as he took his glass and disappeared back into the dressing room. Undaunted, she followed and found him in front of a large oval mirror, breeches unbuttoned as he tucked in his shirt.

"Really, Lion, must you continually strive to embarrass me?"

He pretended innocence. "Does the sight of my naked belly make you blush? Come now, Meagan, I never took you for a hypocrite!"

His candor brought hot blood rushing to her cheeks as the memory of his glorious unclothed body burned in her mind.

"If you expect me to remain here for a month, you cannot do this! I will not be reminded constantly that I have played the fool for you—"

His brown left hand shot out to catch her arm while the right one cupped her delicate chin so that she was forced to meet his eyes.

"Do not say so. Never belittle yourself, do you understand me? You are the one woman I know who does not play the fool, and I will not have you disparage any part of what we have shared!"

Meagan's eyes pooled with tears, but her voice was steady as she replied, "I do not need to belittle myself; you have done it well enough, over and over, by reminding me that I am not good enough to be anything but your servant or your mistress. If I feel debased, Mr. Hampshire, it is because you have made me feel so."

His eyes clouded and the long, taut fingers which gripped her chin relaxed. Meagan knew she was going too far, but it was as if a dam had burst within her and she could not stop.

"I gave myself to you with such innocent trusting! Isn't that a joke! Won't you laugh? Where is your ready laugh?"

"I believed in love, I believed that love was the most important thing a person could acquire in life. How absurd; don't you see the humor? In my ridiculous naïveté, I thought that what I offered you that day at Markwood Villa was more important than a prestigious marriage—or even a seat in the Congress, if it came to that choice!"

Lion held her hands now as he listened, but there was a look of pain and disbelief in his eyes, and Meagan could feel the warmth of his skin being replaced by coldness.

Still, her voice went on, seemingly of its own volition. "You, in your endless charm, could not call halt at taking my virginity and my illusions, though! You had to be certain that I was truly down with my nose pressed in the dirt by offering to *keep* me. A glorified prostitute! However, most insulting of all is Priscilla Wade herself. I might be able to accept your continual, progressive degradations if your prospective wife were some paragon of intelligence and wisdom—but—"

Strong arms enfolded her and her cheek went naturally to the place where his shirt was open. His heart beat against her ear and she felt the same maddening current of passion in her blood that always came when their bodies touched.

Lion lifted her up and carried her to the bed, laying her over the beige and blue counterpane. He stretched out beside her and held her close until she was suffused with a glowing physical warmth that drove all coherent thoughts from her mind.

"Meagan, I am sorry. Truly. I never meant to hurt you this way. I always thought you were too sensible and strong—"

"Oh, Lion, you did not! Don't make excuses!"

He smiled against her glossy hair, heartened by the typically spirited response.

"I have said, though, from the first time we spoke, that I had no place for love in my life at this point. Perhaps I've been too obtuse, but I thought it necessary. And even now, I cannot change.

"I will be honest with you. You are a remarkable girl, a thousand times more intelligent and intriguing than Priscilla, but damn it, I have made the decision to marry for position and I intend to stand by it! And damn it, you are a servant! Why haven't you acclimated yourself to that fact by now? If I have blundered with you, it's partly because I don't expect you to—to expect so much!"

Meagan had pushed away from him during this speech, watching his face and growing more outraged as her own composure returned. Now she flung herself from his embrace and scrambled off the other side of the bed.

"Fine! You have made yourself abundantly clear—sir! You stand by your decision and we'll see who plays the fool!"

Sleep eluded Meagan that night. She did not feel strong enough to grapple with the emotions churning in her heart and mind like water boiling over a blazing fire. Over and over again she saw his face, his body, felt his touch, and worst of all, heard all his bittersweet words.

What was the solution? Lion, and his compromise, at the expense of her pride? Self-respect and resistance, which equaled the dull emptiness of life without him?

Neither choice satisfied her in the slightest.

The walnut tall-clock in the stair hall struck two, and Meagan was still awake. A portion of her consciousness listened for Lion, though she could not admit it even to herself, especially as the hour wore on. Finally she gave up tossing and turning. Plumping up the deep, silk-encased pillows, she sat up in bed and watched the fire slowly die.

Carefully, Meagan attempted to analyze the situation: Instinct told her that her feelings were Lion's as well. Her brain suggested over and over that she simply tell him the truth and end it. A perfectly simple solution! If Lion learned that her own lineage was as noble and respectable as Priscilla's—if not more so—

Meagan was certain that he would break his engagement with a huge sigh of relief and marry her.

It was not the first time such a thought had occurred to her, but it was the first time she had really considered and examined it seriously. And she knew that she could never give him such an easy way out. All their lives she would be brooding over it, thinking that she was not good enough by herself.

So, as she gazed at the flickering orange embers, Meagan chewed at one fingernail and came to a decision.

Before she would consider those two awful alternatives again, she would challenge him at his own game. For the first time, Meagan began to think in positive terms about her future with Lion.

It would be a desperate gamble. If she lost, she knew that she would face ten times the pain and humiliation that she had suffered so far. But, Meagan decided, the dream—if she could achieve it—would be worth the risk. And if Lion couldn't come to choose her as a wife, for love's sake alone, then she knew there would be no place for her in his life.

It would be all or nothing.

Chapter Twenty-four

THE CONFRONTATION WITH Meagan disturbed Lion more than he would admit even to himself. In an effort to banish the persistent recollections of her face and voice which plagued him throughout the theater performance, he deposited Priscilla soon afterward at Mansion House.

His eventual destination was to be City Tavern where his friends quaffed ale and discussed politics.

However, on the way, he decided to stop off on Oriana Street to have a word with Benjamin Franklin. The brick house was dark though the hour was barely ten, and Lion worried anew over the Doctor's health. Their conversations had never failed to lift his spirits and give him hope for the new day, and Franklin's infectious wit was a tonic he craved on this night, but he decided not to disturb his mentor and to use ale as a substitute.

When Lion finally reached his own house on Pine Street, he nearly fell over an old trunk which sat next to the front door. Then he smashed his fingers while reaching too speedily for the knob; his state of insobriety had coupled with the thick darkness to cause him to forget about the box lock which placed a doorknob five full inches from the edge. Nursing his throbbing hand and cursing softly, Lion managed to get the door open and pull the trunk in as well. By the light of the candle Wong had left burning on the pembroke hall table, he could see the trunk label which was written in Anne's graceful hand: "Meagan South."

Lion smiled to himself, deciding instantly that Meagan would be wanting her clothes. Perhaps she is out of clean underthings, he reasoned. After a cursory inspection of his appearance in the nearby oval mirror, Lion heaved the trunk onto one shoulder and set off for Meagan's room.

Quietly he knocked, but when there was no response, he eased the door open. The fire was fast dwindling to red-orange embers which lent the darkened room a warm molten glow. Meagan looked tiny in the middle of her field bed, raven hair splayed upon the silk pillows and fringed lashes lying against her cheeks. Lion's heart turned over at the sight of her. Carefully he grasped the trunk with both hands to set it down where he stood. For a moment, he wavered between leaving and staying, but his ale-induced recklessness won easily over any sense of propriety.

Meagan was clad in the same billowing cambric bedgown which she had worn the night he came to her window. However, this time she had neglected to

214

fasten the buttons which would have covered her neck and Lion thought that her throat looked as soft as ivory rose petals. Gently he kissed her there, his lips brushing upward to press against her cheekbone, then her parted lips.

Meagan awoke slowly, but remained unsure of her actual state of consciousness, for Lion was the one constant in all her dreams.

For the moment, she chose to believe it a delicious fantasy. His face and hair were burnished in the firelight, while well-loved blue eyes sparkled above her like stars. When he bent to kiss her, Meagan clasped her arms around his neck and let the heady magic of his lips sweep away all caution. She caressed the muscles in his shoulders which were easily discernible even through his coat and shirt, reveling in the feel of his hard masculine body pressed to hers.

"I brought your trunk," he whispered, shattering her illusion.

Meagan shifted her hands to his shoulders in an attempt to separate their bodies.

"You have taken advantage of me," she protested without conviction. "I thought you were a dream."

"Why, thank you," Lion grinned, white even teeth flashing in his dark face. "To be honest, you looked rather like a dream yourself, fondling." Tenderly he traced her shell-pink cheek with the edge of his thumb.

"Well," she said, trying to sound brisk while averting her eyes, "I appreciate this late-night delivery. I do need my clothing, for I haven't had a chance to wash that single dress yet. All I had space to bring were my fresh aprons—"

"That reminds me," he interrupted, "I want you to get rid of those awful black dresses. Not that you don't look charming in them, but I do think we might find a more cheerful color. *I'll* choose your new uniform."

"I can imagine," Meagan muttered dryly, and Lion laughed.

"I don't mean to change the subject, but I realized partway through the play's first act tonight that I

215

never did hear what the important matter was that you wished to speak to me about. Will you discuss it now, or are you still angry?"

"I—" her voice faltered and, still sleepy, she let herself smile. "I should be. Deep inside, I always am, but—"

"You are unable to resist such a charming rogue."

"You flatter yourself overmuch."

"Before I suffer a deeper wound from your sharp tongue, let me inquire again what it was that you wished to discuss. Our conversations seem to be plagued by digression."

Meagan wrinkled her nose, aware for the first time of the alcoholic smell which mingled with those other body scents she loved so well. Peering more closely at his face, she discerned subtle changes in his expression, the way his usually firm mouth seemed to tilt down at one side, the brash gleam in his eyes, replacing their generally keen watchfulness.

"Lion, are you intoxicated?"

He grinned, then pretended to be offended, blond eyebrows flying up as he clasped a protective hand to his white shirtfront.

Meagan noticed then that his cravat was slightly askew, an unusual bit of negligence which convinced her more surely than any other piece of evidence. Lion's attire was never any less splendid than the body it covered; even his most casual riding clothes were perfectly tailored, spotless, and unwrinkled.

"No wonder you had the effrontery to burst in here in the middle of the night!" she scolded.

Lion smiled mischievously, but then his expression grew more serious. "I drank tonight to blunt the pain, attempting to banish your face from my mind. The ale helped for a time, but now its only effect seems to be a lessening of all the checks I have kept on my heart and my tongue. I feel as compelled to reveal my emotions to you as you were earlier tonight."

"Perhaps you should leave then," she suggested rather weakly. "I wouldn't want you to say anything that you might regret tomorrow."

"If I were sober," he replied with an ironic smile, "I expect I would leave. I expect I would have overcome the temptation to come in here at all. But, right now, I am sick to death of being strong-willed. I am sick of the role I must play with Priscilla, sick of the deceit, and of forcing myself to recall my ambition whenever I would listen to my heart." A jaw muscle quirked. "You doubt that I have one? Well you might, little one. But I do. I shall tell you something now and I suggest that you listen carefully, for when sobriety returns, so shall my guard." He picked up one of her hands, examining it tenderly. Against his own, so dark and lean, it seemed as tiny as a baby's.

"Soft, sweet . . ." he mused. "As unique as its owner and as incongruous. There could not be another serving-girl alive with delicate, fine hands like these." Looking up, he met her eyes squarely, but the firelight camouflaged her guilty blush.

"Meagan, you imagine that I have used you—as a plaything, a diversion. You think that I toy with your feelings because of the amusement you give me. I am telling you now that you are wrong. My feelings for you are anything but casual though I have tried to convince myself that they were just that. On the occasions when I have made overtures toward you, it was not for the sake of diversion but because my mind could no longer master my heart."

She saw the line of his jaw harden as his eyes mellowed with poignant longing. It was impossible for her to breathe; she could not have made even a finger move, and under the cambric of her bedgown, the downy hairs along her arms stood up.

"Ah, Meagan, if only we had met earlier, before I laid these plans for my life! If I had known you even a season ago, I'd have married you in an instant." Firelight played across his face, and Meagan shivered deliciously at the sight of his rakish grin. "You see, that is the rub. All my life I have thrown caution to the wind, counting on nothing but my incredible good luck to see me through. I've been a devil. Then, for once, I found something that I wanted but could not

217

have. Something of serious substance—a seat in Congress. Can you not understand even a little the forces that pull me from you? That day I arrived at West Hills, I was alive with my dream, excited at the prospect of working toward it. A loveless marriage? It was only a step toward that goal and I was happy to do it for that reason alone. I was happy to have found some meaningful purpose in life beyond accumulating wealth and seeking adventure. I'm no longer young—"

"Oh, Lion!" Meagan could not suppress a delicate snort of laughter.

"I'm not!" he argued defensively. "What do you know about it? What are you? Eighteen?"

"My age is not the issue. You are croaking about your own as if you were in your dotage! Look at this!" Her hand slid under his open jacket as she sought to squeeze his narrow waist. There was not an inch of spare flesh; Meagan could not even pinch him.

"Or this!" Her fingers moved to his arm, which bridged her hips, bracing him against the bed. Under the concealment of his beige coat, she felt the pattern of steely muscles and glanced at him triumphantly. Lion smiled down at her in the secret way that made her feel so uncomfortable.

"Or this!" Her voice faltered a bit. She had thought to save her best point for last, but as she reached out to touch that magnificent face, her nerve seemed to crumble. She had planned to remind him of the firm smoothness of his tan skin, to declare that she knew no boy of eighteen who could boast such a hard-muscled, conditioned body. But her fingers trembled against his cheekbone and strange tingling sensations seemed to pass through those five points of contact. One of Lion's dark hands came up slowly to cover her own, flattening it along his cheek and temple.

"Are you trying to tell me that you like the way I look, or is this inventory of my body being done from a purely objective point of view?"

Meagan blushed so profusely that no amount of flame-hued firelight could disguise it. "I—I—"

"Let me help." The polite tone of his voice mocked

her gently. "I believe I was opening my heart to you; baring my soul, if you will. My guess is that you felt the situation growing rather sticky, particularly as you saw the conversation on the point of being tossed to you, so you grasped at this straw of a distraction—the issue of my age." Lion's eyes began to sparkle now, like sapphires under moonlight, and his mouth curved up slightly. "With your typical enthusiasm you set off to change the subject completely, never realizing—until it was too late—that you were only digging yourself in deeper!"

He allowed himself a soft chuckle as Meagan's face grew hotter. Embarrassment was joined by indignant outrage and she tried to pull her hand from its warm nest, wishing she had the nerve to hit him.

"If you were sober, I should slap you," she announced coldly, thinking that it might be enough that he knew her inclination.

Lion startled her by laughing out and bending to enfold her in his arms. "You are very considerate of my infirmity," he murmured against her ear, obviously highly amused. "It is kind of you not to take advantage of a man in my weakened condition!"

Meagan struggled like a kitten in its first bath; she was totally vehement and totally ineffectual. She had the feeling that Lion could have held her there with one hand if he so desired.

It was perfectly obvious to her what was in his mind and she rebelled at his self-assurance. I will not be aware of his body! she repeated silently, over and over, while continuing to squirm against all those warm muscles.

Lion waited for her to quiet, but when she showed no signs of giving up, he decided to spare her the discomfort of exhausting herself. Smiling at her flushed, piquant face, he bent his head and found her lips.

Meagan wanted to shout, Cheat! but instead she sobbed deep in her throat, pressing her body closer to his, feeling him harden against her even through the quilts as she parted her lips to answer his kiss.

Then Lion's warm breath and firm mouth sent shivers all along her nerve endings as he alternately devoured her and savored her. It was as though he lost control and couldn't get enough fast enough, and then he would remember how long he had yearned to hold her and kiss her so and would wish to make the interlude last forever.

Meagan was born and died a hundred times under the sensuous magic of his mouth, hands, entire body. She pressed hot, sweet kisses over his chiseled face as he flicked open the buttons down the front of her gown and gently slid it off.

To Lion, she was as perfect, as soft and gracefully made as the cream and pink roses in the Binghams' greenery. With every kiss or caress, he felt her silky skin prickle, then warmth would blossom where he had touched and he knew that she responded to him as sentiently as he did to her.

Even in the heat of passion, Lion perceived that Meagan had abandoned restraints, but not permanently. She was indulging them both—because of the things he had said to her? Did she understand, even if she would not say so? He believed, as her lips clung to his, prolonging a kiss even when he would have broken it, that she did. When he was naked beside her, she seduced him with such uninhibited joy that he knew she loved him. Loved him in spite of what he had done to her.

Neither of them could have spoken aloud, but on through the night, Lion and Meagan communicated, again and again, in that most universally eloquent of languages.

Soft, apricot light filtered through the muslin bedhangings and Meagan opened her eyes to the first blush of dawn. Oh, she thought contentedly, this is paradise.

The bed was warm and rumpled, embracing them as they embraced one another. Lion lay almost on his back, one lean-muscled arm holding her against his hard chest while the other fit itself to the curve of her hip. Their legs were entwined, so totally different

220

in every respect that Meagan found herself staring at them. How wondrous is this man-woman phenomenon, she mused. No wonder it has the power to send us to the heights of ecstasy or the depths of despair!

Her violet eyes turned up to drink in the sight of Lion's quiescent face, splendid yet so vulnerable that her heart ached with love.

In all the plans that she had laid the previous night before sleep overtook her, Meagan had not allowed for this contingency. Now as she tried to memorize every detail of his face, she wondered if those glorious hours she had just spent with Lion would prove to be a fatal mistake. It was difficult to concentrate with her body molded to his, but she knew that she must reassess her strategy before he awoke.

She had decided that the only way to win Lion would be to make him realize, during the weeks she would spend in his house, that he could not live without her. The other side of the coin was that he also must be made to believe that she would not remain as his mistress. Somehow the fateful decision laid out in their bargain would have to be reversed to rest with Lion, and reversed so gradually that he would not even realize what she had done. If he comprehended the fact that she was scheming as diligently as he, Meagan knew that all would be lost, for Lion would never allow himself to be manipulated.

She had never intended to let their physical relationship enter in as a factor, at least not to this extent, but now she sensed that her instincts had not betrayed her. When Lion had kissed her, her brain ceased to function and her woman's body had taken control. Meagan had learned her first lesson: all the careful planning in the world could not save her when Lion spun his golden web of magic around her. She knew that her heart could be trusted to follow the right course. When all else failed, the simplicity of love could be the best weapon of all.

Smiling, Meagan nuzzled against the muscled ridges that began between his ribs and continued all the way down his flat belly. Sunrise lent a rosy-orange luster to

Lion's tawny skin and the gilt hairs that shimmered over his arms, chest, and legs.

Meagan edged her way higher, nibbling gently at his collarbone and brushing feather-soft kisses across broad shoulders. She lingered over the hollow at the base of his neck, teasing with her tongue until she felt him harden against her satiny thigh. Slowly Lion's arms encircled her and for a long moment he held her close, breathing in the lilac fragrance of her rich hair.

"You are insatiable!" he teased, his voice husky with sleep.

"I know. I am terrible."

Lion laughed low, rolling her over into the pillows. "On the contrary, sweetheart. You are wonderful."

His mouth grazed her throat, ear, shoulder, burning wherever it touched until Meagan felt the fire spreading downward. Helplessly she arched her hips for closer contact with his bold manhood. Longing kindled anew in her loins; she laced slender fingers into his hair, unaware that she gripped it painfully.

The intensity and quickness of her response heightened Lion's own desire. He came to her, thrusting deeply, and Meagan answered him with fervent passion.

They were consumed by a blazing sun, a searing pleasure that reached far beyond physical need. Afterward, Meagan could not let him go, keeping him within her, her arms around his muscled back. They were both covered with a light sheen of perspiration and their hearts thudded in unison.

Meagan's face was pressed to the place where Lion's neck blended into his shoulder, while he lay against her raven hair. Unexpected tears congealed in her throat. Blinking, she tried to keep them from her eyes, but to no avail. One slid out and fell across the bridge of her nose, then dropped onto Lion's collarbone.

Instantly his head came up. Bracing with his elbows, he stared down at Meagan's face. A warm, surprising tide of emotion swept over him as he gazed at her, wondering how anyone could look so beautiful, winsome, soft, womanly—all at once. She was flushed; a film of moisture clung to her upper lip like dew on a rosebud. Lustrous ebony hair spilled over the pillows, accentuating the delicate translucence of her skin, while her magnificent violet eyes pooled with tears.

"Oh, Lion, don't look at me like that!" Meagan managed at last. But her voice was faint, and her tiny chin trembled even as she bit her lip in an effort to still it.

"I was thinking what an incredible mixture you are. Girl and woman, innocence and sensuousness, classic beauty and piquancy, candor and . . . mystery." She shivered beneath him while her expression grew more anguished. Kissing a tear from her temple, Lion asked gently, "What are *you* thinking? Do you weep out of regret?"

Meagan's hands caressed his back, tracing every muscle, every line that they could reach. When she spoke, her voice was soft and halting. "I could never regret these past hours; I am able to recognize the beauty, purity even, of what we have shared. Part of me cries because of the intensity of my happiness at this moment, but I suppose that there is a sadness, a regret, within me as well. I would like to be the kind of person who could live only in the present instead of complicating things by remembering tomorrow." Her next words were spoken with poignant directness and eyes full of love. "Oh, my great golden lion, I wish I could stay in your arms forever."

"No one is forcing you to leave me, Meagan," he replied quietly. "You are more than welcome to spend the rest of your life with me."

Lion had seen her weakness and could not resist the opportunity to appeal to it. However, he had underestimated, or forgotten, her strength. For a long moment, Meagan gazed at him and her chin steadied, then went up a notch while her entire body stiffened.

"If you think to wear me down by rendering me defenseless, you misjudge me. I would feel less angry if you would stop acting as though you believe I am dim-witted enough to be persuaded to live out my days as any man's whore. Just because I have shed tears for you, that does not mean that I have turned to jelly!" Angrily she swallowed a sob. "See what you have done with your crude charm? You have cheapened a time that I would have treasured—"

Lion was well aware of her body's rejection. As Meagan's eyes closed and she pressed a fist against her lips, he obligingly moved away and left the bed, bending to lightly pick up his breeches from the nearby wing chair. His thoughts were in a whirl, but he knew that he could not accuse her of being proud or stubborn, for he possessed the same traits in equal measure. Also, justice was certainly on her side.

Buttoning the breeches, he shrugged into his shirt and turned back to the bed where Meagan now lay on her side, eyes fixed on the brilliant sunrise. She had pulled the quilts up to her neck, and when Lion brushed loose curls back from her forehead, it seemed that she didn't notice.

"Meagan . . . Meagan, look at me. Are you pouting or is it possible that I have made you this angry? Is this to be my punishment?"

Her head turned and violet eyes met sea-blue.

"I don't mean to be childish if that is what you're implying. There are times, though, when I long to retreat from all these emotions, problems, to become numb. And it is worse now . . . because just a few minutes ago I was soaring so high that it seemed that the joy was too great to contain. I must say that you brought me back to earth quite effectively . . . just like that day at Markwood Villa."

"Meagan, for God's sake, you make me sound like a monster! I am simply human and apparently skilled at putting my foot in my mouth. But I do not see it as you do. To me, it is the only practical solution—you would *not* be a whore! You would be the only woman for whom I care, the greatest delight of my life—"

Meagan couldn't stand it. She stuck out her tongue forcefully, then interrupted, "And Priscilla Wade would be your wife, the mother of your children, the woman who would warm your bed at night and wake with you each morning! What would I get? Hurried lunches? All the business and club meetings you could contrive to sound plausible to your wife?" Her delicate nostrils flared with rage. "No thank you! Forget it! And if you ever bring this proposition up again to me it will be the last conversation we ever share!"

Chapter Twenty-five

AWAY FROM MEAGAN, Lion reviewed their argument in his mind and found that the more he thought of it, the angrier he became.

He had left her room without another word after she had flung that latest threatening ultimatum at him. If he could have produced a suitably scathing retort, he would have employed it, but as it was he had to try for the last word with a well-timed exit. In his haste Lion had forgotten discretion; fortunately no one else seemed to be about except for the inevitable housemaid scrubbing the front steps.

Back in his own rooms, he had again stripped off last night's clothes. The covers on the testered bed were neatly turned back; a brass bed warmer lay cold beneath them. Lion had thought to sleep for an additional hour or two, but his active mind betrayed a suddenly tired body. Wide-eyed, he had watched the sun come up until the sound of Wong's staccato patter in the hall reached his ears. The Oriental had been startled to hear his master bark an order for hot water at such an hour, especially when he knew that he had been out until very late the night before.

Now, clean-shaven and half-dressed, Lion yanked on supple riding boots, gripping the leather so hard that tendons stood out on his hands and wrists. Just who in the hell does she think she is? he wondered for the hundredth time. The chit is a blasted serving-girl and she's got me feeling guilty half the time for not treating her like the Queen of France, and the other half of the time I behave as though she is!

Standing up, he flicked an ash from his biscuit-colored breeches and reached for a fresh muslin cravat. As he tied it with swift, practiced movements, Lion stared into the mirror on his shaving stand, but his gaze was fixed on his own face. The lean line of his jaw hardened; the keen blue eyes took on an icy resolve. I'll be damned, he thought angrily, if I'll turn cartwheels for that little vixen! I should have known better than to ever turn soft toward any woman. She thinks she has me backed into a corner, but she'll learn yet that I am not so easily tamed—or bewitched!

He crossed the dressing room, and after donning a buff waistcoat with narrow walnut-colored stripes, he extracted a soft, nut-brown leather coat from the armoire. Superbly cut, it fit against the hard-muscled shoulders, back, and arms without a wrinkle. If Lion had not been so preoccupied, he might have paused before a mirror to notice his appearance, although he usually took it for granted. He possessed an innate sense of himself and of classic style, concentrating on his physical self only long enough to be assured that his body and the clothes that covered it were flawless. Thoughts in excess of those were a waste of time, particularly if they were spent in self-admiration.

An irresistible aroma wafted out from the kitchen. Meagan rounded the corner to find Prudence, the young cook, crossing the floor with a tin of hot croissants. They were Lion's breakfast favorites and one of the girl's few specialties; exquisitely tender, the rolls were iced with sugar and loaded inside with plump raisins.

"Prudence! Are you aware of the time? Why have you baked the croissants so early?"

Blank, dishwater-gray eyes glanced up and the

cook paused in the midst of transferring the rolls from pan to serving plate. "The master be awake," she replied.

"What do you mean? Has he requested breakfast in bed?"

"Nay. He be in the dining room, drinkin' coffee."

Meagan pondered this news as she moved about the kitchen, seeing that everything was organized for the day ahead. A tiny smile tugged at her lips as she thought, so he was too shaken to go back to sleep! Mr. Cool Indifference!

Her perversity did not extend to the point of ignoring Lion's order not to wear the black uniform anymore. Vanity had won out and she was now happily clad in the soft dove-gray gown she had worn the day they departed from Virginia. It was plain enough, but Meagan had left off a fichu so that the upper curves of her breasts were displayed above the scooped-out neckline. Crisp white ruching trimmed the bodice and elbow-length sleeves, and the soft gray fabric complemented her creamy skin while lending a smoky cast to her violet eyes.

An adolescent kitchen maid had materialized with a silver tray. As Prudence set Lion's breakfast on it, Meagan heard herself blurt, "I will take that in this morning. Do you have the butter?"

The other two females appeared rather startled as she whisked the tray away and departed. Entering the dining room, Meagan saw Lion from behind. He was totally absorbed in a copy of the *Pennsylvania Mercury*, blue eyes riveted to the fine black print as he absently sipped his coffee.

There were seven newspapers available in Philadelphia, staggered throughout the week so that one of them appeared each day. Lion subscribed to all seven, devouring the articles with startling speed and total assimilation. So deeply involved was he now that even the tantalizing fragrance of the croissants did not break his concentration.

Meagan set the tray down and proceeded to lay a place before Lion and the paper barrier. It almost irked her that he hadn't noticed her presence, for she had rather fancied him to be in an emotional turmoil; it seemed that the *Mercury* provided a quick cure! Out of the corner of one eye, she noticed the handsome leather coat and gleaming sweep of blond hair now neatly refastened at his neck. Even through the smells of fresh ink, croissants, and leather, Meagan could detect the masculine essence of the man, and hated herself for being so stirred by it.

Loudly she clattered silver against china, longing to pierce the newspaper with a fork. No reaction. She cleared her throat, then stamped a foot. The *Mercury* moved up a fraction. Meagan peeked under the table to locate Lion's leg and proceeded to deliver a sharp kick to one booted calf. Her thin silk slipper crumpled on impact; her toes felt as though they had struck some tree trunk and it took her last scrap of spirit to refrain from letting out a yelp.

"Is something bothering you, Meagan?" Lion inquired calmly, his face still hidden behind the newspaper.

Her throbbing toes combined with indignant chagrin to set her cheeks aflame as he snapped the *Mercury* into fourths and set it next to his coffee cup. One sun-bleached brow arched over dancing eyes while his mouth twitched with ill-concealed amusement.

Even Meagan's partially exposed breasts were blushing, a fact duly noted and appreciated by her employer.

"Do sit down and catch your breath," he advised, yawning lazily as he stretched out an arm to pull the nearest chair away from the table. Meagan obeyed without a word.

Lion broke a croissant and buttered the middle, confident enough of his own advantage to allow her a moment to cool down. Then, taking a bite of the raisin-studded roll, he turned to meet her eyes and they measured one another in silence.

Several scalding rebukes came to Meagan's mind and hovered on her lips; she itched to wipe the self-satisfied smile from Lion's face. However, she swallowed every epithet. The prospect of another argument or of hearing herself deliver one more harangue was too depressing. Even their quarrel that morning had left her chilled with melancholy, though she knew that it had been necessary. Meagan hoped he was convinced now that she would never become his mistress, because only when he faced that fact would there be a chance for her dream to blossom.

"Could you spare a few minutes?" she inquired primly, maddened by Lion's satirical expression. "I do want to discuss that household matter which I mentioned—"

"Never say that we still haven't gotten around to that! My dear Miss South, please do not leave me in suspense another moment!"

Pretending to ignore his mockery, she began, "It is about Prudence, your so-called cook. I suppose she is competent enough, but obviously there is much room for improvement. I would like your permission to hire someone with real skill—"

"I am flattered that you do not wish to share me . . . After all, the girl is at least as young as you are! However—"

Lion found it difficult to keep a straight face as he watched Meagan spring to take the bait. Gone was the stiff formality of moments before, replaced by hot cheeks and a familiar pulse at the base of her throat.

"You witless coxcomb! Your conceit is ludicrous! Do you imagine that I could actually be jealous of that insipid, paper-brained ninny? Why—" She broke off, angry and humiliated, as she realized his game.

Lion flashed a disarming smile and proffered one of the remaining croissants. "I'm sorry; I shouldn't tease you. You are such a rarity among women, though, that I find myself unable to resist the temptation." He chuckled softly. "Have a croissant. Prudence does have a way with them."

Meagan realized that she was ravenous. It seemed years since she had eaten.

"Thank you. Now, if you are done making sport of me, I would appreciate the opportunity to finish what I wanted to say."

"I promise to behave."

She fought the impulse to smile by nibbling at the roll. "My idea is to keep Prudence in your employ; she can assist the new cook, for Heaven knows there is ample work for two. You see, Lion, I happen to know that Mrs. Bingham is getting a French chef any day now, which means that Bramble will be demoted."

He let out a low whistle and raised both eyebrows. "Bramble! That woman's culinary talents are nearly as sharp as her tongue! And I'll wager that sheer vengeance would prompt her to leave the Binghams' flat—even to work for a miscreant like me." One side of his mouth quirked whimsically. "Wouldn't Anne be in a state! It would almost be worth putting up with Bramble's dour manner just to watch Anne squirm."

"Honestly, Lion, you are as mischievous as a child." Meagan tried to sound disapproving, but a grin broke through. "I must agree, though . . . it would serve her right. If there were justice in this world, she would lose Bramble to us and then discover that her precious Frenchman was a clod in the kitchen!"

Lion tilted his chair back, and at the sight of his knowing smile, Meagan realized the telling slip she had made. Us. Well, let him gloat, she thought, while he still has the confidence to do so.

"This gown is a distinct improvement," he commented, leisurely appraising not only the dress but its wearer. "I have to go out this morning and will send Madame Millet to fit you for a new wardrobe." White teeth contrasted with his tanned face as he admired the swell of her breasts. "Though I heartily approve of this design, I do think we could use more color. Perhaps a bit of lace? Stripes? What is your opinion?"

"You are absolutely dissolute. A lecher. *That* is my opinion."

"Meagan dear, you are obviously still overwrought from your ordeal at the hands of Major Gardner."

"If you are suggesting that I have confused you with him, I suppose that is possible. You do have that one previously mentioned trait in common."

Lion's eyes twinkled as he brushed a napkin across his mouth and stood up. "I do hate to leave in the midst of such a rousing spar, but the morning's duties beckon."

He inclined his head in farewell, but Meagan found herself trailing behind into the entry hall, unwilling to lose sight of him until the last possible moment. Though the sun shone outside, there was a bracing east wind from the river and vestiges of the night's frost still sparkled along the edges of the fanlight.

Lion turned at the door to face her, rubbing a knuckle against his jaw. "Well . . ." he ventured, a trifle bemused by the artless way she had followed in his wake. "I shall do some discreet investigating today concerning Bramble. I'll let you know what I turn up and we can decide on a course of action."

"You might talk to Smith. She is the one who told me the secret plans for the French chef."

"Fine. I will if the opportunity presents itself."

Impulse urged him to take Meagan in his arms; she stood so near that her light fragrance of lilac was temptingly perceptible. Somehow he managed to force one hand to the doorknob, but as it turned, Meagan caught his leather coatsleeve.

"Lion, surely you aren't going out like *that?*"

"Why? Did I neglect to fasten my breeches?"

"It is freezing and you must have a greatcoat! Gloves, and a hat—"

"You warm me well enough with your solicitous concern, fondling. It plays traitor to your frequent declarations of hatred, I think." He touched a finger to her blushing cheek. "You would bundle me up like an infant in its first winter?"

"I only wish that you would be sensible! I have no desire to nurse you through an illness."

"Ah—so your motives are selfish?"

"Lion, stop teasing me. You play like a cat with a mouse. Will you put on a coat or won't you?"

Opening the door, he gave Meagan a last grin that shot to her heart like a burst of sunfire. "No."

Bitter wind caught her skirts and sent goose bumps

up her arms; then the door whipped shut and she was alone. The brief flare of heat sent by Lion's smile dimmed to embers, followed inevitably by cold gray ashes.

Chapter Twenty-six

MADAME MILLET BREEZED in like a tiny, fluttering moth. She was a blend of tans, from her drab brown hair to the hem of her nondescript taupe gown, but the warmth of her manner attracted as many customers as the genuis of her work.

Meagan was drawn to the woman instantly. They spent the entire morning closeted in her bedchamber as Madame Millet measured, then scrawled notes on a sheet of parchment. She had brought a voluminous bag that, once opened, seemed to overflow with material, most of which had been previously chosen by Lion.

Meagan soon perceived that the two of them were old friends. Madame Millet could not praise him enough; his generous nature made it seem natural to her that an ordinary housekeeper should be fitted for a wardrobe that more closely resembled a trousseau than anything else. Her enthusiasm for the task at hand was contagious and Meagan felt her spirits rise as the dressmaker described each potential gown in vivid terms.

The fabrics were perfect. Lion had chosen them with the same unerring taste that showed in his own clothing. There were silks in dusky shades of plum and blue, a light carnation-tinted muslin and several which were sprigged with flowers against white backgrounds. There were striped patterns; black and white, ivory and wine, silver and sapphire. Madame Millet showed her how a plain white muslin would become elegant with the addition of a wide sash of Chinese-red watered silk. Streamers of costly lace were laid across the bed, samples of the ones which Lion had chosen to grace the gowns as well as the underclothes that would match each creation. Meagan blushed as the little dressmaker detailed the array of bedgowns Lion had ordered, declaring that it was a stroke of brilliance on his part to think that they should be fashioned of the sheerest batiste—sleeveless, hip length, and cut deeply at the neckline.

"Women suffer through the heat of summer nights in Philadelphia in the name of modesty," Madame Millet confided. "Only a man as straightforward as Captain Hampshire would put comfort first. You could not wish for a more thoughtful employer."

"Oh, yes. He *is* thoughtful," Meagan replied ironically.

By the time they finished, the sun was high, but Madame Millet could not be persuaded to remain for luncheon. As if by magic, the oceans of fabric were swallowed by the brown bag and she disappeared as quickly as a butterfly.

Alone again, Meagan's mood slid downward and hovered on the brink of that dark pit she had discovered since Lion's appearance in her life. Listlessly, she wandered into the kitchen to check the dinner menu with a sullen Prudence, who reminded her that she had forgotten to discover whether Lion would even be present for that meal.

The familiar rat-a-tat of Wong's footsteps overhead pinpointed his location so Meagan went to seek him out for the necessary information. She found the tiny Chinaman in Lion's chamber, tidying up after his master. The same clothes which had lain across her wing chair at dawn were now being gathered up to be laundered. Next to the door, the pewter ewer and fitted razor case from Lion's shaving stand had been placed; they would be polished downstairs and returned before their owner came home. As she waited to gain Wong's attention, Meagan found herself gazing wistfully at the massive testered bed. It was still unmade, the fine linen sheets twisted in evidence of Lion's early-morning restlessness. An imprint from his head marked the pillow and she remembered with a pang how she had buried her face in the one on her own bed after his abrupt departure. It had still retained the warmth and scent of his body and she wished they could remain there permanently to echo his presence. Why, she wondered now, do I welcome even the pain?

"Missy Meagan, you feel all light?"

Lion's clothes were heaped in Wong's arms so that only his face was visible.

"Oh—oh, yes. I was just . . . thinking."

"You want something?"

"Yes!" She searched her memory. "I need to know whether Mr. Hampshire will be dining at home tonight."

"He not tell me. You with him all the time before he leave—you should have asked!"

Wong gave her a reproving look which he had been waiting to use for four days, and, after attempting to raise an eyebrow in imitation of his master, he started toward the hallway. Unable to find fault with this blunt logic, Meagan felt duly chastised. She gathered up the ewer and razor case and followed him down the stairs, but was thankfully diverted in the entryway by a knock at the door.

Still helplessly spontaneous, she went to answer it with her hands full, balancing the ewer against her hip with an elbow.

Smith stood on the front step, looking incongruous in a dark blue pelisse. The hood was up to protect her hair and face from the biting wind, but there was no mistaking those round pink cheeks or the hazel eyes that shone above them. Meagan could not have wished for a more welcome visitor.

"Oh, Smith! Have you come to see me? Come in! How did you know? Here, let me put these things down and I'll take your pelisse."

The ewer and razor case went directly to the rug

and she reached out impulsively to hug her friend. It seemed years, rather than days, since she had seen her face. Happily, Meagan led Smith back to the kitchen where she assembled a meal of creamed soup, cold chicken, biscuits, and tea. When they were settled at the gateleg table by the fire, Smith patiently answered all questions.

"I spoke with Mr. Hampshire this morning; in fact, he made a point of searching me out when I was alone. He seemed concerned that I should know what had become of you and I'll admit I am grateful to him, for I truly feared for your safety. Mrs. Bingham was very vague about the whole affair—"

"She sent me off with that hideous Major Gardner!"

Smith nodded over her teacup. "So I had heard. It seems curious now, but Mr. Reems of all people told me that first day that you had been sent to work at the major's house! He seemed to be taking great pains to be casual. Stranger still, Mrs. Bingham never said a word even when I asked roundabout questions! And she didn't tell Mr. Hampshire when he arrived, even though you were really his servant. I was pouring tea during their conversation and grew quite angry when I realized she didn't mean to let him know." Smith looked embarrassed by this show of emotion. "So, before he left, I told him. Lord! He was furious. Thank Heaven he was good enough to come to your aid.

"I don't know what happened to cause Mrs. Bingham to do that to you and I don't want you to divulge the story to me. It is no affair of mine, after all! Certainly you are spirited enough to look out for yourself." Then, as an afterthought, Smith asked quickly, "You *are* all right here, aren't you?"

"Oh, yes!" She could not suppress a faint, guilty flush. "Did you know I am housekeeper?"

"Mr. Hampshire mentioned it. I'm certain that you are a charming addition to his household."

"Well, no doubt I could do with a bit more dignity, but Li—Mr. Hampshire appears satisfied." Hastily she tried to cover her slip. "He is in desperate need of help now that he is in permanent residence . . . and about to be married, of course."

"He did speak to me about Bramble." Smith smiled slightly, as if in recollection. "He sounded rather dubious . . ."

"Well, I know that she has a narrow mind and a sour disposition, but she cooks like a dream!" Lowering her voice, Meagan continued, "This Prudence is something short of artistic in the kitchen, and I am convinced that no small amount of natural talent must be involved. Prudence, no doubt after much practice, has learned to make wonderful croissants full of raisins with a sugar icing, and Lion is most impressionable in the morning."

Pausing, she heard his name hang in the air and realized that she could not retrace this misstep. Smith smiled easily while Meagan's cheeks grew redder and redder.

"My dear, do not be embarrassed. Nothing you could say or do would lessen my regard for you. I understand that you are outgoing—engagingly so. You traveled with Mr. Hampshire and Miss Wade for many days on your journey to Philadelphia and I am sure that you had occasion to become his friend as well as his employee. I would worry about you now if you referred to him in a formal way because you only remain distant from people you don't like."

Meagan relaxed, but the guilt lingered. She could not have concocted a more plausible explanation herself and somehow she felt worse hearing it from Smith.

"It would be easy for people to leap to some nasty conclusion . . ." she murmured, trying to phrase her words in a way that reflected truth. After all, nasty was one adjective that could never describe what existed between her and Lion. "It just happens that we are quite—ah—congenial. I think that he finds me amusing, but in spite of his teasing, he likes me. Gradually, I have learned that I may speak my mind and not be tossed into the street. So, I do enjoy being here; I am not as confined by my station."

Smith noticed the way Meagan avoided making direct eye contact when she spoke and felt a twinge of apprehension.

"Well, I am happy then. You must be greatly relieved to express your feelings out loud, and I know that Mr. Hampshire is quite a witty scamp at heart. I imagine that you provide a welcome respite from his new, respectable existence."

The conversation was beginning to probe perilously near some raw and sensitive truths. Meagan feared that a few more sentences in this vein and Smith would see the puzzle pieces fall together.

"I don't know about that," she laughed nervously. "He finds me quite troublesome much of the time— like the other day when I was locked away in Major Gardner's dungeon. I almost hit Lion over the head with a bottle of wine!" Meagan's eyes were radiant and full of laughter until she became conscious of her own expression and Smith's soft, watchful eyes. "So! What is new at Mansion House? I have been wondering whether anyone was aware of my whereabouts; do you suppose Miss Wade knows, or cares?"

"I'm not certain, but my impression is that she thinks you are at Major Gardner's, as I did. I heard her mention your name in the same breath as his two or three days ago, and Mr. Hampshire gave me the feeling that he is not attempting to keep it from Miss Wade, but he will probably not make a point of telling her, either."

"How do you suppose I got my clothes?" Meagan wondered, a frown puckering her brow.

"I couldn't say. I packed them myself and Mrs. Bingham had the trunk sent off—I presumed to Major Gardner's house."

"I don't know . . . I'll wager she knows where I am well enough. I can't imagine that the major kept quiet . . . unless, of course, he was too humiliated." She grinned impishly. "I did a rather thorough job on his swelled head—figuratively *and* literally."

They were silent for a few minutes then, spooning up the last of the lukewarm soup. Meagan artlessly lifted her bowl to let the last stubborn drops trickle into her mouth, and when she lowered it, Smith's eyes were on her.

"Brown has been asking after you. He seems quite upset, besides being curious. More so when he saw me leaving today and I refused to let him drive me. I suppose he must suspect that I was off to see you."

"Has he heard that I went to Major Gardner's?"

"I don't think so. He was rather unwell for a day or two after you left, so he missed the first rush of rumors. He's quite in the dark. As a matter of fact, I saw Brown collar Mr. Hampshire when he first came looking for me in the serving hall. I don't think he gave him a hint; I heard Mr. Hampshire say that he was certain you would make contact when you were ready. The whole exchange appeared quite hostile to me!"

Meagan smiled. Poor Smith was not at all prone to gossip or speculation and obviously was feeling like a spy.

"I appreciate your news. I know that you do not like to talk about people who aren't present."

"Well, this is different; you are so dear to me. I want to help if I can. I wouldn't see you hurt for anything, Meagan . . . You're like a bright little songbird and just as tempting to the hungry cats in this world."

"What would I do without you? If not for you, I would have been a freak at Mansion House, or gone mad."

"We all need someone to keep us in touch with the real world and life's true virtues. The existence there can become so deceptive, like Mrs. Bingham's chairs —bright gilt covering warm, beautiful wood. I have been fortunate to have someone who reminds me that I am a person and not an ornament." Her hazel eyes shone. "I feared from the first that all your lovely, natural joy would be tarnished in time at Mansion House. I am glad that you have left."

Meagan was moved by this soft, gentle speech. Smith was the nearest thing to a saint that she had

238

encountered; a tide of affection rose in her and she grasped the hand that rested nearby on the table.

"Oh, Smith, I wish that you could come here, too! If you feel that way about Mansion House, why don't you leave with Bramble and work here? I would gladly turn over my job to you . . . In truth, I will not be able to remain as housekeeper once Miss Wade becomes Mrs. Hampshire." Smith's eyes widened at this news, but Meagan rushed on. "I'll wager that Bramble would accept the new position much more readily with your persuasion. Do you think she will take it? Oh, it would be so lovely having you here. You bring out all the best in me; I feel strong and good when you are near."

"Meagan, dear, you are sweet to say so, but it is better that you are not influenced by me. We are different people and you must follow your own inclinations. Besides, I cannot leave the Bingham residence. I feel so useful there; I sense that my little light helps in some small way to dispel the darkness. And . . . with all its flaws, Mansion House is my home and I am part of it. I derive great satisfaction from seeing it, in all its complexity, run smoothly, and I like to think that my touch helps to soften the hard edges of its splendor."

"Oh, you are right—it does!" Meagan exclaimed.

"Of course, there is another reason why I could not go away." Her cheeks pinkened. "I am sure that you are aware of my affection for Wickham . . . and his for me. My place is with him.

"As far as Bramble is concerned, I could not predict her reaction! However, I do believe that she will be stung enough by this imminent displacement to wish to inflict a similar hurt on the Binghams. She is the proudest of women—"

"And spiteful!" Meagan grinned.

"That's true . . . So if Mr. Hampshire approaches her at the right moment, immediately after she learns the news—"

"Will you be sure to let us know as soon as she is told? Will you help to convince her to accept him? I

239

know that she thinks Lion is as sinful as the Binghams, but if *you* were to add a word of encouragement . . ."

Smith considered this, touching a hand to her crisp mobcap. "One must proceed carefully with Bramble, for she is stubborn and unpredictable. Often she rebels from advice, suspiciously, but I will wait and watch to see if an appropriate moment arises. If it does, I shall certainly do what I can!"

The tall-clock in the stair hall sounded half after one, distantly, but Smith was ever alert.

"The time has gone so quickly, Meagan, but I must get back. I left them after luncheon was served, but when it is done, I may be missed. Besides, I saw Mrs. Bingham wheedle Mr. Hampshire into accepting a dinner invitation, so she may have some special plans for this evening."

"Well, you've answered a question for me," Meagan observed, reluctantly following suit when Smith stood up. "I forgot to ask him whether or not he was dining here tonight, and now I know."

With a sigh of double sadness, she put her arms around her friend and felt Smith hug her in return. "I can't tell you what your visit has meant."

"I have said before that I am always here if you need me." As they started through the door to the dining room, she inquired hesitantly, "Meagan, do you have some word I might relay to Brown? He has seemed so taken with you—"

"No!" The complication of Brown in her life, especially after that scene on the Binghams' lawn, was too much to contemplate. "I realize that you have hoped there might be some romance between us, but I fear that my heart feels no pull in his direction. That last night, when I put on my new gown during the party, the truth of it became clear. I had hoped that we might be friends, though I should have been more alert to the signs he gave me all along. I suppose I encouraged him, out of my loneliness, but I must not continue."

"But, Meagan, you are very young and unschooled

240

in the ways of love. Perhaps if you gave it a chance . . ."

"No. I know enough of love to recognize the initial spark," she said enigmatically. "There is magic, the same magic that lights your face when you speak of Wickham. When I am with Kevin it is all quite ordinary."

"If you are certain . . ." At the door they paused and Smith looked regretful. "You are made for love, so filled with warmth and joy. You need to give to someone who will cherish you in return."

Meagan's smile was bittersweet, reflecting the pain and ecstasy of her internal passions.

"I believe you are turning into a matchmaker! Don't fret, Smith. The worst thing would be for me to settle for less than the best, wouldn't it?"

"I suppose you are right. Only you can recognize the right man . . . as long as you don't reach for the stars trying to attain that magic you spoke of. We're all hopelessly earthbound, after all. Only in dreams can we touch the sun, and we can't live on those, can we?"

Chapter Twenty-seven

IN THE CARD room Lion and Priscilla sat side by side on a tapestry-covered sofa. Nearby stood a new Hepplewhite gaming table, strewn with cards, and four chairs with shield-shaped backs. The engaged couple had just finished three games of piquet, which Priscilla had lost badly. She had employed every feminine trick she knew to make him let her win; it became the primary game and the defeat of her charm upset her greatly. What sort of man would be so ill-mannered as to purposely beat a lady at cards three times in a row, especially when that lady was his fiancée? Had he no sense of gallantry, no desire to please her? Not even a shred of pride had been spared, for he had played each hand through with an efficient skill that Priscilla found quite ruthless. She may as well have been a child, so inept did she appear, and now her lower lip was thrust out in a way that enhanced that image.

Feeling insulted and wronged, Priscilla thought to prick his conscience by refusing to speak. She was certain that when Lion realized how he had injured her feelings, he would apologize. Perhaps even a kiss might be offered. The infrequency of those was another affront to her ego; she soothed it, however, by reminding herself that he must hold her on a pedestal in his mind. Pure and untouchable. When the thought that Lion hardly seemed the shy and worshipful type nagged her, Priscilla conveniently pushed it away.

She ventured a sideways glance in his direction and found that a copy of the *Columbian Magazine* had materialized in his hands and he was reading quite unworriedly. Momentarily she seethed, but decided that a new approach was in order. Let him resist this! she thought.

After lowering the Italian gauze handkerchief which crossed her breasts, Priscilla edged nearer to Lion, moving with all the sensuousness she could muster. Tentatively she let her arm brush the smooth leather of his coat, then, more boldly, aligned their legs until the lean muscles of his thigh could be felt even through the filmy layers of her yellow gown.

Lion looked up, one blond eyebrow curving high in his dark forehead in a wordless question.

"I was feeling lonely so far away." Her voice oozed babyish, forlorn honey as she melted against his shoulder just in time to miss the distaste that flickered across his face. "Don't you feel even a tiny bit sorry for beating me at piquet?"

"Is it my fault you can't play?" Lion could not keep an edge of irritation from his tone. "Did you want me to cheat?"

242

"Why, what a thing to say! Didn't your mama ever teach you about chivalry?"

He laughed harshly. "Definitely not! Besides, I am not so easily indoctrinated. For God's sake, Priscilla, we're both adults, aren't we? Can't we even have a simple game of cards as equals, or must I treat you like some dim-witted child every minute of every day? Do you really expect me to continually take pratfalls in order to make you look good?"

At what point had she taken a wrong turn? Never before had Priscilla encountered such astonishing obstacles in her dealings with men.

"Marcus always lets me win," she retorted on impulse, pouting anew.

"Marcus is a hypocrite . . . or possibly, even more dense than you are."

Not listening, Priscilla missed the frank insult. "At least Marcus pays attention to me. He even tries to kiss me!"

"Oh, he does, does he?" There was no jealousy in Lion's tone, only cold thoughtfulness. "Is this your coy way of extending an invitation?"

The meaning of "coy" escaped her. After summoning her best demeanor of maidenly shyness, Priscilla turned her face against Lion's shoulder and gazed longingly into his eyes. The expression in their frosty blue depths was strangely familiar; it took her back briefly to the time she had waited for his kiss in the entryway at West Hills. There was something frightening, almost primitive, in those eyes and the set of his mouth and jaw. Cold, tawny fingers closed around her chin, tipping it back, and then he was kissing her.

No one had ever kissed her this way before; she didn't know it was possible. Savagely, his lips twisted over her own, then his tongue was against her teeth and in her mouth. She choked under the brutality of his assault, gasping when the embrace ended, first with relief and then with shock as he devoured her neck and shoulders. The gauze handkerchief was yanked away and Priscilla felt her back bend across a steely arm. Fighting for breath, she realized that

243

his hard lips were on her exposed breasts, scorching the nipples until an unexpected, intense chain of sensation built in her loins. What was happening? she wondered feverishly. How had this come about?

With an abruptness that startled her, Priscilla was released, collapsing into a whimpering heap on the tapestry-covered sofa.

Lion was up and across the room; to Priscilla's amazement he appeared cool and totally unaffected by what had just transpired. Steady, dark hands poured a brandy while she fumbled, trembling, with her bodice and chemise. Deep in her belly, a throbbing heat cried for relief and Priscilla wondered what ailment it could be.

Lion turned to stare at her as she struggled unsuccessfully for composure. His eyes were as icy and dark as the ocean in a winter storm. Flicking out a plain gold watch from his vest pocket, he observed, "I have to be going."

"Going?" she echoed shrilly, her skin red with the heat of frustrated passion. "You would abuse me this way and leave without even a simple apology? What sort of animal are you?"

He walked slowly toward her and bent to press one hand insolently to her most private place, watching as she moaned with instinctive craving.

"I merely accepted your bold invitation, milady," Lion said coolly, straightening to his full height. "I apologize for not having time enough to ease your discomfort."

Every muscle in Lion's body was taut as he strode down Third Street. It had taken the last vestige of his control to behave calmly when he said good-bye to Anne Bingham. Earlier he had promised her that he would stay for dinner and the small evening-party she had planned; it was not easy to back out and do it casually when all he could feel was a consuming blaze of contempt for Priscilla.

Stretching his knotted muscles and inhaling the frigid March wind, Lion relaxed. A smile played over his hard mouth as he remembered Priscilla's tumble into the real world. The disgust he had felt was almost made worthwhile by the transformation of her face from the affected coquette to that of a bitch in heat.

After reaching home, he looked about automatically for Meagan even though common sense told him to avoid her. Still, prompted by curiosity, he asked her whereabouts when Wong came into the stair hall. Could Brown have taken her off? That pup had shown far too much agitated interest over her welfare.

Wong scarcely heard a word Lion said; he jumped up and down, thoroughly rattled, repeating Meagan's assurance that his master would be dining out. Lion finally had to grasp his collar, holding him aloft for the few seconds it took his wiry legs to still.

"For God's sake, Wong, you're as excitable as an old woman! It's not Meagan's fault, though how she learned my plans is a mystery to me. I *was* going to dine at the Binghams', but I changed my mind. Don't worry. I'll be happy with a bowl of soup and a piece of cold meat. Now, where *is* Meagan?"

"She went to clean libelly long time ago."

Lion felt himself pulled off toward that room in spite of his better judgment. Quietly he opened the door and found that a fire had been lit, but there was no sign of her. Then he spotted some patterned silk peeping above the back of the settee. Crossing the room to get a better look, he discovered her, curled up like a child and fast asleep. It was the same spot she had occupied the night of Clarissa's knife attack, and her face in repose held that same exquisite innocence it had then.

Meagan still wore the gray gown of that morning, but she had added a large muslin handkerchief which crossed her bodice and was fastened at the small of her back. One of those familiar white aprons covered the skirt of her dress and she had tied a scarf of figured silk over her curls so that only the most impudent remained free. Dirt smudged her face, hands, and fichu, but the feather duster lay discarded near

Lion's desk. Beside the settee, books were stacked precariously, and two lay open in Meagan's lap, her finger curving near an underlined passage. Grinning, Lion bent to check the bindings. *Tom Jones* and *Common Sense;* choices as paradoxical as their chooser!

He sat back on his heels, level with her face, and sighed. How silken her skin looked, how wonderful she smelled, how enchanting was the expression she wore . . . Her nearness cleansed and soothed him like some sweet nectar and he threaded his fingers through her slender, limp ones, bending to touch his face against the back of her hand. Inches away and blurred by its proximity was the page Meagan had been reading. He recognized the underlined words because of their very familiarity: "The sun never shined on a cause of greater worth."

Meagan opened her eyes slowly, struggling against the heavy fatigue which had engulfed her so suddenly. Lion's hand held hers and his face rested there; she could feel the firm warmth of his mouth on her knuckles. Propped against the corner of the settee, she was high enough to observe his face. The lines of cynicism, so apparent during the early days of their association, were again etched around his mouth, eyes, and forehead, and the tightly coiled tension had returned to his muscles.

Compassion and concern chipped at Meagan's heart until a fissure opened and love streamed out. Her free hand moved to touch flaxen hair. After the slightest of flinches, Lion's head shifted and their eyes met. She watched as the splinters of blue ice melted until it seemed that she would drown in the swirling, vivid sea that replaced them. Wordlessly, he undid her fichu and tenderly kissed her breasts and throat. Bronze hands slid over pink cheeks and azure eyes spoke to violet before Lion bent to find her lips. The books fell unnoticed to the floor as Meagan's arms rounded his shoulders and neck, and she molded her slight body to his lean, hard one. She wanted to tell him how dreary her day had been without him, how his touch had banished all traces of her fatigue and gloom. She wanted to say, I need you!

Lion was thinking many of the same thoughts, but in a more abstract fashion. As he held her and kissed her, it seemed that all the broken, dead places inside him were made whole by the warmth that flowed from her body. He longed to remove the clothing that separated their flesh, not for the sake of passion but out of a need to be as close as possible to Meagan. Minutes passed as they lay fused together, eyes closed and faces touching, kissing occasionally in tender communication.

Finally, completely at ease, they drifted off to sleep. Meagan woke first, with a start, as she realized that anyone could walk in on them at this hour. Gently she rubbed the back of Lion's neck where her hand lay, until he too came awake, grimacing.

"God, I am exhausted!" he moaned, flexing one stiff arm.

As they disengaged and sat up, Meagan replied lightly, "Perhaps you lost sleep last night."

"Ah, yes, it all comes back to me now! Well, I suppose it was worth it."

Blushing, she cuffed his arm. "Cad."

"Nay, sweeting. Merely an innocent lad led astray by a raven-haired enchantress." White teeth flashed in a devilish grin.

"Your imagination is only exceeded by your depravity, sir."

"Smile when you say that."

She did, watching happily as he stretched booted legs and crossed them at the ankles. One arm reached out to draw her against his chest where she rested her cheek on the supple, fragrant leather of his coat.

"So, you have been reading!"

"I thought to, but I fell asleep."

"I noticed. In any case, such ambition is to be admired." Meagan felt him grin above her. "Did you plan to spend the next week in here?"

She glanced at the wobbly piles of books and smiled ruefully. "I might have gotten a bit carried away. I

247

wasn't going to read every *word,* of course. I thought to look them over and choose the most promising ones for the long, lonely nights ahead."

"Ah, I see!" He gave her arm a gentle pinch. "By the way, where did you learn to read?"

Meagan's heart lurched as she realized she had never encountered a literate servant. "A friend taught me the rudiments and I practiced on my own until the deed was done."

"In between rides on your horse? Curiouser and curiouser!"

"Speaking of curious happenings—why are you home? I thought you were supposed to dine with your charming fiancée."

The muscles in his chest tightened. "Who told you that?"

"Smith. She paid me a visit today."

"Hmm. Well, to be honest, I did intend to remain at the Binghams', but Priscilla drove me so near to murder that I was forced to remove myself for her own protection."

Meagan refrained from gloating. "You did look rather bitter earlier."

"I was in the foulest of moods."

"And now?"

Lion tilted her chin up and gave her a long, devastating look.

"Silly minx, you know the answer." He kissed her in a way that stopped her breath. Then, "Meagan, do you suppose that we might find a way to enjoy these next weeks without constantly locking horns over the future? Could you relax and spend some time with me . . . if I promise to behave as a—uhm—gentleman?"

Meagan smiled at the way he had choked on that last word. "Yes, Lion. I would like that."

He shifted her onto his lap, holding her close with both arms. Meagan's face was glowing, cheeks dimpled.

"Thank you," Lion whispered almost inaudibly against her temple.

PART III

And steal one day out of thy life to
live. . .

—ABRAHAM COWLEY
"Ode Upon Liberty"
(1663)

Chapter Twenty-eight

THE FOLLOWING DAY was replete with sunshine and a pleasing, perfect warmth. After breakfast, Lion sought Meagan out and asked if she would join him as he attended to some errands on foot. She had been up since dawn, dragging a lethargic Prudence through the market crush and now felt quite weary as she drew up dinner menus for the next three days. However, Lion's casual sportiveness was a powerful intoxicant, and she was conscious of a strong desire to strengthen the bond that had been formed during those minutes of silent communion the day before.

While changing into a fresh gown, Meagan thought, smiling, I could have been on my deathbed and I'd have managed to struggle off to spend an hour or two with him. And he knows it, the scoundrel.

In spite of the pretty picture she made in the lilac muslin, only the thought of her soon-to-be-delivered new wardrobe kept her from frowning at her reflection. It seemed that he had seen her in this dress a thousand times.

Lion's eyes, when Meagan appeared in the stair hall, gave no hint of this. They were warm with affection and kept desire at bay. He grinned, opening the door with a flourish, and lightly caught her elbow as she passed him.

The flagstones of Pine Street were sun-splashed, the air seemed fresh, and Meagan's raven curls gleamed and danced.

"God, it's a glorious day!" Lion burst out suddenly after minutes of silence.

Surprised by this unaccustomed exuberance, Meagan smiled back.

"Ha!" he laughed. "You look as I must when you start verbalizing your *joie de vivre!*"

"Your behavior *was* rather out of character. Perhaps you've been near me too long?" Her amethyst eyes sparkled with pleasure at the opportunity to tease him. Lion's hand moved to hook her waist and he held her close for a moment before she succeeded in struggling free.

"You think you can soften such a hardened cynic?" Deftly he recaptured her, lifting her off the ground so that they were eye to eye. "Have away, fondling. Do your worst!"

Meagan blushed furiously, wriggling in his iron grasp. "Lion, for Heaven's sake! Would you have us seen? Put me down, lunatic!"

With a grin he obeyed, but appeared amused for the next quarter mile, and Meagan knew that he had done it purposely to set the tone between them for that day. The frantic stimulation made her blood rush and restored her energy; she easily matched his pace and was piercingly aware of his hand on her arm, the richness of the sunshine, and the salty breeze that drew them toward the waterfront.

The scene that met them there was fittingly animated and colorful. Magnificent ships lay close alongside one another, many a hundred feet or more in length with main masts of over seventy feet. Sailors swaggered across the docks, mingling with bales and boxes, ropes and pungent tar.

"That's the *Canton*," Lion gestured toward a stunning vessel, raising his voice to be heard over the din of boisterous shouts. "It began the China trade for Philadelphia and I made my first voyage on it with Thomas Truxton as captain. The next year, I had my own ship."

"Goodness," Meagan breathed, truly awed by the sight before her. Men were calling greetings to Lion and he paused to speak with a few of them, apparently delivering some information.

"I have never seen such ships!" she exclaimed at last, when his attention returned.

"You are not alone; they are splendid. Already these China Traders built in Philadelphia are being called the most beautiful ships on the seas. Notice the figureheads? Several were carved by William Rush, reason enough for the China Traders to be charmed."

A dark, well-dressed man hailed Lion, who excused himself to confer with him. Meagan watched the activity on the waterfront, lost in the elemental panorama as she had been on her first excursion to the market, not even realizing when Lion returned until he took her arm. As they meandered up Front Street, she inquired, "May I ask who that man was? No spy for Anne Bingham, I hope."

Lion chuckled. "No, that was Mordecai Lewis, one of my former backers. I promised William that I would do what I could to help prepare their new ship for sailing since I left him rather flat last month."

They passed some inns; then, as the Crooked Billet came into view, Meagan let out a shout. "Lion! What is *that?*"

Out on the Delaware, among the larger boats, puffed an unquestionably strange contraption which belched smoke and seemed to crawl in the water. Lion laughed in surprise, shading his eyes as he gazed out on the sparkling river.

"By God, if it isn't *Fitch's Folly!* I admire that man's persistence!"

Meagan's expression grew more bewildered. "Don't talk in riddles!"

"It's a steamboat, or so John Fitch has named it. I first saw the thing two summers ago, during the Constitutional Convention. Everyone stood out here on the docks and laughed at him then; the damned thing seemed about to explode! But he's kept at it, trying to perfect this steam engine of his. Doctor Franklin told me that he's got paddle wheels now; the first one employed the *mos*t inept mechanical oars." Remembering it, Lion allowed his mouth to quirk in a wry smile. "According to Doctor Franklin, Fitch has backers now and they hope to start a steamboat service here on the Delaware. As I recall, it's to be five shillings from Philadelphia to Trenton."

"Do you think it will ever happen?" she asked doubtfully, watching the steamboat being passed again and again by other ships.

"Why not? The man is determined and that's half the battle. He has spent close to five hundred pounds since 1785. Do you imagine that he'll stop until he makes the dream a reality?"

"Well, I would say that there is a lesson to be learned from such patience, wouldn't you?" Meagan's eyes belied her conversational tone. "We can't all achieve great success overnight. Goals worth reaching are worth waiting for, aren't they?"

"Damn, but you are quite a philosopher! Do you mean to instruct me? I tremble before such subtlety as yours."

His sarcastic tone made Meagan bite her lips to keep silent. There were moments when she, in her impulsiveness, failed to remember how bitterly cold Lion's blue eyes could become.

Fitch's Folly forgotten, they turned onto Chestnut Street and walked, not speaking, to the corner of Third. Meagan had to nearly run to keep up with him. She thought longingly of his high spirits of an hour ago and raged within over her quick tongue and his temper. Close to tears, she finally caught the sleeve of his coat.

"Oh, Lion, stop!"

Her heart was exposed on her face and he thawed at the sight, trying to ignore the soft fingers which touched his own.

"Devil take it, Meagan, will you never stop interfering with my decisions? Priscilla nags me on every other subject but this and then you make my persecution complete."

She tried to swallow the words, but they wouldn't stay down. "Well, Lion, did it ever occur to you that there might be a reason you have such trouble? Could the original fault be your own?"

They stood there on the corner, oblivious to the curious people who passed, and stared so hard at one another that sparks seemed to fly. Meagan could sense that he longed to strike her, but suddenly a different sort of light appeared in his eyes.

"I keep expecting to react to you the way I do to Priscilla when she begins to complain, but I never do," he said softly. "It is such a relief not to feel that overpowering disgust and boredom. When she irritates me, I cannot wait to get away . . . but when I get mad at you, all I want to do is make love to you."

Devastated, Meagan thought that her knees would buckle. Her skin prickled as hot gusts of love and desire swept her near to fainting. Strong hands encircled her waist and warm breath caressed one ear.

"Would you accept my invitation so readily and have us arrested?" His smile was more dazzling than the midday sun. "You know how weak I am!"

Somehow she righted herself, but could not meet his eyes. As they continued down Third Street, the arm that Lion held shivered as if chilled.

"What if we were seen?" Meagan inquired at length. "Have you no qualms about being seen with me, no matter how innocently?"

"In a word—no."

"You're incorrigible, do you know that?"

"Lovably so, I hope."

Meagan had to shut her eyes against the smile turned down at her. Had the devil no mercy?

At that point, she was saved from total collapse by their arrival at the shop of Robert Bell, bookseller. It was a perfect distraction. The sign which hung outside proclaimed: "Jewels and Diamonds for Sentimentalists." Inside the door was a notice that read: "The Provedore to the Sentimentalists will exhibit food for the mind, where he that buys may reap substantial advantage, because he that readeth much ought to know much."

"Loquacious fellow, isn't he?" Lion whispered in Meagan's ear, amused by her astonished expression.

Robert Bell appeared then on his way to lunch,

but paused long enough to deliver Lion's copy of *The Power of Sympathy* by Anonymous.

"I wish I could stay to chat, Mr. Hampshire, but it's stop I must at the *Packet* to place a grand new advertisement with Dunlap. You will come to the next book auction, won't ye? I would be pleased to converse at length any other day. Come around in the afternoon this week and I'll be letting you know the auction date." He opened the door and looked over one shoulder, adding in his Scottish burr, "Ye've heard, I'll warrant, who the author is of that book?" Although they were alone in the shop, he lowered his voice to a dramatic whisper, eyes twinkling. "'Tis William Hill Brown, neighbor to Perez and Sarah Morton . . . *and* her late sister, of course! Isaiah Thomas fears that he may be forced to cease printing once the word is out, for the Mortons are sure to be in a fury.

"Good fortune to you and your intended, Mr. Hampshire!" With a last impish grin, Robert Bell disappeared out the door, leaving a wide-eyed Meagan staring after him.

"What a unique man!" she said at last.

"He is that!" laughed Lion as he fished out nine shillings to leave for the book's payment.

"Is it true? That *The Power of Sympathy* is about the scandal with the Mortons and her sister?"

"Meagan, for God's sake, how do you know about that?"

Oh dear, she thought, I've done it again. "Never mind how I know. Is it true?"

He eyed her curiously before replying, "So I have heard. Bell should know."

"May I read it? Please?"

"It's rumored to be singularly depressing, but if you want to, you are certainly free."

"If it is so depressing, why did you want it?"

"Incest and suicide are not my favorite subjects, but it *is* the first published novel by an American and I felt that alone made it a valuable addition to my library."

Again her tongue outdistanced her brain. "Another symbol of status?"

Lion gave her a sharp look and turned to the bookshelves. Meagan followed his lead and soon was lost in Bell's extensive collection which covered history, theology, general and polite literature, jurisprudence, medicine, and even household works and the practical arts.

Lion bought her a copy of William Blake's first published volume of poetry, *Songs of Innocence*, but pretended not to see the humor in the two books Meagan had chosen. After pronouncing them "ideally suited" to his needs, she revealed the titles: *Married Libertine* and *Suspicious Lover*.

Chapter Twenty-nine

THE WEATHER IN Philadelphia, notorious for its unpredictable fluctuations, was behaving itself as March drew to a close. It was unfashionable to take exercise; people enjoyed the outdoors by sitting in front of their houses or going for carriage rides in the country. Lion, in his need to defy convention in some small way, spent more and more time walking about town and taking his roan for heartpounding gallops along the Schuylkill. He was filled with dark energy which he attempted to vent in this physical activity, even shedding coat and cravat to work beside the seamen during visits to the waterfront. Only when Meagan was near did he taste life's sweetness or feel inclined to laugh, but she was busy running his house and could seldom be persuaded to ignore her duties. Lion suspected that she was managing from him, throwing herself into work to escape from her thoughts and emotions.

What of me? he wondered bitterly while starting up the Binghams' drive one morning. I have surely been running too, but there's no place to hide.

He had avoided Priscilla, avoided even thinking of her, postponing his responsibilities toward her always just one more day. As April appeared on the horizon, Lion could feel the net begin to close around him. The wedding was supposed to take place before they left for New York and Washington's inauguration; three weeks was the most he could hope for. He could already imagine how Anne and Priscilla would leap upon him when he came through the door, demanding explanations and appropriate apologies for his rude absence, then battering him with plans and details. Teas, assemblies . . . and then the dire event itself.

No jungle cat was ever so desperate when borne to a cage. Lion's suffering was increased by the knowledge that he had set the trap himself, with such blind confidence.

Four days had passed since the scene in the card room. As much as he dreaded seeing Priscilla again, he realized that the inevitable meeting would be more unpleasant the longer he waited. Already he could well imagine the state she must be in.

The ordeal was lessened by Anne Bingham's absence. Lion was thankful he had not sent word ahead of his visit, for she would certainly have stayed home. Priscilla was, surprisingly, out in the garden for a stroll, and it was there that he found her.

Clad in a flattering, low-cut morning gown of lime muslin sashed with lemon silk, she looked like part of the budding greenery that surrounded her. A large-brimmed straw hat, decorated with ribbons to match the gown, covered her auburn curls, and she gazed out from its protective shade to view Lion's approach.

Priscilla's first thought was that he seemed like a wild animal that lived outdoors; there was no longer any hint of his gentleman's disguise. For the first time, he wore no jacket, waistcoat, or cravat—only a muslin shirt, open to reveal his chest, tan breeches, and riding boots. He seemed browner than ever, looking

257

more powerful than any man she had seen in her lifetime, and his hair also seemed to have been sun-bleached to an even lighter gold. Something warned Priscilla—perhaps the dangerous glint in his blue eyes or the aura of recklessness that surrounded him—and she held her tongue when he reached her.

They walked together for a while. Priscilla could not stop remembering the humiliating episode in the card room. She was astonished and outraged by his attitude; first by his failure to apologize immediately and now by the realization that he did not intend to apologize at all! It was incredible, unforgivable, but in spite of her anger, she found herself afraid to throw it up to him. The memory of what he had done to her and her body's explosive reaction left her filled with confused shame. What sort of man was he? What was his game, and what were the rules?

Groping for a foothold, she decided to try to regain some control by raising a subject Anne had urged.

"Lion?"

"Hmm?" He had bent to pull some weeds around a border of crocuses. Priscilla watched in irresistible fascination the play of muscles across his broad back.

"Before—before we discuss the wedding plans, there is another matter I should like to clear up."

"Oh?" Straightening, he brushed his dark hands off and lifted a brow ironically.

"Yes. It's—ah—about this estate I understand you have bought." Nervous under his keen gaze, she re-arranged the folds of her gown. "I think it would have been more considerate of you to have consulted me before you made such a decision."

"Oh?" he repeated, and the brow arched higher.

"Yes. I understand that this place is quite unsuitable. In fact, horrid! Anne says there is a lovely spot available near Landsdowne where we could build a new house. I could have it just the way—"

"God, how cozy that would be!" Lion laughed caustically. "Right on top of the Binghams—or vice versa. What is your point, my dear? Could it be that you want me to cancel the plans for Markwood Villa and

258

acquire a more fashionable summer estate for you?"

"Actually—yes!"

"No!" His eyes were blazing now. "I won't be led about on a leash by you and Anne Bingham like some trained dog—or fawn!" He gestured sharply toward the delicate, long-legged animals on the other side of the grounds. "And now, my precious bride-to-be, I have some news for you. I've been occupied of late with business matters and it looks like it will continue for some time. So, I regret to say that we shall have to postpone the wedding. Perhaps it can be arranged to be held in New York—if not, there will be plenty of time when we return after the inauguration."

Cantering west along Spruce Street, Lion let out a low, incredulous laugh. He still could scarcely believe he had done it. It was crazy! Later, he knew, he would regret the incautious act, but for now he was feeling incredibly free and looking forward to the hard ride to Markwood Villa.

Fate was certainly smiling on him, for suddenly there was Meagan, standing on the brick footpath just ahead. She was handing a coin to a ragged fruit-girl, who then transferred dozens of large strawberries from her hamper to the basket on Meagan's arm.

"You there!" he called, bringing his roan to a prancing standstill. "Black-haired wench!"

Meagan whirled around, eyes flashing indignantly.

"Lion!" she exclaimed in some relief. "Your sense of humor could stand improvement." The sun reflecting off his light hair seemed blinding to her.

"Really? Would you care to lend a hand in its refinement? I crave your advice, as always."

She wrinkled her nose at him and started to turn away, but Lion reached down to capture one of her glossy curls.

"I have an assignment for you, esteemed housekeeper."

"What?" She eyed him suspiciously.

"Come up here. You have some duties to attend to at Markwood Villa."

Before she could react, he braced his knees against the horse and leaned over to whisk her up in front of him, basket and all. With one gentle prod of Lion's boot, the roan broke into an easy trot and Meagan's afternoon was decided.

Secretly she was fired with joy, enchanted by his unpredictable behavior. Each time in his arms was as amazingly stirring for her as that first day they collided at West Hills when his nearness had stopped her breath. The magnetism never lost its potency; now, leaning into his chest and enveloped by his arms, Meagan's intoxication was deeper than any wine could induce.

As they reached the edge of town and the chestnut roan stretched into a gallop, Meagan showed Lion a face alight with the most guileless of smiles.

"You are a devil."

"Yes . . . Wonderful, isn't it?"

"I must say you're looking very pleased with yourself. Is it just because you have abducted a poor defenseless maiden?"

One side of his mouth went up. "Maiden?"

"Until you did your worst!"

"Please—that hurt. I was under the impression I had done rather well!" He flinched, grinning, as she raised a threatening hand. "Actually, like all good villains, I am returning to the scene of my crime."

"Until you get it right?" Her violet eyes were dancing with mischief.

"I'd advise you to guard your tongue, vixen, or you will push me to the point of forgetting my promised role as a gentleman."

"I must say, you are off to a grand beginning, carrying off poor little serving-girls."

"When did I do that? What poor little serving-girl?"

His lips twitched as Meagan averted her face, trying to think of a proper rejoinder. A sudden bump nearly jolted her off the horse and their bantering was forgotten as she scrambled for a steadier position. Lion brought an arm tightly around her waist, and they rode the rest of the way in companionable silence.

It proved to be a delightful afternoon. Together, they wandered through the rooms of Markwood Villa again, but this time they discussed furniture, color schemes, and carpets. Meagan was brimming with ideas, all of which won Lion's favor; they talked until every last corner was explored.

Finally, they headed toward the garden for air and were astonished to find the sky dusk-stained.

"How can it have gotten so late?" Meagan wondered.

"What sort of question is that? Do you expect an answer?" Smiling contentedly, he stretched and put out a hand to ruffle her windblown curls. "I don't know about you, but I am suddenly ravenous."

"Dinner! Prudence will be furious! I was away all morning at Madame Millet's, having my last fitting for those gowns. When I stopped for the strawberries, I intended to go straight home. Prudence can never make a decision alone; if someone doesn't tell her whether or not to cook with the idea of you eating at home, she'll simply throw up her hands and not fix a thing!"

Lion's thoughts were elsewhere. "The strawberries!" he announced dramatically.

All at once they were rushing for the door, but Meagan had no chance in a race with him. By the time she rounded the corner of the entry hall, Lion was brandishing the basket triumphantly.

"Well, they are probably spoiled anyhow," she said airily.

"They look fine to me!" A wicked expression swept across his face.

Beaten, Meagan made a grab for the basket but was held off with one long arm.

"You are insufferable! Selfish, greedy—"

Lion silenced her by slipping the fattest of the berries between her lips. Laughing at her expression, he slid down the wall to the floor. Heedless of her gown, Meagan promptly joined him. They sat there, side by side, eating until the basket was empty and juice reddened Meagan's mouth.

"I think I may be ill," she moaned.

Lion gave her tummy a solicitous caress that was immediately slapped away, then rose to his feet and extended a hand to her.

"I fear we shall have to chance it. I just remembered that I am due at a meeting of the Library Company in less than two hours."

Meagan had always enjoyed solitude, so the frequent, painful bouts of loneliness she had suffered of late were difficult to come to terms with. After Lion departed for his meeting, her buoyant mood seemed to deflate instantly. She sat in the kitchen and stared at Wong until she could not bear the sight of his face another moment, then remembered the undone household accounts. Grateful for any diversion, she set off for the library.

The evening had turned chilly and a cheerful fire blazed in the room. Meagan lit some candles, then crossed to Lion's desk to assemble her materials. The accounts she sought were in a spot already known to her but there was no quill or ink in sight. Pulling open the top drawer, she reached for them as her eye fell on a worn-looking Bible tucked toward the back.

Some instinct compelled her to take it out and open it, for Lion had never struck her as a religious man. Certainly not a Bible reader.

Inside, on the fly leaf, was a faded, delicately written name: "Sarah Hampshire." His mother! Meagan thought, suddenly consumed with curiosity as she realized he had never mentioned his family or background. Since the subject was not one she cared to pursue in their conversations, she had never broached it.

Knowing that she should not, Meagan turned the pages until she came to the record of family marriages, births, and deaths. There were only two entries, the first made in that same fragile hand:

"Born: Thomas Lional, on April the Nineteenth, 1756, at six o'clock in the afternoon."

On the second line was handwriting Meagan recognized, though it lacked its present boldness. Lion had made this terse entry:

"Died: Sarah Elizabeth Hampshire, September 2, 1770."

Slowly Meagan replaced the Bible, gathered her papers, quill, and ink, and moved to the escritoire near the fireplace. The figures swam before her eyes; all she could think of was that enigmatic Bible. No marriage entered, no maiden name inserted for Sarah Hampshire, no other children mentioned . . . and Lion left motherless at the age of fourteen. Was there no father? If not, what had become of Lion at that age?

When Meagan finally began on the household accounts, concentration eluded her and the work progressed slowly. With a start, she heard the tall-clock in the entryway strike twelve, followed within minutes by the sounds of Lion's arrival. Almost immediately, he appeared in the doorway.

"Meagan! What are you doing up? I wondered what the reason was for the roaring fire in here . . ."

She turned in her chair, smiling sleepily at the sight of him, resplendent in a sage green coat and amber breeches.

"I was trying to bring the household accounts up to date."

"Egad! Now she's a mathematician!" He crossed the room to look over her shoulder. "You didn't have to do this, little one. You have too much work as it is."

"Oh, I don't mind. Besides, I know how busy you have been."

Lion lifted a nearby candle to light his cheroot, then stretched out in a wing chair. Firelight flickered over his hard body and dark face as he smoked in silence for a long minute; Meagan gathered up the papers and waited.

"Something happened this morning that I meant to tell you about," he said at length, turning to meet her eyes. In the warm fireglow, she looked so sweet to him, drowsy and soft and indescribably lovely. He had meant to tell her about his announcement to Priscilla, to laugh about the nerve of it and hear her scold, teasingly, in response. But now he wondered if it was wise, just yet, even as he had second thoughts about his rash postponement of the wedding. Was he only prolonging his agony, and did he want to prolong Meagan's as well?

"Lion, do have your say!" she prodded softly. "Another minute and I shall be asleep!"

"Well, the news is that I saw Smith this morning. The French chef is due to arrive in two days and Bramble has already been told. She rather resembled a chicken that had been plucked and boiled alive— she'll be here in time to cook breakfast."

Chapter Thirty

LION SPENT THE better part of two days searching out the perfect horse for Meagan. On the first morning of April, a filly was delivered to the small stable behind the Pine Street house.

Meagan was in her room, trying on the new clothes which Madame Millet had left an hour before. Most of the wardrobe was completed and Meagan felt like a child at Christmas. When Lion knocked at her door, she had just finished fastening a gown of damask rose silk, one of the most elaborate of the group. Its square neckline enhanced the curves of her breasts while ivory lace had been sewn lavishly over every finished hem. Meagan tied a band of matching lace around her neck before answering the door.

The expression on Lion's face flooded her with happiness and stained her cheeks appealingly.

"Meagan! I am dazzled! Turn around."

Self-consciously she obeyed, feeling his eyes burn through the silk which was molded so closely to her body.

"You look absolutely exquisite. I shall be consumed by impatience until I see you in the rest of the gowns."

Meagan allowed him to take her hands and kiss them in several tender spots. "Thank you. It isn't a bit proper for me to accept these, but . . ."

"You will. The reward will be mine, actually, for I shall be the one to enjoy your beauty. Now, come with me. I have a surprise for you."

As he led her through the garden and over the lawn, Meagan realized their destination.

"Oh, Lion, I hope you haven't—"

"Shh! No guessing allowed."

"Stop this!" She twisted free from the hand that guided her arm, calling out in frustration as he continued to walk ahead, "I am warning you that if there is another horse in there, you may as well forget it. Taking these dresses is bad enough, but—"

Her voice broke as Lion brought the filly out into the sunlight. She was so lovely that Meagan felt tears prick her eyes.

Her gleaming coat was the color of richest sable. Elegantly built, she had expressive, intelligent eyes below the small heart-shaped blaze on her forehead and graceful white-stockinged legs.

It was love at first sight. Meagan put a hand out, which the horse nosed gently; then they met—Meagan caressing, the filly nuzzling.

When at last she looked back to seek out Lion, two silvery tears sparkled on each cheek.

Bramble retained her customary bad temper, and Meagan soon understood what had brought gentle Smith to complain about the cook's high-handedness. Bramble made her presence and her opinions known each minute of each day; she seemed more sour than ever since her demotion at Mansion House. When she wasn't discoursing on the many flaws of the Binghams and their contemporaries, she was making Meagan feel like a fool. Bramble expected her to be involved in some type of work from dawn to dusk and when she wasn't, the old woman shot her looks more deadly than poison.

Lion thought it all highly amusing. Only his balancing influence kept Meagan from turning into a guilty wreck, for he laughingly reminded her several times a day that she, and not Bramble, was in charge.

After her weeks as lowly serving-girl, this was a hard fact to remember. She succumbed to habit once again as Lion led her back from the stables. Bramble was waiting for them in the kitchen, obviously irked by Meagan's all-morning absence. With one critical eye, she took in the new rose gown and said, "Would ye have a minute to spare as housekeeper?"

Meagan blushed automatically, conscious of Lion's hand at the small of her back. He removed it and left the room, giving her a smile of mingled amusement and sympathy.

"I never saw a servant wear such clothes," Bramble observed. "Have ye misplaced the gowns from Mansion House?"

"Perhaps," Meagan said, slightly irritated. In fact, Lion had left the black dresses for the poor.

"Ye have been away a great amount." Her tone belied the simplicity of the statement. "I would have some information as to the master's preferences. The other girl—Prudence—is too dull to be of help, and I had a notion ye might be the one to ask."

Oh Lord, thought Meagan, I never felt so guilty before my parents or my governess, no matter how I misbehaved. Why now?

"Certainly, Bramble. I should have thought of it myself."

Together, they sat down at the gateleg table and Meagan wrote down Lion's favorite foods, including squash, cornpone, succotash, Indian pudding, turkey stuffed with oysters, and hominy. It was Bramble, in her perceptiveness, who made her see the significance of that list.

"Hmm! He must come from the country! I never knew a city-bred gentleman partial to such dishes."

It was one more piece for Meagan's puzzle.

When she left the kitchen to finish unpacking the new dresses, she found Lion waiting in the hallway.

"There is much to do, sweeting," he announced with that dazzling, resistance-melting grin. "And your poor horse is waiting to be exercised."

Meagan succumbed to his persuasion, begging only a few minutes to change into her new plum velvet riding habit. After issuing instructions to Bramble and Wong, she fairly ran to join Lion at the stables. He had saddled the lovely filly, who divided her affectionate gaze between her mistress and Lion's chestnut roan.

"Does your horse have a name?" Meagan inquired.

"To be honest, no, although when I acquired him in January, Brown called him Hellfire."

"Oh! That is perfect! It shall be Hellfire and Heaven!" Her face grew pensive as she thought of leaving the filly behind in a few weeks. When Lion spoke, it seemed that he read her mind.

"You understand that Heaven is your horse, come what may? I would not separate you. She is a gift, a token of love, if you will."

Meagan looked up sharply, meeting his clear blue eyes. It was the first time he had ever used the word love, however lightly, and its cut was both deep and sweet.

They rode back to Markwood Villa, where Lion wrote down their final plans for each room's contents. The afternoon was advanced when they left but Lion seemed energetic, and Meagan felt active as well. They gave the horses their heads along the Schuylkill until the great estates north of Philadelphia came into view.

Lion showed her Landsdowne, the Binghams' magnificent summer home, as well as the nearby estate owned by Robert Morris. They then passed Mount Pleasant, designed in the manner of Markwood Villa, which Benedict Arnold had acquired for his bride,

Peggy Shippen. Lion explained that Arnold had been charged with treason before they ever passed a night in the house.

The Schuylkill shimmered in the spring sunlight as they rode along past the fashionable summer homes of Philadelphia's elite. The grounds to the right were like parks, watered and clipped to perfection, unlike the wild riotousness of Markwood Villa. Heaven was proving an ideal horse, obedient yet frolicsome. She followed Hellfire's lead as he galloped along the riverside road. When they passed Woodlands, Lion told her that the Hamiltons, who owned it, were the first to bring the Lombardy poplar and the weeping willow to the Colonies. The family had greatly advanced botany by importing large numbers of unique trees and shrubs from England, the Continent, and even the Far East.

His voice broke off as he recognized a carriage full of people who drew near to them and called a greeting. The open carriage slowed, then stopped, and a magnificent man jumped down.

He had black hair and vivid turquoise eyes; his body was as tall, lean, and tanned as Lion's, and they clasped hands as old friends.

"Meagan, this is Alexandre Beauvisage and his wife, Caroline. In the back are their children, ah . . ."

"Étienne and Natalya," called the honey-haired Mrs. Beauvisage.

A boy of around five, his father's miniature, and a blond toddler peeked out and smiled. Meagan grinned back, feeling instantly drawn to this attractive quartet and to Caroline in particular. There was a candor in her friendly, caramel eyes that Meagan thought rare.

The two men conversed for a few moments, apparently about ships, then Beauvisage grinned broadly at her and returned to his Caro. When they started off in the opposite direction, Meagan drew Heaven alongside Lion to ask, "Who *were* they? What lovely people!"

"You would be delighted by their story," he answered, as Hellfire began to trot up the road. "Alec brought Caro here as his ward after the war ended.

He launched her into society, but eventually married her himself. Theirs is one of the few happy endings I know of."

Meagan saw the cynical spark of disbelief flicker in his eyes and decided not to comment. There would be no use in her defending true love if he refused to accept its existence.

They continued northward until Meagan sighted a castle perched above the river, lush, trimmed greenery encircling it like a necklace.

"Lion! Is that a castle, or are my eyes playing tricks?"

"It is. We must turn back now, but I brought you this far so that you could see State in Schuylkill. This is the gathering place for that incredible organization from May to October. The food, notably the beefsteak, is superlative; there is a secret, potent punch, and the meetings have no time limits. I've attended as a guest in the past, but I hope to be asked to join this summer. Fashion dictates membership in endless organizations, but there are only a handful—three, probably—that interest me. This is one."

"Isn't it a shame that women can never belong to these? I consider it grossly unfair." Meagan cast a final, longing look over her shoulder as they turned the horses about and Lion headed straight for Kingressing.

This was the location of John Bartram's botanical gardens. Meagan knew of it well but pretended ignorance as Lion pointed out the various species of plants and shrubs discovered by Bartram.

John, once Royal Botanist of the Colonies, had been dead ten years. His son, William, came out to meet them. Again Meagan was amazed by the number of friends Lion had acquired, despite his many months at sea. All who hailed him showed genuine respect and liking.

Lion introduced her as casually as if she were his groom, then just as easily included her in their conversation. The fiftyish William Bartram was as enthusiastic a botanist as his late father had been, tend-ing the vast gardens lovingly and traveling out to the untamed lands beyond the thirteen states to hunt new species of plant life. He listened with interest to Lion's story of Markwood Villa and his plans for a crazy-quilt garden. Skillfully, Lion edged into a request for some of Bartram's prized flowers and plants, most particularly the rare tree Franklinia, discovered and named by the father and son after the one and only Benjamin.

Graciously, Bartram offered to present Lion with two of the trees as a wedding gift and was persuaded to relinquish, for a price, slips of Lion's other favorite plants to ensure a spectacular beginning for the new garden.

As they talked, the sun was dipping low over the Schuylkill, a molten coral arc that bled fire into the water. Meagan finally nudged Lion with an elbow to his waist, thinking in spite of all her firmest intentions, of Bramble's disapproval and silent, accusing glares which would await them at home. Fortunately, he took the hint and minutes later they bade Mr. Bartram a warm good-bye.

Hellfire and Heaven cantered toward Philadelphia in smooth harmony. Meagan cast worried glances at the vehicles which they passed on the road, remembering what a popular recreation spot Bartram's Gardens was.

"Starting tomorrow," said Lion suddenly, "we shall begin to organize Markwood Villa in earnest. The painting and carpets must be attended to, and we can investigate the shops of every cabinet-maker before choosing all the funiture. We want to have each room perfect; just the way you've envisaged.

"I'll send Joshua round to Bartram's to fetch the Franklinia trees and the rest. Don't you think that it will be safe to begin by next week? God knows I wouldn't want to see them freeze as soon as they're replanted—"

"You are really looking forward to working on the house, aren't you?" Meagan asked, vaguely surprised by his verbal enthusiasm.

"Damn—it's true! It is the challenge, I suppose, and I seem to feel oddly attached to the place. Perhaps we are both misfits . . . black sheep . . ." His eyes turned thoughtful for a moment, then a harsh laugh broke the silence. "I may as well tell you—it's partly that rebellious side of me. Priscilla tried to make me change my mind and buy some property near Landsdowne. Had visions of me building a dream house for her."

"I gather you refused?"

Lion lifted a satirical eyebrow. "Did you doubt it? Poor girl . . . she'll have to make do with a haunted, broken-down villa unfashionably south of Philadelphia."

"You are a blackhearted wretch," Meagan said matter-of-factly, and Lion's mouth curved upward at her demeanor. "By the way, I simply do not see how you can propose to take me with you on these shopping excursions! Even today, we could have been recognized by dozens of people at Bartram's Gardens and here on the road. You can't just flaunt me in front of the entire town, especially in these new gowns of mine—"

Her violet eyes widened, sparkling like amethysts in the smoky-pink light of sunset, and she sat up straight on Heaven's back as a grin spread over her face.

"Lion! Oh, Lion, listen! I have the most inspired idea; it is the perfect solution. Why didn't I think of it earlier?"

Chapter Thirty-one

BUBBLING WITH AN excitement that smacked of anticipated risk, Meagan buttoned Wong's breeches up to her waist and hurried toward the mirror. The figure staring back laughed out loud, appearing on the verge of an impromptu dance.

Only the creaminess of her complexion and the thick lashes which fringed brilliant violet eyes could possibly betray her sex, but who would take the time to suspect a small, plainly-dressed groom? Wide lace ribbons, thoughtfully supplied by an unwitting Madame Millet, bound her ripe breasts. Aided by a loose-fitting shirt and black coat, her curves were effectively hidden.

Meagan had spent a full quarter-hour pinning silky, endless curls against her head, and still a man's bicorne hat barely fit around the ebony mass. It did cover her forehead, however, lending shade and a slightly gauche look to the face below.

Perfect, thought Meagan. Thank God for little Wong and his unremarkable taste in clothes! In the black suit, white stockings, and buckled shoes, she cut the ideal figure of a dullwitted, adolescent groom. No one would give her a second glance.

She sauntered around the room a few times, marveling at how wonderful it felt to be back in breeches. How could she have borne the sidesaddle these past weeks? Perhaps Lion would consent to a hard ride in the country; it would be glorious to sit properly on Heaven's back!

Wong's clothing had been confiscated while the Chinaman was busy upstairs, and Meagan shuddered at the thought of discovery. No possible explanation would placate him.

So she had left word for Lion to fetch her at her room; together they would be able to escape safely from the house. At that moment, his familiar knock sounded, and after one last jaunty glance in the mirror, Meagan went to meet him.

It was a rare treat to see Lion so nonplussed. Giggling softly, she pulled him in and closed the door.

"Do you like it?" she inquired, pirouetting on the toe of one buckled shoe. "I'll allow that Wong and I may not curve in quite the same places, but the fit will do."

Lion continued to look dazed. "Meagan—"

"I know, I am a genius!"

"You are mad! Look at you! Breeches!"

"Well, honestly, you act as though I am some sort of freak! Women do have legs, you know, just like men."

"Come over here."

She could see a glint in his eyes that betrayed admiration and pure delight. Her own happiness was such that she stood still and continued to beam as he ran tawny hands over her hips, then under the jacket. His touch was warm through the fabric of her shirt, almost causing her to forget to draw back before he reached her breasts.

But Lion was quicker. "For God's sake, Meagan, what have you done to yourself?"

"Well, boys don't have . . . those—do they?" she argued defensively. "It's a costume, after all, and it should be authentic."

Lion raked a hand through his bright hair. "This is insane! There is not another woman alive who would cheerfully garb herself in breeches, let alone—"

"I'm not any other woman. I am me. If I am odd, then so be it."

"Oh, Meagan," he groaned, feeling his lips twitch helplessly at the sight of her.

"It will be fun! An adventure! Please, don't scold me anymore. If we are going to do all that you

273

planned, we must be off, so let's not waste another moment." She dashed back for one last appraisal in the mirror, adding as she pulled down her hat, "You must go and scout the rear hallway, Lion. It wouldn't do for me to bump into Wong!"

And so it went. Every morning, Meagan donned her groom's disguise and she and Lion combed the shops of Philadelphia until all the furnishings for Markwood Villa were chosen. The simple pleasure of shopping was transformed into something of a daring escapade by Meagan's masquerade. There was always the chance that someone would look too closely at her face or that she would forget to deepen her voice —a practice which gave Lion great amusement—or that he would thoughtlessly embrace her. His own role became crucial to the success of hers, for he had to remember to treat her as he would Joshua. Considering his feelings and a strong physical attraction that persisted no matter what clothing Meagan wore, this was a tall order.

The conspiracy brought them closer together than ever. In the evening, Meagan would take unusual pains with her appearance; she never wore the same gown twice, and her skin glowed from the scrubbing it received. No longer were her curls pinned up helter-skelter; in fact, she arranged them over and over and never felt satisfied with the results. It was as though she needed to remind Lion regularly that in spite of her fondness for breeches, she was still very much a female.

Lion needed no reminding. He burned night and day with desire and was somewhat astonished at his newly discovered control. Unable to leave her side, he virtually ignored Priscilla and dined at home, yet wondered why he subjected himself to such unceasing torment. Meagan seemed to be unaware of his agony, obviously expecting him to behave since he had given his promise. No longer wary, she happily shared his company, and Lion marveled that all the other aspects of their relationship were enough in themselves to compensate for not only the absence of physical communication but his own accompanying painful yearnings.

Even during the day, the sight of her mischievous, piquant face under that ridiculous hat made him long to lift her up and kiss her. Each moment they were together reminded him of moments past; the abandon of her response when her control was washed away, the sweetness of her lips, the satiny warmth of the body now constantly hidden, the thump of her heart against his chest. The days of denial drove him mad, yet he could not bring himself to leave the cause of his suffering any more than he could break down and take her by force. He guessed, rightly, that she would not have refused him a simple kiss, but Lion knew that after one taste there would be no turning back.

The first week of April was gone before Markwood Villa's purchases were complete. Only the master bedchamber remained to be filled, a task Meagan had purposely postponed. Priscilla's furnishings had been difficult enough, but Lion had casually refrained from mentioning the room's future occupant when they picked out the new Hepplewhite four-poster and its various accessories. There was no way to camouflage the purchase of his own bed, however, and Meagan was tortured throughout by images in her mind of Priscilla curled up on it, her head resting on Lion's hard brown chest. By the time they decided on a suitably handsome bed and gray and ivory drapes for it, she felt physically ill.

Leaving John Folwell's shop, Lion took one look at her drawn face and sensed the problem.

"Well, that's that! All we have to do now is stand back and tell them where everything should go."

"When will the men bring the carpets?" she asked weakly.

"Tomorrow. I hope that dubious crew I hired to paint the interior is done. You are right. I do need a bigger staff. Someone should have been out there to supervise more often."

"Well, there is time yet for that. You would have no

problem finding servants if you kept slaves like every-one else."

"Not everyone." He smiled slightly at her dubious expression. "All right, almost everyone, but not I. You know how I feel—"

"Yes, Lion, and I agree! You don't have to argue the point with me. Save that speech for your future wife."

He put a tentative hand on her arm in spite of the people milling about. "Meagan, you look a bit pale. Would you like a walk? We could head toward the State House—"

"Yes. Yes, I would like that."

They left Heaven and Hellfire tethered to a post and started off in a westerly direction. The weather was fine and Philadelphia's citizens were out; the poplar-shaded footpaths were crowded with the lower classes while the more wealthy passed in their open carriages.

Meagan's innate good spirits were revived by the sunshine and Lion's presence. They strolled past every sort of shop, from apothecary and blacksmith to milliner and bootmaker. There was even a comb shop, with hand-carved combs of tortoiseshell and horn displayed in its window.

Lion made easy, distracting conversation, pointing out every building of interest and answering all Meagan's questions as her curiosity returned. He showed her Jefferson's corner room at the Indian Head Tavern where he had labored over the Declaration of Independence while noisy parties and meetings continued downstairs. Farther on, they made a detour up the cobbled lane to Carpenter's Hall, originally the site of the First Continental Congress, and now the meeting place for the Library Company.

"The Company pretty much grew out of Doctor Franklin's Junto Club," Lion explained. "We have a room up there for our books and another for a collection of objects the Doctor has christened 'Philosophical Apparatus.' "

"His inventions, I suppose!" Meagan added, laughing as Lion allowed one side of his mouth to quirk.

"The Junto Club was for discussion, wasn't it? Morals and philosophy and such?"

"Basically. The Library Company was born when they added books. It is still essentially a gathering of good minds for the free exchange of ideas; the guiding principles are freedom of opinion and truth for its own sake. Heady stuff! Doctor Franklin drew up most of the rules and one of them is that there must be intermittent pauses in each meeting for the wine glasses to be refilled and drained."

Meagan laughed. "Isn't he wicked!"

"You sound terribly disapproving," he mocked.

"Oh, I love wickedness. You should know that by now!"

One of Lion's champagne eyebrows shot up at that remark; he had to clench his fists to keep from grabbing her right there on the street. Meagan, however, was unaware of her imminent peril, for she was eyeing a Negro who wheeled his oyster barrow a few houses away.

"Could we get some?" she pleaded.

It was Meagan's first taste of this famous Philadelphia food, and at first she shuddered at the slimy texture. The oysters were gray, with the tang of ocean salt still noticeable, and Lion showed her how to add just the right amounts of lemon and horseradish. Meagan's pluck won out. She ate the things until it seemed natural, like any other native who had been raised on them. Lion watched, smiling, as she conquered her revulsion with typical enthusiasm but finally pulled her away when he feared she would be sick from downing too many.

They passed a host of other vendors on their way to the State House: youngsters hawking fragrant bread or papers or flowers, fruit-girls with their hampers of cherries and strawberries, more oyster-men, and Negroes selling steaming pepper pot. Lion was thankful that Meagan had not brought her basket, for he knew that she would stop and buy until it was full.

All around was the Federal spirit. Signboards had been painted over to include the word so that every-

277

where Meagan looked were Federal livery stables, Federal taverns, shops boasting Federal hats or furniture. The birthplace of that intoxicating word was located a square down Fifth Street and halfway through the next on Chestnut. The State House was far enough from Society Hill that Meagan had yet to see it, though her childhood was rich with tales of the place. It seemed that every man who ever visited her family had just come from there, after the Continental Congress signed the Declaration of Independence when she was only four, or after the Constitutional Convention just three years earlier. She had heard descriptions of Philadelphia and its State House from everyone from Washington to Jefferson to the Lees to Madison, but none of it had prepared her for the throb she felt in her breast when Lion said, "There it is."

So handsomely constructed, the building seemed haloed with idealism and pride. Within it had been formed concepts that men had fought for and died to win; intangibles made tangible, "inalienable rights." Staring at the cream-trimmed bricks, Meagan recalled a snatch of Thomas Paine's *The Crisis*:

> Heaven knows how to put a proper price on its goods; and it would be strange indeed, if so celestial an article as FREEDOM should not be highly rated.

Robert Morris, punctual as always, had been in New York for a month, waiting for the rest of Congress to arrive. In fact, the ballots for the election of President and Vice President had only just been counted two days ago, on April the sixth, and Robert had sent a letter to his wife by special messenger to relay the news.

When the boy arrived, grimy and breathless, a liveried servant intercepted him in the doorway. The letter was then properly delivered on a silver salver to the elegant parlor where Mary Morris poured tea for her guests, Anne Bingham, Priscilla Wade, and Eliza Powel. The women clustered together when Mary recognized her husband's seal, all of them anxious for the final word and some hint of when they might expect to journey to New York.

"He says that it is official; General Washington was elected unanimously, and Mr. Adams shall be Vice President, though his margin of votes was considerably narrower!" The women laughed knowingly at that. "The inauguration shall take place on the thirtieth day of this month and Mr. Thomson is leaving immediately for Mount Vernon to convey the news of victory to the General."

The conversation was thick with plans and predictions from then on. Unfamiliar with New York City, the main topic, as well as most of the people being discussed, Priscilla soon grew bored. Finally, she reached over to tap Anne's satin sleeve and smothered a yawn.

"Couldn't you show me the house? I am finding this conversation awfully dull!"

Anne was in a good mood and so agreed quite readily.

"You know, there is speculation that the new President himself may be living here before the year is out," she confided to Priscilla when they reached the stair hall. "Robert has a great deal of influence and he has already begun coaxing General Washington to locate the capital here instead of in New York."

"And he would turn over his house?"

"He has done so before, during the General's periods of residence in Philadelphia. You know, the various conventions and such. You may be sure that if this becomes the seat of government, so shall his home be here." She pointed to the glossy floor.

It was a beautiful mansion, in keeping with Morris's reputation for wealth rivaling the Binghams'. Everything was polished to the highest possible shine; brass fittings had been used lavishly throughout the house. Mary Morris was a lovely woman with a sweet face and temperament; the decor reflected her own understated elegance. Little of the opulence of Mansion House was in evidence, but each piece of furniture proclaimed its value in the richness of the wood and excellence of its craftsmanship.

Upstairs, on the second of three floors, Anne led Priscilla through a sitting room to view the charming gardens and orchard below which were surrounded by a red-brick wall. The front of the house looked out over the fifty-foot-wide High Street and its intersection with Sixth, an area of town quite different and far away from Society Hill. Anne paused at a window in Hester Morris's bedchamber, watching the parade of rich and poor on Philadelphia's busiest street, while Priscilla inspected the daughter's furnishings.

"Well, well . . ." said Anne at length, "if it isn't the ever-absent Lion Hampshire, walking the footpath amongst the chimney sweeps and pigs! Someone told me that one can never see him in his carriage anymore. It's a wonder he hasn't contracted some hideous disease." Narrowing her eyes, she leaned closer. "It would seem that he has acquired more new servants than just my Bramble . . . I'm certain I have never seen that boy before."

Lion had lately begun to seem like a myth to Priscilla, she saw him so seldom. Her curiosity pricked by Anne's comments, she went to the window and immediately located the sunlit blond hair of her fiancé.

The next moment she froze; her green eyes became fixed and unblinking. Without seeing the shadowed face of his companion, she knew who it was as surely as she knew her own name. There was no mistaking those petite legs in their once familiar garb of breeches, or the energetic walk and animated gestures of their owner. Even the distant lilt of laughter could be recognized amidst the shouts of the urchins and vendors on the street below.

Conscious of a creeping, chilling dread, Priscilla shifted her eyes back to Lion. Part of her would have preferred to turn away, for some instinct warned her what she would see in the expression on his walnut face.

And truly, this was a man she had never so much as glimpsed or imagined could exist. The near-animal brilliance of Lion, gold and bronze and sapphire, had been somehow transformed into the most warm and dazzling sort of magic. Even Priscilla could recognize that his laughter, as fire-charged as the sun overhead, could only be a product of love.

Chapter Thirty-two

MARKWOOD VILLA WAS finished, for the present at least, and Meagan experienced an uneasy twinge as she opened her armoire door to choose clothing for the day ahead. Every morning for over a week, she had gaily pulled on breeches, but now they were only a dark lump in the corner.

What lay ahead for them now? she wondered. Their excuse for spending every waking hour together was gone, crushed under the last piece of furniture put in place at the villa. Though Lion infrequently mentioned Priscilla, and had never spoken a word about the wedding, Meagan realized that it could not be more than a fortnight away. Surely there were parties planned, and Lion would have to start behaving like an attentive fiancé. It seemed that the best days were over for Meagan and him . . . The charade was truly in its last act.

Blindly, she dressed in a pretty gown of gauzy white muslin banded by a wide velvet sash the color of heather, then sat down at her dressing table and frowned into the mirror. Great violet eyes stared back, more beautiful than ever, their newly blazed depths partially obscured by iridescent mists of pain. No matter how poorly she slept, the love that flourished within lent its warmth to her body so that her cheeks and lips retained their rosy glow. Absently, Meagan pinned her long curls up over her head so that they spilled down randomly, one or two falling free to the small of her back. After encircling her neck with another band of heather velvet, she was off to the door without a backward glance.

In the hall a fresh vase of blue phlox caught her eye. The flowers were so small and tender that she reached out for them irresistibly, plucking out a handful. One by one they touched her tilted nose and were nestled amongst the gleaming raven curls; a quick pause before the mirror confirmed her suspicion that the blue blossoms made better accessories than anything Madame Millet could create.

Through the hours of early morning, Meagan remained pensive and preoccupied. Bramble and Wong sensed the problem at once when she failed to respond to their barbs. Two new housemaids arrived to be interviewed, but Meagan was so surprisingly vague with them that Wong had to step in to ask the necessary questions. While he was busy with this task, a knock sounded at the front door, and Meagan went to answer. A footman wearing the Bingham livery stood on the step.

"Good day, South! Didn't know you was here, too! I've a message for Cap'n Hampshire."

He fished in his coat to locate the letter and handed it to her with a grin. Touching a hand to his tricorne hat, he turned to leave, but Meagan called, "Wait, Pierce! Shouldn't you stay for an answer?"

"Mistress Wade says there won't be one," the footman replied and leaped to the back of the waiting carriage.

Puzzled, Meagan closed the door and regarded the envelope with the Binghams' seal on it. She glanced up at the tall-clock to be certain of the hour, then started up the stairs.

Her tentative knock drew an immediate response.

"Come in!"

Peeking around the door, Meagan caught her breath at the sight of him. Lion sat up in bed, teak brown against a backdrop of snowy pillows with the linen sheet drawn negligently over his legs to his hips. The window curtains had been parted to allow the entrance of a wide sunbeam which lent a brilliant haze to his hard-muscled torso and chiseled face. A newspaper was spread across his thighs, which accounted for the long moment before Meagan's presence was acknowledged.

When Lion glanced up, he looked irritated, but that expression was instantly replaced by one much softer.

"I thought you were Prudence," he said ironically. "It seems to be a time-consuming task—bringing me coffee."

"No doubt," Meagan smiled, her eyes on the tendons of his arms and neck, the luster of the sun-gilded hair covering his broad chest. Moving closer, she could see the engaging remnants of recent sleep in his expression, a drowsy sparkle in the blue eyes and a faint pattern of pillow creases on his cheek.

"This just came for you."

Lion accepted the letter, breaking the seal and glancing over the page. His smile was enigmatic.

"Her Highness informs me that she will be otherwise occupied until further notice."

"What? What does that mean? Lion, how can you look so complacent? Why, the wedding is barely a fortnight away—"

Meagan stopped short, cheeks burning as she felt his eyes caressing her. Her breasts tingled in warning.

"I imagine Priscilla is still mad at me about Markwood Villa," he explained in a low voice, the barest smile curving his mouth. Meagan stood frozen, near enough for him to kiss, and Lion stared at her long and hard with a hungry gaze that seared her flesh right through the muslin gown. A part of her brain wondered if the magic rode in on the sunbeam as it had danced down on a shaft of moonlight outside William Shippen's house. Frantically, she thought of closing the curtains, but it was too late. Weakness born of longing most desperate had already set in, causing her to tremble even before she met Lion's eyes.

God save me, she thought, lost in his mesmerizing gaze. For the first time, she saw the flecks of gold dust that sparkled in the depths of his clear sapphire eyes amongst a swirl of emotions that he did not trouble to mask.

With agonizing slowness, one of Lion's tawny hands moved toward her, lean fingers about her waist. Gently, they slid up her side and across her narrow back so that she shivered visibly. Meagan was unable to coordinate the simple act of breathing; she thought that his veins must run with fire, certainly not ordinary blood, for when his hand grazed her bare shoulder her flesh burned and burned . . . He traced the line of her throat, her trembling chin, then downward to the creamy, lush curves of her breasts. Meagan gasped, dissolved, and dropped to one knee on the edge of the bed. She heard him draw a ragged breath before leaning forward to take her in his arms; the newspaper and Priscilla's letter crackled between them and Lion ripped them away along with the linen sheet. Meagan's own skirts rode up her thighs as Lion dragged her face up to his. She felt the long muscles and crisp hair on his legs against her own soft skin, then the shock of contact with his manhood, warm and rock hard. His hands were in her hair and their mouths came together in a ravenous kiss, devastating in its intensity. Meagan's lips parted eagerly; blue phlox blossoms spattered the white pillows as she felt the hot tingling ache between her thighs become an exquisite torture. Lion cupped her breasts and they swelled against his hands. Meagan thought she would die when he bent her over into the pillows, pulling her low-cut bodice down. Slowly, his firm lips traced the curves and soft valley between her breasts until they reached one taut, rosy nipple. First a light kiss; then his tongue touched it with fire.

Meagan gripped Lion's shoulders, nails biting into tanned skin until she felt his face touching hers, kissing her tremulous lips as his fingers moved to unfasten her gown with unfailing deftness.

The rapping at the door went on for several seconds before they heard it.

"I be out here with your tray, Mister Hampshire!" Bramble called in her sharpest, most suspicious tone.

"For God's sake, not now!" Lion's voice was menacing.

During the heavy pause which followed, Meagan scrambled up and off the bed, tears welling in her eyes as she fumbled with the fastenings on her gown.

Lion's jaw was set angrily. In seconds, he had her muslin bodice back in place and hastened to retrieve the sheet as Bramble warned, "For the girl's sake, I be comin' in!"

Lion was sitting in bed, reassembling the newspaper, and Meagan had turned away to arrange the window curtains when Bramble entered. Her thin lips worked for a moment as she surveyed the bedchamber and its occupants.

"Devil's spawn!" she hissed at Lion.

"Madame, I hired you to cook my meals and for no other purpose. I find your intrusion here and your attitude incredible!" The anger in his voice seemed to cut the air like a sword.

"I be a God-fearing woman. I could not stand by and see you ruin a young maiden." She thrust out her pointed chin. "I smell the heat of you in this room. Vile! Like animals—"

"That's enough," Lion ground out.

Bramble narrowed her eyes as she noticed the blue flowers strewn on the sheets. "South, you may depend on me to keep you safe from this—man. My responsibility as a Christian is clear."

Meagan turned to face her, ready to protest, to admit the truth, but Bramble would not be interrupted.

"I have feared for you, for I know the bestial nature of this man. I have heard of the attack Mistress Wade suffered at his hands. The poor girl was nearly taken against her will, right in the card room in the full light of day!"

Heaven stretched out her elegant legs, seeming to

285

fly as Meagan urged her on toward Markwood Villa. It was almost an adequate release for her angry pain; the muscular force of Heaven's movements against her legs, the sting of a suddenly chill wind that pierced her muslin gown and pricked the softness of her throat and face. As they topped a hill, Meagan automatically pressed her heels into the horse's flanks, anticipating a familiar length of straight road.

However, the sight that met her eyes on the far-off horizon was a shock. What had seemed to be an innocent April shower brewing now gave signs of a different nature. Enormous black clouds rose above the distant tree-lined hills like thick smoke from some terrible fire. They sent a stunningly powerful wind northward to announce their approach, while darkness seeped over the sky like ink poured on pale blue muslin.

Sheer fright and sudden cold prickled Meagan's skin. Heaven modified her pace without being told, nearly coming to a standstill as her mistress wondered wildly what to do. Was there time to return to the house on Pine Street? If so, did she want to flee from the storm like some helpless child? Somehow, the fury of the elements seemed to offer a challenge to the bitter passion that coursed through her veins, a passion that smothered her better judgment.

Heaven seemed to give Meagen a wondering glance when she nudged her sides almost fiercely, calling above the rising wind, "We must not stop until we reach Markwood Villa!"

The storm swept out chilling dark arms to welcome them as they advanced, and the wind grew so powerful that Meagan was forced to press her body along the length of Heaven's flanks to keep her seat. The spirited filly bowed her head and fought the cold blasts, winning steady, if slow, progress. Meagan felt the pins loosen in her hair, then escape, as the long sable curls flew out behind her.

They had almost reached the winding approach to the villa when the clouds seemed to split open, sending down wild, drenching torrents of rain. Heaven never wavered, picking her way down the path in spite of whipping branches, sheets of rain backed by a fierce wind, and the wet ground at her feet. Meagan simply held on as cold rivulets of water ran down her face, neck, and breasts, while her clothing and unbound hair grew icily saturated, pasting themselves to her shivering body. Several times it seemed that they would never make it. Heaven began to stumble and the force of the storm seemed unconquerable.

But each time she slipped on the mud and was driven to her knees by the punishing wind, Meagan would cry out to her to keep fighting. Heaven's graceful head would rise, her heart-shaped blaze turned toward the hidden sun, and somehow she would clamber up to her feet and struggle on.

At last, the circular drive came into view. Meagan's heart pounded with sheer relief as she slid from Heaven's back. Together they ran down the hill, defeating the storm with the aid of basic gravity.

Meagan did not hesitate. Opening the white front door, she took the reins and pulled her horse over the threshold. Heaven seemed startled and reluctant, but one glance in the other direction convinced her to accept her mistress's hospitality. When Meagan threw trembling arms around the filly's neck, a soft nose nuzzled her in return.

"Oh, Heaven, you are the bravest creature, animal or human, male or female!" Meagan said huskily, half-sobbing. "We two frail beings are living proof that determination is more powerful than simple strength." A hard suggestion of a smile curved her lips. "Mr. Hampshire shall learn that I will not be claimed like some prize for his library shelf. The victor in a man-woman confrontation need not be predictable!"

She drew back to give Heaven a rather weak, if determined, grin. The elation Meagan felt at their safe arrival began to fade as she became conscious of her physical state. The gauzy muslin of her gown looked like soaked tissue; her pretty heather velvet sash was wilted, ruined. Her skin was blue-tinged and numb from the wet and cold, while drops of water fell from her hair, collecting on the patterned brick floor.

"We are both chilled to the bone, Heaven! You poor thing. Let me go and get some blankets."

Pulling off wet silk slippers, Meagan wriggled her toes and scampered up the stairway. She knew exactly where the bedding was stored since she had personally picked out the blanket chest for Priscilla's room and stocked it with plush quilts and sheets.

Outside, the fury of the storm seemed to increase. Meagan could hear tree branches slapping the stucco exterior of the house while other limbs broke with loud snaps. The wind howled eerily over the noisy tattoo of the rain. Meagan lifted the lid of the blanket chest, peering closer in the darkness as she chose three carefully folded quilts.

Suddenly, a loud creak on the planked floor sent a chill up her spine. The chest's lid dropped with a bang and Meagan spun around just in time to see the dressing-room door swing closed. The pounding of her heart was deafening. For a moment, fear immobilized her, then, clasping the blankets, she ran out into the hall and down the long stairway.

Heaven's presence was reassuring, but Meagan had a feeling that her horse would be little protection from a ghost.

"It would probably serve me right," she muttered, spreading a quilt on the floor beneath Heaven and putting a second one over her back. "A fitting reward for a girl who runs away from home, who lies, who lets herself be bedded by some libertine, who thinks she can defeat a storm . . ."

Miserably, she wrapped a down-filled comforter around her own shivering body and perched on the stairway. "It would serve Lion right as well. 'Devil's spawn!' For once, Bramble was not too severe in her judgment! I wonder if he would have the decency to feel guilty if I were killed by Markwood's ghost?" She smiled rather diabolically. "I could haunt this place as well! Wouldn't that make for an interesting marriage between Lion and Priscilla!"

There was a crashing noise almost directly above

them that wiped the smile from Meagan's face, replacing it with a look of wide-eyed terror. Perhaps, she thought wildly, it had come from the roof. A large branch could have been blown against it . . .

She clenched her teeth to still her trembling chin, pulling the blanket closer. The only sound was the pounding of her heart, which seemed to fill her head as well as her breast, until Heaven suddenly pricked her ears in the direction of the front door.

Fear cascaded over her when she saw the doorknob begin to turn . . .

Chapter Thirty-three

LION BURST THROUGH the door, looking like a wild, wet animal. His eyes were as stormy as the sea; rain highlighted the planes of his bronzed face, while his quickly donned clothing clung to every steely muscle.

Relief and joy warred with fury and outrage in Meagan. She wanted to fly into his arms and hold fast to his broad shoulders, but pride forced her to remember the injury so recently dealt her.

So Lion was rewarded for his perilous ride by the sight of Meagan lifting her chin. The violet eyes he loved so well were narrowed, their soft color hidden behind a barrier of lush black lashes.

How tiny she appeared! The stairs surrounding her seemed endless, and Meagan looked like a pitiful waif all wrapped in her blanket, wet ebony hair drying into a wealth of curls, until Lion's eyes reached her face and saw that stubborn, challenging expression. She might be a female, fragile in appearance, but her spirit was proving to be as strong as his own.

"What do you want?" Meagan demanded in a voice that quavered only slightly.

"What the hell do you mean?" he shouted. "I risked my life to come after you—to make certain you hadn't gotten yourself killed in this storm! And you act as though I'm dropping by at an inconvenient moment! I regret that I was unable to send word of my imminent arrival!"

Meagan stood up, wishing she could match his imposing height as he strode nearer. "Oh, that's right! Pretend as though you weren't the cause of my coming out today! The reason why I couldn't turn back—"

"Have you taken leave of your senses? You would kill yourself over that ridiculous story spread by Bramble?"

"Bramble is not addlebrained. Would you tell me that she made it up?"

"No, but "

Eyes spitting purple fire, Meagan turned to run up the stairway, dropping the blanket en route. Lion took the steps three at a time and, halfway up, caught her elbow. Angrily, he spun her around.

"Have you no faith at all in me?"

"Faith? Why should you expect that? After all, *I* have been the one to deny your fidelity to Priscilla! I should be well aware of your weaknesses—"

"Bitch!" He gripped her other arm, shaking her once so that her head snapped back painfully. "You insist on soiling the one fine thing in either of our lives! Perhaps it's time you learned the difference between sweet and sour . . ."

One long, lean arm moved to hook behind her knees. Meagan's head was spinning against Lion's hard shoulder as he carried her into his future bedchamber and tossed her on the huge bed. Her clothing was still wet; thin muslin molded itself to her body and Meagan blushed under his bold scrutiny, conscious of her cold, wet nipples so plainly outlined against the sheerness of her bodice.

There was something in his eyes, in the tension of his hard-muscled body, that frightened her. She had seen this side of him before, but always in relation to some third person—Priscilla, Kevin, Clarissa, or Marcus. His eyes were blue diamond chips, fire and ice clashing. His jaw was set ominously, and Meagan saw a muscle move across it; a bad sign. His wet darkened skin was stretched over a network of muscles and tendons, each one taut with some bitter rage that Meagan felt powerless to diminish.

Shrugging out of his leather coat, Lion walked closer to the bed, his eyes never leaving her. She was feeling quite alarmed by this time and made an instinctive attempt to escape off the other side of the bed, but he easily caught her arm, pulling her back roughly.

"My dear, I think you may have failed to perceive the true extent of my past gallantry toward you. Obviously you believe that this behavior has been substandard for me; you have persisted in the notion that I regard you as a plaything, or if I may quote you—a prostitute. It would seem that my repeated denials have not been taken seriously. I am beginning to chafe under your constant vilification of my character and my motives.

"This morning has broken my patience. Since you refuse to be persuaded by gentler means, you force me to change my tactics. Perhaps this argument will convince you that my *past* treatment of you has not been as mean-spirited as you suppose . . ."

His grip tightened on her arm and for a moment their eyes met and locked, as charged with dark emotion as the angry storm outside. Meagan was chilled and baffled by Lion's speech; his deadly calm frightened her more than any amount of shouting.

"Take your hands off me."

Lightning white teeth flashed when Lion laughed coldly in response. "Not this time, fondling. I am about to give you a lesson in the true nature of the relationship between a man and his whore." Another humorless smile. "Rule One: the woman keeps her mouth closed unless she is being kissed. Naturally, since she is being used, her feelings are immaterial."

"Lion! You scurrilous beast! If you think I am going

291

to stay here and put up with this insanity, you have another think coming! Now, let me go!"

"No." His eyes were so hard, like a cat stalking its prey. Already wet and chilled, Meagan began to shake; she had never been in a situation where she felt so powerless and ineffectual.

"I will hate you forever if you do this," she cried hotly, struggling against the dark hands which held her forearms like iron bands. Lion did not reply, merely narrowing his eyes before pulling her up to meet his lips. When Meagan twisted her head back and forth to avoid the kiss, he let go of her arms and transferred his hands to her head. The pressure of his palms was like a vise, but still Meagan felt a sharp, searing response as their mouths came together. Helplessly, she tried to keep her lips pressed coldly together under the fiery roughness of Lion's, but it was impossible. As she kissed him back, angry tears of frustration sprang up in her eyes, and somehow she managed to stop her arms from embracing his neck.

Instead, she struck out, alternately hitting and scratching, but seldom making contact. Within seconds, Lion caught both her wrists with his left hand and cuffed her across the face with his right. The blow carried more humiliation than pain. Meagan's cheeks burned; she prepared to spit at him, but he cupped her chin hard.

"I wouldn't do that." Still holding her delicate wrists, Lion calmly unfastened the damp muslin gown with his free hand. Her flesh was thoroughly chilled, and his lean fingers seemed warm and dry in contrast. The leather coat and boots, doeskin gloves, and fawn breeches had done much to protect Lion's body from the drenching rain, though his champagne hair and upper torso remained damp.

The gauzy dress was removed. Lion's eyes remained opaque as he gripped Meagan's waist over her thin chemise and pulled her against the length of his body. Steely arms enfolded her, pinning her own at her sides as he yanked her raven hair to force her head back.

The kiss which followed was impersonal, hot, and

degrading. Meagan felt as though she were in the arms of some cruel stranger, yet she was still beset by familiar currents of fire when his mouth moved along the line of her throat. The rational part of her brain was determined to surpass Lion's coolness, but it was impossible.

The shift in mood came so gradually that neither of them noticed. Lion had planned to push Meagan back into the bed, but when they moved onto it together, it didn't even register with him. His touch was gentler when he slid her chemise down, and it was no stranger's mouth that grazed her breasts.

She wanted to pull his hair or kick between his legs, but flying would have been more possible. The chemise was being eased over her hips, then warm lips touched her cold belly. Desire was a consuming ache that throbbed wherever his hands or mouth touched. When Meagan reached up helplessly to trace the familiar lines of his face and shoulders, the depth of her plight hit her like the stab of a knife. Salty tears filled her eyes and spilled down her temples.

"I hate you!" she choked. "Hate you! Hate—" Her voice broke on a sob as Lion parted her legs to find the eager sweetness awaiting him.

To the casual observer, Marcus Reems seemed to possess an exceptional quantity of confidence at all times. However, this aura of self-assurance was usually contrived; Marcus had spent twenty years learning to camouflage his emotions. No one could have guessed, except Lion Hampshire perhaps, that he was constantly plagued by insecurity. It ate at him insidiously, chewing up the small amounts of warmth he had once possessed. Whenever he accomplished something he thought he wanted, he had only to look for Lion to discover that he remained always a step behind, and until he had what Lion had, until Lion was envying *him,* Marcus would never be satisfied.

Tonight, however, his cool self-confidence was genuine. At last, luck seemed ready to shine on him and cast its shadow over Lion. Even the storm seemed an appropriate omen . . . Marcus took another long drink of Claussen's exceedingly fine cognac, enjoying the sensation of it running down his throat. Hot velvet, he thought, and welcome on a night as black and rainy as this.

His gold tiger eyes swept the room, cynically appraising the carved furniture with its bright, flame-stitched upholstery. At length, he located the clock. The chit had kept him waiting nearly half an hour! If his news were not so juicy, Marcus wouldn't have bothered to stay, but . . .

The double doors leading to the stair hall swung open and Clarissa swept into the room. She was clad in a stylish gown of Ming green muslin over cream silk, but the smile she gave Marcus was tight and forced.

"Well, I see Daddy has furnished you with ample refreshment."

"Little enough in return for my patience," he observed sardonically.

"I don't recall inviting you."

"You'll wish you had when you hear my news. Sit down, darling, and try not to look so disagreeable."

"Lovely weather we're having," Clarissa said peevishly as she lay back on a daybed and watched as Marcus refilled his glass. When he turned to meet her eyes again, she was startled by the wicked smile that lit his face.

"You have not met with Lion alone since our ill-fated kidnap attempt—am I right? How long has it been? Three, four weeks? No wonder you look so . . . pinched."

"You know perfectly well how long it's been!" Clarissa snapped, pulling nervously at the edges of her gown. "And don't remind me, for your own sake! You *promised* me, Marcus, that you would find another way, and thus far—"

"You really must curb these shrewish tendencies, darling, if you plan to be a suitable wife for our Lion." He paused, smiling catlike over the rim of his glass as he took a slow drink. "Did you truly imagine that I

294

would fail? Clarissa, my sweet, we shall both see this affair to a happy conclusion."

His dark face was so cool and confident that Clarissa felt a bright spark of hope flare in her heart. Suddenly, her cheeks grew pink, her movements animated, and she crossed the room to sit beside Marcus.

"Don't tease me!" she implored. "Tell me your news!"

"That is better." He caressed her cheek lightly with cold fingers. "I have just come from Mansion House. The library was so cozy and intimate tonight . . . I hadn't seen Priscilla for a few days and it seems that there have been a number of new developments in her life."

"Yes?" Clarissa's eyes were almost feverishly bright.

"My sweet Southern charmer has been keeping things from me. If she had confided in me earlier, it would have saved you and me many days of worry." Marcus paused to light a long cigar, obviously enjoying the increased suspense.

"If I wished to witness dramatics, I could go to the theater! Do be brief!"

"You are lovely when you're in a temper, darling. Now, where were we?"

"About to hear about the secret developments in Priscilla's life!"

"Oh, Clarissa, it is *rich*. It seems that the ardent bridegroom is not so ardent after all. In fact . . . he has postponed the wedding until after the journey to New York. He told Priscilla that it may be arranged during their stay in the capital. Otherwise, the grand event will have to wait until they return here." He grinned satanically. "Eager, isn't he?"

Clarissa matched Marcus's smile. "That *is* lovely news. When did this happen?"

"Apparently, over a week ago. But, darling, there is more . . . much more. Lion's 'reason' for this delay was a mountain of business which supposedly demanded his immediate attention. Priscilla was hurt and slightly suspicious. Of course . . . if I had known about this, I could have told her days ago that the only business Lion has been engaged in has been that little serving-wench—along with furnishing that unfashionable villa he's bought. Incidentally, Priscilla is none too pleased about that, either; he refused her pleas to get something near Landsdowne."

"You say he's still seeing that girl?" Clarissa queried, pricked by the mention of the chit who had outwitted her with a tree branch.

"Constantly. As a matter of fact, though Anne Bingham thought she had managed to dispose of her in Henry Gardner's hands, I have reason to suspect that Lion has her in his house now. You know how ridiculously understaffed he was."

"She couldn't be—"

"Housekeeper, yes. That's what I've heard. But that's neither here nor there. We both know better than anyone that Lion would *never* marry a serving-girl. That is the one mistake he could *not* afford . . ."

"It won't last," Clarissa sniffed.

"No, but neither did you. Ah, ah! No tantrums. At any rate, we digress; the issue here is Lion's betrothal to Priscilla." He licked his lips, savoring the rest of the story while thunder rumbled outside to punctuate the silence. "You see, I believe that Lion, in his consummate self-assurance, has played right into our hands. It seems that Priscilla is not as malleable as he presumed. He has virtually ignored her from the beginning, but when he placed so little value on their wedding date, it was a slap in the face that truly stung her pride."

"Poor thing," Clarissa laughed.

"She plays the wronged maiden most engagingly," he agreed. "The climax to all this has convinced me that our luck has changed; the game is all but won.

"A day or two ago, Priscilla was having tea at Mary Morris's house, and whom do you suppose she saw from an upstairs window?"

"Not—?"

"Precisely. Priscilla's all-business fiancé and her erstwhile lady's maid, walking together on High Street and laughing quite gaily. The girl was disguised as a stableboy!"

"Is she truly angry? I mean, angry enough to actually break the engagement?"

Marcus puffed on his cigar. "Probably not—if she had no alternate course of action. However, I mean to show her that she does. Skillfully, of course . . . I must tread with caution. There is one more hopeful sign. Priscilla sent Lion a message today saying that she would be busy 'indefinitely' and that he should not call on her. I imagine that she hoped he would dash right over, the picture of repentance, but instead there was no word at all. I think that—and this wonderful storm—drove her to telling me all." He laughed noiselessly. "It is a priceless situation, though. Poor, poor Lion . . . he'll be so busy enjoying his last days with that kitchen wench that he won't see the trap until it is sprung. And, after Priscilla is safely mine and the inauguration is at hand, there will be only one thing he can do to regain some of his lost ground and save face in New York . . ."

Clarissa giggled, chewing on one long, lacquered nail. "You are a genius! *This* time it will work—and before the month is out, I will be Mrs. Lional Hampshire!"

Chapter Thirty-four

BY SOME MIRACLE, the long, black, storm-swept night became a most glorious morning. Meagan awoke, wrapped in Lion's embrace under layers of cozy quilts, to find the bedchamber awash with lemony sunshine.

Tentatively, she worked herself out of Lion's arms and was surprised when he groaned and dropped over on his back, still asleep. Meagan crept out of bed, naked, to find the air cool, but refreshingly so. The drenching light took the edge off the chill, as did the persistent fire across the room. There, before it, her ruined muslin gown had been spread over two comb-back chairs.

When had Lion lit the fire and taken care of her dress? she wondered. If he had been up puttering around during the night, that surely accounted for the depth of his slumber now. Teasing the back of her mind was the question of why he had been restless . . . Could he have been troubled by conscience, or perhaps even more profound emotions?

Meagan donned her underclothes and dress, refastening the wilted heather sash as best she could. She slipped into Priscilla's future bedchamber through the connecting door and appraised her appearance in the dressing-table mirror. Hopelessly disheveled . . . but radiant, somehow. Her hair was soft and full with unruly curls; many of which had formed as she squirmed beneath Lion in bed. Her lips were so rosy as to appear bruised, and they very nearly were. Muscles in her thighs ached wonderfully. And her cheeks and eyes . . . Meagan couldn't repress a grin as she noted the way they glowed. Dear God, she thought, any fool could see I'm in love and have been involved in that very act for hours and hours!

Slowly she made her way barefoot down the white trellised stairway. Heaven was no longer in the entry hall, obviously having been moved when the storm subsided. Had Lion been up all night?

How much of what had passed between them had been real and how much a dream?

Sunlight flooded the parlor, illuminating all the new pieces of furniture in a room that had been bare and musty only a fortnight before. A lump rose in Meagan's throat as she remembered the many happy hours spent planning and working to achieve this effect— warmth mingling with tastefulness. The wide–planked floor was glossy; a stunning Kuba rug in shades of blue, gray, cranberry, and tan replaced the worn

Turkey carpet. The paneled walls were painted gray and white and the fireplace was newly faced with snowy white marble. Flanking a long window were two wing chairs upholstered in blood-red moreen, while the draperies around the room had been fashioned of the same material. Several brass candlesticks added fire and warmth on the mantelpiece and each table.

Meagan was proud of the room. It was part of her, part of Lion, part of their time together. It hurt her to think of Priscilla as mistress of Markwood Villa, knowing that she could never feel the proper love and affinity for the house.

Turning around, she crossed to the dining room, but paused only briefly. This was their best achievement, Lion's enthusiastic creation. It was his piece of the past, reflecting the best of the Orient. A rich Chinese Ch'ien Lung rug in jade tones covered the floor, while the walls were papered with an enchanting pattern of bamboo, tree peonies, and butterflies on a muted green surface. All the furniture was simply beautiful, each piece the finest Chinese Chippendale, skillfully decorated with exquisite latticework and fretwork. Already, Lion had begun to fill the velvet-lined breakfront shelves with his porcelains and other treasures.

Tears brimmed in Meagan's eyes as she ran slim fingers along the carved back of a chair, remembering the day they had arranged the furniture. Lion had stepped back to appraise the final picture, then abruptly let out a shout of happiness more eloquent than any words. His eyes, seeking hers, had spoken volumes, and when he caressed the sweep of hair down her back, Meagan knew that he felt as she did about their joint transformation of Markwood Villa.

Now, she withdrew her hand from the chair's latticeback and walked quickly through the house to the garden door. The weather was as celestial this morning as it had been satanic the day before. Spring gave its full embrace to the garden, and after the intensity of the storm, the plants seemed lush beyond belief.

The air was poignantly fresh and cool; rain droplets glittered on every leaf and blade of grass.

Meagan strolled over the brick footpaths which divided the huge flowerbeds. They had hired men to weed the garden, but did most of the planting themselves. The boxwood, neatly trimmed into square borders, lent its dry, pungent scent to the air, mixing with the richly fragrant wisteria which was just beginning to open its white and violet blossoms. Soon the bees will be swarming over it, Meagan thought.

She made her way toward the place where the ground bent into a gentle hill, in the opposite direction from the woods and the tiny schoolroom. The garden had been tiered to follow the incline downward and the footpath gave way to flagstone steps. Meagan's bare feet descended into the wildness of this hidden paradise where leafy arbors went unpruned and there was no boxwood to mask the sweet aromas of the spring flowers.

Blushing moss-pink roses stained the terraces, but it was impossible for them to obscure the other multi-hued blooms struggling back toward the sun after the beating they had suffered under the lashing rain. Proud, blazing yellow daffodils danced above the trailing borders of grape hyacinths and bright pansies. Southernwood shrubs grew along the end of the steps, trimmed by cheerfully striped ribbon grass. Weeping willow and honey-locust trees hovered over the masses of greenery yet to bloom: hollyhocks, larkspur, moss roses, honeysuckle, jessamine, sweet cinnamon roses, and curling grapevines.

Meagan spread her skirts and sat down on the damp flagstone, grieving anew for the colors, the shapes, and the fragrances she would miss in months to come. Her pain was keen and of such complexity that it defied analysis.

Threading her fingers through the tangled black hair which haloed her face, Meagan leaned down to rest against her drawn-up knees. Slowly, she attempted to fit together the pieces from yesterday's puzzle. Hours went unaccounted for; could they have spent so much time entwined in the warmth of Lion's quilted bed? She could remember little else besides endless soft caresses, luxurious kisses, dozing fused to Lion's body, and his eyes, smile, magic touch. Fire . . .

It was like a day outside of time, outside of the world they knew. What had it meant?

Meagan was too bewildered, disoriented, and pained to think of any strategy. Her relationship with Lion was no longer so simple; she doubted that a solution existed or that either of them would ultimately claim a victory.

It was unseasonably hot for the eighteenth of April; in fact, each day of the week following the storm had grown warmer.

At noon, Lion and Meagan shared a light luncheon of fish soufflé, baked carrots, and wilted spinach salad. Both of them turned down Bramble's almond cheesecake in favor of yesterday's butter thins, drawing from the cook the first sour expression that Lion had noticed in days. As he and Meagan walked out to the garden, slowly eating their dessert, he remarked, "Is it my imagination, or has Bramble's attitude actually softened toward me?"

"She hasn't said a cross word for days. In fact, I can't recall seeing her frown in our direction." Meagan's smile faded slightly. "I have an idea that she feels sorry for me . . . for us."

Lion looked up sharply, but Meagan had turned to cut a cluster of white wisteria from the trellis next to the back door. Dreamily, she smiled and buried her nose in the fragrant blossoms.

It was their custom these days to stroll in the small, neat garden after lunch. Meagan kept ribboned shears to fasten at her waist so that she might assemble a bouquet for the dinner table. The narrow brick walkways passed miniature box-edged flowerbeds lined with bright tulips and daffodils. Meagan liked to relax on the tree-shaded bench; sometimes she and Lion would sit there for over an hour, totally unaware of the passage of time.

"My dear," Lion began with a wry smile, "I would take exception to your premonitions of impending doom—"

"But you are already due at Dr. Franklin's," she finished, grinning.

"True." He led her behind the great shade tree. "Also, I have no heart for quarreling with you."

His hands were on her back, warm through the pale lavender of her dress. They stood close together, quietly burning with unquenchable love. Meagan laid her cheek against the linen of his shirt until he tipped her chin up for a slow, stirring kiss.

"You should go," she whispered softly.

"I know."

But instead, Lion kissed her again and seemed far from eager to depart.

Except for the high voices of Franklin's playing grandchildren, all was peaceful in the rear yard. Lion leaned against a familiar mulberry tree, listening to the birds sing and the children shout. From time to time, a door would slam as the trio, who ranged within a birthday or two on either side of ten years of age, dashed out. Lion could almost time the appearance, moments later, of five-year-old Richard, squealing in outrage at having been left behind.

When acquaintances, even friends, spoke in hushed tones of the Doctor's decline, they frequently mentioned Sally Bache's "undisciplined, irritating" children. Lion smiled as he thought of this, for he knew well enough that the youngsters' exuberance was Franklin's favorite tonic.

Sally Bache threw open a window and called to Lion to come in. Her father was awake. After much coaxing, she allowed Lion to take the tray of scones and tea that she had assembled, saving her at least one of her numerous daily treks up the stairs.

"I suppose you are going to be married any day now, hmm?" she inquired with a motherly smile. "You must know that we were all most charmed by your intended."

Lion winced inwardly at her innocent reminder of the mire of quicksand in which he had immersed himself. "Ah—I agree that she is a lovely girl." A neutral statement; no more lies.

On the stairway, Lion was astonished to feel his hands go clammy at the thought of the long confession he was about to make to his mentor. When he paused on the landing, an encouraging voice called, "Lion, are you ill or merely slow? I have better things to do than listen to your halting approach."

Lion was caught off guard by the sight of him, as he had been on the occasion of their first meeting. This time, Dr. Franklin was reclining complacently in his custom-made sitz bath. The tub was shaped like a great copper shoe; Franklin sat in the heel, while his pale legs nearly reached the toe. A convenient rack had been fitted in the instep to hold his books.

Apparently spring had proven to be an effective medicine, for not since the warm autumn of 1787, when Lion had left on his year-long journey to the Orient, had he seen Franklin looking this well. Of course, he appeared thin and weak, but there was reassuring color in his face.

"Doctor, I am pleased to see you looking so fit! That is, if you haven't been rouging your cheeks on the sly."

Franklin chuckled, extending a hand for Lion to clasp. "Sit down, my boy, and pour me a bit of that tea." He closed the book on his rack and slid it to one side. "No, I haven't been rouging my cheeks . . . I may love the French, but I can't say I agree with all their fashions!" After sipping gratefully from his cup, he continued, "I am feeling rather better. It's been a while since I had any attacks of the stones. My only complaint is this damned weather; it's giving me a chill I cannot be rid of."

Lion raised both eyebrows in perplexity. He thought the room stiflingly hot and had been on the verge of opening the windows.

"Well, I'm happy you've had relief from the pain. Have you given any thought to venturing out when

General Washington arrives? If not to Gray's Ferry, perhaps you might attend the dinner at City Tavern—"

"Don't tempt me, Lion. Sally would horsewhip you if she heard such words from your mouth!" His eyes were twinkling, yet sad. "As they say, the spirit is willing . . ."

"I'm sorry I mentioned it. It is difficult for me to know what you are capable of, since you seem to be so able verbally," Lion smiled gently.

"Quite true. My tongue is the equal of any twenty-year-old man! But, since you ask, physically I am capable of traveling downstairs on a good day, after a large dose of laudanum. If I am feeling exceptionally adventurous, I might sit in the garden and share tea with a guest or two." The Doctor paused, staring at his bony knees, and let out a ragged sigh. "To be honest . . . for my personal comfort, I should have died two years ago."

Those words, void of Franklin's usual humor, wrenched Lion so that he could not speak or move. Finally, he bent beside the copper tub and took the old man's hand. It was cold; the skin was white and flabby against Lion's lean, tan fingers.

"It's selfish of me to say, but I must tell you how thankful I am you did *not* die two years ago. If you had, we would never have met—our association has changed my life."

"Time will tell if your outcome will be favorable or not!" The weary eyes were dancing again. "My boy, would you help me up? I should like to dry myself and return to bed. We can chat until you work up the courage to challenge me at cribbage."

They were silent for a few minutes as Lion assisted the Doctor back to bed, then sat tensely in a plush wing chair nearby. There seemed to be no easy way to confess his problems, so the conversation focused on the older man for nearly half an hour. Relaxed after the interlude in his sitz bath, Franklin spoke at length, candidly, about his current activities and feelings.

Lion learned that he had finally heeded the urgings

of his friends and begun work again on the autobiography. Benny, the oldest of the Bache children and his grandfather's adoring protégé, had been taking down the newest installments when Franklin was in too much pain, or too tired, to write.

"The account has passed my fiftieth year now," he confided, "but I worry about the quality. Somehow, I fear that I am not saying the right things in the right way . . ."

"Ridiculous! I have never heard you voice an insecurity before today."

"My boy, after eighty-three years of perfection, there *is* the possibility that certain of my abilities might erode."

"You spend too much time imagining the worst."

"On the contrary." His eyes moved to gaze out the window, as if seeing beyond time and space. "I would rather think of anything but my own decline. I dwell on the past, the decades of challenge, other cities and countries . . ." He smiled. "Even during my catnaps, I dream of wonderful women. Daily I yearn for my dear Madame Helvétius and her thousand sofas . . ."

"Doctor Franklin, if your attachment to her was so great, why did you leave France?"

"I felt an instinctive wish to draw my last breath in America; to see my Philadelphia again." He drained his second cup of tea. "So! Enough about me. Since we speak of women, tell me how your lovely Priscilla fares. What great good fortune for you to have found such an enchanting minx on pure chance!"

Lion smiled miserably, searching for the right words. "Ah—actually, I do want to talk to you about this. You see—" he loosened his cravat "—the fact is, the girl you met was not Priscilla. I mean, there *is* a Priscilla and we *are* betrothed, but I don't love her. Worse, I can barely endure her company."

Franklin's pale brows were raised in his high forehead; his expression combined gentle, amused tolerance with sharp concern. "I gather that you *can* endure the company of the mysterious young lady I met?"

Lion began to pace. "I did not set out to deceive

you in this matter. I meant to introduce her to you correctly, but you assumed . . . and she seemed to cheer you up . . ."

"She was delightful." There was a meaningful pause. "Who was she?"

Lion clenched his fist. "Her name is Meagan South. She was Priscilla's lady's maid. She traveled with us from West Hills."

Slowly, then, Lion divulged the truth, one painful fact at a time, until the whole story was made known to Dr. Franklin. He finished by relating the events of the past week.

"Somehow, it has changed. The bargain we struck, I mean. The anger and determination are gone . . . I'm certain that she loves me, and it's as if she's resigned to it, but I am uneasy about the way she behaves."

"Are you worried that she still won't agree to be your mistress?"

"I don't know!" The hard muscular outline of Lion's back showed through his coat as he pressed his hands against the door frame. "She screamed and fought like a tiger the day of the storm. We had an argument. Christ, I was furious at some of the things she said to me! She was unfair, but I was worse, I suppose—I forced her, I wanted to teach her a lesson, but she wouldn't give in.

"Anyway, in the end, we spent hours together in that bed, waiting out the storm. After she quit fighting me, it was as if she were on fire. We both were. We still are—it's like being consumed by hell and heaven all at once." He looked back to the bed, turning tortured eyes on Franklin. "Do you know what I mean?"

"Yes."

"Well, for God's sake, what am I going to do?" Lion began to pace again, but the older man remained calm.

"Obviously, you are aware of your choices."

"I'm telling you that I am in no condition to analyze this situation objectively!"

"All right, then, let me assist you. First, we both

306

know that in view of your own beginnings, it would be fatal politically speaking for you to marry a serving-girl. Could you give up your career dreams for Meagan? And I don't mean just for this month or year. Could you forfeit your plans for the rest of your life and not regret the decision or resent her?"

"Why don't you stop asking questions I can't answer and give me some advice, damn it! You are the one who pushed me into this fiasco with Priscilla!"

"Lion, you are certainly imposing, blazing like that over me, but you should know better than to try intimidating me into accepting the guilt or responsibility for your situation. You are very much an adult. You could have married any woman you chose, but you made the decision to avoid a love match, not I. Just because you had no proof of love's reality, you denied its existence. The lesson has been cruelly learned, *n'est-ce pas?*"

Lion did not answer. His face was averted once more, his body absolutely taut.

"I would not make the same mistake again by giving you more advice. I can only help you see the questions you must answer before a choice can be made. Those answers, and the ultimate decision, must be yours alone."

Lion turned back and their eyes met. Compassion soothed pain.

Finally, Dr. Franklin spoke again, softly. "I cannot influence you, my boy. We are different people and you must not live your life by my rules or inclinations. There is one bit of wisdom I will pass on. This was written by the late husband of Madame Helvétius. He said that 'by annihilating the desires, you annihilate the mind. Every man without passions has within him no principle of action, no motive to act.'

"So, it is up to you to decide which of your passions is stronger—more important. Apparently, you will be denied the pleasure of satisfying them both."

Chapter Thirty-five

THE SCENE THAT evening in the Binghams' card room was cozy and civilized—on the surface. Anne and William were engaged in a rare game of whist, but Anne's long fingernails clicked nervously on the table-top as she watched Priscilla.

Marcus Reems was watching her as well, seated on the same tapestry-covered sofa where Lion had kissed her so savagely. Priscilla was upset tonight; possibly just angry enough to act in haste. She moved agitatedly around the room, stopping at different windows, fingering the drapes as she peered outside. Marcus's tiger eyes were cunningly alert, glowing with pleasure as he perceived the last pieces of his plan falling so effortlessly into place. *It is almost too easy,* he thought.

Their game done, William and Anne left the room to kiss their children goodnight. Marcus was careful in his nonchalant silence, watching Priscilla take one last look outside.

"Were you hoping for a visit from Lion?"

She spun around, surprised and confused. "What? Why, no! At least—well, it would certainly seem proper! Even though I wrote him that I would be too busy to see him for a long time, he might have protested a bit, don't you think?" Her voice broke, and Marcus was on his feet silently, putting his strong arms around her as the first tear escaped.

"Darling Priscilla, how I despise him for treating you so shabbily! You deserve so much more. I could kill him for hurting you this way!"

Priscilla turned wet emerald eyes up to him and al-

308

lowed her lower lip to tremble. His reaction was all she could wish for. "Oh, Marcus, I simply don't understand why he should be so cruel to me! What have I done?" She sobbed sweetly against his broad chest. "Do you know, tomorrow is his birthday and I have had a present ready for over a week. I bought him the handsomest pearl stickpin for his stock . . . I thought we could make up our differences if he would promise me to send Meagan away." She paused to sniffle delicately into Marcus's snowy handkerchief. "I could never admit this to anyone but you . . . but I have not had so much as a note from Lion for days and days. I was so certain that he would come tonight—that he would invite me to share his birthday—"

"My darling, it is wrong of me to say it, but I cannot help myself! Seeing you in such pain—all because of that villain—makes me wild with rage. My sweet, I cannot allow you to marry such a cad. I love you, Priscilla! I will soon be as wealthy as Lion. With you beside me, I shall overtake him immediately! Please—" He kissed her with studied tenderness. "Please, my love, say that you will be my wife. You deserve a man who loves you as I do . . . and Lion deserves the ruin this will bring to him!"

Priscilla was faint with emotion. She had tried so hard and long to make Lion respond to her as Marcus did. Such success at last was dizzying.

"Yes! Oh, yes, Marcus!"

They kissed for several minutes; Priscilla was lightheaded with power.

"It is terrible of me to do this to Lion, but as you say, he deserves it. Besides, he will have Meagan now. I'm certain she will finally come forward with the truth—"

"What truth?" Marcus nibbled on one soft alabaster ear.

"Why, the truth about who she is! But, that's right —I never told you! Why, Meagan's surname isn't South at all; it's Sayers!" Priscilla giggled, but Marcus's face had frozen to stone. She turned back to the parted drapes, seeming to see past the streets off

Society Hill to the plantations of Fairfax County, her face softer than it had been in weeks. "You see, Meagan's daddy was richer than mine—her blood is bluer. She's related to titles in England. But, Mr. Sayers spent his money by the bucket—not that he was any different from all the other rich men in Virginia. Meagan's mama had the best of everything; her parties were famous, her home was more beautiful than any house I ever saw . . . except this one, of course!

"But then, Mr. and Mrs. Sayers died last year, and Meagan took the punishment for their extravagance. Pecan Grove, their plantation, was going to be sold to pay the debts . . . every last rug and chair and slave. Meagan was supposed to go north to Boston to live with some old aunt, but she came running to West Hills—"

"Don't tell me the two of you *knew* each other!" Marcus ejaculated.

"Don't be silly! We were best friends." She continued to look out over the darkened rooftops. "Not really. We were more like sisters who didn't get along very well. I never understood Meagan; she was as outrageous and rebellious as an unbroken horse. Only *she* could have masqueraded as a maid to keep from going to live with that aunt . . ." Priscilla felt a strange lump form in her throat and it was necessary for her to swallow a few times before her voice returned. "It was all her idea. She nearly forced me to go along with it. I can't be responsible for the mess she's made!"

She looked back to find Marcus watching her broodingly and attempted a lighthearted smile. "Well, perhaps she and Lion are right for each other, just as you are right for me. Thank the good Lord we all found out before it was too late!"

Priscilla clung to Marcus's shoulders again, searching out his lips, but his response was suddenly distant.

Lion spent his thirty-third birthday at Markwood Villa with Meagan. It had never crossed his mind to visit his fiancée; already he dreaded having to take her to Gray's Garden the next day to view Washington's arrival.

In the meantime, he and Meagan took a long walk through the budding woods around the villa and ate a picnic lunch on the garden lawn. Meagan wore a simple frock of clover-sprigged muslin, its wide leaf-green sash tied at one side. The neckline was cut deep to reveal ivory breasts occasionally obscured by glossy, unbound raven curls. Lion loved every moment spent in her company, as fascinated by her appearance and gestures as she was by his. He thought he had never known a high-born woman with an innate grace and alert, witty mind to match Meagan's. Every smile, blush, and toss of her curls seemed lovelier than the last. In her company under the dazzling April sun, Lion forgot the problems so clearly spelled out by Dr. Franklin.

At twilight, they prepared a light supper in the huge kitchen, bantering back and forth over the correct cooking procedures. Lion opened a bottle of champagne so that they might toast the day, and they ate and drank side by side in the Oriental dining room.

Evening hung overhead, blue-gray and waiting. Meagan knew Lion would want to return to the house on Pine Street before total darkness set in, but she managed to put him off with one last glass of champagne. Slipping into the parlor after dinner, she retrieved her reticule which bulged suspiciously. Meagan had saved scrupulously for Lion's birthday gift, combing the shops every day since the storm to find the perfect token of her feelings.

Lion was stunned and deeply moved when she presented him with the package. It was a small lion, fashioned of Staffordshire pottery, with a body of ocher and a brown mane, standing on a pale green base. Its head was tilted in proud arrogance; even the muscles in the back and legs were carefully detailed.

"It seemed just the thing . . ." Meagan offered after a long minute of silence.

He looked up, clearly touched. "Only you—" he began, breaking off in what might have been a tide of

311

emotion. One hand went out to pull her onto his lap and they kissed with bittersweet fervor, the pottery lion wedged between them.

A silvery slice of moon hung suspended in the ebony sky, shooting down sharp, diamond-bright rays that pierced muslin bed-hangings of the field bed in Meagan's own room. Only moments ago, the tall-case clock in the entry hall had struck midnight, ending Lion's birthday, but he and Meagan didn't notice. They lay naked between the cool linen sheets, making love with the same poignant intensity that had marked their first coupling and each interlude since.

When they lay still at last, hearts pounding in exhilarated unison, Meagan turned her face just enough to seek out Lion's eyes. The fierce emotion blazing from deep within them almost startled her.

Impulsively, she accused him in a hoarse whisper, "You love me!"

Lion turned his head and slowly moved away from her. The fireplace was dark, leaving only the blue-white moonbeams to illuminate his body as he stood up and walked over to the window. Meagan felt oddly detached observing him. The best sculptor could not chisel out a more splendid male form, she thought, or a more classic profile. The sweep of hair caught casually at Lion's neck gleamed in the moonlight; his clear sapphire eyes were serious as they contemplated the wisteria-drenched trellis outside.

"You may be right," he said at length. After a moment, he returned to bed and gathered Meagan into his lean, dark arms. "I think it is time for me to tell you the truth about myself. I never see a birthday that doesn't remind me of my childhood, my origins. Perhaps, when you've heard my story, you will understand why I hesitate to believe in love. It has always been a phenomenon I thought never to experience ..."

"Are you certain that you want to tell me?" Meagan could scarcely believe she had questioned him after all the time she had spent puzzling over this very subject.

"Don't interrupt. I might change my mind!" Lion admonished softly, pearlescent teeth sparkling in the darkness.

After pulling her back with him into the pillows, the crisp hair on his chest tickling Meagan's soft back, he closed his eyes and began, "I was born thirty-three years ago tonight in the countryside of New York. The details are not important now, so I will just give you the facts. My mother was not married to my father; people have called me a bastard, but I never felt like one . . . not until later. My mother was lovely, educated. It seemed that she met my father when she was too young not to trust a man who said he loved her. He was married, of course."

Meagan could hear the tenseness in his voice flare into hatred when he mentioned his father.

"I didn't know it then, but he was giving her money throughout my childhood, though I never met the man."

"What was your mother like?"

"She was clever, warm—but frequently ill. She was only sixteen when I was born and it seemed to break her health. She loved me, but I cost her a very different future that would have been hers if not for my father—and my birth. Her parents never forgave her and she had no true friends, so there was a sadness beneath every smile."

"Oh, Lion . . ." Meagan turned her face, nuzzling his hard upper arm. "Did you look like her?"

"No." He seemed to choke on the word. "I do have her eyes, but her hair was brown. Her features were fine and she was delicately built."

"And she died?" Meagan supplied gently. She felt his heart beating against her back before he answered.

"Yes. When I was fourteen."

"And . . ."

"And my father arrived, terribly uncomfortable about having to relocate me. To his amazement, I turned out to be nearly his double. God, I could have

313

died the first time we came face to face! He was disgustingly elated and decided to take me home and raise me as his son. What a joke! His son! Totally ignored for fourteen years—with no excuse whatever. He couldn't have lived more than twenty miles away."

"You went to live with him?"

"I had to. I went from poor fatherless boy to favorite son of a wealthy estate-owner. I arrived to find a dark, temperamental stepmother and a stepbrother whose hair was as black as mine and my father's was blond. The only physical trait he inherited from our father was the one I did not possess. They both had piercing gold eyes."

He paused while realization dawned on Meagan.

"Gold eyes? Do you mean . . . is *Marcus Reems* your stepbrother?" She twisted in his arms, scrambling onto her knees.

Lion leisurely cupped her breasts, kissing them, before responding, "Yes."

He went on to describe the following years in the Reems's household while his hands told Meagan a different story.

It seemed that Marcus had been ill-fated from birth. Nothing he ever tried was executed well enough to earn his father's approval. He lacked the indefinable qualities of luck and finesse as well as the ability to draw people to him. Thomas Reems was constantly frustrated by this son who resembled only his disagreeable wife.

Then he found Lion. Without even trying, the illegitimate youth outshone his stepbrother in every way, from schoolwork to his effortlessly magnetic personality. The elder Reems warmed enthusiastically to him and to the challenge of winning his love.

He never did.

"I have never been a hater by nature," Lion told Meagan, "but I could not find any seeds of affection within me for my father. He was calculating, like Marcus, and they both possessed ambition flawed by selfishness. My father's feelings for me were rooted in his own ego, not in honest love for *me*. He was ob-

314

sessed by the dreams of glory I might bring to his later years."

"How awful for you. How did you manage?"

"I persuaded him to send me away to school almost immediately. I attended the Academy of Philadelphia, then began at Harvard until the war demanded my attention. I hated being dependent on my father, but at that age it seemed I had no choice. At least, there was no other way to get the education I craved."

"And Marcus?"

"Oh, he was right there beside me all along, despising me more with each year. One can hardly blame him—for me to have suddenly appeared on the scene, almost a duplicate of our father, and winning the approval Marcus never could." Lion laughed bitterly. "Good God, what ludicrous irony. The last thing I desired was that man's approval. If it weren't so pathetic, it would have been funny."

They were silent for a few minutes, Lion lost in memories and Meagan watching the shadowy, cynical lines of his face, grieving for the young boy who had been embittered by those around him.

"At any rate," he continued softly, "I fought in the war, which seemed to be a good release for much of my anger, and after Yorktown, I went 'home' to straighten out some matters with my father. I wanted to finish at Harvard, but not with his money, so I decided to claim my mother's possessions—her furniture, jewelry, and the small amount of money she had put aside.

"But . . . when I arrived, I found Marcus waiting for me with the news of our father's death. He and my stepmother seemed to be certain that I would be falling down in my haste to claim my share of the estate. She informed me that my father had written a new will before he died, leaving me over half of his property . . . then they began laughing like maniacs and said they had witnessed it for him—and burned it later.

"I don't think Marcus ever hated me more than at that moment when I said that I wouldn't have soiled my hands with that money . . . That, if they hadn't burned the will, I would have. For years, he had lived to hurt me the way I had—by my very presence— hurt him. But it was the crowning blow to have his plan for revenge turned to dust."

"Lion! You feel sorry for him!" Meagan turned to face him again. "The man has hounded you for over half your life—"

"Oh, don't imagine that I harbor some secret fondness for Marcus!" he replied dryly. "Undoubtedly, he was shallow and flawed long before my arrival on his doorstep, and I certainly dislike him nearly as much as he dislikes me. Let us just say that I can see his point of view. And, yes, I pity him in some ways."

"I always wondered why you never got mad at him —especially that night he and Clarissa were ready to kidnap me! Everyone talks of you being enemies—"

"I simply hope that one day he will get over this and leave me alone." A muscle moved in his jaw. "Each time I see Marcus, I am reminded of my origins . . . of the father who branded me forever as his bastard son with his face, his body, and hair so blond that no one can ever forget it. Even my smile is his—"

"No! Your smile is your own. Perhaps on the surface, it seems similar, but yours is so special. As for the rest, you may look like him, but his touch, his scent, his movements could never have compared—" She broke off, blushing, under his keen scrutiny. "Well, now I understand why you don't use the name Thomas."

"How did you know that was my true name?" Lion asked sharply.

"Well—I saw your mother's Bible the night I did the accounts in your library."

"And you never asked about it?"

"It was not my affair. Your past is your own, to share as you wish." Her eyes began to twinkle then. "I will admit to curiosity!"

The hard lines softened in Lion's face and he lifted her up, slipping his arms around her slender back. He began kissing her with deliberate slowness until her fingers twisted in his hair. Meagan could barely hear the husky words spoken against her throat, "My love, you are delicious . . ."

Chapter Thirty-six

MEAGAN DOZED FITFULLY through the night but came fully awake before the dawn broke. There was no avoiding it; the time had come to reach a decision. The new day would bring General Washington to Philadelphia and that was the beginning of the end. Lion was taking Priscilla to the festivities at Gray's Ferry, followed by the dinner at City Tavern given in Washington's honor by Philadelphia's elite. Then, in days to come, the exodus to New York would begin, and Meagan knew that the dreaded wedding must be sandwiched in somewhere.

It was impossible to think clearly with Lion's warm, walnut-brown body against her own. The scent of him clung to the sheets and pillows, intoxicating her, yet intensifying the tight knot of melancholy in her chest. Just being near him made the idea of becoming his mistress seem plausible; she could barely hear the voice within that said such an arrangement would rub every facet of her personality the wrong way. It would mean the sacrifice of her identity and independence. The voice grew stronger, warning her that eventually she would begin to hate herself—then Lion, as well.

Carefully she slipped out of her bed, deciding that the only way to think clearly would be to separate herself from the powerful magnet of Lion's presence. Drawing on a silk wrapper, Meagan padded through the house to the cozy library. She sat down behind

Lion's desk and surveyed the room, letting the memories of other days return. The first meeting with Clarissa . . . the night Lion brought her here after her arm was cut . . . the time she had fallen asleep on the sofa and woke to find Lion kneeling on the floor, his cheek against her hand. So many kisses, so much laughter—even the memories of their fiery arguments made her nostalgic.

The sun was beginning to rise; a golden-pink glow lightened the library. Meagan pressed her hands to her temples and forced herself to think.

One painful conclusion was clear. After what Lion had told her last night, she could not hope to be his wife. The reasons for his "respectable" marriage were apparent now. She thought, I should have known he could not be so cold-bloodedly ambitious without a reason! All the things I have thought and said were so unfair and cruel . . .

The only question remaining was whether the love they shared might be of greater importance than his dream of government service. What would Lion decide to do if she revealed her *own* past to him? Was there any chance at all that his reputation could survive the scandal of a broken engagement on the eve of the wedding?

Later she would wonder at the twist of fate which left the book by Thomas Paine on Lion's desk, only inches from her hand. It was well-thumbed and marked with a scrap of newspaper. She opened it to that page and read a passage that seemed to shout directly at her:

> We have it in our power to begin the world again . . . 'Tis not the concern of a day, a year, or an age; posterity are virtually involved in the contest, and will be more or less affected to the end of time by the proceedings now. Now is the seed-time of the Continental union.

The words had as much effect on Meagan as her first view of the State House. Tears stung her eyes as

318

she reread the eloquent paragraph, feeling smaller and more insignificant with each line.

Kevin Brown was feeling more chipper than he had in weeks. The memory of his confidence's downfall the night on the Binghams' lawn was painful, even for a man with a nature as resilient as his. Meagan was a perfect rose in a field of wild flowers, so perhaps it should not have surprised Brown that not only did she fail to succumb to his charms, but that Lion Hampshire would have designs on the girl himself.

Since the night Hampshire had knocked him out cold with one superhuman punch, Brown had made a few false starts at tracking Meagan down. It did not take long to learn that she was living at the captain's Pine Street house; the question was: what did it mean? Kevin had idealized Meagan to the point where she seemed incapable of loose conduct, and he knew Hampshire well enough to feel fairly certain that he would not ravish her against her will.

It was a month today since their last meeting, since Meagan had left Mansion House. Brown thought of her every day, wondering and wondering until his mind seemed tied in knots. This morning, he had learned that Lion would be accompanying Priscilla Wade to Gray's Ferry. Mr. Bingham had given him the day off so that he might attend the festivities, but Kevin, caught in a holiday mood of impulsive bravery, decided to pay a visit to a certain house on Pine Street instead.

All I want to do, he thought defensively, is to find out what her feelings really are. Then, if she truly doesn't care for me, we might be friends . . .

He dressed in his best brown suit with its waistcoat of green and gold figured silk. His hair was powdered for the occasion, his shoe buckles polished. After watching Captain Hampshire drive away with Priscilla, Brown set off on foot at a near trot for Pine Street, stopping only long enough to purchase an armful of pink azaleas from a flower vendor.

The sun was bright in the clear blue sky and the

streets were nearly deserted except for a few distant vehicles heading west toward Gray's Garden. Brown could hear his heels click on the brick footpath and the cadence of his breathing, which quickened as Hampshire's dwelling came into view. So total was his nervous excitement at the prospect of seeing Meagan again, that he failed to note the lone black coach opposite the house or the three pairs of eyes that watched from inside as he knocked at the door.

If anything, Brown thought, she looks like the lady of the house—more beautiful than ever.

Meagan wore an elegant gown of black-and-white striped silk, edged with crisp white ruching. Her shiny curls were pinned up carefully; only one long ringlet escaped down her back, a perfect white hot house rose pinned at its source.

She seemed pleased to see him, if a trifle preoccupied. How different she looks! thought Kevin. The gown and neat coiffure made her appear older, but the helter-skelter, animated serving-girl Kevin had known remained in all her gestures, smiles, and candid remarks. They sat at the table in the kitchen as she poured his Madeira and he tried to see past her guard into the depths of her violet eyes.

Meagan drank tea as he downed two glasses of wine. She spoke of Mansion House, of Smith, and of how fondly she remembered Kevin and his many kindnesses. When the tall-case clock in the entry hall struck the hour, she went pale.

"Meagan, did you want to go to Gray's Garden? Smith and Wickham will be there; we could make a celebration of it!"

Her smile seemed sad. "You are far too kind to me. And you've certainly no reason to be." Her small hand touched his arm across the table. "I am sorry, Kevin, about that night. It was my fault to a degree for leading you on. I should have realized your intentions from the start and explained my own more clearly. I was self-centered and lonely. And, I know

320

Lion is sorry for hitting you so hard; he has meant to mend things between you himself."

Brown's chest burned when he tried to breathe. She talks as if I am some overeager boy and Captain Hampshire is her husband! he thought incredulously.

"It's true, isn't it!" he choked. "He's bedded you! And I suppose you'll let him keep you after Mistress Wade is his wife!"

Meagan's face went chalk white, deepening the purple of her eyes. "Kevin, I won't discuss it if you are going to fly into a fit. Whatever your feelings are, you have no claim on me or my affections. I had hoped we could be friends—" Unexpected tears welled in her eyes. "God knows I could use one today!"

His anger was dissolved by the expression on her face. When he went to her chair, Meagan let him hold and comfort her, and he breathed in the lilac fragrance of her hair.

Suddenly, she straightened up and gained control. "Well, perhaps that will help me make it through the day. I have some time yet . . . Could we talk?"

Artlessly, she pulled her chair around the table next to Brown's, and slowly revealed the outline of her relationship with Lion.

"No matter what you or anyone else thinks," she finished, "he does love me. This morning, before breakfast, he pinned this rose in my hair, and he gave me this ring." She extended her hand to reveal an exquisite, carved gold band studded with rubies. "It was his mother's—a gift on her fifteenth birthday. It even has her initials engraved in it."

Meagan paused, staring down at the ring. "I am leaving here today, Kevin. I don't mean to be melodramatic, but I have given it a great deal of thought, and I know it is the only way. Even if Lion were prepared to break off with Priscilla for my sake—which he is not—I have to think of him first. I've spent so many hours trying to weigh this question of what *is* best for Lion . . . a much-desired career in government or my love. Last night I read something that Thomas Paine wrote and it made me realize that more is at stake than just the two of us. The future of this country hangs in the balance, and from what I hear about this First Congress, they will need all the extraordinary men they can get. Lion could make such a difference . . ."

"Aye," Brown agreed softly. "But, where will you go?"

"Boston, I think. I—ah—know someone there." She tried to repress a shudder at the thought of Aunt Agatha. "I would like to stay out of the way for a time—until Lion's situation settles down. Then, well, time will tell."

"Meagan, I would come with you. I would take care of you—always." His black eyes were tragically hopeful, but Meagan only smiled bleakly and touched his cheek.

"No, Kevin. That would not be fair to either of us. But I will always treasure my memories of our friendship . . . and perhaps we will meet again someday."

"How will you travel? On the stage?"

"No. That would be like leaving a trail! I'll take my horse—she's a gift from Lion. I have a suit of clothes belonging to Wong that I used to wear when Lion and I went out to the shops, and I plan to wear it. I play quite a convincing boy when I put my mind to it!"

"No!" Brown's mouth slashed into a grave frown. "I'll not be a party to *that!* I'll go right home and get one of the Binghams' chaises. Your horse can pull it, and I'll pick a stableboy to go along for protection. The Binghams will be off tomorrow for New York, so they won't be around to miss the chaise *or* the boy."

Meagan laughed, obviously relieved. "You are so good! I am certain I could have made the trip safely, but this will make me feel less apprehensive."

"So, you aren't as brave as you let on?" Brown teased lightly.

"When the need arises, I can summon up the courage to accomplish any task. My secret is that I truly believe that!"

322

Gray's Ferry was actually a floating toll bridge which crossed the Schuylkill River and today it was barely recognizable. The rickety frame was hidden behind cedar branches, while a tall laurel arch stood at either end. Enormous crowds of people were gathered around the Philadelphia road, straining to see into the distance, each person longing to be the first to sight General Washington.

Lion was helping Priscilla to alight from his yellow post-chariot, some distance from the throngs near the bridge. They were both rather subdued, waiting for the chance to speak on matters of considerable importance. Lion looked startlingly handsome in polished black boots and a tailored coat of dove-gray over white breeches and a snowy white shirt. His hair, neatly queued, gleamed in the sunshine like newly minted gold.

"Would you care to walk for a few minutes? I have something I need to speak with you about and I find I cannot wait."

"I was just going to ask you for the same privilege!" Priscilla exclaimed, staring at him with a twinge of regret. He was such a man—but, unfortunately, beyond her ken. "Will you allow me to speak first?"

Lion nodded shortly, waiting as she opened her apple-green sunshade. It was made to match the leaves which sprigged her delicate muslin gown, but he barely noticed the soft pale curves of her breasts or the fragrance of cologne water surrounding her. Together they walked up a rolling hill that overlooked the decorated bridge and the crowds of waiting citizens. Priscilla paused beneath a chestnut tree, fingering the lace on her bodice.

"I suppose there is only one way to tell you. It is rotten of me to do it, but you've been quite rotten yourself, Lion Hampshire!" Her green eyes sought his challengingly, but he only nodded amused agreement. "Marcus Reems has declared his love for me— which is considerably more than you ever did! I have agreed to marry him."

Lion's ocean-blue eyes widened. It took all the

will power he possessed to keep from shouting his joy and relief, but instead, he took Priscilla's hand in a warm grasp. His smile turned her heart over.

"My dear, you have every right in the world to do this. I have treated you shamefully and you deserve better than that." One brow went up in his chiseled face. "No doubt you and Marcus Reems will suit very well."

Suddenly, a shout went up from the crowd. On the crest of a distant hill across the river, a column of men riding horses came into view. At the head was a magnificent white stallion ridden by none other than the President-elect himself. Elegantly garbed in his buff and blue uniform, General Washington was solemn and erect, his simply arranged hair white against the bright sky.

"He looks rather sad," Priscilla commented as the white horse clattered onto the bridge.

"The feeling of not having control over one's own life would make any man sad" was Lion's grim reply.

Eleven banners, one for each state which had ratified the Constitution, waved cheerily in a row along the bridge's north side, while the flag of the American Union flew alone on the south side. As Washington passed under the near laurel arch, a young girl leaned out from above to hold a wreath of laurel over his head. The crowd intensified its cheers, and the General began to bow gravely in response.

Behind him followed the procession of honor guards, made up of Pennsylvania assemblymen and the City Troop of Horse. The latter group was resplendent in high-top boots, snowy breeches, and silver-bound black hats.

The mob of citizens crowded closer as their hero passed under the second arch and onto the dusty road lined with flags bearing such slogans as "The New Era" and "Don't Tread on Me." Washington continued to bow as hands reached out to touch him, allowing himself to smile with a mixture of affection and melancholy. The crowd followed the procession toward the city where cannon were already beginning to thunder.

Lion and Priscilla remained on the hill, watching, until the dust had settled around the bridge.

At length, she asked, "What was it you wanted to say to me?"

"Hmm? Oh! Well, it doesn't matter now. There's no need. All I need to know now is whether or not you still wish to accompany me to City Tavern?" Lion's tone was the friendliest Priscilla had ever heard.

"Yes! That is, if you agree. Marcus is busy elsewhere today. Making arrangements for the wedding, I suppose."

Lion held her arm as they descended the grassy slope. "Thoughtful, isn't he?"

"Yes, he is!" Priscilla agreed, glancing up at the note of mockery in his voice. "I must say, you certainly don't seem very upset by all this. Marcus had visions of you challenging him to a duel!"

Lion laughed out loud at that, white teeth brilliant in his brown face. "Oh he did, did he? That's wonderful; it makes my day! Dear Priscilla, you must be sure to describe my carefree, cheerful demeanor to your new fiancé. I'm confident he will be greatly relieved to hear that I am not suffering!"

She waited until he stopped laughing before speaking again. "Would you do a favor for me as well? If I do not see Meagan before Marcus and I leave for New York, I would appreciate it if you could tell her how sorry I am for the way I've behaved. Perhaps the day will come when we can be friends again."

Lion was startled by this speech, but his good spirits were such that he did not pause to question it. Helping Priscilla into the post-chariot, he could think only of how superbly things were working out.

Bramble and Wong stood side by side, blinking back tears as they watched Meagan cross the garden on her way to the stable.

"She some lady!" the Chinaman sniffed, too emotional to mind the fact that she was wearing his suit.

" 'Tis truth ye speak. The goings-on of the pair of

325

them were Satan's work, but I believe the girl was misled."

"She love Missa Lion!" Wong protested. Bramble's face grew longer with skepticism, but for once she refrained from arguing the point. The two of them watched Meagan disappear into the stable, then returned to their rooms to prepare to walk to Market Street. General Washington was just the thing to keep them from noticing how gray and colorless the house suddenly seemed.

Meagan carried only a tiny deerskin trunk, small enough to fit easily under the chaise's seat. She had packed two dresses, two bedgowns, her original mauve pelisse, and the books Lion had given her. On her left hand she wore the ruby ring.

Heaven was prancing in her stall, unnerved not only by the chorus of church bells which had begun chiming around the city but also by the absence of Hellfire from her side.

"Sweetheart," Meagan soothed, laying her cheek against Heaven's glossy neck, "you and I are going for a little trip together. In a minute, a nice boy will arrive with a chaise, and he'll hitch you up to it—"

"Not today he won't," a deep voice announced from behind her. As she spun around to confront the man, someone snapped a cloth over her eyes with such force that her neck seemed to crack. In quick succession, she was blindfolded, gagged, and bound, then hoisted off the ground and carried away by two rough pairs of hands.

"Shouldn't we take her trunk?" asked one gravelly voice.

The other man, who had spoken earlier, laughed in a way that sent chills up Meagan's spine.

"Where she's goin', she won't be needin' it."

PART IV

And there the lion's ruddy eyes,
Shall flow with tears of gold ...

—WILLIAM BLAKE
"Night," from *Songs of Innocence*
(1789)

Chapter Thirty-seven

THE MUSLIN STRIP that covered Meagan's eyes was gauzy enough that she eventually was able to discern the images of her captors. The coach they shared was huge and heavy; it smelled disgusting and couldn't have been more uncomfortable.

After wrapping her in a foul woolen cape, the two men had carried Meagan around the back of the stables to the spot on Fifth Street where the black coach waited. In the distance, the cannon were booming, church bells rang, and the hum of cheering and applause could be heard. Twenty thousand people swelled up Washington's route to City Tavern, but Fifth Street was deserted.

Meagan was most terrified by the restraints; her inability to fight back, or even see and talk, left her paralyzed with panic. Her insane courage before any foe was her best weapon. Time and time again she had proven that attitude and strength of presence could triumph over size or even numbers.

But now she was powerless.

The coach had rumbled out of town; Meagan could feel the character of the road change and smell the greenery. After only a mile or so, they stopped. She remained motionless, listening to the men talk, and gradually they seemed to forget she was alive or capable of understanding them.

The first light of hope blinked in the darkness of her brain as she realized how totally dim-witted both men were. The one who was apparently in charge had a manner and voice tone that suggested shrewdness, but this proved to be an illusion. The two of them talked as if they were incapable of constructing any plan of action.

It seemed that they were waiting for further instructions from someone in charge. This person, referred to as B, was past due, and the later it got the more confused they became about what they would do if B did not arrive.

A few more minutes passed. Shrewd-voice suggested that the other man probably had the time wrong. Gravelly-voice somehow managed to whine in denial, and Meagan thought that she would probably be highly amused under different circumstances.

There was a sharp rap at the coach door, followed by a scuffle as her inept captors outdid each other in their efforts to get out first. Meagan strained her ears, but it seemed that they had moved off for the conference.

She knew it was Marcus. The question was: what purpose did this serve? Would he blackmail Lion? There were a number of possibilities along that line, involving Lion's money or political plans or both. Or was Marcus after more serious revenge? If he knew what she and Lion had actually shared, he may have guessed a way to wound Lion enough to make up for all the times in the past when he had tried and failed.

Gravel and Shrewd, as Meagan had dubbed them in her mind, were both quite fat and smelled bad. Through her muslin blindfold, she could not discern any more than their shapes, except to notice how clumsy they were.

The roads were badly rutted so that whenever a particularly gaping hole appeared in the distance, the driver would shout, "Now, folks, to the left!" or the right, as the situation demanded.

Meagan could sense the stealthy approach of twilight and knew that it was time she did something. So far, she had made no move to struggle or attract attention of any kind, so she hoped they thought her a limp and docile female. With luck, they would also believe it took just these few hours for such a fragile flower to reach her breaking point.

Her captors were snorting with laughter as they made plans to spend their payment for this night's work. Meagan was almost ready to go into her act when she heard a cork squeal and pop from a bottle, followed by the sound of liquid splashing against glass as the coach thundered along the road.

She remained quiet, listening to them swill what smelled like bad whisky. Gravel hiccupped and launched into another of his many confusing brainstorms for spending the money. He was sitting next to her, across from Shrewd, and Meagan decided there was a better way to slip into her role. Holding her breath to keep from gagging, she put her head on his shoulder. He stiffened and went silent. She could almost feel them staring at one another; she whimpered. The cork slid back into the bottle.

"Hey! What's wrong with you?" Gravel demanded, apparently afraid to touch her or remove her head.

Meagan began to cry, almost silently at first, working her way up to pitiful sobs.

"Maybe she's hurt?" Gravel wondered in total confusion.

"Hurt? She's been sittin' right here for hours. How'd she get hurt?"

"How should I know? Lookit her! She's as little as —as a little girl, almost. All tied up—"

"Some little girl!" Shrewd retorted nastily, reaching over to grip one of Meagan's breasts and giving it a painful twist. She fell in the other direction, pretending to go faint.

"Hey! What's wrong with you?" Gravel accused the other man.

"What's wrong with *you?* Whatta you care if she's hurt? She's gonna be dead pretty soon anyway! Let's have some fun with her!"

Meagan felt hands pulling at Wong's black coat; the first button was torn off. Then, the seat heaved beside her, followed by the thud of a blow, and the coach lurched forward as a body fell. Fingers closed around

330

her waist and arm; gratefully she recognized Gravel's repulsive odor. He fumbled with her blindfold and gag until they were off, and Meagan rewarded him with a smile that lit up the darkness.

Shrewd was slumped sideways on the opposite seat. Blood trickled from his nose, and he lay so motionless as to appear dead if not for his labored breathing. Meagan looked away, searching her defender's face as he concentrated on untying her wrists and ankles. Even in the dark, she could see his bulbous nose and the heavy folds of fat that encircled his tiny eyes and mouth. His skin was shiny with grime; his clothes looked as if they had not been off since the first cold day last autumn.

"Thank you, sir," she murmured in a weak, frightened voice.

"I don't like to see a little girl like you treated bad," he growled. "There's nothin' worse."

"But—he said you were going to kill me . . . ?"

Gravel looked up, pained. "Oh, no, ma'am! Not me! He promised I wouldn't have to do anything. I wasn't even gonna watch! I was—"

"But you would let him?" Meagan pressed softly. Her hands were free and she began to rub them.

"All that money! That's all. I just wanted to get drunk enough—maybe I'd forget. I'd never have another chance to get money like that. All I had to do was help him take you so you wouldn't get away. You know, like a guard—" His gravelly voice was whining again.

"Don't feel bad," Meagan soothed. "There's a way you can get your money without killing me at all, more than what you were promised. I'll give you this ring!" She spread her fingers under a moonbeam to display the ruby ring. Her only sure chance of success was to play on his greed. "Tell me, how were you to kill me?"

Gravel swallowed several times. His face was covered with beads of sweat. "We—he—was supposed to drown you in the Delaware up by Trenton, so

331

somebody'd find you on the way up to New York town."

"A pleasant surprise for someone," Meagan observed grimly. "Well, I have a better idea. I will give you my ring and you may also keep my horse—"

When she paused to gulp at the thought of handing over Heaven, Gravel interrupted, "We was go na keep her anyway. Uh—B wants the horse back as part of the proof."

"Oh, he does, does he? Well, if that's all the proof he demands—"

"That, and you floatin' in the river!"

Meagan made a face. "This B of yours is not as clever as I thought if he believes a drowning victim just lies in the same spot of the river waiting to be discovered! My disappearance can easily be explained. I've been swept away into the ocean!"

Gravel was squinting his raisin eyes, obviously in awe of Meagan and conveniently not noticing what a radical change she had undergone in just a minute or two.

"Now," she was saying, "I want you to leave me here. You just drive on to the Delaware then, or turn around now, and when your friend wakes up you can say he slept through it all."

"But you couldn't. What'd you do without a horse? At night—"

Meagan's eyes gleamed enigmatically in the darkness. "Don't worry about me. I am very good at adapting!"

"He'll never believe me. He knows *I* couldn't—"

"Just tell him you got courage from the bottle. Or I made you mad. Besides, why should he care as long as he gets his money? He'd never believe a frail little thing like me could last out here all night anyway."

Gravel was leaning forward to shout to the driver, but at Meagan's last words, he looked back over his beefy shoulder. "I don't believe you can either! I think you're mad! But, then, it's your life . . ."

She grinned. "Well said, sir."

The evening was well advanced. Luminous silver clouds drifted back and forth across the moon as showers of fireworks lit up the sky in a last gasp of celebration. Usually the streets were quiet by ten o'clock, but tonight there was still activity, as if the people realized that this was a holiday which could never be repeated.

Lion was walking home from Mansion House, having sent Joshua on alone with the post-chariot. He was keenly impatient to see Meagan and deliver the news which would change both their lives, but he felt the need to be alone with his thoughts first, to reflect on the day's events and their meanings.

The banquet at City Tavern had been lavish, the atmosphere saturated with gaiety. Fourteen toasts were drunk, each one larger and more enthusiastic than the last. Lion and Priscilla sat next to the Binghams, and he was amazed to find his attitude toward the two women quite altered. Priscilla drank a great deal and, now that she felt no further need to play games or roles with him, became relaxed. She was as trite and childish as ever, but Lion found himself reacting to her tolerantly, rather like an older brother.

After her third glass of wine, Priscilla drew Anne into the conversation. She had already told her, briefly, of her plans to marry Marcus. A heated quarrel had begun, interrupted almost immediately by William's entrance into the room. Since that incident, the two women had exchanged only the briefest civilities, but Priscilla proceeded to pour out all her feelings and reasons for her decision. Lion provided cool, quiet support, and eventually Anne was making peace with them both. She had only wanted the best for Priscilla, she insisted, and everything she had done or said was motivated by that desire.

Lion doubted that, but it seemed an appropriate time to call a truce with the world in general. Furthermore, Anne Bingham was not a person he cared to have angry with him and Meagan.

The streets were well-lighted, as always, with watchmen at regular intervals, so there seemed no reason to be wary of anyone on this night further illuminated by fireworks and moonbeams. Emboldened by wine or ale, people who normally would have dropped their eyes when passing a man like Lion now greeted him exuberantly. He grinned in return, for it almost seemed that they must know his secret and be congratulating him on his good fortune and future.

The house on Pine Street was dark except for the usual candle burning in the entryway.

Walking the few blocks home had heightened Lion's anticipation of this meeting with Meagan. If she was upset with him for spending so many hours with Priscilla, it would mean even greater joy for her when she heard the news. It seemed like a year had passed since that morning when he had given her the ruby ring. She had wept, and he could guess the reason for her tears, but he had resolved not to tell her his intentions until the break with Priscilla had been made. The torment he had suffered was ended now, for the time had come at last to offer Meagan the position in his life they both wanted. Lion felt as if a tremendous weight had been lifted from him.

He was covered with a layer of dust, and his clothes smelled of smoke and liquor and sweat. It took only a moment to reach his chamber, where he quickly peeled off the gray and white garments. After washing with cold water, Lion pulled on sunshine-fresh beige breeches and a crisp, open-necked shirt. He was reaching for a pair of polished boots when his eye caught sight of the flower-filled vase on the lowboy. Every day it held blossoms to match Meagan's mood, but it was the first time he had seen this variety. The pottery lion had been placed there as well, and Lion paused, smiling, to pick it up. Then he reached for the vase in order to get a better look at these mystery flowers.

Slowly, as recognition dawned, the smile faded from his tan face and all his muscles began to tighten and grow hot, like molten steel. These flowers were not in bloom outdoors yet and wouldn't be until May or

June, so Meagan had obviously gone to some trouble to acquire them.

They were blue forget-me-nots.

Closing his eyes, George Washington leaned back against the finely upholstered interior of his coach. A light rain began to fall, pattering against the windows, while the newly risen sun struggled for attention behind a veil of gray clouds.

Colonel David Humphreys, friend and secretary to the General, exchanged glances with Charles Thomson, the third passenger in the coach. The Irish-born Thomson, who was Secretary of the Congress, had been dispatched two weeks earlier to Mount Vernon. He had been given the unlucky duty of breaking the news Washington had been dreading, then seeing that he got back to New York City in one piece.

As if sensing the looks that passed between his two companions, the General opened an eye.

"I was not asleep, but simply enjoying my own company. And the quiet."

"Yes, sir," Thomson agreed.

David Humphreys, who was counted among the President-elect's most constant companions and friends, felt more sure of himself. Most people were intimidated by Washington's seemingly austere manner, but Humphreys knew that the real man enjoyed laughter and witty conversation as much as anyone. At least that was true at Mount Vernon, but it seemed those times were past. Already, he was tense, pensive, withdrawn . . . Would the Presidency bring back the somber man Humphreys had served during the War for Independence?

"General, I must say I admire the way you disposed of the City Troop this morning! Telling them you could not have borne traveling covered while others got wet—all Philadelphia will be talking of your modest unselfishness."

Washington's deep-set gray-blue eyes met Humphreys', which were openly twinkling, and allowed himself an ironic smile.

"One begins to feel confined . . . pressed. All this bowing and clanking beside the carriage . . . At times I wonder if the world hasn't gone mad."

Thomson spoke up defensively. "Everyone holds you in such *high* regard, sir, that I fear they may overdo—"

At that moment, the coach suddenly swerved to the left and Colonel Humphreys landed nearly in Thomson's lap. Someone was yelling outside, so General Washington swiveled to look out the back.

"Why, there is someone jumping about in the road! It almost looks like a servant—buckled shoes and all —but certainly a *filthy* one."

The person was running in a wobbly fashion after them as the driver began to gain speed again.

"Tell him to stop!" Washington ordered Humphreys. "Perhaps it is a servant from a nearby farm. Someone could be in trouble."

The colonel leaned out the window and shouted to the driver, who reined in the six horses with a frown.

As the bedraggled figure ran toward the coach, where the driver waited atop the box with one hand on his pistol, Washington glanced out through the window with growing apprehension. It appeared to be a boy, wet, muddy, and quite wild-eyed.

Charles Thomson cleared his throat. "Sir, I am not at all certain that we should be—"

But the General's eyes were riveted on the figure pulling at the door, and David Humphreys' expression had altered as well.

"I could swear . . ." the aide muttered in disbelief.

"Open the door," intoned Washington.

The order was obeyed, and suddenly the elegant, dry interior of the coach was filled with the animated presence of a dripping, grubby urchin whose violet eyes sparkled like huge amethysts. Off came the crumpled bicorne hat, followed by a spill of curling black hair.

"Oh, General! And Colonel!" she sobbed. "Thank God you came. No one else would have stopped for me—or believed my story!"

336

Washington forgot his immaculate blue and buff uniform. His arms enfolded her and one big hand patted her hair.

"Meagan Sayers, if it were anyone but you, I would name this episode a trick of my old mind!"

Chapter Thirty-eight

WONG SCURRIED ALONG the paneled hallways, his ears tuned to any sound that might warn of his employer's approach. When a tall kitchen maid rounded a corner in front of him, Wong skidded into the nearest bedchamber without a second thought.

In all the time Wong had known Lion Hampshire, he had seen him forbiddingly angry on many occasions, but this mood was something else again. Always, one could feel safe in the knowledge that the core of the man was good and there was no room for cruelty in his nature.

But this person, born during last night, seemed terrifyingly alien. All the power that Lion usually kept under tight control had been released; his steely body emanated currents of danger that Wong felt as tangibly as his own alarmed heartbeat.

Lion's menacing, black mood was rooted in unbearable pain. Even Bramble was ready to admit that he must have truly loved Meagan to be so devastated by this loss. He was like a great wild animal, now mortally wounded and capable of striking out at anyone unfortunate enough to cross his path.

The unnerving sound of Lion pacing in his bedchamber could be heard at frequent intervals all night long. Neither Wong nor Bramble had slept either. Lion had kept them up until nearly three o'clock with a barrage of questions, repeating himself as if his mental powers had been crippled. Then, the other servants had been roused, even the ones who had left before Lion to go to Gray's Garden.

Bramble, immune to fear, admitted from the start that Meagan had told them good-bye, that Wong and she had watched the girl's breeches-clad figure disappear into the stables. Meagan had not revealed either her destination or mode of transportation.

Lion released a stormy tide of verbal abuse, yelling at them for allowing her to go in a dozen different ways. Bramble stared back stoically, but Wong began to quake in his chair and his slanted eyes widened to a point that would not have seemed possible. Grasping for a straw that might save him, he had remembered the visit of Kevin Brown that morning. Perhaps, he squeaked, there was a clue?

And so, by dawn, Brown had been delivered to the house on Pine Street. Wong paused now outside the library door, listening fearfully to be certain not only that the two men were still conferring, but that Brown was safe.

Inside, Lion strode around the room, unable to sit down. Kevin occupied a brocade wing chair, but sprang up and down throughout their conversation.

His own elfin face was lined with real concern and something akin to surprise. It had never occurred to him that his former captain, the consummate rake, could have actually fallen in love with Meagan.

"I can't believe that she put so little value on herself!" Lion was shouting. "You say that she reached the conclusion the country needed me most?" He paused, raking a lean hand through his fair hair for what seemed like the hundredth time, then turned back to Brown, ready for the story's finish. "Tell me then—you left her to go after a chaise and a boy to drive it—"

"It seems she panicked, or never intended to wait at all. By the time I got back here, she'd taken her horse and gone on her way. I went to the house to ask what had happened, but everyone was off to Gray's

Garden except for some paper-brained chit stirring the stew."

Lion crossed the room to grip Brown's arm. "Do you mean that she's alone on Heaven? She's been out there all night?" His head turned to the window where a light rain drummed the panes. Backing up against his kneehole desk, he let his knees go as he sat on the edge. Fiercely, he tried to clear his mind and think, but it was as if a fire had been lit behind his eyes. A scalding tear escaped to trace the chiseled lines of his cheekbone and jaw. "Sweet Jesus, what have I done?"

"Clarissa, this had better be important! I do not have time for any more scheming conversations with you." Marcus stalked into his study, where Clarissa waited, perched on the edge of a fashionable Hepplewhite easy chair. "I told you night before last that you would have to engineer the rest of your plans without my assistance. Priscilla has me rushing toward the altar at full tilt."

"I hope you are enjoying yourself, Marcus dear, after working so hard for this!" She smiled archly. "Let me assure you that I have everything under control. Your information was more than enough help!"

In the act of pouring himself a brandy, Marcus looked back at Clarissa curiously. "What have you done with the girl?"

"She is out in the Delaware River—without a boat, of course!"

His black eyebrows went up. "Rather drastic measures, eh?"

"I wanted to leave no room for error this time. That wench was far too crafty. At any rate, the deed is done, so further discussion is a waste of time." Her perfect pink and white face was pinched, the sky-blue eyes flinty. "The swine I hired to do her in have returned for the remainder of their payment, and more. That is why I am here. They have a ring that they claim she wore; the chit said it was originally a possession of Lion's mother and begged them to leave it to her. It *does* have his surname inscribed in the band,

and it is set with several small rubies. They want me
to buy it from them, at a horrible price, to ensure it
won't 'fall into the wrong hands.' "

"Are you asking for a loan?" Marcus inquired
coldly.

"Yes."

"Done. Now, I am due at Mansion House. Is there
anything else?"

"Only my dilemma of how to leak the news of the
girl's death—without casting Lion's suspicions on you
or me. They said the river had a strong current and
she was taken off at once, so there is no chance of
anyone discovering the body, as I had hoped . . ."

Marcus was counting money at his desk, obviously
in a hurry. "You are not as clever as you insist, my
dear. Send the men to the servants' entrance of Mansion House where they may beg a meal and tell their
tale to Smith. Let them take the girl's horse to show
and say they saw her thrown from its back into the
river last night. Swept away by the current. The ever-
good Smith will undoubtedly take over from there."
He leaned across the desk to hand her a small leather
pouch bulging with guineas. "You may wait until you
become Mistress Hampshire to repay me. In the meantime, it would behoove both of us to avoid one another,
don't you agree? Especially with the death of the girl
—suspicion is one thing we can do without."

Marcus's improvised strategy worked with such
smooth efficiency that even Clarissa was astounded at
how well things were going. Except for the ruby ring,
there had not been a single tangle in her design.

Seated at her graceful dressing table, she replaced
the top on her orange flower water while regarding
her flawless reflection in the mirror. Every blond curl
was in place. She practiced the smile that had always
entranced Lion and adjusted her décolletage so that
just enough white flesh was revealed.

It was April twenty-third. Clarissa had suffered
through two torturous days since Lion had been told
of Meagan's death, waiting until the perfect moment

to approach him. Now she could not take the chance of letting another hour pass in case he should suddenly leave for New York to seek solace in the celebrations there.

Carefully, she felt into the corner of her jewel case to be certain that the dearly bought ruby ring was safe. Then, she unfolded the letter delivered that morning by Marcus's disguised valet, and reread it.

11 o'clock April 22, 1789

Tomorrow, I shall be married. That knowledge, combined with brandy, has softened me sufficiently to compose one *last* message to you. I feel compelled to relay any new information to you, since your failure and discovery could lead to my own. (I have an idea that you would like company in your descent.)

Events proceed splendidly. As I understand, your two "swine" carried off their performance at Mansion House quite convincingly. (Thank God for Bramble's transfer! She would have closed the door on their snouts.) A grief-stricken Smith heard them out, then identified the filly. Wickham extracted Brown from the Bunch of Grapes where he was deep into ale and winning at Pharaoh, and proceeded to destroy his jolly little world. (Yes, he was enamored of the girl as well!) Brown delivered the news to Lion. It seems he is taking it very hard; Smith goes over regularly, for the situation appears rather desperate. The servants are actually frightened of him though he's spent the better part of the past thirty-six hours closed up in one room or another. Bramble is telling anyone who will listen that Lion has become more beast than man.

Doubtless, that is not the reaction you hoped for, but it rather satisfies me.

Priscilla and I shall be leaving the twenty-fifth for New York. She wishes to begin our marriage at the estate I've just purchased above Woodlands, so I shall indulge her, however briefly. I want to allow at least two days in New York before the inauguration.

Perhaps, if this astonishing good fortune continues, we shall meet there, both enjoying the first week of wedded bliss. I remain, in spirit—

Your Obed. Servant.

M.

Clarissa folded the letter and wedged it into a compartment inside her dressing table. Her face was serene with confidence in her one talent—enchantment of the male animal, the most splendid of which was Lion Hampshire.

No matter how bewitched he had been by that kitchen wench, Lion had never been a man who bemoaned the past. He would be ready to pull himself together, which meant he'd crave a female to warm his empty bed. Clarissa meant to be in the right place at the right time.

Wong was close to hysteria as he tried to stop Clarissa Claussen from ascending the stairs.

"Please, missy! He say he no see anybody! He kill us both if you go in. Oh, please!"

She ignored him. On the tenth step, Wong reached wildly for her skirt, and Clarissa turned to deliver a savage blow with the flat side of her hand. Wong, already frantic, stumbled and fell against the stair rails. By the time he recovered his equilibrium, Clarissa had reached the top step and was turning down the hall.

She knocked, receiving an angry growl in response. Obviously, the man was in no mood for company, but it was up to her to remind him of what he was missing.

Lion tensed, instantly erect, when the door to his bedchamber opened the first inch. He had been staring out the window at the garden below, but his mood switched from pensive to hostile in the space of a heartbeat.

Clarissa stood on the threshold, a vision in ivory and peacock blue. Her rosebud mouth smiled.

"Get out" was Lion's terse greeting.

She made a moue, widened her sky-blue eyes, and inhaled slowly so that her breasts swelled temptingly above her neckline.

"Get out!" Sparks began to flash in his eyes; tendons stood out on his neck. Clarissa felt a sharp twinge between her legs at the sight of him outlined in sunshine and she burned with passions that she longed to channel in the right direction.

"Darling, I know you need me now, even though you aren't aware of it yourself. Your fiancée has been stolen from you and—you've lost a—a mistress—"

That brought him to her side, but the expression on his dark face gave her true cause for alarm. He gripped her arm to the bone. "Shut your mouth and get out of my house!"

Clarissa tried tears next. "Oh, Lion, I am only trying to help! Can't you see you need me? I can make you well again, I know I can. Please—"

Lion shook her off savagely, causing Clarissa to fall on the bed, and headed toward the wardrobe. "When a man cannot find peace in his own home, the time is come for a change of scene! Excuse me while I pack; Wong will show you the door."

As he pulled clothing out, piling the random choices on the nearest chair, Clarissa was struggling to rise from where she had landed.

"No! You cannot ignore me this way! I know you want me as much as I want you! Oh, Lion, don't you know I haven't slept through a night since we parted because of my need for you?"

He brushed past her on his way to the bureau, not even glancing in her direction.

The pink and white face grew flushed; the sky-blue eyes became cloudy. "You imbecile! Do you think you can deny your true feelings to *me*? Listen to me! Look at me!" She was back at his elbow, breathing in gasps of rage. "Would you deny that you have missed my body?" Feverishly, she tore at the hooks on her

343

bodice to expose her shaking breasts, but Lion seemed completely oblivious. When Clarissa clawed at his coat with her long fingernails and pressed her naked flesh against his arms and wide back, he finally looked down, but his expression was one of sickened fury.

"Get away from me!"

Before Clarissa could remember to fight, she had been literally pitched into the hallway, where she collided with a thud against the far wall. The door slammed, and her tears began in earnest.

"I will show you, Lion Hampshire. The day will come when you beg for my body and for my forgiveness! I *will* become your wife!"

Chapter Thirty-nine

To THE FEMALES who were acquainted with George Washington, his chivalrous nature was legendary. He loved women, with restraint, and showed to them the most charming aspects of his personality.

Meagan knew that she could not have encountered a more ideal rescuer, for in spite of the conspicuous, paradelike nature of this journey, he never considered deserting her. She explained, in the sketchiest of terms, what had befallen her since Christmas, revealing little more than the fact that she had gone with Priscilla to escape Aunt Agatha. Washington tactfully refrained from pressing the issue. He had known Meagan all her life and had been shocked by her antics in the past just as he been enchanted. Never for a moment did he question the quality of her character, not even now.

David Humphreys was given the job of blending Meagan into the scenery. This was fraught with risks,

344

for there were no women included in the entourage and it would be a catastrophe if she were discovered. Humphreys transformed her into his valet. They sneaked her into the inn at Princeton that first day and sent her one suit of clothes out to be cleaned. The next morning, Humphreys labored to make her look as boyish and inconspicuous as possible; even General Washington stopped in to approve the disguise.

Meagan looked adorable, just as she had the first time she donned the suit to go shopping with Lion, but they planned to use her size to advantage by keeping her hidden behind the other men. Charles Thomson agreed that discovery was unlikely, if only because everyone's eyes would be riveted on the idolized President-elect.

The morning of the twenty-third found Meagan in Elizabeth Town, peering around corners at the hotel of Samuel Smith in search of her shield—Colonel Humphreys. The men had just returned from Boxwood Hall and a meeting of the Committee of Congress, and were ready to embark on the fifteen-mile journey by water that would bring them to Manhattan Island.

Through a window, Meagan could see the distinguished-looking crowd that milled about in the spring sunshine, but there was no sign of David Humphreys. She was about to creep into the next room when a hand caught her elbow and spun her around. Meagan swallowed a startled cry at the sight of her tall protector.

"I was beginning to fear that you had forgotten me!" she exclaimed in relief.

Humphreys smiled. He was an attractive man with almost beautiful eyes and mouth, a prominent nose, and neatly arranged gray hair which curled naturally. Meagan thought he looked splendid in his buff and blue uniform.

"Little elf, you would be most difficult to forget!"

"Well, it is almost time to leave, and I haven't the faintest notion what I'm to do!"

"All is arranged. The General has given this a great deal of thought, as you know. I opted for the Hamiltons—"

"Do you mean as my final destination?" she queried, eyes twinkling. Humphreys was amused as well.

"Yes. The idea is to find a wife who has a temperament sufficiently capricious to accept this insanity. And, of course, most of the men who have just moved to New York as part of the new government have not brought their wives in yet. So that narrowed the field down to a family already settled in the city. The General resists the Hamiltons, since he and Alexander are rather on the outs, so the final decision is to put you with John and Sarah Jay. At your age, she nearly matched you in enthusiasm and impulsiveness, so you should be great friends.

"Jay is here now, as part of the escort from New York, and the General has discussed the matter with him. He assures us that his wife will welcome you with open arms."

"And later . . . ?"

"There's no need to worry about the future, Meagan. Just relax and enjoy yourself, and when things quiet down after the inauguration, we can all decide what to do next." He smiled reassuringly. "You know how the General loves children. Perhaps after Mrs. Washington arrives, they will have you come to live with them!"

Meagan looked bleak. "The only problem is that I am no longer a child!"

It was a long day. Meagan had grown accustomed to the extravagant displays of adulation that met General Washington at every bend in the road, but the journey by barge to New York outdid all the rest.

The custom-built barge was grand, complete with an awning festooned with red curtains and the thirteen identically dressed harbor pilots who manned the oars. As it started out through Kill van Kull into the bay, a naval parade formed behind. Meagan was deposited on a boat with John Jay and Henry Knox, though they were generally too preoccupied to pay much attention to her. Mr. Jay had the look of an aristocrat; a slender build, long chin, hawk nose, and

346

arching eyebrows. He was polite when introduced to Meagan, but she thought him aloof, even forbidding, and hoped his manner did not reflect the way he felt about taking her into his home.

Dressed in her breeches, it seemed a wise idea to stand off to one side and keep quiet. She watched General Washington's barge progress toward Staten Island as more and more boats came out to crowd the water. At one point, cannon began to fire a thirteen-gun salute from a Spanish ship-of-war and banners spiraled out on dozens of boats. Answering shots boomed from the far-off shore. A sloop sailed alongside the barge so that four of its passengers faced the General, whereupon they began singing to the tune of "God Save the King":

> Joy to our native land,
> Let every heart expand
> For Washington's at hand,
> With glory crowned.

More music-producing boats followed. Meagan could scarcely believe her eyes as she watched the spectacle. A school of porpoises performed next, and then a vessel appeared carrying Philip Freneau, the Anti-Federalist writer, and two orangutans.

Even General Washington seemed startled by this. Frequently during the boat trip, he had turned to seek out the faces of Jay and Knox, who were familiar friends in an ocean of strangers. As Freneau passed by, the President-elect looked back with an expression of startled confusion. Meagan caught his eye and gave him her brightest grin, which seemed to have the desired effect.

That smile had taken all her willpower, for in the midst of the day's contagious excitement, Meagan was feeling desperately lonely. Ever since Washington had taken her under his wing, the overpowering nature of her will to survive had gradually been replaced by misery. Now that she was safe, and returned to her true name and position, it began to seem that her past with

Lion was only a bittersweet dream. He was lost to her forever . . . and she had no idea what, or whom, the future would hold for her.

As the boat neared Manhattan Island, she forced herself to concentrate. All along the shore, deafening cheers went up from crowds that stood so close together that little was visible but hats. People were clinging to the masts of ships and hanging out of windows; thousands of arms waved to and fro. It seemed to Meagan that every person in the city, and then some, must have assembled on the docks today. She watched as the white-uniformed pilots skillfully brought the barge into a landing on Murray's Wharf at the foot of Wall Street.

The next hour was a blur of cheers, faces, shoves, and confusion. Once General Washington mounted the carpeted stairs to the dock, where he was greeted by Mayor Duane and Governor Clinton, Meagan was not destined to see him again that day. Wedged in among the men, she could not get a proper view, and the cheering crowd made it impossible to even think. John Jay took her arm, but once they were off the boat, handed her over to his coachman.

Washington had begun to walk through the crowds on his way to the home which had been procured for him on Cherry Street, but Meagan bounced along a different route—up Broadway in the Jay carriage. She was exhausted and utterly fed up with the crowds. A man had been crying nearby when she and John Jay stepped off the boat, sobbing that he could die contented now that he had seen the Saviour of his Country.

It seemed too much. In fact, the entire period of her life since she had left Virginia was taking on the quality of a grand, mad illusion.

New York City had been ravaged during the Revolution by two terrible fires and seven years of British occupation. After the war's end, the island seemed suspended in a state of shock which lasted through most of the 1780s. Lately, however, there had been much improvement. Damaged buildings were being restored, fine new homes were built, and improvements were begun on the narrow, crooked streets. The city and its management were still noticeably flawed, but there was no shortage of pleasure. New Yorkers loved to socialize, often to excess, and there was more than enough entertainment to satisfy every taste.

John and Sally Jay were at the center of the elite social whirl in New York. Their mansion on Broadway was a gathering place for distinguished people from all over the world, known for the excellent wine and French food served by a hostess who charmed every guest.

Meagan was no exception. She and Sally were immediately drawn to each other by certain shared physical traits: clear sparkly eyes, small frames, and creamy skin which was prone to blush. Sally Jay, however, was quite pregnant and possessed beautiful chestnut hair and dimples.

Meagan felt at home instantly. The Jay mansion, centrally located on the east side of Broadway, was handsome and dignified, yet warm. The combination reminded Meagan of the marriage of John and Sally— opposites bringing out the best in each other.

She was given a lovely room on the second floor, a hot bath, and a collection of dresses from Sally's pre-pregnancy collection. The children, ranging in age from four to fourteen, danced in and out of her room until she felt like an older sister.

There was a share of other relatives, mostly Sally Jay's unmarried sisters. So many people rushed about the house that Meagan never did learn the exact dividing line between family and friends. Sally took it all in stride, her mood serene yet gay, so that Meagan just let herself fall into the group and hoped she was not making extra work for anyone.

When General Washington explained Meagan's circumstances to John Jay, he began with the tale of her wealthy parents and their untimely deaths, intimating that the spirited girl was now in the process of escaping Aunt Agatha's guardianship and had encountered the General quite by chance. Jay passed this explanation on to his curious household, which had been dying to learn the secret of this gamine in boy's clothing. Sally was delighted by the entire situation.

For three days, she let Meagan relax. There was a constant stream of callers at the mansion; it seemed that the only time someone wasn't visiting was when Sally and John were out at an assembly somewhere else. Meagan was invited to join in as though she were another sister, but she was reluctant to leave the house, and often remained in her room when there were visitors. The day the Binghams came for tea, Meagan was adamant about not meeting them, despite Sally's vivid description of Philadelphia's most wealthy and beautiful lady.

Sally Jay worried about her young houseguest, especially since her reticence seemed so at odds with the adventurous spirit in breeches. Meagan was quiet, her huge violet eyes misty with hidden emotions.

Then, James Madison and Edmund Randolph came for luncheon and Sally glimpsed the girl Meagan had been. She seemed overjoyed to see them, her happiness translated into rosy cheeks, dancing eyes, and a smile so bright that Sally was startled by the sight of it. Over lunch, the three Virginians spoke of times gone by at Pecan Grove, Mount Vernon, and their own plantations. They discussed General Washington and his reluctant return to public life as well as Madison and Randolph's moves to New York and their own futures. Meagan was particularly anxious for news about Edmund's wife Betsy and their four children.

Finally, Jay took his guests off to the library so that they could discuss government affairs, and Meagan and Sally were left with their tea. The dining room overlooked a garden which stretched like a bright spring carpet back to New Street. Violets lent their perfume to the breeze that swirled through the open window, and Sally inhaled appreciatively.

"I didn't know you could laugh like that! Seeing Mr. Randolph and Representative Madison seems to have been the perfect tonic for your spirits."

Meagan looked up to meet clear blue eyes that reminded her so much of Lion's her heart twisted in pain. Her hostess's eyes were open, though, revealing pure motives of concern and affection.

"I have felt so unsettled lately," Meagan told her carefully. "Since my father and mother died, I have had moments when I've been unsure of my own identity. My whole life has been turned upside down. I've never been frightened. But just now—being with those two men—was like falling backward in time—very reassuring . . ."

"You used to laugh like that?"

Meagan smiled crookedly. "I hope I didn't offend either you or Mr. Jay. I've never been good at holding my enthusiasm in check! But yes, I used to laugh like that—regularly. Often at all the wrong times!"

"That sounds like me a dozen years ago! I'm still rather incorrigible, but time has toned me down." Sally inclined her head to one side, looking out over the garden. "And I know how you feel, losing your family, your home, and the environment you loved. About ten years ago, John was chosen to be the emissary to Spain and I went with him. The usual adjustments one makes in a foreign country—cut off from friends and relatives—were bad enough . . . but then, I gave birth to our second child. She was a beautiful little girl, but she fell ill when she was just a few days old and died." The blue eyes pooled with tears. "I could find little to console me in a country whose customs, language, and religion were all the very reverse of our own, and where I had no ties. How I longed for a familiar face or voice! So you see, I have an idea of what you feel now."

Meagan blinked back tears of her own, unable to frame a reply. When Sally Jay took her hand, it was the first bond of their warm friendship; their eyes met in understanding.

"Meagan, I liked you from the moment you entered my house, and I feel closer to you the more I learn of your personality. It breaks my heart to think you no longer crave laughter and gaiety.

351

"Would you make an attempt, just once, for me? There is so much excitement in New York right now and I think you deserve to share in it."

Meagan considered this. The dull pain of yearning for Lion never left her, but hearing of Sally's loss seemed to diminish the size of her own problems. Besides, she had never been one to sink into gloom; life was too precious to waste in self-pity.

"You are right. I suppose the time has come for me to plunge ahead. What did you have in mind?"

Sally leaned forward in her chair, wearing the excited look of a matchmaker who seldom had the chance to act. "There is an assembly Tuesday night at the home of Henry and Lucy Knox. It should be a splendid affair, and I have the perfect gown for you. Isn't it wonderful that we are the same size?" Dimples appeared in her pink cheeks as she patted the curve of her abdomen. "Well, we were once, and shall be again! At any rate, I should confess all . . ."

Meagan was puzzled, but Sally laughed and rushed on.

"When John came home yesterday, he said that he had met a most interesting man at City Tavern. Apparently this fellow possesses every physical and mental virtue, including a facility for sarcasm—a trait much admired by my husband! In John's opinion, he is destined for greatness . . . but he did seem lonely. Now, in *my* opinion, you and this mystery man sound ideally suited!"

Chapter Forty

WEARING ONLY HER chemise and petticoats, Meagan lay stiffly on the pencil-post bed, afraid to move lest her coiffure be ruined. A cool afternoon breeze played with the linen ruffle on the canopy frame and caused her bare throat and arms to prickle.

I must have lost my senses to have agreed to this, she thought desperately. It is bound to be one of the major gatherings; the Binghams are sure to attend! I'm not ready yet for confrontations . . .

She closed her eyes in an attempt to keep Lion from invading her mind, but it was no use. She had been gone a week, and he and Priscilla were certainly married by this time. Her thoughts had only to touch on the subject of their wedding night and her brain recoiled as if scalded. She practiced again at making her mind a blank.

There was a knock at the door, followed by the cheerful entrance of Sarah Jay, who wore a loose, skillfully cut gown of cinnamon brocade shot through with gold threads. The colors were perfect against her chestnut curls.

Sally's maid followed. Meagan saw that she held a beautiful dress fashioned of smoky-violet taffeta in one hand, silk slippers in the other.

"Do you like it?" Sally inquired anxiously.

"Oh, it is lovely!"

"Good! That color never flattered me half as much as it will you. Oh, Meagan, I haven't been so excited since the night John proposed to me!

"As soon as you finish dressing, join us downstairs. The cook is fixing lobster tonight, so we shall feast before leaving for General Knox's. We also have an entire tray of eclairs from Mr. Pryor's shop, but the children will devour them if you aren't quick!"

She paused, noting Meagan's position and expression.

"I do hope you are well. John tells me the young man with the scathing wit will certainly attend—as well as a girl you may know. Her name is Priscilla Wade, and I understand her family also lives near Mount Vernon. Anne Bingham said that she and her brand-new husband were due to arrive in New York at any time!"

Sally could not have been more surprised when, at the end of her cheerful announcement, she saw Meagan's face go as white as her petticoats.

General Henry Knox lived in a handsome four-story brick house located not far from Bowling Green, on the west side of Broadway. Tonight, it was ablaze with light and an assemblage of dazzling notables who were enjoying their chance to play a role in this week-long fairy tale. Women and men alike wore costly imported silks, satins, and brocades, as well as a profusion of jewels. To Sally Jay, it was like returning to Versailles.

There was at least one person present who was not opulently garbed. He stood away from the groups of people who drank and danced and laughed. His expression was indifferent; cool and cynical. Steely blue eyes watched the performances of others, and although one golden brow arched in seeming amusement, the hard line of his mouth never softened.

John and Sarah Jay were coming in from the piazza when she spotted the stranger whose unpowdered hair appeared more golden than the glittering light of the chandeliers. He was magnificent. Clad in a well-cut coat of indigo blue over white breeches, a pearl silk waistcoat, and a spotless linen shirt with a froth of lace against his brown jaw, the man seemed to mock the extravagant clothes worn by others. He lounged against the wall, sipping brandy, and Sally thought that

354

even in repose, he appeared more powerful than any man she had ever seen.

"John!" she hissed, pulling at her husband's arm as he started off toward Alexander Hamilton. "Who is that ferocious-looking fellow over there? Do you know?"

He followed her gaze and broke into a rare smile. "That is the man I was telling you about! The one Meagan was to meet—Lion Hampshire."

"Are you joking?"

"No, of course not. And stop staring, Sally."

"Well, introduce us, then! I am consumed by curiosity!"

A moment later, Lion was greeted by the tall figure of John Jay, who lost no time in presenting his wife. Lion nearly closed his eyes after one look at her. The rosy cheeks, gleaming dark curls, and dancing eyes were wrenchingly familiar.

Sally felt the tawny hand that held hers tighten almost reflexively and saw the pain that flared in his eyes.

"Mr. Hampshire, are you all right?"

Lion waited for the agony to subside and his wall of ice to slip back into place, protecting him from those emotions that made living worse than hell. Mrs. Jay's anxious gaze was like a steady flame that prevented the ice from setting.

"I—" A muscle moved in his jaw. "To be honest, Mrs. Jay, your enchanting face and manner remind me of someone I loved—and lost, recently."

"Oh, my! Mr. Hampshire, I am so sorry! That must be the reason why you look so bitter—"

"Sally—" interjected John.

"You poor man. This is simply dreadful, especially at your age. Were there any children?"

"Sally!"

"It's all right, Mr. Jay." Lion's mouth hinted at a smile, the first in days. "No, there were no children. We were just on the verge of marriage."

Sally's great blue eyes shone with compassion. It seemed a tragedy beyond belief that two people as

355

young and splendid as Lion Hampshire and Meagan Sayers should be so sad during this wonderful, festive week.

John was watching Sally, his high forehead creased as he sensed her busy mind at work. He took full advantage of the opportunity to interrupt.

"Mr. Hampshire, are you acquainted with Mr. Hamilton?"

"Yes, though I am sure he would not remember our meeting. I attended the Constitutional Convention, where he was a delegate."

Sally would not be turned aside so easily. "Mr. Hampshire, I do hope you will forgive me for daring to interfere, but it breaks my heart to hear of your misfortune and to see you harden toward the rest of the world.

"It just so happens that we have a guest in our house whose circumstances are very similar to yours. She is a *lovely* girl. Perhaps you have heard John speak of Miss Sayers? The ordeal she has been through this winter has driven out all her natural gaiety. Even tonight—I had persuaded her to come along, but at the last minute, she couldn't face the crush."

Lion was afraid to reply, sensing what was ahead. "That does sound like a sad situation, Mrs. Jay," he murmured at last.

"Oh, Mr. Hampshire, I know you will believe me hopelessly romantic, but I cannot help thinking that you and Miss Sayers might be able to help each other! At least, it couldn't do any harm for you to meet—"

"Sally!" pleaded John.

"Well, it couldn't! Mr. Hampshire, won't you agree to come home with us later tonight for a bit of brandy? If my friend could meet just one person, it might be the first step back into society for her."

Lion felt cornered. He was too charmed by Sally Jay to deliver the curt refusal any other woman would have received.

"Mrs. Jay, I am at your disposal."

As the clock struck ten, the white-wigged major domo intoned, "Mr. and Mrs. Marcus Reems!"

A radiant Priscilla moved beside her husband to meet Henry Knox, the convivial giant of a man who was called Washington's closest friend, and his wife, Lucy, followed by a dozen other socially prominent couples. They had been in New York only a few hours, but Marcus had been determined to make an appearance at General Knox's.

The President-elect was due to arrive at any moment. Marcus stood in the large parlor, flawlessly attentive to his beautiful bride, but all the while looking for Lion. If he could have seen his brother through the walls, Marcus would have burned anew with frustrated rage.

Lion was in the library, in the middle of a group of the country's most influential men. Alexander Hamilton, graceful and courtly, stood to his left; John Adams, the plump and often pompous Vice President-elect to his right. Also present were James Madison, slight of build and calm; and John Jay.

They were involved in a heated discussion concerning the issue of the month: presidential etiquette. They argued back and forth, each with a different idea for General Washington's title. Hamilton commented that a Senate committee had voted for "His Highness the President of the United States of America and Protector of the Rights of the Same."

Madison wrinkled his nose and inquired reasonably, "What is wrong with simply, 'President of the United States'?"

His round cheeks flushed, Adams launched into a speech that all had heard before. "What will the common people of foreign countries, what will the soldiers and sailors say when asked to speak to George Washington, President of the United States? They will despise him. The title 'Mr. President' would put him on a level with the governor of Bermuda!"

Lion stifled a yawn, remembering that Adams wanted the President to be known as "His Most Benign Highness." It was a variation on the same conversation at the Shippens' dinner over a month ago and Lion was still amazed that the men with whom he had longed to fraternize could waste their time on such a trivial subject. Why, Hamilton, Madison, and Jay were the authors of *The Federalist Papers!*

For his own part, he had drunk too much brandy and sunk back into his abyss of indifferent bitterness. He had hoped that coming to New York and mingling with the people who had inspired him in the past would rekindle the fires of his ambition. How desperately he needed a reason to live, or as Dr. Franklin had said, a *passion.*

Lion pressed a hand against his forehead, wishing he could remember how to cry. Alexander Hamilton was speaking in a most persuasive tone, but the words blurred by the time they reached his ear.

I can't go to the Jays' tonight, he thought wearily. The last thing I need is an introduction to some paper-brained chit who is afraid to leave her room!

He could feel someone watching him. Turning his head, he looked past Hamilton in the direction of the doorway. There, in the brightly lit hall, stood Clarissa, a vision in silver brocade and diamonds.

Clarissa had brought her abigail to New York, hoping to pass her off as a chaperone if anyone were to question her conduct. She had to pay an exorbitant price to get a pair of rooms in Widow Bradford's Coffee House, but suddenly it was worth it.

Lion had made a shockingly brief apology to John Jay and none at all to Sally. He even failed to notice the gold tiger eyes that followed his every move. Within moments of first sighting Clarissa, he was walking with her out the front door of General Knox's house to the place where his post-chariot waited.

Clarissa was astonished. She wondered what could have happened to totally reverse her luck, but there was little time to ponder this mystery, for as soon as they were inside the carriage Lion reached for her.

Being in his arms after so long released such a flood of sharp pleasure in Clarissa that she thought she would faint. Hungrily, she touched his hard shoulders, chest, neck, and face, stroked his gilded hair, inhaled his intoxicating scent, and met his lips with feverish ardor. So absorbed was she in her own need that she failed to notice Lion's response. He thrust her away at the same moment the post-chariot lurched to a stop before the coffee house which stood on the southeast corner of Wall and Water Streets.

By the time they entered her rooms, a vague fear had begun to take shape in Clarissa's breast. Lion had not met her eyes even once, though she watched him anxiously all the way upstairs. His handsome, arrogant face was as cold as a piece of sculpture, his eyes like splintered sapphires. He shut the door and reached out to catch her wrist, pulling her against him. Immediately, his mouth was on hers in a kiss as degrading as a stranger's rape while lean hands opened the priceless silver gown and found her breasts.

Lion's fingers had always been wickedly sensuous; the memory of their touch had haunted Clarissa's dreams for weeks. But now, he was taking her with deliberate cruelty. She pushed away just long enough to glimpse his face and was devastated by what she saw. There was no love, or even passion, in Lion's blue eyes—only contempt and raw pain.

Tears closed her throat. She began to tremble as the totality of all she had done assailed her, followed by the realization that she could never win Lion or his love.

"What the hell is wrong with you?" Lion demanded harshly.

She stumbled to the bed, choking back sobs. Lion turned his back and looked for a bottle of brandy or wine. Some brandy stood on Clarissa's dressing table, along with two glasses, but he filled only one. Briefly, he glanced back at the bed, but she continued to moan.

Damn it all, I can't even indulge my despicable impulses anymore! Lion thought. Who could have guessed that the most ready and eager wench of all would go to pieces on me?

Deciding to leave, he drank deeply of the brandy. Her jewelry case was open on the table and Lion momentarily entertained thoughts of reclaiming all the gems he had given her. A long emerald necklace hung over the side of the box, but when he reached for it, desiring nothing more than a closer look, Clarissa gasped a protest.

She looked absolutely panic-stricken, scrambling up to her feet. The silver gown was twisted and crumpled, her elaborate powdered coiffure disheveled, and her face was even paler than fashion dictated. Lion's brow furrowed as he looked back at the necklace with sudden interest.

When he lifted it from the case, the reason for Clarissa's agitation was clear. Under the chain of emeralds lay the gold and ruby ring he had given to Meagan before she left Philadelphia.

Chapter Forty-one

LION STARED AT the ring for a long minute. In his mind the truth came like a storm, beginning with one gray cloud and thundering into a full-fledged tornado. When he turned on Clarissa, she cringed fearfully, emitting low animal-like sounds from deep in her throat. She stumbled over the silver gown as she tried to flee, and he grabbed one soft arm, snapping her around with all his considerable strength.

"You did it, didn't you?" he demanded. The force of his rage and torment was like an erupting volcano. His eyes burned; tendons stood out on his neck that seemed to run on through that splendid, terrifying dark face. Clarissa broke out in a panic-stricken sweat.

Lion gripped both her arms until she whimpered

with pain. "Say it, damn you, you rotten slut! You killed her! Didn't you!"

He shook her until she began to scream "Yes!" hysterically. Lion was full of demons, past reason or conscience as his powerful hands went to her neck, encircling it like steel bands.

In that moment of unbearable pain and fury, the civilized man somehow gained control over the primitive beast. Slowly, his hands relaxed their grip on her slender, bruised neck, and she crumpled to the floor. Lion looked into her wild eyes for a moment, then headed for the door. An old woman stood in the hall, poised to knock, and when he brushed past, racing down the stairs, she followed to shout complaints about the commotion at his back.

Outside on Wall Street, the nearest street lamp had gone out again, and the night was dark and cool. Lion took long, harsh breaths, clenching and unclenching his fists, until the fire in his blood dropped to a temperature he could bear. Tears, ages-old and strong as acid, scalded his eyelids.

Lion knew nothing about the penal system in New York City. However, he had no intention of letting Clarissa go free after what she had done, and planning her arrest kept his mind occupied so that he would not have to think about Meagan. He fully intended to learn the complete truth of Meagan's disappearance and death . . . but at that moment, hearing about it would have driven him over the brink into an endless chasm of madness.

No. 58 Wall Street was the residence of Alexander Hamilton. From where Lion stood outside Bradford's Coffee House, he could see the lights burning in the downstairs windows and set off at a blind sprint, hoping against hope that the Hamiltons had returned early from General Knox's.

Alexander Hamilton was one person Lion felt he could take into his confidence. As a lawyer, he would be able to tell Lion where and how to go about getting Clarissa arrested. Just as important at this moment

361

was the fact that both men shared the stigma of illegitimacy. Hamilton had worked with zealous precision to achieve his current position, being as passionately ambitious as Lion had been so recently. Lion was certain that Hamilton would understand how that chaos involving Meagan had evolved, particularly since he himself had taken great care to marry into a powerful and respectable family.

When a servant answered the door Lion stood there looking like one of the wild animals that roamed in the nearby woods. Low voices came from the room which opened off the stair hall, and before the footman could close the door on him, he had pushed his way in.

Alexander and Betsey Hamilton both stood up at once, equally surprised. Hamilton, elegant as always in burgundy velvet, had loosened his cravat, and he and his wife both held glasses of wine.

"Why—it is Lion Hampshire, isn't it? Betsey, this is Mr. Hampshire. He was with us in the library tonight—"

"How do you do, Mrs. Hamilton." Lion nodded briefly in her direction, then ran an agitated hand through his untidy gold hair. "Mr. Hamilton, I would not burst in like this except in the case of a true emergency. I am in desperate need of your help."

Betsey seemed to disappear into thin air and Lion told his story to Hamilton quickly and candidly.

"You were right to come to me. You need an impartial third party." Hamilton stood up. "Let us return to Miss Claussen. I suggest that we take her to prison without delay."

It seemed that barely five minutes had passed since Lion left the coffee house, and if he knew Clarissa, she would still be swooning on the floor. The two men crossed Wall Street at an angle, entered the coffee house, and dashed up the stairs.

Clarissa's room was empty.

Lion glanced around wildly, and when he saw that the jewelry case was gone, cursed himself for leaving the ring behind.

The innkeeper had seen nothing; none of the celebrants they questioned in the taproom remembered any girl. Only the old woman Lion had encountered in the hall on his way out had any statement at all to make, but she quavered and rambled so much that Alexander Hamilton barely took the time to hear her out. She said something about having seen a black-haired man take a limp girl down the hall toward the back stairs.

"Probably some other lodger trying to sneak by with a prostitute," Hamilton told Lion in a matter-of-fact tone. "I don't like to crush your hopes, but right now it will be awfully easy for Miss Claussen to make her escape. The city is teeming with strangers; she will have no trouble hiding, or finding a way out. By tomorrow night, she could be on a ship bound for another country."

Lion nodded; however, the dark-haired man was not so easily dismissed from his thoughts.

On the eve of the inauguration, Fraunces Tavern was crowded with the best sort of men. Twilight veiled the city with pink and gray, and candles were being lit around the long room.

Lion sat at a round, polished table with four men who traded stories of their escapades during the last few days and talked over their plans for the morrow. General Washington would become President at two o'clock, and a second tide of visitors had begun today, swelling New York nearly to the point of bursting.

Sipping brandy, Lion wished that he could absorb some of the high spirits that charged the air. He wished that the inauguration were over and he were home. And then what? Gradually, he was forcing himself to think and attempt to feel again, for the intensity of his despair had begun to pull him down further and further. It had become a life battle, and now he was feeling the first stirring of infection by the challenge. The past could not be altered—but his response to it could be.

He still held out hope for overtaking Clarissa. Since

giving up the search the night before, he had not slept or eaten. There was too much thinking to be done, and now he was finally beginning to feel as though it was straight in his mind. He felt hope for the future, and something new—patience. It would take time . . . Part of him wondered if he could ever stop hurting for Meagan.

Chairs scraped; two of the men got up to leave and someone else sat down.

"Well, well, what do you know. Lion Hampshire!"

Lion looked up and his ocean-blue eyes widened in genuine surprise. It was James Wade.

"This must be a case of *déjà vu*," Lion murmured, raising a brow ironically as he recalled the night they had met at Indian Head Tavern in Philadelphia and made the arrangement for him to marry Priscilla. "Or is it simply that you and I spend all our time in tap-rooms?"

James settled his corpulent body more snugly in the bow-back chair and grinned. Rather drunkenly, Lion thought, I am surprised to see you! Would have thought you'd be afraid to show your face after losing my sister to another man!

"I am happy that she found someone more compatible. I realize now that the whole plan—our marriage—was ridiculous."

James narrowed his green eyes, trying to focus on Lion. The man seemed as cool as ever, with that cynical, handsome face, and clothes that looked fresh no matter how sweaty the tavern air became.

"You're singing a different tune these days! What happened to your marriage of convenience?"

Lion almost didn't answer. He swirled the brandy around in his glass and for a moment he could almost see Meagan's face in it. "I met someone who made me aware of what I had missed in my relationships with women."

"Must be quite a girl! Or is she just adept in bed?" James asked cunningly between gulps of ale.

Lion stared at him, his body hard and taut under a suit of amber broadcloth.

"That is a slanderous lie. The girl was Meagan—"

"Meagan!" Wade spluttered, coming partway out of his chair. "Meagan! So that's where the chit got off to!"

"What are you babbling about? You sent her with us!"

"*I?* I couldn't have sent Meagan to the *garden* without having her put her tongue out at me. What makes you think that I had anything to do with it?"

Lion's golden brows met as he frowned. "Why shouldn't I think it? She was in your employ—"

In his surprise, James choked, showering ale all over Lion's white shirt. "In my employ? Oh, that's rich! Hoo! Just what did the wench tell you?"

Lion was almost reluctant to continue. If there was one thing he hated, it was the feeling that he'd been made a fool of. "Well . . . they said she was Priscilla's maid. Actually, that's about it."

"Maid? Maid? Har—har—har!" It seemed he might strangle in his fit of laughter.

Lion's face grew darker.

"Meagan a maid? Oh, that's rich! Really rich! Har —har! Wait till they hear this at home! So that's what the vixen did to get away!"

"Will you kindly tell me what the hell you are talking about?"

"Your little Meagan the maid is actually the daughter of one of the wealthiest men in Virginia—he was to look at him, anyway. Russell William Sayers owned the plantation Pecan Grove, not far from West Hills, and Priscilla and Meagan have been friends—of a sort —since they were babies. Har—har! Wish you could see your face!" James wiped his oily, perspiring forehead with a scented handkerchief. "Her parents were killed in a shipwreck last autumn. You know how we Southern men overextend. General Washington had to borrow five hundred pounds to pay off his creditors before he left Virginia and a hundred more for traveling expenses to get here!"

"Will you get on with it?" Lion ground out.

"Don't get hot and bothered. Let's see now . . . as I

recall, when Meagan disappeared, I didn't know what the situation was, but soon afterward, this man Bumpstock showed up. Her father's attorney. That's when we all learned that Pecan Grove was going to be sold off to pay the debts and Meagan had been scheduled to be shipped off to some spinster aunt of hers in Boston. Didn't surprise me a bit, then, that she'd flown the cage. Just her style."

Lion sat there looking like someone had dropped a ton of bricks on his head. Dazedly, he gulped brandy. "Is this your idea of a joke, Wade?"

"Joke! You're a fine one to suspect jokes at this late date! A maid! I'd love to have seen that!"

Lion flushed under his tan.

"By the way," James continued conversationally, "after the inauguration, I'll be looking Meagan up. She's got to go home and sign a lot of papers before Pecan Grove can change hands. Bumpstock, not to mention every one of Russell Sayers's creditors, have been looking all over for the minx. When General Washington told me how she'd—"

"Listen, Wade, haven't you heard that Meagan is dead?" Lion demanded hoarsely.

"Hoo! Hampshire, for a man in love, you are certainly misinformed all around! I saw General Washington at luncheon yesterday and he told me he brought Meagan with him to New York last week! Something about finding her running about on the road outside Philadelphia! When I filled him in on the situation at Pecan Grove, he told me Meagan has been installed with the Jays for the time being."

Lion's heart was thundering in his ears. He clenched his hands to keep them from shaking, and when he closed his eyes, red and orange sparks danced behind his eyelids.

"What did you say her true surname is?" he asked hoarsely.

"Sayers." James gave him a benign smile, showing wine-stained teeth.

Lion's mind spun back to his introduction to Sally

Jay the night before. "Miss Sayers" she had called the bashful house guest.

"I've got to go—get some air . . ."

He stood up and threaded his way out of the taproom, only to nearly collide with John Jay as he emerged on Pearl Street. Jay had just stepped out of his carriage and started toward the door of Fraunces Tavern, but at the sight of Lion's gleaming hair he stopped in pleased recognition.

The irony of all this is stretching credibility to new limits! thought Lion.

"Well, Mr. Jay," he said aloud, "what a coincidence! I was just talking about you!"

"Nothing too libelous, I trust?"

Suddenly Lion realized that he felt alive and vital for the first time since the night he walked home from City Tavern in Philadelphia.

John Jay was studying him, noticing the change in his eyes, gestures, smile, the tone of his voice.

"As a matter of fact, the subject was actually your house guest . . . Miss Sayers, wasn't it?"

"That's right. Who—"

"James Wade, a neighbor of hers in Virginia. I understand she is quite a girl."

"Lovely, yes, though sadly lacking these days in the spirit she is known for. I gather she has been through a great deal."

"No doubt," Lion agreed in a voice leaden with sarcasm.

"Would you be interested in meeting her after all?"

"I can't imagine that Mrs. Jay would still allow that —after my conduct last night. Breaking my word—"

Jay smiled wryly. "Sally thinks you a dashing libertine, and your conduct only served to enhance that romantic image in her mind. As a matter of fact, she was urging me only an hour ago to ask you to join her and Miss Sayers tomorrow. I will be part of the President's entourage, but the ladies will go to Federal Hall in our carriage."

"Perhaps I could meet them there."

"Splendid! Sally will be thrilled at the prospect.

367

However, I think it best not to tell Miss Sayers that your meeting has been prearranged. Sally has been moving heaven and earth to persuade her to attend the ceremonies at all, and the idea of being thrown together with a man might scare her off again."

Nodding somberly, Lion stifled an impulse to laugh. "A wise decision. May I ask if that was the reason she backed away from the party last night?"

"Oh, no. I'm certain your name never came up, for I neglected to mention it to Sally until she saw you at General Knox's. As I recall, Sally felt Meagan grow skittish at the prospect of meeting some girlhood friend of hers who has recently married."

Lion bit his lip, eyes snapping merrily. "I see. Poor girl. Well, I shall do my best to break through her apathy . . ."

Chapter Forty-two

MEAGAN WAS AWAKE before dawn. Her self-imposed confinement was beginning to chafe and she longed to get outside, if only to breathe the sweet, dewy air and see the sights of New York.

Standing at her window, clad in an exquisitely embroidered lawn bedgown, she stared out over the dark, still city. Where is Lion now? she wondered. Is he sleeping with Priscilla? Does she lie in the circle of his arm, with her head on his chest . . . as I used to do?

The constant flow of pain was turning sour. Jealousy made her angry, more at herself than anyone else, and she was weary of the sadness that lay on her heart like a great weight. All the emotions she had been experiencing the past few days were part of a natural process, but foreign to her nonetheless. Never before had she known even a moment's depression— she was too feisty.

I think the time has come to tell the rest of the world to go to hell! she thought rebelliously. At least the people who knew me as Meagan South. So what if I meet the Binghams—or even Lion and Priscilla? I have never been afraid of anyone before, or any situation, either! And, after all, I have a right to a life, too. I can't keep skulking around like a scared kitten.

Outside, a molten orange sun began to edge its way up over the bay and Meagan saw the first in a long line of Negro slaves on their way to the river, each with a tub of sewage on his head. A cart driven by a tea-water man clattered around the corner next, and drowsy-looking serving-girls came out of houses to purchase a hogshead of the excellent spring water.

It looked like the weather would cooperate; only a few clouds drifted across the glowing sky. Meagan started as the cannon shots began from the Battery. There were thirteen of them, reminding anyone who might have forgotten that today George Washington would become the first President of the United States.

Meagan was excited and ready for this newest adventure. Who could tell what might happen?

Lion shrugged into his newest coat, of a shade known as "London smoke." It fit to perfection, skillfully cut to accommodate his shoulders without hanging in folds around his lean, narrow hips. He also wore a crisp muslin shirt and cravat, a dull gray satin waistcoat, oyster-white breeches, and black knee-boots. What truly pleased him, though, was the sparkle in his eyes. Ultramarine, Meagan had called them once. Beyond the sea.

The sea on a windy, sunny day with a hurricane on the horizon! Lion thought now. He grinned at his reflection, gratified to see that his teeth were still blindingly white.

The pottery lion stood on the worn tea-table in this room on City Tavern's second floor. He reached out to touch the statue, remembering Meagan's face when she presented it to him.

Part of himself was furious with her for the deceit she had practiced on him—though he thought he understood what had prompted it. He was looking forward to their confrontation today with diabolical glee. One eyebrow went up as he stared at his mirror image, recalling things she had said: "I am only a waif who knows no life but service to my betters" . . . followed by an endless stream of evasions. So much that had perplexed him in the past was clear now, but a new set of questions simmered in his mind.

Clenching his teeth, Lion thought of what both of them had suffered because of her pride. It had nearly cost Meagan her life.

"Ah, fondling," he whispered, "today I shall have my turn. Prepare to be stalked!"

The sudden pounding at the door startled him. Lion opened it to find James Wade standing there, and for a moment he failed to remember the note he had sent the night before.

"Well?" demanded Wade, whose breath already smelled of wine.

"James, come in! Your revelations yesterday have made me see you in a new light. I have a favor to ask of you." Lion was at his ironically courteous best.

"A favor? Today? Why should I—"

"I don't mean to take advantage of your friendship, of course. I thought that, in return, I might pay whatever debts you have yet outstanding—and then some."

Wade's expression changed immediately from surly to elated. As Lion well knew, the man would sell his sister for money.

"Well then! What did you have in mind? By the way, you wouldn't have something to drink—?"

Lion poured a generous glass of brandy which James took eagerly in his pudgy hand.

"Neither of us has time to spare on this of all days, so I shall come directly to the point. I learned last night that a—lady friend of mine was killed in a carriage accident yesterday morning, some miles south of

New York City. There is reason to believe that the carriage-wheel may have been tampered with, but of course that is difficult to prove."

James gulped his brandy, looking utterly confused.

"Suffice it to say that I suspect that your dear brother-in-law was involved, at least in helping the young lady leave town. Certain articles that were in her possession are missing, and I am hoping you can help me trace them to Marcus."

"Trace them . . .?" James drained the glass and Lion refilled it.

"Yes. All I ask is that you keep your eyes and ears open. What I am looking for is a ring—a carved gold band inlaid with seven small, perfect rubies. There is also a large emerald necklace that I would recognize. If you can discover either or both of these pieces in Marcus's possession, the money I mentioned earlier will be yours. Do you understand?"

James' little eyes glittered greedily. "'Believe me, Hampshire, if he's got that jewelry, I'll find out!"

The Jay coach was full to the brim with Sally, Meagan, the three children, and Sally's sisters. Everyone was dressed in their finest, including the little girls, who wore tailored dresses and coats of white silk, and fourteen-year-old Peter, garbed in a suit of gray that matched his father's in every detail. Sally was cloaked in the same gray broadcloth, while her sisters wore green brocade and cinnamon taffeta.

Meagan had been shocked when Sally brought a dress from her wardrobe for Meagan to wear. Fashioned of cream silk overlaid with soft lilac muslin, it was so lovely that she had protested. They argued; Sally won, and Meagan emerged from her room looking truly beautiful. For the first time in months, a maid had dressed her hair, leaving it unpowdered, with a spray of lilacs inserted into the shining curls at the back of her head. Her cheeks glowed with excitement, and her violet eyes seemed larger and more thickly-lashed than ever. When she appeared at the top of the stairs, the group of Jays in the vestibule broke into spontaneous applause.

Shortly after noon, they all set out in the coach, bound for the newly refurbished Federal Hall. The streets were crowded with troops, carriages, riders, carts, and pedestrians, and people were beginning to line the windows of houses within view of Federal Hall. The Jay carriage wound its way down Wall Street until it could go no farther. The well-trained horses stood still, in spite of all the chaos around them, and the passengers settled back to wait for the procession.

Peter was particularly anxious, since he knew his father would be passing on horseback behind General Washington's carriage and the committee of the House. Meagan was chatting with the little girls, telling them stories about her childhood adventures at Mount Vernon, while Sally looked nervously out into the crowded street.

How in the world will Mr. Hampshire ever find us? she wondered. Her excitement was fading quickly into disappointment. It seemed fortunate that she had not told Meagan about Mr. Hampshire after all, for it had appeared extremely unlikely that they would meet today.

When Meagan saw the yellow post-chariot from her window, drawn by Hellfire and Heaven, all the blood drained from her face.

How did he get Heaven? she wondered wildly, remembering Gravel's statement about Heaven serving as "proof."

Then, the light carriage drew to a halt right next to their own and Meagan thought her heart would stop. Sally Jay was beaming in relief as the door opened and Lion stepped down to the street. She called a greeting to him.

Merciful God, turn him in another direction! Meagan prayed feverishly. She huddled into her corner and pretended to look for someone in the crowd. Sally was opening the door, greeting Lion again. By some miracle Meagan prayed that she would not be noticed or introduced and Lion would see only the back of her head. She felt giddy, hot, and nauseous; voices came through a blur. Peter nudged her.

"Meagan! Have you gone deaf?" Sally was asking. "Do turn around and say hello to Mr. Hampshire."

There was no escape. Slowly, she turned, dreading the expression she knew would appear on his face.

His physical presence had a stunning effect on Meagan; she had forgotten the intensity of his magnetic pull. Their eyes met, but Lion's flashed with mischief rather than shock; Meagan blinked and focused on a wicked grin of dazzling brilliance.

"Meagan, are you feeling ill?" Sally asked anxiously.

Lion reached for her hand; his tanned skin was warm and dry.

She began to tremble.

"My dear Miss Sayers, I have waited so long for this moment. You must promise to revive." His gaze wandered over her, lingering on the places a gentleman's eyes would avoid. "I must say, you are certainly a lovely representative of Virginia's aristocracy."

Meagan tried to speak, but when her lips parted, only a tiny squeak came out. Her mind spun so that each time she tried to catch a thought, it eluded her. Only one phrase repeated itself over and over, until her ears seemed to ring . . . I must be dreaming. I *must* be dreaming!

Sally was watching her with anxious concern, while Lion continued to hold her hand, tightening his grip whenever she attempted to pull away.

"Meagan has been through a trying time," Sally was explaining. "She is weak, and shy around strangers."

Lion's expression was sympathetic in the extreme. Only Meagan could see the mocking lights in his eyes. "I shall certainly keep that in mind, Mrs. Jay. As a matter of fact, I am partial to shy, soft-spoken women, so we should deal quite well together." He looked directly into Meagan's wide eyes. "Miss Sayers, if it would help you to talk to someone, I should be pleased to provide a sympathetic ear. I am a very good listener!"

373

Meagan's blood was beginning to flow again as she reacted instinctively to Lion's taunting. Her voice returned.

"Mr. Hampshire, shouldn't you be getting back to your wife?"

To her chagrin, his smile only widened.

"Meagan!" Sally interjected. "What a thing to say. Mr. Hampshire is not married!"

"Not yet," he agreed.

Meagan glowered back, but before she could speak again, Peter let out a shout from the street, where he had gone to get a better view. Other people had begun to point to the distant figures, while the faint sound of music could finally be heard.

"Peter!" called Sally, "You had better get back inside this instant."

The drumbeats were louder now; the grand marshal, Colonel Lewis, was close enough to recognize. As Peter scrambled up into the crowded carriage, Lion moved in with silent, deadly grace for the first attack.

"I think I may have a solution for this overcrowding problem, Mrs. Jay." His smile could have lit a bonfire. "It would give me great pleasure to offer Miss Sayers a seat in my carriage—"

"No!" Meagan snapped, glaring at him.

Sally was startled, confused, and embarrassed. The poor man! She had badgered him so about meeting Meagan . . . and he couldn't be more charming! "Meagan, it *is* rather close in here. I see nothing wrong with you sharing Mr. Hampshire's carriage. I am certain that we may count on him to behave as a gentleman."

"Absolutely!" Lion could scarcely contain his mirth as he put out a hand to help Meagan down.

Her cheeks were burning with anger and humiliation; she longed to pummel him, to push him over backward into the street for the cavalry troops to trample.

Sally's two sisters, both over thirty and unmarried, leaned forward to watch the couple cross to the yellow post-chariot.

374

"I have never seen such a man before in all my life!" breathed one of them, spellbound. "Did you see the way Meagan behaved? You'd think he had leprosy! I would give anything to change places with her right now."

Sally started to speak but was interrupted by the shouts of the children, who jumped up and down on the carriage seat to herald the procession's approach. The cavalry troop of dragoons came alongside them, horses prancing and swords glinting in the sunlight. The artillery passed next, followed by the grenadiers, resplendent in blue uniforms and hats with towering white feathers. Sally forgot about Meagan and Lion Hampshire, losing herself in the pageantry with an enthusiasm to match that of her children. Bagpipes, played by kilt-garbed troops, wailed eerily, and Peter exclaimed that he could see the carriages which held the committee of the Senate.

The yellow post-chariot might as well have been the only vehicle on a deserted street for all the attention it was paid. Everyone's eyes were riveted on the impressive, handsomely uniformed troops; then they were cheering as they recognized the more illustrious new senators who waved from the plush carriages.

Meagan and Lion were oblivious to the pandemonium that swept from the figures atop Wall Street's roofs all the way through the roaring sea of heads and arms to the cream-colored coach carrying George Washington. Meagan saw nothing but Lion, and heard no sound but his voice.

"It would seem that there is a great deal for us to discuss," he said, when they sat facing one another in the familiar brown leather environment from their past.

Meagan was enraged by his insolence, his arrogance. The smile had disappeared. He stretched out his legs so that the handsome leather boots brushed her skirts, flicked a bit of dust from his white-clad thigh, and stared at her.

"You pompous ass! How dare you!"

Lion raised a tawny hand and pretended to cringe. "Oh, please, Miss Sayers! Don't call me names!"

She swept her muslin and silk skirts away from his boots. "Of all the high-handed behavior! The only position you could fill in this government would be Secretary of Arrogance!" Her eyes were sparkling amethysts, framed by soft black tendrils escaping from her coiffure.

"I didn't know ladies of the upper class could speak like that," Lion observed dryly.

"Will you stop it! Can I never find any peace from you? Have you sought me out now to take Priscilla's place as your political asset? Has she been cast aside now that you've learned your kitchen-slut has nobler ancestry? One of my uncles is a duke, you know—"

"Shut up." Lion's voice was dangerous.

"Why don't you leave me alone? You didn't want me before and you must think me a bigger fool than Priscilla if you imagine I'll marry you *now!* Now that my lineage has been given the Hampshire seal of approval—"

Lion leaned over and roughly cupped her trembling chin. Their faces were inches apart; his eyes opaque and icy, hers brimming with bitter tears. Meagan tried to strike him, but he deftly caught her wrist. The lilac scent that clung to her feverish body filled his nostrils and shot powerful currents of desire through his loins.

The questions which they both had been waiting to ask found a common answer as Lion's mouth met hers. She was sobbing, clinging to his shoulders and letting her fingertips wander over the planes of his face. Lion's arms were like iron across her back, crushing her slight body against him as though he could absorb her. They kissed, over and over, tasting until their cravings abated enough for a pause. Lion held her face between his lean, dark hands and met her tearful gaze with eyes no longer icy.

"Don't you know, you foolish vixen, how much I love you?"

General Washington stood on the balcony of Federal Hall in full view before a low railing and repeated the oath of office after Chancellor Robert R. Livingston. His voice was fervent with emotion as he spoke, and after proclaiming, "So help me God!" he bent and kissed the Bible.

Livingston turned to the endless crowd and cried out. "Long live George Washington, President of the United States!"

The cheers of the crowd intensified into a deafening roar that seemed capable of reaching every corner of the new country. Cannon thundered from the harbor, church bells rang in celebration; and in the midst of the tumult, Lion and Meagan were conscious only of each other.

EPILOGUE

A single man resembles the odd half of a pair of scissors.

—BENJAMIN FRANKLIN

BIRDSONG AND SUNLIGHT abounded the first Sunday in May as the Jay family strolled home from church. Broadway's footpath was crowded with parishioners who chattered noisily after the long, enforced silence at St. Paul's Chapel, but Sally was quiet as she continually looked over her shoulder for Meagan and Lion.

"Darling, what could he do in broad daylight?" John inquired, reading her mind.

"I don't trust him. Look! They are deliberately losing themselves in the crush—"

"I don't blame them," he said with growing irritation. "You probably make them nervous, ever watching and following. It is not like you! They're in love and probably desperate for a moment alone."

"They have looked just that desperate since they emerged from his carriage Thursday, barely an hour after they were introduced!" Sally argued. "Something is just not right."

"Well, tomorrow they will be married and you can stop worrying."

"Fine, John. In the meantime, if Lion Hampshire gets cold feet on his wedding day, my vigilance shall be the reason why Meagan loses nothing but her heart!"

Though separated from Sally Jay by four families and a pair of plump dowagers, Lion could guess what she was saying. The expression on her face was becoming familiar.

"Your duenna is upset, fondling," he murmured to

Meagan. Feeling her hand slip under his coat, he could scarcely refrain from tossing her onto the nearest bit of greenery and having her. His loins, hands, mouth had ached unceasingly for four days—and it was Sally Jay's fault.

"Let her stew," Meagan remarked. "Some friend she has turned out to be!"

"You might tell her the truth about us and set her mind at ease." He smiled devilishly, drawing her nearer as they walked. "That is . . . if you absolutely cannot wait until tomorrow to have me!"

"Conceited beast!" she accused happily. Violet eyes turned up to gaze at the hard, tantalizing lines of his mouth. "It's a tempting thought, but I could never unravel all of the truth to Sally; she might think worse of us both if she heard it. No . . . I'm certain that this is the better way. 'Bachelor rogue laid low by true, tempestuous love!'" Meagan laughed in the spring sunshine. "When she sees you at the church tomorrow, her mind will be at rest."

"I'll try not to disappoint either of you," Lion grinned, and Meagan cuffed his arm. The number of pedestrians had thinned considerably by this time as people turned in different directions, and Lion looked ahead to see Sally conversing with little Peter. Quickly, he pulled a startled Meagan off into the tiny court to their left. A large willow tree obligingly offered concealment.

"Lion!" Meagan exclaimed. "What are you—"

Hard-muscled arms encircled her, drew her against the length of his body and upward to meet lips that seared her own. Eagerly she responded, starved for the delicious savagery of his kiss, her fingers tracing the familiar pattern of muscles on his back. Lean fingers sought swelling breasts; aroused maleness pressed the sobbing core of her own desire.

"Christ! It has been so long! This is the worst torture I have ever been subjected to!" Lion whispered, his breath fiery against her soft neck.

Meagan was flushed with feverish yearning, but she realized that it was impossible to ease their desire now. "I know what you mean!" she moaned, managing a shaky smile that pierced Lion's heart.

"I may not live until tomorrow," he predicted dramatically, fingers teasing her spine. "They may have to carry me into the church . . . I'll be permanently disabled and you will be too embarrassed to claim me!"

"Lion, you could arrive in a sedan chair, wearing a British uniform and white periwig, powdered and patched and taking snuff, and I would still claim you!"

They grinned at one another; then Lion feigned a scowl. "I had planned to turn you over my knee the first moment we were alone, dear *South*. Do not imagine that you can use your charms to divert me indefinitely, for that masquerade which you practiced on me shall not—" He swallowed as Meagan stood on tiptoe to brush her lips against his jaw above the snowy cravat. "That is—the deception—" She pulled his head down, her tongue touched his teeth, and the conversation was ended.

Eventually, they managed to straighten their clothes and emerge into the sunlight. In the distance, a voice called, "Meagan? Meagan!"

Lion groaned. "Let's go for a walk," he proposed to his startled companion.

"But Sally will be worried sick!"

"Meagan, I am a grown man and little Sally Jay does not frighten me in the least." He paused. "I'll simply have John lock her in her room until the wedding!"

Laughing, Meagan allowed him to lead her between the houses, away from Broadway toward Greenwich Street. Since their reunion, they had had little or no opportunity for extended conversation, for there was always a chance that they might be overheard. They began to walk aimlessly, interrupting one another as they discussed all that had transpired in the past fortnight. Lion had dozens of questions about her abduction and escape, after which he answered all of hers about Clarissa and her mysterious ending. The touchy part came when he tried to explain the reason for his presence in Clarissa's New York room, but Meagan was not anxious for an argument. He had thought Meagan dead and was in pain—it was easy enough for her to understand. Knowing that he had broken his engagement to Priscilla with the intent of marrying Meagan South, housekeeper, lit a fire in her soul that nothing could dim.

After two hours, they finished their conversation on a bench next to Bowling Green, where the Dutch had once set up their Tenpins. Meagan held Lion's hand, rested her cheek against his shoulder, and told him the story of Meagan Sayers. Her voice caught when she spoke of Pecan Grove, describing it vividly. No flower or horse or friend among the slaves was omitted, and by the time she had finished, Lion's mind was busy.

"Sweetheart, in these past days of blinding love, I seem to have forgotten to tell you something. James Wade gave me some news about your Pecan Grove that is seeming more interesting by the moment . . ."

May fourth was a glorious day. New York had quieted down as the visitors returned to their hometowns, and now there was a residue of hope and friendliness in the spring sunshine.

St. Paul's Chapel bordered Broadway on the west, but the west porch faced the Hudson River and all that separated the church from the glistening blue water was a series of grassy slopes. Although there was no spire, the building was an excellent example of the Georgian-Classic Revival style with a handsome columned portico. Farther down Broadway stood the charred ruins of Trinity Church, a victim of the fire of 1776.

Anxiously, Meagan waited in an anteroom. Smith, who had been summoned by a rider paid well by Lion, stood behind her arranging the fragile, Belgian lace veil. Meagan positively glowed. Her gown was simple, fashioned of soft white muslin with a lace-on-silk sash that merely served to emphasize her unique, natural beauty. Her skin had never looked creamier, her hair glossier, or her cheeks more becomingly rosy. Impulsively, she turned to embrace Smith.

"Thank you so much for coming. You have been such a loyal friend. I am only sorry I couldn't tell you the truth about myself—or Lion."

"Don't worry about that!" Smith admonished. "All's well that ends well . . . and besides, I never felt any reason to pry into your personal affairs. All I ever wanted was to see you happy."

"No one in the world could be happier than I am!" exclaimed Meagan.

"Will you be returning to Philadelphia soon?"

"Yes, but only for a short while. As much as I hate to be away from Markwood Villa, Lion is determined that we should spend some time at Pecan Grove. He is paying off all of Daddy's debts, so the plantation remains in my name. Lion wants to see it and take care of whatever work needs to be done."

"What about his political ambitions?"

Meagan made a face. "He claims that it is no longer important—that when he thought he had lost me because of his ambition, it just withered away. But I know better. He is just worn out emotionally. At least he has learned to be patient, and I am certain that after a few months he will begin to crave politics again." Her eyes danced as she leaned closer. "Actually, I am rather set on the idea myself. I got quite excited about the new government—enough to leave Lion so that he might have his chance—and I hope that one day he will be able to serve. I know he would be brilliant!"

"I'm sure you are right," Smith agreed, smiling. "With you by his side, he cannot lose."

"Oh, it's good to hear you say that! I've worried so about this mess he's made of his private life . . ."

"Don't be silly!" A voice chided from the doorway. It was Priscilla Reems, lovely as usual in bottle-green silk. "It's been a fortunate end for us all. Meagan . . . I've been wanting to apologize to you for . . . everything."

Feeling warm toward the world, Meagan went and

hugged her oldest friend. "Never mind. As Smith says, 'All's well that ends well.' Are you happy?"

"Oh, yes. Happier than I could have been with Lion. He despised me, Meagan, because I stood between you two and he knew it was his own fault. Marcus explained to me. He says, 'Whatever you cannot understand, you cannot possess.' I was miserable with Lion because I couldn't begin to understand him."

"And Marcus?"

"Marcus is good to me. He likes me, I think, and he wants the life I want. We sort of think alike."

Meagan grinned in relief. "Good. You know, we are going back to Fairfax County for a while, so Marcus will have a clear field until Lion returns."

"I'll tell him," Priscilla smiled. "Perhaps when you two return, you can pay us a visit. Our new summer home isn't too far from—what is it? Markville? At any rate, I see no reason why Marcus and Lion shouldn't be good friends, just like you and me. I would think that they would have a great deal in common!"

"Well, that may be the problem. Perhaps they have too much in common," Meagan smiled ironically. "By the way, don't you think you can woo Bramble away from me while we are gone, because she and Wong will be coming with us!"

"Anne is the person who will be hatching that scheme! You'll have to tell her; she's right outside in the chapel."

Meagan's mouth dropped open in surprise, just as there was a knock at the door. Smith opened it to admit Brown. He was dressed in his best tan suit, blushing and holding a small bouquet of flowers.

"Kevin!" Meagan exclaimed in delight. "How sweet of you to come all this way!"

"I just wanted to tell you congratulations, Miss Sayers." It was killing him, remembering how he had kissed her on the Binghams' lawn. "The captain asked me to give you these."

He thrust the nosegay into her hands and Meagan saw that the flowers, mixed with baby white roses, were blue forget-me-nots. Oh, Lion! she thought, then turned to kiss Brown's cheek.

"Thank you, Kevin. You're a special friend, and I don't want anything to change that. No matter what my surname is—South, Sayers, or Hampshire—you must always call me Meagan."

The organ began to play then and everyone rushed around the room at once, while Meagan laughed. Smith checked her veil, then the three visitors hastened back to their pews. The chapel was nearly empty, but the guests that were present made an impressive group. The Jays were there, the Hamiltons, the Powels, James Wade, David Humphreys, Charles Thomson, Madison, and Randolph, as well as assorted relatives of the guests. Priscilla slipped into a space between her brother and William Bingham.

"Where's your precious Marcus Reems today?" James hissed.

Priscilla gave him a haughty glance, immediately rising to her own defense. She was certain that James thought her a fool for allowing Lion to escape, and she was determined to prove him, as well as Anne Bingham, wrong.

"He wanted to come, of course, but he and Lion are not the warmest of friends. I shouldn't be telling you this, but . . . I think he is out arranging a surprise for me. He is so good—a thousand times more attentive than your precious Lion ever could be! I just feel sorry for Meagan . . ."

"What's this grand surprise?" James prompted skeptically.

"Well . . . I think he is having some jewelry made for me. "I saw him counting something last night when I came in to dress for dinner, but he hid them in a handkerchief in his drawer. I confess I peeked, and what do you think was inside? A half-dozen of the sweetest little rubies! I'm certain he is going to buy some other larger ones and then have a necklace or bracelet made—possibly an entire parure! It would be just like him!"

James, shocked and delighted by this revelation,

opened his mouth to speak, but at that moment the music intensified and all heads turned to seek out the bride.

Meagan stood at the far end of the center aisle, looking enchantingly radiant, one tiny hand resting on the arm of President Washington. Clad in the same brown broadcloth suit he had worn on Inauguration Day, he appeared solemn but for the gentle twinkle in his deep-set eyes.

At the end of the aisle, Lion waited, and Meagan's heart turned over at the sight of him. The elaborate pulpit and surrounding columns were white and gold, colors that made a perfect backdrop for Lion. He wore a frock coat the color of champagne, with a tawny vest, and elegant linen shirt and cravat. His hair was a burnished gold against bronzed skin and he seemed incredibly tall and handsome. The morning sun poured like fire through the stained glass windows, and when Meagan reached Lion's side, she looked up at him and smiled with all the love that burned within her heart.

President Washington stood back as Lion reached for her hand.

About the Author

Twenty-five-year-old Cynthia Challed Wright interrupted her college education in 1972 to marry her high school sweetheart, Richard, and follow where the Navy took him. Their daughter, Jennifer, was born in 1973, after which Cynthia decided to redirect her old writing hobby into the creation of a book. She never did return to college, but, to her endless pleasure, she now has the career she dreamed of since childhood.

The Wrights currently live in New London, Connecticut, where Richard is an officer on a nuclear submarine. Cynthia enjoys antiques, photography, traveling, her old house, but most of all her husband and daughter.

Caroline, her first attempt at a full-length novel, was written during spare moments while raising her daughter. Most of Cynthia's family and friends tried to dissuade her from submitting the manuscript to publishers, but encouraged by Richard, she put it in the mail. Initially it was rejected, but on a spring day she received a phone call from a publishing house that *was* interested. *Caroline* was published a year ago. Due to its success and an enormous amount of requests from delighted readers, she wrote *Touch the Sun.* Cynthia is currently finishing her third book.

NEW FROM BALLANTINE!

FALCONER, John Cheever   27300 $2.25

The unforgettable story of a substantial, middle-class man and the passions that propel him into murder, prison, and an undreamed-of liberation. "CHEEVER'S TRIUMPH . . . A GREAT AMERICAN NOVEL."—*Newsweek*

GOODBYE, W. H. Manville   27118 $2.25

What happens when a woman turns a sexual fantasy into a fatal reality? The erotic thriller of the year! "Powerful."—*Village Voice.* "Hypnotic."—*Cosmopolitan.*

THE CAMERA NEVER BLINKS, Dan Rather with Mickey Herskowitz   27423 $2.25

In this candid book, the co-editor of "60 Minutes" sketches vivid portraits of numerous personalities including JFK, LBJ and Nixon, and discusses his famous colleagues.

THE DRAGONS OF EDEN, Carl Sagan 26031 $2.25

An exciting and witty exploration of mankind's intelligence from pre-recorded time to the fantasy of a future race, by America's most appealing scientific spokesman.

VALENTINA, Fern Michaels   26011 $1.95

Sold into slavery in the Third Crusade, Valentina becomes a queen, only to find herself a slave to love.

THE BLACK DEATH, Gwyneth Cravens and John S. Marr   27155 $2.50

A totally plausible novel of the panic that strikes when the bubonic plague devastates New York.

THE FLOWER OF THE STORM, Beatrice Coogan   27368 $2.50

Love, pride and high drama set against the turbulent background of 19th century Ireland as a beautiful young woman fights for her inheritance and the man she loves.

THE JUDGMENT OF DEKE HUNTER, George V. Higgins   25862 $1.95

Tough, dirty, shrewd, telling! "The best novel Higgins has written. Deke Hunter should have as many friends as Eddie Coyle."—*Kirkus Reviews* /

LG-2